D0946547

THE FUTURE IS *FEMALE!*

THE FUTURE IS *FEMALE!*

25 CLASSIC SCIENCE FICTION STORIES BY WOMEN, FROM PULP PIONEERS TO URSULA K. LE GUIN

LISA YASZEK, EDITOR

A Library of America Special Publication

THE FUTURE IS FEMALE!

Published in the United States by Library of America.
www.loa.org

Jacket art: Jean Shrimpton, jumpsuit by Loomtogs,
DIMAR Construction Co., Route 84, Ft. Lauderdale, Florida, January 11, 1965.
Photography by Richard Avedon.

Some of the material in this volume is reprinted with the permission of holders
of copyright and publishing rights. Acknowledgments are on page 528.

Distributed to the trade in the United States by Penguin Random House Inc.
and in Canada by Penguin Random House Canada Ltd.

Library of Congress Control Number: 2018935008
ISBN 978–1–59853–580–8

1 3 5 7 9 10 8 6 4 2

Printed in the United States of America

CONTENTS

INTRODUCTION

BY LISA YASZEK

Stories speculating about the future of science, technology, and society began to appear across the globe over the course of the nineteenth century. But science fiction (SF) only came into its own in the American SF magazines of the early and mid-twentieth century. Tantalizing readers with sensational cover art and even more sensational titles like *Amazing Stories*, *Fantastic Universe*, and *Astounding Science Fiction*, dozens of new periodicals promised to reveal the shape of things to come. They offered not only action-packed adventure narratives but informed, even sometimes prescient, accounts of real-world scientific discovery and technological innovation. Along the way, they became laboratories for aesthetic exploration as well. Authors used these magazines to test the themes and techniques that would become associated with the genre, probing and expanding the limits of fiction; editors distilled the results of these experiments, commenting on shared histories and future trajectories for SF; and fans volunteered ideas and opinions about everything from scientific accuracy to the necessity of sex in speculative writing. This truly collaborative process, still ongoing, has established SF as the premier story form of techno-scientific modernity.

As the title of this book asserts, SF was never just about boys and their toys. Instead, the future has always been female as well. This collection presents twenty-five stories written by three generations of American women between the launch of the first specialist genre magazines in the 1920s and the emergence of self-identified feminist SF in the 1970s. Adopting personae ranging from warrior queens and heroic astronauts to unhappy housewives and sensitive aliens, women were pioneers in developing our sense of wonder about the many different futures we might inhabit, partners in forging the creative practices associated with the best speculative fiction, and revolutionaries who blew up the genre when necessary to address the hopes and fears of American women.

So who were the women of early SF? The story of women in this field has long been celebrated by fans, who do the important cultural work of preserving genre history amongst themselves, and, more recently, by authors and scholars who share this history with others outside the SF community. However, such efforts are often overshadowed by "commonsense" assumptions about the historic relations of gender and genre. These assumptions have all but taken on the status of myth and posit that: (1) Mary Shelley's 1818 novel *Frankenstein* is a foundational SF text, but few other women participated in the genre until the advent of feminist SF; (2) women sometimes wrote SF before the 1970s but had to disguise themselves as men to get published in a community that was inherently hostile to their sex; and (3) even when early women SF authors did write under their own names, they followed the lead of their male counterparts, celebrating science and technology in ways that reinforced rather than transformed our understanding of science and society.

These myths remind us of what we value in the present moment, and enjoy in increasing abundance: women who write scientifically responsible and socially daring fiction that encourages us to see our own world and its many possible futures in startling new ways. But they also beg an important question. Where did all these modern wonder women—writers like C. J. Cherryh, N. K. Jemisin, Ann

Leckie, Nnedi Okorafor, Jo Walton, and Martha Wells, to name just some—come from in the first place?

As it turns out, women have been involved in shaping SF all along. Between the mid-1920s and the late 1960s, nearly 300 women published in the principal genre-specialist magazines—about 15 percent of all contributors, just going by the numbers.[1] Most were fiction writers but some also helped to develop their chosen genre as editors, critics, poets, artists, and science journalists. Still others made their mark in the harder-to-quantify and still-understudied realm of fandom: publishing zines, sharing fan fiction, exerting significant influence on SF as its keenest audience. Women were active within professional organizations (helping to found the Science Fiction and Fantasy Writers of America, the Fantasy Amateur Press Association, and the Milford and Clarion Writers' Workshops), and won every award and honor the community had to confer (see the Biographical Notes to this volume for individual Hugos, Nebulas, and other distinctions).

While it is true that women in SF occasionally met resistance from male writers, editors, and fans who disliked their presence in the field, most recall such incidents as isolated ones. From the start, SF magazine editors appear to have encouraged women's contributions—as Leigh Brackett put it, "editors aren't buying sex, they're buying stories."[2] At *Amazing Stories*, the pioneering Hugo Gernsback "liked the idea of a woman invading the field he had opened," as Leslie F. Stone remembered.[3] C. L. Moore "never felt the least bit downed because I was a woman"—indeed *Weird Tales* editor Farnsworth Wright is reported to have closed his office for the day in celebration when he received Moore's now-famous story "Shambleau."[4] For Zenna Henderson, Anthony J. Boucher and Francis J. McComas of *The Magazine of Fantasy and Science Fiction* seemed like "midwives" to her career.[5]

And so the question remains: if women were a small but generally welcome part of the early SF world, why did so many adopt androgynous or male pseudonyms? The short answer is that most didn't—and those who did had good reasons for their deception that had little to do with their SF careers. Almost all of the twenty-six authors featured in this anthology published primarily under their own, clearly feminine names, or under female pseudonyms; others (Leslie F. Stone, Leigh Brackett, Marion Zimmer Bradley) were given androgynous names at birth but published as women. (Throughout this volume, we've used each story's original byline; real names are provided in the Biographical Notes.) In the few well-known cases where women deliberately concealed their true identities, they did so for complex professional reasons. Catherine Lucille Moore became "C. L." so as not to jeopardize her banking job during the Great Depression. Alice Mary Norton reinvented herself as Andre Norton (also writing occasionally as Allen Weston or Andrew North) when she first launched a career writing boys' adventure tales. Alice Sheldon, spotting a jar of Tiptree marmalade on a supermarket shelf, came up with the pseudonym James Tiptree, Jr., to protect her identity as a former CIA agent and budding experimental psychologist. As each of these examples suggests, the problem was not the reception of women in SF per se, but patterns of sexual discrimination across American culture. Pseudonymous authorship was common practice for male SF writers as well, and is one of the genre's fascinating quirks; a couple of the apparently female authors we considered for the present volume turned out in fact to be men.

The first generation of women writing within the American SF magazine community began their careers in what is commonly known as the Pulp Era: the period from 1926 to 1940, approximately, when genre periodicals were often printed on cheap wood-pulp paper. SF was not, at this point in its history, a genre that radiated social prestige, like the lyric poem or the realist novel. Indeed C. L. Moore, a writer credited then and now with bringing newfound character depth to the pulps, later remembered it as "a great act of daring" for her to purchase her first SF magazine, happening upon *Amazing Stories* at an Indianapolis newsstand. Her parents "had *very* definite ideas about literature" and "didn't approve of 'trashy' fiction," she recalled.[6]

Readers today with similarly definite ideas about literature, who are looking for subtle allusions or the artful defamiliarization of ordinary language, could certainly describe Pulp Era writers like Clare Winger Harris, Leslie F. Stone, and Moore herself as "pulpy." Less interested in sentence-by-sentence literariness than in big *what if* questions and the seemingly boundless imaginative possibilities of futures to come—for optimism was one of the hallmarks of the era—these women bravely and collaboratively broke all sorts of new generic ground, trying out speculative themes that now seem like basic elements of American culture. How many of our current SF movie blockbusters still more or less fit the sixteen "Possible Science Fiction Plots" that Harris casually tossed off back in 1931?

1. Interplanetary space travel.
2. Adventures on other worlds.
3. Adventures in other dimensions.
4. Adventures in the micro- or macrocosmos.
5. Gigantic insects.
6. Gigantic man-eating plants.
7. Time travel, past or future.
8. Monstrous forms of unfamiliar life.

9. The creation of supermachines.
10. The creation of synthetic life.
11. Mental telepathy and mental aberration.
12. Invisibility.
13. Ray and vibration stories.
14. Unexplored portions of the globe: submarine, subterranean, etc.
15. Super intelligence.
16. Natural cataclysms: extraterrestrial or confined to the earth.[7]

The first woman to publish in an SF-specialist magazine, Harris seems to have been the first writer of any sex to offer such a taxonomy, and she wrote stories based on several of these possible plots herself. Her contemporary Leslie F. Stone imagined the first woman astronaut, the first black SF hero, and the first alien civilization to win a war against humans, helping to build a new kind of American literature from its foundations up.

Science fiction's Golden Age—from 1940 to 1960, approximately—saw the genre move from the margins of the culture toward its center. In the wake of Hiroshima and Nagasaki, the stakes involved in speculation about the future increased exponentially, drawing mainstream authors and critical attention to the genre. For women who began writing during these years, including Judith Merril, Carol Emshwiller, Andre Norton, and others who have been all but lost to history, SF magazines proliferated and paid them increasingly well for their work; a new generation of editors demanded better-crafted sentences and new approaches to already established themes. Book publishers, both genre-specialist and mainstream, increasingly sought story collections, novels, and anthologies. Enabling professional literary careers for some of the writers included here, growing audiences also enjoyed SF radio shows, comic books, and movies; Merril became the first woman—and one of the first authors of any gender—to have her SF adapted for television. (Her post-apocalyptic novel, *Shadow on the Hearth*, appeared as *Atomic Attack* for the prestigious Motorola Television Hour in 1954.)

By the 1960s, with the advent of the Space Age, some of the wildest imaginings of the genre's pioneers had become matters of fact: computers, robots, lasers, and lunar exploration programs were now entirely real. For the generation of women beginning their careers during these years—writers including Sonya Dorman, Ursula K. Le Guin, and Joanna Russ—changing times seemed to have overtaken much of the SF they had grown up reading. Rethinking their predecessors' often utopian investments in the world-altering potential of the hard sciences, they turned to psychology, anthropology, and sociology, and to modernity's many discontents, exploring themes like consumerism, overpopulation, virtual reality, corporatism, and the technoscientific manipulation of sex and gender. Most notably, these New Wave writers (as they came to be called) experimented not only with more contemporary subject matter but with form, style, and modes of expression. For inspiration, some looked to avant-gardes in art, music, and literature, as well as to futurity. More than ever before, they saw their stories appear in literary or mainstream magazines, and deliberately crossed genres; the "science fiction" of earlier generations became, more popularly, "speculative fiction."

So what drew women to SF, and what were their contributions to it? As they recall in lectures, interviews, and their own writing, women loved the openness of the genre. Leigh Brackett cherished the "sense of wonder" associated with speculative fiction, asking, "where else can I voyage among the 'great booming suns of outer space' . . . shoot the fiery nebulae, and make planetfall anywhere I want?"[8] Margaret St. Clair valued SF for leading "human attention into areas of experience that might not have otherwise been explored."[9] Still others turned to the future in order to confront social and political issues in the imperfect present. Indeed, for Judith Merril SF seemed like "virtually the only vehicle of political dissent" available to artists during the Cold War, enabling expressions of protest that publishers or audiences might otherwise have rejected.[10] Joanna Russ believed similarly that SF could "crystallize an awful lot of things [people are] already feeling," and could be particularly useful to minority authors hoping to convey new perspectives on science and society to wider audiences.[11]

As they staked claims for themselves in the American future, early women SF authors made three major contributions to their chosen genre. First and foremost, they made complex character development a priority in a genre that initially excelled in big ideas and impressive gadgetry rather than emotional depth. As Andre Norton put it, hard science and technology might well be crucial to making a story SF, but what really interested her was "why people do things and how they might react."[12] To better explore these questions, women revised one of the oldest and most central relationships in SF: that of humans and aliens. Over the course of the nineteenth and early twentieth centuries, authors drew on widespread assumptions about Darwinian competition between species to cast aliens as bug-eyed monsters whose horrifying appearance reflected their equally horrifying desire to steal scarce resources from humans. But as early as 1928, Clare Winger Harris's "The Miracle of the Lily" challenged such representations with its depiction of a man who struggles against his innate antipathy toward aliens upon meeting sympathetic, intelligent insects from Venus. Other early SF authors included in this volume who elaborate on the startling notion that humans might cooperate rather than compete with those who differ from them include Zenna Henderson, Rosel George Brown, and Ursula K. Le Guin. Women also challenged extant ideas about the natural hostility between species by telling tales from alien points of view. Leslie F. Stone pioneered this technique in her 1931 battle-of-the-sexes tale "The Conquest of Gola," which invites readers to side with the female inhabitants of Venus as they ward off attack by their male Earthly neighbors. Subsequent authors, including Margaret St. Clair, Carol Emshwiller, and Sonya Dorman, refined this reversal of perspective to explore a host of issues, including sexism, racism, environmentalism, colonialism, and capitalism.

Not surprisingly, women revised science fictional representations of male-female relations as well. "Readers are tired of the yarn based on the super-hero and the ravishing babe," Leigh Brackett warned would-be SF writers in 1944. For her, stereotypical Pulp Era romance narratives, full of stalwart space jocks with their requisite ray-guns saving hysterical damsels in distress from monstrous aliens, were simply "old stuff." Fortunately, Brackett and many other contributors to this anthology felt that "you can get away with practically anything [in SF] as long as it's well and subtly done."[13] Well before their explicitly feminist successors (or in a few cases their explicitly feminist future selves), many of the women included here were rethinking the gender roles that their male counterparts and the broader culture usually took as given—sometimes to an extent that might have been difficult to express without the imaginative freedom or allegorical cover of SF.

Instead of wish-fulfilling fantasies of masculine heroism, Doris Pitkin Buck, Kate Wilhelm, and James Tiptree, Jr., offer stories in which male protagonists not only fail to save the women they love but turn out themselves to be responsible for the scientific and social situations that have endangered these women in the first place. Katherine MacLean, Andre Norton, and others cast women as experts who embrace alternate modes of science emphasizing intuition and empathy with the natural world. C. L. Moore, Leslie Perri, and Joanna Russ transform the damsels of SF cliché into "sheroes" who engage in quests and fight for truth and justice with almost superhuman strength, but who reject the stoicism, rugged individualism, and separation from nature that define the classic male hero. Still other stories by Judith Merril, Rosel George Brown, and Alice Eleanor Jones introduce readers to an entirely new character type: the housewife heroine whose relative happiness or unhappiness in the future becomes a barometer for evaluating the relative merits of our technocultural arrangements in the present. (Jones's "Created He Them"—published in 1955, two years before the debut of *Leave It to Beaver*—is a striking example of the latter class. Darkly dystopian and profoundly antipatriarchal, it sounds a housewife's note of protest against the expectations and conformities of the baby boom years. Jones is one of those authors, and there are others in this collection, who almost no one has heard of but whom many will find worth reading.)

Traversing interstellar voids, piloting vast spaceships, and exploring exotic planets as nimbly as male SF writers, the women of early SF also built more intimate, down-to-earth worlds for speculation and reflection. The revelations of Wilmar H. Shiras's mutant-child story "In Hiding"—an influential text for the X-Men comics—unfold in an ordinary, present-day office and suburban home, spaces that seem as exciting in Shiras's hands as any high-tech lab. Judith Merril's midcentury classic "That Only a Mother" tackles the consequences of nuclear proliferation without special effects, in modest, near-future interiors. Zenna Henderson's "Ararat" transforms a typical rural schoolhouse and its surroundings into a scene of alien and paranormal encounter. (A first-grade teacher for all of her adult life, Henderson saw Kim Darby and William Shatner portray her characters in *The People*, made for TV in 1972.)

Motherhood, community survival, and the future of human reproduction are significant concerns in these and other stories featured here, both early and late. The ways in which science and technology might be used to literally reconstruct sex, overturning readers' assumptions about "natural" gendered behavior and enabling radical new modes of living, are a third prominent theme throughout women's speculative fiction. Anticipated on occasion in stories of the Pulp Era and Golden Age, it is particularly evident in the New Wave stories of Sonya Dorman, Marion Zimmer Bradley and John Jay Wells (Juanita Coulson), and Ursula K. Le Guin, all of whom extrapolate from current scientific and technological developments to imagine worlds in which sex, gender, sexual orientation, and individual humanity have been profoundly altered. How will cohorts of clones address each other? How will military men feel about their pregnancies? Shape-shifting and protoplasmic, will we look back with nostalgia on bodies, or on love? From provocative thought-experiments such as these, the overtly feminist SF of the 1970s began to take form. It is one thing to map the limits of traditional gender roles and the damage they do to women and men alike, as many authors in this volume do implicitly. It is another to envision and articulate new arrangements that might have some positive bearing on the present—as several New Wave authors, including Ursula K. Le Guin in *The Left Hand of Darkness* (1969) and Joanna Russ in *The Female Man* (1975), went on to do over the course of their subsequent careers.

And this is why we need to remember the women of early SF: they are the missing link between the pioneering experiments of Mary Shelley and the finely honed, radiant results we see increasingly in the work of women writing today. Even more consciously than their famous foremother, the twenty-six women included here were dedicated to creating a new kind of fiction that could communicate individual hopes and fears about life in a technoscientific world across centuries, continents, and cultures. In doing so, they identified some of the most pressing issues facing women —and indeed, all people—at the beginning and middle of the twentieth century, laying the groundwork for the contemporary women authors we continue to celebrate, and for the writers of tomorrow. So we learn that women who dream about new and better futures for all did not come from outer space, 20,000 leagues under the sea, or even a swiftly tilting planet. Instead, they have always been with us, always insisting that the future is female.

---

[1] See Pamela Sargent, "Women in Science Fiction," in *Women of Wonder* (New York: Vintage, 1975), and Eric Leif Davin, *Partners in Wonder: Women and the Birth of Science Fiction, 1926–1965* (Lanham, MD: Lexington Books, 2006).

[2] Paul Walker, "Leigh Brackett: Interview," *Speaking of Science Fiction* (Oradell, NJ: Luna Publications, 1978), 371–83.

[3] In a 1974 speech to the Baltimore Science Fiction Society, published as "Day of the Pulps," *Fantasy Commentator* 9.50 (Fall 1997): 100–101.

[4] Jeffrey M. Elliot, "C. L. Moore: Poet of Far-Distant Futures," *Pulp Voices; or, Science Fiction Voices #6: Interviews with Pulp Writers and Editors* (San Bernardino, CA: Borgo Press, 1983), 45–51.

[5] Zenna Henderson, "The People Series," in Joseph Olander, Martin Harry Greenberg, and Frederik Pohl, eds., *The Great Science Fiction Series* (New York: Harper & Row, 1980), 173–74.
[6] Elliot, "C. L. Moore: Poet of Far-Distant Futures."
[7] Clare Winger Harris, "Possible Science Fiction Plots," *Wonder Stories* 3.3 (August 1931): 426–27.
[8] Walker, "Leigh Brackett: Interview."
[9] Margaret St. Clair, "Wight in Space: An Autobiographical Sketch," in Martin H. Greenberg, ed., *Fantastic Lives: Autobiographical Essays by Notable Science Fiction Writers* (Carbondale: Southern Illinois University Press, 1981), 144–56.
[10] Judith Merril, "What Do You Mean: Science? Fiction?" *Extrapolation* 7, 8 (May 1966, December 1966): 30–46; 2–19.
[11] "Joanna Russ," in Charles Platt, *Dream Makers II: The Uncommon Men & Women Who Write Science Fiction* (New York: Berkley, 1983), 191–202.
[12] Paul Walker, "Andre Norton: Interview," *Speaking of Science Fiction* (Oradell, NJ: Luna Publications, 1978), 264–70.
[13] Leigh Brackett, "The Science-Fiction Field," *Writer's Digest*, July 1944, 20–27.

THE FUTURE IS *FEMALE!*

CLARE WINGER HARRIS

The Miracle of the Lily

I. The Passing of a Kingdom

SINCE the comparatively recent resumé of the ancient order of agriculture I, Nathano, have been asked to set down the extraordinary events of the past two thousand years, at the beginning of which time the supremacy of man, chief of the mammals, threatened to come to an untimely end.

Ever since the dawn of life upon this globe, life, which it seemed had crept from the slime of the sea, only two great types had been the rulers; the reptiles and the mammals. The former held undisputed sway for eons, but gave way eventually before the smaller, but intellectually superior mammals. Man himself, the supreme example of the ability of life to govern and control inanimate matter, was master of the world with apparently none to dispute his right. Yet, so blinded was he with pride over the continued exercise of his power on Earth over other lower types of mammals and the nearly extinct reptiles, that he failed to notice the slow but steady rise of another branch of life, different from his own; smaller, it is true, but no smaller than he had been in comparison with the mighty reptilian monsters that roamed the swamps in Mesozoic times.

These new enemies of man, though seldom attacking him personally, threatened his downfall by destroying his chief means of sustenance, so that by the close of the twentieth century, strange and daring projects were laid before the various governments of the world with an idea of fighting man's insect enemies to the finish. These pests were growing in size, multiplying so rapidly and destroying so much vegetation, that eventually no plants would be left to sustain human life. Humanity suddenly woke to the realization that it might suffer the fate of the nearly extinct reptiles. Would mankind be able to prevent the encroachment of the insects? And at last man *knew* that unless drastic measures were taken *at once*, a third great class of life was on the brink of terrestrial sovereignty.

Of course no great changes in development come suddenly. Slow evolutionary progress had brought us up to the point, where, with the application of outside pressure, we were ready to handle a situation, that, a century before, would have overwhelmed us.

I reproduce here in part a lecture delivered by a great American scientist, a talk which, sent by radio throughout the world, changed the destiny of mankind: but whether for good or for evil I will leave you to judge at the conclusion of this story.

"Only in comparatively recent times has man succeeded in conquering natural enemies; flood, storm, inclemency of climate, distance, and now we face an encroaching menace to the whole of humanity. Have we learned more and more of truth and of the laws that control matter only to succumb to the first real danger that threatens us with extermination? Surely, no matter what the cost, you will rally to the solution of our problem, and I believe, friends, that I have discovered the answer to the enigma.

"I know that many of you, like my friend Professor Fair, will believe my ideas too extreme, but I am convinced that unless you are willing to put behind you those notions which are old and not utilitarian, you cannot hope to cope with the present situation.

"Already, in the past few decades, you have realized the utter futility of encumbering yourselves with superfluous possessions that had no useful virtue, but which, for various sentimental reasons, you continued to hoard, thus lessening the degree of your life's efficiency by using for it time and attention that should have been applied to the practical work of life's accomplishments. You have given these things up slowly, but I am now going to ask you to relinquish the rest of them *quickly*; everything that interferes in any way with the immediate disposal of our enemies, the insects."

At this point, it seems that my worthy ancestor, Professor Fair, objected to the scientist's words, asserting that efficiency at the expense of some of the sentimental virtues was undesirable and not conducive to happiness, the real goal of man. The scientist, in his turn, argued that happiness was available only through a perfect adaptability to one's environment, and that efficiency *sans* love, mercy and the softer sentiments was the short cut to human bliss.

It took a number of years for the scientist to put over his scheme of salvation, but in the end he succeeded, not so much from the persuasiveness of his words, as because prompt action of some sort was necessary. There was not enough food to feed the people of the earth. Fruit and vegetables were becoming a thing of the past. Too much protein food in the form of meat and fish was injuring the race, and at last the people realized that, for fruits and vegetables, or their nutritive equivalent, they must turn from the field to the laboratory; from the farmer to the chemist. Synthetic food was the solution to the problem. There was no longer any use in planting and caring for food stuffs destined to become the nourishment of man's most deadly enemy.

The last planting took place in 2900, but there was no harvest, the voracious insects took every green shoot as soon as it appeared, and even trees, that had previously withstood the attacks of the huge insects, were by this time, stripped of every vestige of greenery.

The vegetable world suddenly ceased to exist. Over the barren plains which had been gradually filling with vast cities, man-made fires brought devastation to every living bit of greenery, so that in all the world there was no food for the insect pests.

II. Man or Insect?

Extract from the diary of Delfair, a descendant of Professor Fair, who had opposed the daring scientist.

From the borders of the great state-city of Iowa, I was witness to the passing of one of the great kingdoms of earth—the vegetable, and I can not find words to express the grief that overwhelms me as I write of its demise, for I loved all growing things. Many of us realized that Earth was no longer beautiful; but if beauty meant death; better life in the sterility of the metropolis.

The viciousness of the thwarted insects was a menace that we had foreseen and yet failed to take into adequate account. On the city-state borderland, life is constantly imperiled by the attacks of well organized bodies of our dreaded foe.

(*Note*: The organization that now exists among the ants, bees and other insects, testifies to the possibility of the development of military tactics among them in the centuries to come.)

Robbed of their source of food, they have become emboldened to such an extent that they will take any risks to carry human beings away for food, and after one of their well organized raids, the toll of human life is appalling.

But the great chemical laboratories where our synthetic food is made, and our oxygen plants, we thought were impregnable to their attacks. In that we were mistaken.

Let me say briefly that since the destruction of all vegetation which furnished a part of the oxygen essential to human life, it became necessary to manufacture this gas artificially for general diffusion through the atmosphere.

I was flying to my work, which is in Oxygen Plant No. 21, when I noticed a peculiar thing on the upper speedway near Food Plant No. 3,439. Although it was night, the various levels of the state-city were illuminated as brightly as by day. A pleasure vehicle was going with prodigious speed westward. I looked after it in amazement. It was unquestionably the car of Eric, my co-worker at Oxygen Plant No. 21. I recognized the gay color of its body, but to verify my suspicions beyond the question of a doubt, I turned my volplane in pursuit and made out the familiar license number. What was Eric doing away from the plant before I had arrived to relieve him from duty?

In hot pursuit, I sped above the car to the very border of the state-city, wondering what unheard of errand took him to the land of the enemy, for the car came to a sudden stop at the edge of what had once been an agricultural area. Miles ahead of me stretched an enormous expanse of black sterility; at my back was the teeming metropolis, five levels high—if one counted the hangar-level, which did not cover the residence sections.

I had not long to wait, for almost immediately my friend appeared. What a sight he presented to my incredulous gaze! He was literally covered from head to foot with the two-inch ants, that next to the beetles, had proved the greatest menace in their attacks upon humanity. With wild incoherent cries he fled over the rock and stubble-burned earth.

As soon as my stunned senses permitted, I swooped down toward him to effect a rescue, but even as my plane touched the barren earth, I saw that I was too late, for he fell, borne down by the vicious attacks of his myriad foes. I knew it was useless for me to set foot upon the ground, for my fate would be that of Eric. I rose ten feet and seizing my poison-gas weapon, let its contents out upon the tiny black evil things that swarmed below. I did not bother with my mask, for I planned to rise immediately, and it was not a moment too soon. From across the waste-land, a dark cloud eclipsed the stars and I saw coming toward me a horde of flying ants interspersed with larger flying insects, all bent upon my annihilation. I now took my mask and prepared to turn more gas upon my pursuers, but alas, I had used every atom of it in my attack upon the non-flying ants! I had no recourse but flight, and to this I immediately resorted, knowing that I could outdistance my pursuers.

When I could no longer see them, I removed my gas mask. A suffocating sensation seized me. I could not breathe! How high had I flown in my endeavor to escape the flying ants? I leaned over the side of my plane, expecting to see the city far, far below me. What was my utter amazement when I discovered that I was scarcely a thousand feet high! It was not altitude that was depriving me of the life-giving oxygen.

A drop of three hundred feet showed me inert specks of humanity lying about the streets. Then I knew; *the oxygen plant was not in operation!* In another minute I had on my oxygen mask, which was attached to a small portable tank for emergency use, and I rushed for the vicinity of the plant. There I witnessed the first signs of life. Men equipped with oxygen masks, were trying to force entrance into the locked building. Being an employee, I possessed knowledge of the combination of the great lock, and I opened the door, only to be greeted by a swarm of ants that commenced a concerted attack upon us.

The floor seemed to be covered with a moving black rug, the corner nearest the door appearing to unravel as we entered, and it was but a few seconds before we were covered with the clinging, biting creatures, who fought with a supernatural energy born of despair. Two very active ants succeeded in getting under my helmet. The bite of their sharp mandibles and the effect of their poisonous formic acid became intolerable. Did I dare remove my mask while the air about me was foul with the gas discharged from the weapons of my allies? While I felt the attacks elsewhere upon my body gradually diminishing as the insects succumbed to the deadly fumes, the two upon my face waxed more vicious under the protection of my mask. One at each eye, they were trying to blind me. The pain was unbearable. Better the suffocating death-gas than the torture of lacerated eyes! Frantically I removed the head-gear and tore at the shiny black fiends. Strange to tell, I discovered that I could breathe near the vicinity of the great oxygen tanks, where enough oxygen lingered to support life at least temporarily. The two vicious insects, no longer protected by my gas-mask, scurried from me like rats from a sinking ship and disappeared behind the oxygen tanks.

This attack of our enemies, though unsuccessful on their part, was dire in its significance, for it had shown more cunning and ingenuity than anything that had ever preceded it. Heretofore, their onslaughts had been confined to direct attacks upon us personally or upon the synthetic-food laboratories, but in this last raid they had shown an amazing cleverness that portended future disaster, unless they were checked at once. It was obvious they had ingeniously planned to smother us by the suspension of work at the oxygen plant, knowing that they themselves could exist in an atmosphere containing a greater percentage of carbon-dioxide. Their scheme, then, was to raid our laboratories for food.

III. Lucanus the Last

A Continuation of Delfair's Account.

Although it was evident that the cessation of all plant-life spelled inevitable doom for the insect inhabitants of Earth, their extermination did not follow as rapidly as one might have supposed. There were years of internecine warfare. The insects continued to thrive, though in decreasing numbers, upon stolen laboratory foods, bodies of human-beings and finally upon each other; at first capturing enemy species and at last even resorting to a cann*ibalistic procedure. Their rapacity grew in inverse proportion to their waning numbers, until the meeting of even an isolated insect might mean death, unless one were equipped with poison gas and prepared to use it upon a second's notice.

I am an old man now, though I have not yet lived quite two centuries, but I am happy in the knowledge that I have lived to see the last living insect which was held in captivity. It was an excellent specimen of the stag-beetle (*Lucanus*) and the years have testified that it was the sole survivor of a form of life that might have succeeded man upon this planet. This beetle was caught weeks after we had previously seen what was supposed to be the last living thing upon the globe, barring man and the sea-life. Untiring search for years has failed to reveal any more insects, so that at last man rests secure in the knowledge that he is monarch of all he surveys.

I have heard that long, long ago man used to gaze with a fearful fascination upon the reptilian creatures which he displaced, and just so did he view this lone specimen of a type of life that might have covered the face of the earth, but for man's ingenuity.

It was this unholy lure that drew me one day to view the captive beetle in his cage in district 404 at Universapolis. I was amazed at the size of the creature, for it looked larger than when I had seen it by television, but I reasoned that upon that occasion there had been no object near with which to compare its size. True, the broadcaster had announced its dimensions, but the statistics concretely given had failed to register a perfect realization of its prodigious proportions.

As I approached the cage, the creature was lying with its dorsal covering toward me and I judged it measured fourteen inches from one extremity to the other. Its smooth horny sheath gleamed in the bright artificial light. (It was confined on the third level.) As I stood there, mentally conjuring a picture of a world overrun with billions of such creatures as the one before me, the keeper approached the cage with a meal-portion of synthetic food. Although the food has no odor, the beetle sensed the man's approach, for it rose on its jointed legs and came toward us, its horn-like prongs moving threateningly; then apparently remembering its confinement, and the impotency of an attack, it subsided and quickly ate the food which had been placed within its prison.

The food consumed, it lifted itself to its hind legs, partially supported by a box, and turned its great eyes upon me. I had never been regarded with such utter malevolence before. The detestation was almost tangible and I shuddered involuntarily. As plainly as if he spoke, I knew that Lucanus was perfectly cognizant of the situation and in his gaze I read the concentrated hate of an entire defeated race.

I had no desire to gloat over his misfortune, rather a great pity toward him welled up within me. I pictured myself alone, the last of my kind, held up for ridicule before the swarming hordes of insects who had conquered my people, and I knew that life would no longer be worth the living.

Whether he sensed my pity or not I do not know, but he continued to survey me with unmitigated rage, as if he would convey to me the information that his was an implacable hatred that would outlast eternity.

Not long after this he died, and a world long since intolerant of ceremony, surprised itself by interring the beetle's remains in a golden casket, accompanied by much pomp and splendor.

I have lived many long years since that memorable event, and undoubtedly my days here are numbered, but I can pass on happily, convinced that in this sphere man's conquest of his environment is supreme.

IV. Efficiency Maximum

In a direct line of descent from Professor Fair and Delfair, the author of the preceding chapter, comes Thanor whose journal is given in this chapter.

Am I a true product of the year 2928? Sometimes I am convinced that I am hopelessly old-fashioned, an anachronism, that should have existed a thousand years ago. In no other way can I account for the dissatisfaction I feel in a world where efficiency has at last reached a maximum.

I am told that I spring from a line of ancestors who were not readily acclimated to changing conditions. I love beauty, yet I see none of it here. There are many who think our lofty buildings that tower two and three thousand feet into the air are beautiful, but while they are architectural splendors, they do not represent the kind of loveliness I crave. Only when I visit the sea do I feel any satisfaction for a certain yearning in my soul. The ocean alone shows the handiwork of God. The land bears evidence only of man.

As I read back through the diaries of my sentimental ancestors I find occasional glowing descriptions of the world that was; the world before the insects menaced human existence. Trees, plants and flowers brought delight into the lives of people as they wandered among them in vast open spaces, I am told, where the earth was soft beneath the feet, and flying creatures, called birds, sang among the greenery. True, I learn that many people had not enough to eat, and that uncontrollable passions governed them, but I do believe it must have been more interesting than this methodical, unemotional existence. I can not understand why many people were poor, for I am told that Nature as manifested in the vegetable kingdom was very prolific; so much so that year after year quantities of food rotted on the ground. The fault, I find by my reading, was not with Nature but with man's economic system which is now perfect, though this perfection really brings few of us happiness, I think.

Now there is no waste; all is converted into food. Long ago man learned how to reduce all matter to its constituent elements, of which there are nearly a hundred in number, and from them to rebuild compounds for food. The old axiom that nothing is created or destroyed, but merely changed from one form to another, has stood the test of ages. Man, as the agent of God, has simply performed the miracle of transmutation himself instead of waiting for natural forces to accomplish it as in the old days.

At first humanity was horrified when it was decreed that it must relinquish its dead to the laboratory. For too many eons had man closely associated the soul and body, failing to comprehend the body as merely a material agent, through which the spirit functioned. When man knew at last of the eternal qualities of spirit, he ceased to regard the discarded body with reverential awe, and saw in it only the same molecular constituents which comprised all matter about him. He recognized only material basically the same as that of stone or metal; material to be reduced to its atomic elements and rebuilt into matter that would render service to living humanity; that portion of matter wherein spirit functions.

The drab monotony of life is appalling. Is it possible that man had reached his height a thousand years ago and should have been willing to resign Earth's sovereignty to a coming order of creatures destined to be man's worthy successor in the eons to come? It seems that life is interesting only when there is a struggle, a goal to be reached through an evolutionary process. Once the goal is attained, all progress ceases. The huge reptiles of preglacial ages rose to supremacy by virtue of their great size, and yet was it not the excessive bulk of those creatures that finally wiped them out of existence? Nature, it seems, avoids extremes. She allows the fantastic to develop for awhile and then wipes the slate clean for a new order of development. Is it not conceivable that man could destroy himself through excessive development of his nervous system, and give place for the future evolution of a comparatively simple form of life, such as the insects were at man's height of development? This, it seems to me, was the great plan; a scheme with which man dared to interfere and for which he is now paying by the boredom of existence.

The earth's population is decreasing so rapidly, that I fear another thousand years will see a lifeless planet hurtling through space. It seems to me that only a miracle will save us now.

V. The Year 3928

The Original Writer, Nathano, Resumes the Narrative.

My ancestor, Thanor, of ten centuries ago, according to the records he gave to my great grandfather, seems to voice the general despair of humanity which, bad enough in his times, has reached the *nth* power in my day. A soulless world is gradually dying from self-inflicted boredom.

As I have ascertained from the perusal of the journals of my forebears, even antedating the extermination of the insects, I come of a stock that clings with sentimental tenacity to the things that made life worth while in the old days. If the world at large knew of my emotional musings concerning past ages, it would scarcely tolerate me, but surrounded by my thought-insulator, I often indulge in what fancies I will, and such meditation, coupled with a love for a few ancient relics from the past, has led me to a most amazing discovery.

Several months ago I found among my family relics a golden receptacle two feet long, one and a half in width and one in depth, which I found, upon opening, to contain many tiny square compartments, each filled with minute objects of slightly varying size, texture and color.

"Not sand!" I exclaimed as I closely examined the little particles of matter.

Food? After eating some, I was convinced that their nutritive value was small in comparison with a similar quantity of the products of our laboratories. What were the mysterious objects?

Just as I was about to close the lid again, convinced that I had one over-sentimental ancestor, whose gift to posterity was absolutely useless, my pocket-radio buzzed and the voice of my friend, Stentor, the interplanetary broadcaster, issued from the tiny instrument.

"If you're going to be home this afternoon," said Stentor, "I'll skate over. I have some interesting news."

I consented, for I thought I would share my "find" with this friend whom I loved above all others, but before he arrived I had again hidden my golden chest, for I had decided to await the development of events before sharing its mysterious secret with another. It was well that I did this for Stentor was so filled with the importance of his own news that he could have given me little attention at first.

"Well, what is your interesting news?" I asked after he was comfortably seated in my adjustable chair.

"You'd never guess," he replied with irritating leisureliness.

"Does it pertain to Mars or Venus?" I queried. "What news of our neighbor planets?"

"You may know it has nothing to do with the self-satisfied Martians," answered the broadcaster, "but the Venusians have a very serious problem confronting them. It is in connection with the same old difficulty they have had ever since interplanetary radio was developed forty years ago. You remember, that, in their second communication with us, they told us of their continual warfare on insect pests that were destroying all vegetable food? Well, last night after general broadcasting had ceased, I was surprised to hear the voice of the Venusian broadcaster. He is suggesting that we get up a scientific expedition to Venus to help the natives of his unfortunate planet solve their insect problem as we did ours. He says the Martians turn a deaf ear to their plea for help, but he expects sympathy and assistance from Earth who has so recently solved these problems for herself."

I was dumbfounded at Stentor's news.

"But the Venusians are farther advanced mechanically than we," I objected, "though they are behind us in the natural sciences. They could much more easily solve the difficulties of space-flying than we could."

"That is true," agreed Stentor, "but if we are to render them material aid in freeing their world from devastating insects, we must get to Venus. The past four decades have proved that we can not help them merely by verbal instructions."

"Now, last night," Stentor continued, with warming enthusiasm, "Wanyana, the Venusian broadcaster, informed me that scientists on Venus are developing interplanetary television. This, if successful, will prove highly beneficial in facilitating communication, and it may even do away with the necessity of interplanetary travel, which I think is centuries ahead of us yet."

"Television, though so common here on Earth and on Venus, has seemed an impossibility across the ethereal void," I said, "but if it becomes a reality, I believe it will be the Venusians who will take the initiative, though of course they will be helpless without our friendly cooperation. In return for the mechanical instructions they have given us from time to time, I think it no more than right that we should try to give them all the help possible in freeing their world, as ours has been freed, of the insects that threaten their very existence. Personally, therefore, I hope it can be done through radio and television rather than by personal excursions."

"I believe you are right," he admitted, "but I hope we can be of service to them soon. Ever since I have served in the capacity of official interplanetary broadcaster, I have liked the spirit of good-fellowship shown by the Venusians through their spokesman,

Wanyana. The impression is favorable in contrast to the superciliousness of the inhabitants of Mars."

We conversed for some time, but at length he rose to take his leave. It was then I ventured to broach the subject that was uppermost in my thoughts.

"I want to show you something, Stentor," I said, going into an adjoining room for my precious box and returning shortly with it. "A relic from the days of an ancestor named Delfair, who lived at the time the last insect, a beetle, was kept in captivity. Judging from his personal account, Delfair was fully aware of the significance of the changing times in which he lived, and contrary to the majority of his contemporaries, possessed a sentimentality of soul that has proved an historical asset to future generations. Look, my friend, these he left to posterity!"

I deposited the heavy casket on a table between us and lifted the lid, revealing to Stentor the mystifying particles.

The face of Stentor was eloquent of astonishment. Not unnaturally his mind took somewhat the same route as mine had followed previously, though he added atomic-power-units to the list of possibilities. He shook his head in perplexity.

"Whatever they are, there must have been a real purpose behind their preservation," he said at last. "You say this old Delfair witnessed the passing of the insects? What sort of a fellow was he? Likely to be up to any tricks?"

"Not at all," I asserted rather indignantly, "he seemed a very serious minded chap; worked in an oxygen-plant and took an active part in the last warfare between men and insects."

Suddenly Stentor stooped over and scooped up some of the minute particles into the palm of his hand—and then he uttered a maniacal shriek and flung them into the air.

"Great God, man, do you know what they are?" he screamed, shaking violently.

"No, I do not," I replied quietly, with an attempt at dignity I did not feel.

"Insect eggs!" he cried, and shuddering with terror, he made for the door.

I caught him on the threshold and pulled him forcibly back into the room.

"Now see here," I said sternly, "not a word of this to anyone. Do you understand? I will test out your theory in every possible way but I want no public interference."

At first he was obstinate, but finally yielded to threats when supplications were impotent.

"I will test them," I said, "and will endeavor to keep hatchings under absolute control, should they prove to be what you suspect."

It was time for the evening broadcasting, so he left, promising to keep our secret and leaving me regretting that I had taken another into my confidence.

VI. The Miracle

For days following my unfortunate experience with Stentor, I experimented upon the tiny objects that had so terrified him. I subjected them to various tests for the purpose of ascertaining whether or not they bore evidence of life, whether in egg, pupa or larva stages of development. And to all my experiments, there was but one answer. No life was manifest. Yet I was not satisfied, for chemical tests showed that they were composed of organic matter. Here was an inexplicable enigma! Many times I was on the verge of consigning the entire contents of the chest to the flames. I seemed to see in my mind's eye the world again over-ridden with insects, and that calamity due to the indiscretions of one man! My next impulse was to turn over my problem to scientists, when a suspicion of the truth dawned upon me. These were seeds, the germs of plant-life, and they might grow. But alas, where? Over all the earth man has spread his artificial dominion. The state-city has been succeeded by what could be termed the nation-city, for one great floor of concrete or rock covers the country.

I resolved to try an experiment, the far-reaching influence of which I did not at that time suspect. Beneath the lowest level of the community edifice in which I dwell, I removed, by means of a small atomic excavator, a slab of concrete large enough to admit my body. I let myself down into the hole and felt my feet resting on a soft dark substance that I knew to be dirt. I hastily filled a box of this, and after replacing the concrete slab, returned to my room, where I proceeded to plant a variety of the seeds.

Being a product of an age when practically to wish for a thing in a material sense is to have it, I experienced the greatest impatience, while waiting for any evidences of plant-life to become manifest. Daily, yes hourly, I watched the soil for signs of a type of life long since departed from the earth, and was about convinced that the germ of life could not have survived the centuries, when a tiny blade of green proved to me that a miracle, more wonderful to me than the works of man through the ages, was taking place before my eyes. This was an enigma so complex and yet so simple, that one recognized in it a direct revelation of Nature.

Daily and weekly I watched in secret the botanical miracle. It was my one obsession. I was amazed at the fascination it held for me—a man who viewed the marvels of the thirty-fourth century with unemotional complacency. It showed me that Nature is manifest in the simple things which mankind has chosen to ignore.

Then one morning, when I awoke, a white blossom displayed

its immaculate beauty and sent forth its delicate fragrance into the air. The lily, a symbol of new life, resurrection! I felt within me the stirring of strange emotions I had long believed dead in the bosom of man. But the message must not be for me alone. As of old, the lily would be the symbol of life for all!

With trembling hands, I carried my precious burden to a front window where it might be witnessed by all who passed by. The first day there were few who saw it, for only rarely do men and women walk; they usually ride in speeding vehicles of one kind or another, or employ electric skates, a delightful means of locomotion, which gives the body some exercise. The fourth city level, which is reserved for skaters and pedestrians, is kept in a smooth glass-like condition. And so it was only the occasional pedestrian, walking on the outer border of the fourth level, upon which my window faced, who first carried the news of the growing plant to the world, and it was not long before it was necessary for civic authorities to disperse the crowds that thronged to my window for a glimpse of a miracle in green and white.

When I showed my beautiful plant to Stentor, he was most profuse in his apology and came to my rooms every day to watch it unfold and develop, but the majority of people, long used to business-like efficiency, were intolerant of the sentimental emotions that swayed a small minority, and I was commanded to dispose of the lily. But a figurative seed had been planted in the human heart, a seed that could not be disposed of so readily, and this seed ripened and grew until it finally bore fruit.

VII. Ex Terreno

It is a very different picture of humanity that I paint ten years after the last entry in my diary. My new vocation is farming, but it is farming on a far more intensive scale than had been done two thousand years ago. Our crops never fail, for temperature and rainfall are regulated artificially. But we attribute our success principally to the total absence of insect pests. Our small agricultural areas dot the country like the parks of ancient days and supply us with a type of food, no more nourishing, but more appetizing than that produced in the laboratories. Truly we are living in a marvelous age! If the earth is ours completely, why may we not turn our thoughts toward the other planets in our solar-system? For the past ten or eleven years the Venusians have repeatedly urged us to come and assist them in their battle for life. I believe it is our duty to help them.

Tomorrow will be a great day for us and especially for Stentor, as the new interplanetary television is to be tested, and it is possible that for the first time in history, we shall see our neighbors in the infinity of space. Although the people of Venus were about a thousand years behind us in many respects, they have made wonderful progress with radio and television. We have been in radio communication with them for the last half century and they shared with us the joy of the establishment of our Eden. They have always been greatly interested in hearing Stentor tell the story of our subjugation of the insects that threatened to wipe us out of existence, for they have exactly that problem to solve now; judging from their reports, we fear that theirs is a losing battle. Tomorrow we shall converse face to face with the Venusians! It will be an event second in importance only to the first radio communications interchanged fifty years ago. Stentor's excitement exceeds that displayed at the time of the discovery of the seeds.

Well it is over and the experiment was a success, but alas for the revelation!

The great assembly halls all over the continent were packed with humanity eager to catch a first glimpse of the Venusians. Prior to the test, we sent our message of friendship and good will by radio, and received a reciprocal one from our interplanetary neighbors. Alas, we were ignorant at that time! Then the television receiving apparatus was put into operation, and we sat with breathless interest, our eyes intent upon the crystal screen before us. I sat near Stentor and noted the feverish ardor with which he watched for the first glimpse of Wanyana.

At first hazy mist-like spectres seemed to glide across the screen. We knew these figures were not in correct perspective. Finally, one object gradually became more opaque, its outlines could be seen clearly. Then across that vast assemblage, as well as thousands of others throughout the world, there swept a wave of speechless horror, as its full significance burst upon mankind.

The figure that stood facing us was a huge six-legged beetle, not identical in every detail with our earthly enemies of past years, but unmistakably an insect of gigantic proportions! Of course it could not see us, for our broadcaster was not to appear until afterward, but it spoke, and we had to close our eyes to convince ourselves that it was the familiar voice of Wanyana, the leading Venusian radio broadcaster. Stentor grabbed my arm, uttered an inarticulate cry and would have fallen but for my timely support.

"Friends of Earth, as you call your world," began the object of horror, "this is a momentous occasion in the annals of the twin planets, and we are looking forward to seeing one of you, and preferably Stentor, for the first time, as you are now viewing one of us. We have listened many times, with interest, to your story of the insect pests which threatened to follow you as lords of your planet.

As you have often heard us tell, we are likewise molested with insects. Our fight is a losing one, unless we can soon exterminate them."

Suddenly, the Venusian was joined by another being, a colossal ant, who bore in his fore-legs a tiny light-colored object which he handed to the beetle-announcer, who took it and held it forward for our closer inspection. It seemed to be a tiny ape, but was so small we could not ascertain for a certainty. We were convinced, however, that it was a mammalian creature, an "insect" pest of Venus. Yet in it we recognized rudimentary man as we know him on earth!

There was no question as to the direction in which sympathies instinctively turned, yet reason told us that our pity should be given to the intelligent reigning race who had risen to its present mental attainment through eons of time. By some quirk or freak of nature, way back in the beginning, life had developed in the form of insects instead of mammals. Or (the thought was repellent) had insects in the past succeeded in displacing mammals, as they might have done here on earth?

There was no more television that night. Stentor would not appear, so disturbed was he by the sight of the Venusians, but in the morning, he talked to them by radio and explained the very natural antipathy we experienced in seeing them or in having them see us.

Now they no longer urge us to construct ether-ships and go to help them dispose of their "insects." I think they are afraid of us, and their very fear has aroused in mankind an unholy desire to conquer them.

I am against it. Have we not had enough of war in the past? We have subdued our own world and should be content with that, instead of seeking new worlds to conquer. But life is too easy here. I can plainly see that. Much as he may seem to dislike it, man is not happy, unless he has some enemy to overcome, some difficulty to surmount.

Alas my greatest fears for man were groundless!

A short time ago, when I went out into my field to see how my crops were faring, I found a six-pronged beetle voraciously eating. No—man will not need to go to Venus to fight "insects."

1928

LESLIE F. STONE

The Conquest of Gola

HOLA, my daughters (sighed the Matriarch) it is true indeed, I am the only living one upon Gola who remembers the invasion from Detaxal, I alone of all my generation survive to recall vividly the sights and scenes of that past era. And well it is that you come to me to hear by free communication of mind to mind face to face with each other.

Ah, well I remember the surprise of that hour when through the mists that enshroud our lovely world, there swam the first of the great smooth cylinders of the Detaxalans, fifty *tas** in length, as glistening and silvery as the soil of our land, propelled by the man-things that on Detaxal are supreme even as we women are supreme on Gola.

In those bygone days, as now, Gola was enwrapped by her cloud mists that keep from us the terrific glare of the great star that glows like a malignant spirit out there in the darkness of the void. Only occasionally when a particularly great storm parts the mist of heaven do we see the wonders of the vast universe, but that does not prevent us, with our marvelous telescopes handed down to us from thousands of generations before us, from learning what lies across the dark seas of the outside.

*Since there is no means of translating the Golan measurements of either length or time we can but guess at these things. However, since the Detaxalan ships each carried a thousand men it can be seen that the ships were between five hundred and a thousand feet in length.

Therefore we knew of the nine planets that encircle the great star and are subject its rule. And so are we familiar enough with the surfaces of these planets to know why Gola should appear as a haven to their inhabitants who see in our cloud-enclosed mantle a sweet release from the blasting heat and blinding glare of the great sun.

So it was not strange at all to us to find that the people of Detaxal, the third planet of the sun, had arrived on our globe with a wish in their hearts to migrate here, and end their days out of reach of the blistering warmth that had come to be their lot on their own world.

Long ago we, too, might have gone on exploring expeditions to other worlds, other universes, but for what? Are we not happy here? We who have attained the greatest of civilizations within the confines of our own silvery world. Powerfully strong with our mighty force rays, we could subjugate all the universe, but why?

Are we not content with life as it is, with our lovely cities, our homes, our daughters, our gentle consorts? Why spend physical energy in combative strife for something we do not wish, when our mental processes carry us further and beyond the conquest of mere terrestrial exploitation?

On Detaxal it is different, for there the peoples, the ignoble male creatures, breed for physical prowess, leaving the development of their sciences, their philosophies, and the contemplation of the abstract to a chosen few. The greater part of the race fares forth to conquer, to lay waste, to struggle and fight as the animals do over a morsel of worthless territory. Of course we can see why they desired Gola with all its treasures, but we can thank Providence and ourselves that they did not succeed in "commercializing" us as they have the remainder of the universe with their ignoble Federation.

*

Ah yes, well I recall the hour when first they came, pushing cautiously through the cloud mists, seeking that which lay beneath. We of Gola were unwarned until the two cylinders hung directly above Tola, the greatest city of that time, which still lies in its ruins since that memorial day. But they have paid for it—paid for it well in thousands and in tens of thousands of their men.

We were first apprised of their coming when the alarm from Tola was sent from the great beam station there, advising all to stand in readiness for an emergency. Geble, my mother, was then Queen of all Gola, and I was by her side in Morka, that pleasant seaside resort, where I shall soon travel again to partake of its rejuvenating waters.

With us were four of Geble's consorts, sweet gentle males, that gave Geble much pleasure in these free hours away from the worries of state. But when the word of the strangers' descent over our home city, Tola, came to us, all else was forgotten. With me at her side, Geble hastened to the beam station and there in the matter transmitter we dispatched our physical beings to the palace at Tola, and the next moment were staring upward at the two strange shapes etched against the clouds.

What the Detaxalan ships were waiting for we did not know then, but later we learned. Not grasping the meaning of our beam stations, the commandants of the ships considered the city below them entirely lacking in means of defense, and were conferring on the method of taking it without bloodshed on either side.

It was not long after our arrival in Tola that the first of the ships began to descend toward the great square before the palace. Geble watched without a word, her great mind already scanning the brains of those whom she found within the great machine. She transferred to my mind but a single thought as I stood there at her side and that with a sneer, "Barbarians!"

Now the ship was settling in the square and after a few moments of hesitation, a circular doorway appeared at the side and four of the Detaxalans came through the opening. The square was empty but for themselves and their flyer, and we saw them looking about surveying the beautiful buildings on all sides. They seemed to recognize the palace for what it was and in one accord moved in our direction.

Then Geble left the window at which we stood and strode to the doorway opening upon the balcony that faced the square. The Detaxalans halted in their tracks when they saw her slender graceful form appear and removing the strange coverings they wore on their heads they each made a bow.

Again Geble sneered for only the male-things of our world bow their heads, and so she recognized these visitors for what they were, nothing more than the despicable males of the species! And what creatures they were!

Imagine a short almost flat body set high upon two slender legs, the body tapering in the middle, several times as broad across as it is through the center, with two arms almost as long as the legs attached to the upper part of the torso. A small column-like neck of only a few inches divides the head of oval shape from the body, and in this head only are set the organs of sight, hearing, and scent. Their bodies were like a patch work of a misguided nature.

Yes, strange as it is, my daughters, practically all of the creature's faculties had their base in the small ungainly head, and each organ was perforce pressed into serving for several functions. For instance, the breathing nostrils also served for scenting out odors, nor was this organ able to exclude any disagreeable odors that might come its way, but had to dispense to the brain both pleasant and unpleasant odors at the same time.

Then there was the mouth, set directly beneath the nose, and here again we had an example of one organ doing the work of two for the creature not only used the mouth with which to take in the food for its body, but it also used the mouth to enunciate the excruciatingly ugly sounds of its language forthwith.

Guests From Detaxal

Never before have I seen such a poorly organized body, so unlike our own highly developed organisms. How much nicer it is to be able to call forth any organ at will, and dispense with it when its usefulness is over! Instead these poor Detaxalans had to carry theirs about in physical being all the time so that always was the surface of their bodies entirely marred.

Yet that was not the only part of their ugliness, and proof of the lowliness of their origin, for whereas our fine bodies support themselves by muscular development, these poor creatures were dependent entirely upon a strange structure to keep them in their proper shape.

Imagine if you can a bony skeleton somewhat like the foundations upon which we build our edifices, laying stone and cement over the steel framework. But this skeleton instead is inside a body which the flesh, muscle and skin overlay. Everywhere in their bodies are these cartilaginous structures—hard, heavy, bony structures developed by the chemicals of the being for its use. Even the hands, feet and head of the creatures were underlaid with these bones, ugh, it was terrible when we dissected one of the fellows for study. I shudder to think of it.

Yet again there was still another feature of the Detaxalans that was equally as horrifying as the rest, namely their outer covering. As we viewed them for the first time out there in the square we discovered that parts of the body, that is the part of the head which they called the face, and the bony hands were entirely naked without any sort of covering, neither fur nor feathers, just the raw, pinkish-brown skin looking as if it had been recently plucked.

Later we found a few specimens that had a type of fur on the lower part of the face, but these were rare. And when they doffed the head coverings which we had first taken for some sort of natural covering, we saw that the top of the head was overlaid with a very fine fuzz of fur several inches long.

We did not know in the beginning that the strange covering on the bodies of the four men, green in color, was not a natural growth, but later discovered that such was the truth, and not only the face and hands were bare of fur, but the entire body, except for a fine sprinkling of hair that was scarcely visible except on the chest, was also bare. No wonder the poor things covered themselves with their awkward clothing. We arrived at the conclusion that their lack of fur had been brought about by the fact that always they had been exposed to the bright rays of the sun so that without the dampness of our own planet the fur had dried up and fallen away from the flesh!

Now thinking it over I suppose that we of Gola presented strange form to the people of Detaxal with our fine circular bodies, rounded at the top, our short beautiful lower limbs with the circular foot pads, and our short round arms and hand pads, flexible and muscular like rubber.

But how envious they must have been of our beautiful golden coats, our movable eyes, our power to scent, hear and touch with any part of the body, to absorb food and drink through any part of the body most convenient to us at any time. Oh yes, laugh though you may, without a doubt we were also freaks to those freakish Detaxalans. But no matter, let us return to the tale.

On recognizing our visitors for what they were, simple-minded males, Geble was chagrined at them for taking up her time, but they were strangers to our world and we Golans are always courteous. Geble began of course to try to communicate by thought transference, but strangely enough the fellows below did not catch a single thought. Instead, entirely unaware of Geble's overture to friendship, the leader commenced to speak to her in most outlandish manner, contorting the red lips of his mouth into various uncouth shapes and making sounds that fell upon our hearing so unpleasantly that we immediately closed our senses to them. And without a word Geble turned her back upon them, calling for Tanka, her personal secretary.

Tanka was instructed to welcome the Detaxalans while she herself turned to her own chambers to summon a half dozen of her council. When the council arrived she began to discuss with them the problem of extracting more of the precious tenix from the waters of the great inland lake of Notauch. Nothing whatever was said of the advent of the Detaxalans for Geble had dismissed them from her mind as creatures not worthy of her thought.

In the meantime Tanka had gone forth to meet the four who of course could not converse with her. In accordance with the Queen's orders she led them indoors to the most informal receiving chamber and there had them served with food and drink which by the looks of the remains in the dishes they did not relish at all.

Leading them through the rooms of the lower floor of the palace she made a pretence of showing them everything which they duly surveyed. But they appeared to chafe at the manner in which they were being entertained.

The creatures even made an attempt through the primitive method of conversing by their arms to learn something of what they had seen, but Tanka was as supercilious as her mistress. When she thought they had had enough, she led them to the square and back to the door of their flyer, giving them their dismissal.

But the men were not ready to accept it. Instead they tried to express to Tanka their desire to meet the ruling head of Gola. Although their hand motions were perfectly inane and incomprehensible, Tanka could read what passed through their brains, and understood more fully than they what lay in their minds. She shook her head and motioned that they were to embark in their flyer and be on their way back to their planet.

Again and again the Detaxalans tried to explain what they wished, thinking Tanka did not understand. At last she impressed upon their savage minds that there was nothing for them but to depart, and disgruntled by her treatment they reentered their machine, closed its ponderous door and raised their ship to the level of its sister flyer. Several minutes passed and then, with thanksgiving, we saw them pass over the city.

Told of this, Geble laughed, "To think of mere man-things daring to attempt to force themselves upon us. What is the universe coming to? What are their women back home considering when they sent them to us. Have they developed too many males and think that we can find use for them?" she wanted to know.

"It is strange indeed," observed Yabo, one of the council members. "What did you find in the minds of these ignoble creatures, O August One?"

"Nothing of particular interest, a very low grade of intelligence, to be sure. There was no need of looking below the surface."

"It must have taken intelligence to build those ships."

"None aboard them did that. I don't question it but that their mothers built the ships for them as playthings, even as we give toys to our 'little ones,' you know. I recall that the ancients of our world perfected several types of space-flyers many ages ago!"

"Maybe those males do not have 'mothers' but instead they build the ships themselves, maybe they are the stronger sex on their world!" This last was said by Suiki, the fifth consort of Geble, a pretty little male, rather young in years. No one had noticed his coming into the chamber, but now everyone showed their surprise at his words.

"Impossible!" ejaculated Yabo.

Geble however laughed at the little chap's expression. "Suiki is a profound thinker," she observed, still laughing, and she drew him to her gently hugging him.

A Nice Business Deal

And with that the subject of the men from Detaxal was closed. It was reopened, however, several hours later when it was learned that instead of leaving Gola altogether the ships were seen one after another by the various cities of the planet as they circumnavigated it.

It was rather annoying, for everywhere the cities' routines were broken up as the people dropped their work and studies to gaze at the cylinders. Too, it was upsetting the morale of the males, for on learning that the two ships contained only creatures of their own sex they were becoming envious, wishing for the same type of playthings for themselves.

Shut in, as they are, unable to grasp the profundities of our science and thought, the gentle, fun-loving males were always glad for a new diversion, and this new method developed by the Detaxalans had intrigued them.

It was then that Geble decided it high time to take matters into her own hands. Not knowing where the two ships were at the moment it was not difficult with the object-finder beam to discover their whereabouts, and then with the attractor to draw them to Tola magnetically. An *ous* later we had the pleasure of seeing the two ships rushing toward our city. When they arrived about it, power brought them down to the square again.

Again Tanka was sent out, and directed the commanders of the two ships to follow her in to the Queen. Knowing the futility of attempting to converse with them without mechanical aid, Geble caused to be brought her three of the ancient mechanical thought transformers that are only museum pieces to us but still workable. The two men were directed to place them on their heads while she donned the third. When this was done she ordered the creatures to depart immediately from Gola, telling them that she was tired of their play.

Watching the faces of the two I saw them frowning and shaking their heads. Of course I could read their thoughts as well as Geble without need of the transformers, since it was only for their benefit that these were used, so I heard the whole conversation, though I need only to give you the gist of it.

"We have no wish to leave your world as yet," the two had argued.

"You are disrupting the routine of our lives here," Geble told them, "and now that you've seen all that you can there is no need for you to stay longer. I insist that you leave immediately."

I saw one of the men smile, and thereupon he was the one

who did all the talking (I say "talking" for this he was actually doing, mouthing each one of his words although we understood his thoughts as they formed in his queer brain, so different from ours).

"Listen here," he laughed, "I don't get the hang of you people at all. We came to Gola (he used some outlandish name of his own, but I use our name of course) with the express purpose of exploration and exploitation. We come as friends. Already we are in alliance with Damin (again the name for the fourth planet of our system was different, but I give the correct appellation), established commerce and trade, and now we are ready to offer you the chance to join our federation peaceably.

"What we have seen of this world is very favorable, there are good prospects for business here. There is no reason why you people as those of Damin and Detaxal can not enter into a nice business arrangement congenially. You have far more here to offer tourists, more than Damin. Why, except for your clouds this would be an ideal paradise for every man, woman and child on Detaxal and Damin to visit, and of course with our new cloud dispensers we could clear your atmosphere for you in short order and keep it that way. Why you'll make millions in the first year of your trade.

"Come now, allow us to discuss this with your ruler—king or whatever you call him. Women are all right in their place, but it takes the men to see the profit of a thing like this—er—you are a woman aren't you?"

The first of his long speech, of course, was so much gibberish to us, with his prate of business arrangements, commerce and trade, tourists, profits, cloud dispensers and what not, but it was the last part of what he said that took my breath away, and you can imagine how it affected Geble. I could see straightway that she was intensely angered, and good reason too. By the looks of the silly fellow's face I could guess that he was getting the full purport of her thoughts. He began to shuffle his funny feet and a foolish grin pervaded his face.

"Sorry," he said, "if I insulted you—I didn't intend that, but I believed that man holds the same place here as he does on Detaxal and Damin, but I suppose it is just as possible for woman to be the ruling factor of a world as man is elsewhere."

That speech naturally made Geble more irate, and tearing off her thought transformer she left the room without another word. In a moment, however, Yabo appeared wearing the transformer in her place. Yabo had none of the beauty of my mother, for whereas Geble was slender and as straight as a rod Yabo was obese, and her fat body overflowed until she looked like a large dumpy bundle of *yat* held together in her furry skin. She had very little dignity as she waddled toward the Detaxalans, but there was determination in her whole manner and without preliminaries she began to scold the two as though they were her own consorts.

"There has been enough of this, my fine young men," she shot at them. "You've had your fun, and now it is time for you to return to your mothers and consorts. Shame on you for making up such miserable tales about yourselves. I have a good mind to take you home with me for a couple of days, and I'd put you in your places quick enough. The idea of men acting like you are!"

For a moment I thought the Detaxalans were going to cry by the faces they made, but instead they broke into laughter, such heathenish sounds as had never before been heard on Gola, and I listened in wonder instead of excluding it from my hearing, but the fellows sobered quickly enough at that, and the spokesman addressed the shocked Yabo.

"I see," said he, "it's impossible for your people and mine to arrive at an understanding peaceably. I'm sorry that you take us for children out on a spree, that you are accustomed to such a low type of men as is evidently your lot here.

"I have given you your chance to accept our terms without force, but since you refuse, under the orders of the Federation I will have to take you forcibly, for we are determined that Gola become one of us, if you like it or not. Then you will learn that we are not the children you believe us to be.

"You may go to your supercilious Queen now and advise her that we give you exactly ten hours in which to evacuate this city, for precisely on the hour we will lay this city in ruins. And if that does not suffice you we will do the same with every other city on the planet! Remember ten hours!"

And with that he took the mechanical thought transformer from his head and tossed it on the table. His companion did the same and the two of them strode out of the room and to their flyers which arose several thousand feet above Tola and remained there.

The Triumph of Gola

Hurrying into Geble, Yabo told her what the Detaxalan had said. Geble was reclining on her couch and did not bother to raise herself.

"Childish prattle," she conceded and withdrew her red eyes on their movable stems into their pockets, paying no more heed to the threats of the men from Detaxal.

I, however, could not be as calm as my mother, and I was fearful that it was not childish prattle after all. Not knowing how long ten hours might be I did not wait, but crept up to the palace's beam station and set its dials so that the entire building and as much of the surrounding territory it could cover were protected in the force zone.

Alas that the same beam was not greater. But it had not been put there for defense, only for matter transference and whatever other peacetime methods we used. It was the means of proving just the same that it was also a very good defensive instrument, for just two *ous* later the hovering ships above let loose their powers of destruction, heavy explosives that entirely demolished all of Tola and its millions of people and only the palace royal of all that beauty was left standing!

Awakened from her nap by the terrific detonation, Geble came hurriedly to a window to view the ruin, and she was wild with grief at what she saw. Geble, however, saw that there was urgent need for action. She knew without my telling her what I had done to protect the palace. And though she showed no sign of appreciation, I knew that I had won a greater place in her regard than any other of her many daughters and would henceforth be her favorite as well as her successor as the case turned out.

Now, with me behind her, she hurried to the beam station and in a twinkling we were both in Tubia, the second greatest city of that time. Nor were we to be caught napping again, for Geble ordered all beam stations to throw out their zone forces while she herself manipulated one of Tubia's greatest power beams, attuning it to the emanations of the two Detaxalan flyers. In less than an *ous* the two ships were seen through the mists heading for Tubia. For a moment I grew fearful, but on realizing that they were after all in our grip, and the attractors held every living thing powerless against movement, I grew calm and watched them come over the city and the beam pull them to the ground.

With the beam still upon them, they lay supine on the ground without motion. Descending to the square Geble called for Ray C, and when the machine arrived she herself directed the cutting of the hole in the side of the flyer and was the first to enter it with me immediately behind, as usual.

We were both astounded by what we saw of the great array of machinery within. But a glance told Geble all she wanted to know of their principles. She interested herself only in the men standing rigidly in whatever position our beam had caught them. Only the eyes of the creatures expressed their fright, poor things, unable to move so much as a hair while we moved among them untouched by the power of the beam because of the strength of our own minds.

They could have fought against it if they had known how, but their simple minds were too weak for such exercise.

Now glancing about among the stiff forms around us, of which there were one thousand, Geble picked out those of the males she desired for observation, choosing those she judged to be their finest specimens, those with much hair on their faces and having more girth than the others. These she ordered removed by several workers who followed us, and then we emerged again to the outdoors.

Using hand beam torches the picked specimens were kept immobile after they were out of reach of the greater beam and were borne into the laboratory of the building Geble had converted into her new palace. Geble and I followed, and she gave the order for the complete annihilation of the two powerless ships.

Thus ended the first foray of the people of Detaxal. And for the next two *tels* there was peace upon our globe again. In the laboratory the thirty who had been rescued from their ships were given thorough examinations both physically and mentally and we learned all there was to know about them. Hearing of the destruction of their ships, most of the creatures had become frightened and were quite docile in our hands. Those that were unruly were used in the dissecting room for the advancement of Golan knowledge.

After a complete study of them which yielded little we lost interest in them scientifically. Geble, however, found some pleasure in having the poor creatures around her and kept three of them in her own chambers so she could delve into their brains as she pleased. The others she doled out to her favorites as she saw fit.

One she gave to me to act as a slave or in what capacity I desired him, but my interest in him soon waned, especially since I had now come of age and was allowed to have two consorts of my own, and go about the business of bringing my daughters into the world.

My slave I called Jon and gave him complete freedom of my house. If only we had foreseen what was coming we would have annihilated every one of them immediately! It did please me later to find that Jon was learning our language and finding a place in my household, making friends with my two shut-in consorts. But as I have said I paid little attention to him.

So life went on smoothly with scarcely a change after the destruction of the ships of Detaxal. But that did not mean we were unprepared for more. Geble reasoned that there would be more ships forthcoming when the Detaxalans found that their first two did not return. So, although it was sometimes inconvenient, the zones of force were kept upon our cities.

And Geble was right, for the day came when dozens of flyers descended upon Gola from Detaxal. But this time the zones of force did not hold them since the zones were not in operation!

And we were unwarned, for when they descended upon us, our world was sleeping, confident that our zones were our protection. The first indication that I had of trouble brewing was when awakening I found the ugly form of Jon bending over me. Surprised, for it was not his habit to arouse me, I started up only to find his arms about me, embracing me. And how strong he was! For the moment a new emotion swept me, for the first time I knew the pleasure to be had in the arms of a strong man, but that emotion was short lived for I saw in the blue eyes of my slave that he had recognized the look in my eyes for what it was, and for the moment he was tender.

Later I was to grow angry when I thought of that expression of his, for his eyes filled with pity, pity for me! But pity did not stay, instead he grinned and the next instant he was binding me down to my couch with strong rope. Geble, I learned later, had been treated as I, as were the members of the council and every other woman in Gola!

That was what came of allowing our men to meet on common ground with the creatures from Detaxal, for a weak mind is open to seeds of rebellion and the Detaxalans had sown it well, promising dominance to the lesser creatures of Gola.

That, however, was only part of the plot on the part of the Detaxalans. They were determined not only to revenge those we had murdered, but also to gain mastery of our planet. Unnoticed by us they had constructed a machine which transmits sound as we transmit thought and by its means had communicated with their own world, advising them of the very hour to strike when all of Gola was slumbering. It was a masterful stroke, only they did not know the power of the mind of Gola—so much more ancient than theirs.

Lying there bound on my couch I was able to see out the window and trembling with terror I watched a half dozen Detaxalan flyers descend into Tubia, guessing that the same was happening in our other cities. I was truly frightened, for I did not have the brain of a Geble. I was young yet, and in fear I watched the hordes march out of their machines, saw the thousands of our men join them.

Free from restraint, the shut-ins were having their holiday and how they cavorted out in the open, most of the time getting in the way of the freakish Detaxalans who were certainly taking over our city.

A half *ous* passed while I lay there watching, waiting in fear at what the Detaxalans planned to do with us. I remembered the pleasant, happy life we had led up to the present and trembled over what the future might be when the Detaxalans had infested us with commerce and trade, business propositions, tourists and all of their evil practices. It was then that I received the message from Geble, clear and definite, just as all the women of the globe received it, and hope returned to my heart.

There began that titanic struggle, the fight for supremacy, the fight that won us victory over the simple-minded weaklings below who had presumptuously dared to conquer us. The first indications that the power of our combined mental concentration at Geble's orders was taking effect was when we saw the first of our males halt in their wild dance of freedom. They tried to shake us off, but we knew we could bring them back to us.

At first the Detaxalans paid them no heed. They knew not what was happening until there came the wholesale retreat of the Golan men back to the buildings, back to the chambers from which they had escaped. Then grasping something of what was happening the already defeated invaders sought to retain their hold on our little people. Our erstwhile captives sought to hold them with oratorical gestures, but of course we won. We saw our creatures return to us and unbind us.

Only the Detaxalans did not guess the significance of that, did not realize that inasmuch as we had conquered our own men, we could conquer them also. As they went about their work of making our city their own, establishing already their autocratic bureaus wherever they pleased, we began to concentrate upon them, hypnotizing them to the flyers that had disgorged them.

And soon they began to feel of our power, the weakest ones first, feeling the mental bewilderment creeping upon them. Their leaders, stronger in mind, knew nothing of this at first, but soon our terrible combined mental power was forced upon them also and they realized that their men were deserting them, crawling back to their ships! The leaders began to exhort them into new action, driving them physically. But our power gained on them and now we began to concentrate upon the leaders themselves. They were strong of will and they defied us, fought us, mind against mind, but of course it was useless. Their minds were not suited to the test they put themselves to, and after almost three *ous* of struggle, we of Gola were able to see victory ahead.

At last the leaders succumbed. Not a single Detaxalan was abroad in the avenues. They were within their flyers, held there by our combined wills, unable to act for themselves. It was then as easy for us to switch the zones of force upon them, subjugate them more securely and with the annihilator beam to disintegrate completely every ship and man into nothingness! Thousands upon thousands died that day and Gola was indeed revenged.

Thus, my daughters, ended the second invasion of Gola.

Oh yes, more came from their planet to discover what had happened to their ships and their men, but we of Gola no longer hesitated, and they no sooner appeared beneath the mists than they too were annihilated until at last Detaxal gave up the thought of conquering our cloud-laden world. Perhaps in the future they will attempt it again, but we are always in readiness for them now, and our men—well they are still the same ineffectual weaklings, my daughters . . .

1931

C. L. MOORE

The Black God's Kiss

THEY brought in Joiry's tall commander, struggling between two men-at-arms who tightly gripped the ropes which bound their captive's mailed arms. They picked their way between mounds of dead as they crossed the great hall toward the dais where the conqueror sat, and twice they slipped a little in the blood that spattered the flags. When they came to a halt before the mailed figure on the dais, Joiry's commander was breathing hard, and the voice that echoed hollowly under the helmet's confines was hoarse with fury and despair.

Guillaume the conqueror leaned on his mighty sword, hands crossed on its hilt, grinning down from his height upon the furious captive before him. He was a big man, Guillaume, and he looked bigger still in his spattered armor. There was blood on his hard, scarred face, and he was grinning a white grin that split his short, curly beard glitteringly. Very splendid and very dangerous he looked, leaning on his great sword and smiling down upon fallen Joiry's lord, struggling between the stolid men-at-arms.

"Unshell me this lobster," said Guillaume in his deep, lazy voice. "We'll see what sort of face the fellow has who gave us such a battle. Off with his helmet, you."

But a third man had to come up and slash the straps which held the iron helmet on, for the struggles of Joiry's commander were too fierce, even with bound arms, for either of the guards to release their hold. There was a moment of sharp struggle; then the straps parted and the helmet rolled loudly across the flagstones.

Guillaume's white teeth clicked on a startled oath. He stared. Joiry's lady glared back at him from between her captors, wild red hair tousled, wild lion-yellow eyes ablaze.

"God curse you!" snarled the lady of Joiry between clenched teeth. "God blast your black heart!"

Guillaume scarcely heard her. He was still staring, as most men stared when they first set eyes upon Jirel of Joiry. She was tall as most men, and as savage as the wildest of them, and the fall of Joiry was bitter enough to break her heart as she stood snarling curses up at her tall conqueror. The face above her mail might not have been fair in a woman's head-dress, but in the steel setting of her armor it had a biting, sword-edge beauty as keen as the flash of blades. The red hair was short upon her high, defiant head, and the yellow blaze of her eyes held fury as a crucible holds fire.

Guillaume's stare melted into a slow smile. A little light kindled behind his eyes as he swept the long, strong lines of her with a practised gaze. The smile broadened, and suddenly he burst into full-throated laughter, a deep bull bellow of amusement and delight.

"By the Nails!" he roared. "Here's welcome for the warrior! And what forfeit d'ye offer, pretty one, for your life?"

She blazed a curse at him.

"So? Naughty words for a mouth so fair, my lady. Well, we'll not deny you put up a gallant battle. No man could have done better, and many have done worse. But against Guillaume——" He inflated his splendid chest and grinned down at her from the depths of his jutting beard. "Come to me, pretty one," he commanded. "I'll wager your mouth is sweeter than your words."

Jirel drove a spurred heel into the shin of one guard and twisted from his grip as he howled, bringing up an iron knee into the abdomen of the other. She had writhed from their grip and made three long strides toward the door before Guillaume caught her. She felt his arms closing about her from behind, and lashed out with both spiked heels in a futile assault upon his leg armor, twisting like a maniac, fighting with her knees and spurs, straining hopelessly at the ropes which bound her arms. Guillaume laughed and whirled her round, grinning down into the blaze of her yellow eyes. Then deliberately he set a fist under her chin and tilted her mouth up to his. There was a cessation of her hoarse curses.

"By Heaven, that's like kissing a sword-blade," said Guillaume, lifting his lips at last.

Jirel choked something that was mercifully muffled as she darted her head sidewise, like a serpent striking, and sank her teeth into his neck. She missed the jugular by a fraction of an inch.

Guillaume said nothing, then. He sought her head with a steady hand, found it despite her wild writhing, sank iron fingers deep into the hinges of her jaw, forcing her teeth relentlessly apart. When he had her free he glared down into the yellow hell of her eyes for an instant. The blaze of them was hot enough to scorch his scarred face. He grinned and lifted his ungauntleted hand, and with one heavy blow in the face he knocked her half-way across the room. She lay still upon the flags.

2

Jirel opened her yellow eyes upon darkness. She lay quiet for a while, collecting her scattered thoughts. By degrees it came back to her, and she muffled upon her arm a sound that was half curse and half sob. Joiry had fallen. For a time she lay rigid in the dark, forcing herself to the realization.

The sound of feet shifting on stone near by brought her out of that particular misery. She sat up cautiously, feeling about her to determine in what part of Joiry its liege lady was imprisoned. She knew that the sound she had heard must be a sentry, and by the dank smell of the darkness that she was underground. In one of the little dungeon cells, of course. With careful quietness she got to her feet, muttering a curse as her head reeled for an instant and then began to throb. In the utter dark she felt around the cell. Presently she came to a little wooden stool in a corner, and was satisfied. She gripped one leg of it with firm fingers and made her soundless way around the wall until she had located the door.

The sentry remembered, afterward, that he had heard the wildest shriek for help which had ever rung in his ears, and he remembered unbolting the door. Afterward, until they found him lying inside the locked cell with a cracked skull, he remembered nothing.

Jirel crept up the dark stairs of the north turret, murder in her heart. Many little hatreds she had known in her life, but no such blaze as this. Before her eyes in the night she could see Guillaume's scornful, scarred face laughing, the little jutting beard split with the whiteness of his mirth. Upon her mouth she felt the remembered weight of his, about her the strength of his arms. And such a blast of hot fury came over her that she reeled a little and clutched at the wall for support. She went on in a haze of red anger, and something like madness burning in her brain as a resolve slowly took shape out of the chaos of her hate. When that thought came to her she paused again, mid-step upon the stairs, and was conscious of a little coldness blowing over her. Then it was gone, and she shivered a little, shook her shoulders and grinned wolfishly, and went on.

By the stars she could see through the arrow-slits in the wall it must be near to midnight. She went softly on the stairs, and she encountered no one. Her little tower room at the top was empty. Even the straw pallet where the serving-wench slept had not been used that night. Jirel got herself out of her armor alone, somehow, after much striving and twisting. Her doeskin shirt was stiff with sweat and stained with blood. She tossed it disdainfully into a corner. The fury in her eyes had cooled now to a contained and secret flame. She smiled to herself as she slipped a fresh shirt of doeskin over her tousled red head and donned a brief tunic of link-mail. On her legs she buckled the greaves of some forgotten legionary, relic of the not long past days when Rome still ruled the world. She thrust a dagger through her belt and took her own long two-handed sword bare-bladed in her grip. Then she went down the stairs again.

She knew there must have been revelry and feasting in the great hall that night, and by the silence hanging so heavily now she was sure that most of her enemies lay still in drunken slumber, and she experienced a swift regret for the gallons of her good French wine so wasted. And the thought flashed through her head that a determined woman with a sharp sword might work some little damage among the drunken sleepers before she was overpowered. But she put that idea by, for Guillaume would have posted sentries to spare, and she must not give up her secret freedom so fruitlessly.

Down the dark stairs she went, and crossed one corner of the vast central hall whose darkness she was sure hid wine-deadened sleepers, and so into the lesser dimness of the rough little chapel that Joiry boasted. She had been sure she would find Father Gervase there, and she was not mistaken. He rose from his knees before the altar, dark in his robe, the starlight through the narrow window shining upon his tonsure.

"My daughter!" he whispered. "My daughter! How have you escaped? Shall I find you a mount? If you can pass the sentries you should be in your cousin's castle by daybreak."

She hushed him with a lifted hand.

"No," she said. "It is not outside I go this night. I have a more perilous journey even than that to make. Shrive me, father."

He stared at her.

"What is it?"

She dropped to her knees before him and gripped the rough cloth of his habit with urgent fingers.

"Shrive me, I say! I go down into hell tonight to pray the devil for a weapon, and it may be I shall not return."

Gervase bent and gripped her shoulders with hands that shook.

"Look at me!" he demanded. "Do you know what you're saying? You go—"

"Down!" She said it firmly. "Only you and I know that passage, father—and not even we can be sure of what lies beyond. But to gain a weapon against that man I would venture into perils even worse than that."

"If I thought you meant it," he whispered, "I would waken Guillaume now and give you into his arms. It would be a kinder fate, my daughter."

"It's that I would walk through hell to escape," she whispered back fiercely. "Can't you see? Oh, God knows I'm not innocent of the ways of light loving—but to be any man's fancy, for a night or two, before he snaps my neck or sells me into slavery—and above all, if that man were Guillaume! Can't you understand?"

"That would be shame enough," nodded Gervase. "But think, Jirel! For that shame there is atonement and absolution, and for that death the gates of heaven open wide. But this other—Jirel,

Jirel, never through all eternity may you come out, body or soul, if you venture—down!"

She shrugged.

"To wreak my vengeance upon Guillaume I would go if I knew I should burn in hell for ever."

"But Jirel, I do not think you understand. This is a worse fate than the deepest depths of hell-fire. This is—this is beyond all the bounds of the hells we know. And I think Satan's hottest flames were the breath of paradise, compared to what may befall there."

"I know. Do you think I'd venture down if I could not be sure? Where else would I find such a weapon as I need, save outside God's dominion?"

"Jirel, you shall not!"

"Gervase, I go! Will you shrive me?" The hot yellow eyes blazed into his, lambent in the starlight.

After a moment he dropped his head. "You are my lady. I will give you God's blessing, but it will not avail you—there."

3

She went down into the dungeons again. She went down a long way through utter dark, over stones that were oozy and odorous with moisture, through blackness that had never known the light of day. She might have been a little afraid at other times, but that steady flame of hatred burning behind her eyes was a torch to light the way, and she could not wipe from her memory the feel of Guillaume's arms about her, the scornful press of his lips on her mouth. She whimpered a little, low in her throat, and a hot gust of hate went over her.

In the solid blackness she came at length to a wall, and she set herself to pulling the loose stones from this with her free hand, for she would not lay down the sword. They had never been laid in mortar, and they came out easily. When the way was clear she stepped through and found her feet upon a downward-sloping ramp of smooth stone. She cleared the rubble away from the hole in the wall, and enlarged it enough for a quick passage; for when she came back this way—if she did—it might well be that she would come very fast.

At the bottom of the slope she dropped to her knees on the cold floor and felt about. Her fingers traced the outline of a circle, the veriest crack in the stone. She felt until she found the ring in its center. That ring was of the coldest metal she had ever known, and the smoothest. She could put no name to it. The daylight had never shone upon such metal.

She tugged. The stone was reluctant, and at last she took her sword in her teeth and put both hands to the lifting. Even then it taxed the limit of her strength, and she was strong as many men. But at last it rose, with the strangest sighing sound, and a little prickle of goose-flesh rippled over her.

Now she took the sword back into her hand and knelt on the rim of the invisible blackness below. She had gone this path once before and once only, and never thought to find any necessity in life strong enough to drive her down again. The way was the strangest she had ever known. There was, she thought, no such passage in all the world save here. It had not been built for human feet to travel. It had not been built for feet at all. It was a narrow, polished shaft that cork-screwed round and round. A snake might have slipped in it and gone shooting down, round and round in dizzy circles—but no snake on earth was big enough to fill that shaft. No human travelers had worn the sides of the spiral so smooth, and she did not care to speculate on what creatures had polished it so, through what ages of passage.

She might never have made that first trip down, nor anyone after her, had not some unknown human hacked the notches which made it possible to descend slowly; that is, she thought it must have been a human. At any rate, the notches were roughly shaped for hands and feet, and spaced not too far apart; but who and when and how she could not even guess. As to the beings who made the shaft, in long-forgotten ages—well, there were devils on earth before man, and the world was very old.

She turned on her face and slid feet-first into the curving tunnel. That first time she and Gervase had gone down in sweating terror of what lay below, and with devils tugging at their heels. Now she slid easily, not bothering to find toeholds, but slipping swiftly round and round the long spirals with only her hands to break the speed when she went too fast. Round and round she went, round and round.

It was a long way down. Before she had gone very far the curious dizziness she had known before came over her again, a dizziness not entirely induced by the spirals she whirled around, but a deeper, atomic unsteadiness as if not only she but also the substances around her were shifting. There was something queer about the angles of those curves. She was no scholar in geometry or aught else, but she felt intuitively that the bend and slant of the way she went were somehow outside any other angles or bends she had ever known. They led into the unknown and the dark, but it seemed to her obscurely that they led into deeper darkness and mystery than the merely physical, as if, though she could not put it clearly even into thoughts, the peculiar and exact lines of the tunnel had been carefully angled to lead through poly-dimensional space as well as through the underground—perhaps through time, too. She did not know she was thinking such things; but all about her was a blurred dizziness as she shot down and round, and she knew that the way she went took her on a stranger journey than any other way she had ever traveled.

Down, and down. She was sliding fast, but she knew how long it would be. On that first trip they had taken alarm as the passage spiraled so endlessly and with thoughts of the long climb back had tried to stop before it was too late. They had found it impossible. Once embarked, there was no halting. She had tried, and such waves of sick blurring had come over her that she came near to unconsciousness. It was as if she had tried to halt some inexorable process of nature, half finished. They could only go on. The very atoms of their bodies shrieked in rebellion against a reversal of the change.

And the way up, when they returned, had not been difficult. They had had visions of a back-breaking climb up interminable curves, but again the uncanny difference of those angles from those they knew was manifested. In a queer way they seemed to defy gravity, or perhaps led through some way outside the power of it. They had been sick and dizzy on the return, as on the way down, but through the clouds of that confusion it had seemed to them that they slipped as easily up the shaft as they had gone down; or perhaps that, once in the tunnel, there was neither up nor down.

The passage leveled gradually. This was the worst part for a human to travel, though it must have eased the speed of whatever beings the shaft was made for. It was too narrow for her to turn in, and she had to lever herself face down and feet first, along the horizontal smoothness of the floor, pushing with her hands. She was glad when her questing heels met open space and she slid from the mouth of the shaft and stood upright in the dark.

Here she paused to collect herself. Yes, this was the beginning of the long passage she and Father Gervase had traveled on that long-ago journey of exploration. By the veriest accident they had found the place, and only the veriest bravado had brought them thus far. He had gone on a greater distance than she—she was younger then, and more amenable to authority—and had come back white-faced in the torchlight and hurried her up the shaft again.

She went on carefully, feeling her way, remembering what she herself had seen in the darkness a little farther on, wondering in spite of herself, and with a tiny catch at her heart, what it was that had sent Father Gervase so hastily back. She had never been entirely satisfied with his explanations. It had been about here—or was it a little farther on? The stillness was like a roaring in her ears.

Then ahead of her the darkness moved. It was just that—a vast, imponderable shifting of the solid dark. Jesu! This was new! She gripped the cross at her throat with one hand and her sword-hilt with the other. Then it was upon her, striking like a hurricane, whirling her against the walls and shrieking in her ears like a thousand wind-devils—a wild cyclone of the dark that buffeted her mercilessly and tore at her flying hair and raved in her ears with the myriad voices of all lost things crying in the night. The voices were piteous in their terror and loneliness. Tears came to her eyes even as she shivered with nameless dread, for the whirlwind was alive with a dreadful instinct, an animate thing sweeping through the dark of the underground; an unholy thing that made her flesh crawl even though it touched her to the heart with its pitiful little lost voices wailing in the wind where no wind could possibly be.

And then it was gone. In that one flash of an instant it vanished, leaving no whisper to commemorate its passage. Only in the heart of it could one hear the sad little voices wailing or the wild shriek of the wind. She found herself standing stunned, her sword yet gripped futilely in one hand and the tears running down her face. Poor little lost voices, wailing. She wiped the tears away with a shaking hand and set her teeth hard against the weakness of reaction that flooded her. Yet it was a good five minutes before she could force herself on. After a few steps her knees ceased to tremble.

The floor was dry and smooth underfoot. It sloped a little downward, and she wondered into what unplumbed deeps she had descended by now. The silence had fallen heavily again, and she found herself straining for some other sound than the soft padding of her own boots. Then her foot slipped in sudden wetness. She bent, exploring fingers outstretched, feeling without reason that the wetness would be red if she could see it. But her fingers traced the immense outline of a footprint—splayed and three-toed like a frog's, but of monster size. It was a fresh footprint. She had a vivid flash of memory—that thing she had glimpsed in the torchlight on the other trip down. But she had had light then, and now she was blind in the dark, the creature's natural habitat. . . .

For a moment she was not Jirel of Joiry, vengeful fury on the trail of a devilish weapon, but a frightened woman alone in the unholy dark. That memory had been so vivid. . . . Then she saw Guillaume's scornful, laughing face again, the little beard dark along the line of his jaw, the strong teeth white with his laughter; and something hot and sustaining swept over her like a thin flame, and she was Joiry again, vengeful and resolute. She went on more slowly, her sword swinging in a semicircle before every third step, that she might not be surprized too suddenly by some nightmare monster clasping her in smothering arms. But the flesh crept upon her unprotected back.

*

The smooth passage went on and on. She could feel the cold walls on either hand, and her upswung sword grazed the roof. It was like crawling through some worm's tunnel, blindly under the weight of countless tons of earth. She felt the pressure of it above and about her, overwhelming, and found herself praying that the end of this tunnel-crawling might come soon, whatever the end might bring.

But when it came it was a stranger thing than she had ever dreamed. Abruptly she felt the immense, imponderable oppression cease. No longer was she conscious of the tons of earth pressing about her. The walls had fallen away and her feet struck a sudden rubble instead of the smooth floor. But the darkness that had bandaged her eyes was changed too, indescribably. It was no longer darkness, but void; not an absence of light, but simple nothingness. Abysses opened around her, yet she could see nothing. She only knew that she stood at the threshold of some immense space, and sensed nameless things about her, and battled vainly against that nothingness which was all her straining eyes could see. And at her throat something constricted painfully.

She lifted her hand and found the chain of her crucifix taut and vibrant around her neck. At that she smiled a little grimly, for she began to understand. The crucifix. She found her hand shaking despite herself, but she unfastened the chain and dropped the cross to the ground. Then she gasped.

All about her, as suddenly as the awakening from a dream, the nothingness had opened out into undreamed-of distances. She stood high on a hilltop under a sky spangled with strange stars. Below she caught glimpses of misty plains and valleys with mountain peaks rising far away. And at her feet a ravening circle of small, slavering, blind things leaped with clashing teeth.

They were obscene and hard to distinguish against the darkness of the hillside, and the noise they made was revolting. Her sword swung up of itself, almost, and slashed furiously at the little dark horrors leaping up around her legs. They died squashily, splattering her bare thighs with unpleasantness, and after a few had gone silent under the blade the rest fled into the dark with quick, frightened pantings, their feet making a queer splashing noise on the stones.

Jirel gathered a handful of the coarse grass which grew there and wiped her legs of the obscene splatters, looking about with quickened breath upon this land so unholy that one who bore a cross might not even see it. Here, if anywhere, one might find a weapon such as she sought. Behind her in the hillside was the low tunnel opening from which she had emerged. Overhead the strange stars shone. She did not recognize a single constellation, and if the brighter sparks were planets they were strange ones, tinged with violet and green and yellow. One was vividly crimson, like a point of fire. Far out over the rolling land below she could discern a mighty column of light. It did not blaze, nor illuminate the dark about. It cast no shadows. It simply was a great pillar of luminance towering high in the night. It seemed artificial—perhaps man-made, though she scarcely dared hope for men here.

She had half expected, despite her brave words, to come out upon the storied and familiar red-hot pave of hell, and this pleasant, starlit land surprized her and made her more wary. The things that built the tunnel could not have been human. She had no right to expect men here. She was a little stunned by finding open sky so far underground, though she was intelligent enough to realize that however she had come, she was not underground now. No cavity in the earth could contain this starry sky. She came of a credulous age, and she accepted her surroundings without too much questioning, though she was a little disappointed, if the truth were known, in the pleasantness of the mistily starlit place. The fiery streets of hell would have been a likelier locality in which to find a weapon against Guillaume.

When she had cleansed her sword on the grass and wiped her legs clean, she turned slowly down the hill. The distant column beckoned her, and after a moment of indecision she turned toward it. She had no time to waste, and this was the likeliest place to find what she sought.

The coarse grass brushed her legs and whispered round her feet. She stumbled now and then on the rubble, for the hill was steep, but she reached the bottom without mishap, and struck out across the meadows toward that blaze of far-away brilliance. It seemed to her that she walked more lightly, somehow. The grass scarcely bent underfoot, and she found she could take long sailing strides like one who runs with wings on his heels. It felt like a dream. The gravity pull of the place must have been less than she was accustomed to, but she only knew that she was skimming over the ground with amazing speed.

Traveling so, she passed through the meadows over the strange, coarse grass, over a brook or two that spoke endlessly to itself in a curious language that was almost speech, certainly not the usual gurgle of earth's running water. Once she ran into a blotch of darkness, like some pocket of void in the air, and struggled through gasping and blinking outraged eyes. She was beginning to realize that the land was not so innocently normal as it looked.

On and on she went, at that surprizing speed, while the meadows skimmed past beneath her flying feet and gradually the light drew nearer. She saw now that it was a round tower of sheeted luminance, as if walls of solid flame rose up from the ground. Yet it seemed to be steady, nor did it cast any illumination upon the sky.

Before much time had elapsed, with her dream-like speed she had almost reached her goal. The ground was becoming marshy underfoot, and presently the smell of swamps rose in her nostrils and she saw that between her and the light stretched a belt of unstable ground tufted with black reedy grass. Here and there she could see dim white blotches moving. They might be beasts, or only wisps of mist. The starlight was not very illuminating.

She began to pick her way carefully across the black, quaking morasses. Where the tufts of grass rose she found firmer ground, and she leaped from clump to clump with that amazing lightness, so that her feet barely touched the black ooze. Here and there slow bubbles rose through the mud and broke thickly. She did not like the place.

Half-way across, she saw one of the white blotches approaching her with slow, erratic movements. It bumped along unevenly, and at first she thought it might be inanimate, its approach was so indirect and purposeless. Then it blundered nearer, with that queer bumpy gait, making sucking noises in the ooze and splashing as it came. In the starlight she saw suddenly what it was, and for an instant her heart paused and sickness rose overwhelmingly in her throat. It was a woman—a beautiful woman whose white bare body had the curves and loveliness of some marble statue. She was crouching like a frog, and as Jirel watched in stupefaction she straightened her legs abruptly and leaped as a frog leaps, only more clumsily, falling forward into the ooze a little distance beyond the watching woman. She did not seem to see Jirel. The mud-spattered face was blank. She blundered on through the mud in awkward leaps. Jirel watched until the woman was no more than a white wandering blur in the dark, and above the shock of that sight pity was rising, and uncomprehending resentment against whatever had brought so lovely a creature into this—into blundering in frog leaps aimlessly through the mud, with empty mind and blind, staring eyes. For the second time that night she knew the sting of unaccustomed tears as she went on.

The sight, though, had given her reassurance. The human form was not unknown here. There might be leathery devils with hoofs and horns, such as she still half expected, but she would not be alone in her humanity; though if all the rest were as piteously mindless as the one she had seen—she did not follow that thought. It was too unpleasant. She was glad when the marsh was past and she need not see any longer the awkward white shapes bumping along through the dark.

She struck out across the narrow space which lay between her and the tower. She saw now that it was a building, and that the light composed it. She could not understand that, but she saw it. Walls and columns outlined the tower, solid sheets of light with definite boundaries, not radiant. As she came nearer she saw that it was in motion, apparently spurting up from some source underground as if the light illuminated sheets of water rushing upward under great pressure. Yet she felt intuitively that it was not water, but incarnate light.

She came forward hesitantly, gripping her sword. The area around the tremendous pillar was paved with something black and smooth that did not reflect the light. Out of it sprang the uprushing walls of brilliance with their sharply defined edges. The magnitude of the thing dwarfed her to infinitesimal size. She stared upward with undazzled eyes, trying to understand. If there could be such a thing as solid, non-radiating light, this was it.

4

She was very near under the mighty tower before she could see the details of the building clearly. They were strange to her—great pillars and arches around the base, and one stupendous portal, all molded out of the rushing, prisoned light. She turned toward the opening after a moment, for the light had a tangible look. She did not believe she could have walked through it even had she dared.

When that tremendous portal arched over her she peered in, affrighted by the very size of the place. She thought she could hear the hiss and spurt of the light surging upward. She was looking into a mighty globe inside, a hall shaped like the interior of a bubble, though the curve was so vast she was scarcely aware of it. And in the very center of the globe floated a light. Jirel blinked. A light, dwelling in a bubble of light. It glowed there in midair with a pale, steady flame that was somehow alive and animate, and brighter than the serene illumination of the building, for it hurt her eyes to look at it directly.

She stood on the threshold and stared, not quite daring to venture in. And as she hesitated a change came over the light. A flush of rose tinged its pallor. The rose deepened and darkened until it took on the color of blood. And the shape underwent strange changes. It lengthened, drew itself out narrowly, split at the bottom into two branches, put out two tendrils from the top. The blood-red paled again, and the light somehow lost its brilliance, receded into the depths of the thing that was forming. Jirel clutched her sword and forgot to breathe, watching. The light was taking on the shape of a human being—of a woman—of a tall woman in mail, her red hair tousled and her eyes staring straight into the duplicate eyes at the portal. . . .

"Welcome," said the Jirel suspended in the center of the globe, her voice deep and resonant and clear in spite of the distance between them. Jirel at the door held her breath, wondering and afraid. This was herself, in every detail, a mirrored Jirel—that was it, a Jirel mirrored upon a surface which blazed and smoldered with barely repressed light, so that the eyes gleamed with it and the whole figure seemed to hold its shape by an effort, only by that effort restraining itself from resolving into pure, formless light again. But the voice was not her own. It shook and resounded with a knowledge as alien as the light-built walls. It mocked her. It said,

"Welcome! Enter into the portals, woman!"

She looked up warily at the rushing walls about her. Instinctively she drew back.

"Enter, enter!" urged that mocking voice from her own mirrored lips. And there was a note in it she did not like.

"Enter!" cried the voice again, this time a command.

Jirel's eyes narrowed. Something intuitive warned her back, and yet—she drew the dagger she had thrust in her belt and with a quick motion she tossed it into the great globe-shaped hall. It struck the floor without a sound, and a brilliant light flared up around it, so brilliant she could not look upon what was happening; but it seemed to her that the knife expanded, grew large and nebulous and ringed with dazzling light. In less time than it takes to tell, it had faded out of sight as if the very atoms which composed it had flown apart and dispersed in the golden glow of that mighty bubble. The dazzle faded with the knife, leaving Jirel staring dazedly at a bare floor.

That other Jirel laughed, a rich, resonant laugh of scorn and malice.

"Stay out, then," said the voice. "You've more intelligence than I thought. Well, what would you here?"

Jirel found her voice with an effort.

"I seek a weapon," she said, "a weapon against a man I so hate that upon earth there is none terrible enough for my need."

"You so hate him, eh?" mused the voice.

"With all my heart!"

"With all your heart!" echoed the voice, and there was an undernote of laughter in it that she did not understand. The echoes of that mirth ran round and round the great globe. Jirel felt her cheeks burn with resentment against some implication in the derision which she could not put a name to. When the echoes of the laugh had faded the voice said indifferently,

"Give the man what you find at the black temple in the lake. I make you a gift of it."

The lips that were Jirel's twisted into a laugh of purest mockery; then all about that figure so perfectly her own the light flared out. She saw the outlines melting fluidly as she turned her dazzled eyes away. Before the echoes of that derision had died, a blinding, formless light burned once more in the midst of the bubble.

Jirel turned and stumbled away under the mighty column of the tower, a hand to her dazzled eyes. Not until she had reached the edge of the black, unreflecting circle that paved the ground around the pillar did she realize that she knew no way of finding the lake where her weapon lay. And not until then did she remember how fatal it is said to be to accept a gift from a demon. Buy it, or earn it, but never accept the gift. Well—she shrugged and stepped out upon the grass. She must surely be damned by now, for having ventured down of her own will into this curious place for such a purpose as hers. The soul can be lost but once.

She turned her face up to the strange stars and wondered in

what direction her course lay. The sky looked blankly down upon her with its myriad meaningless eyes. A star fell as she watched, and in her superstitious soul she took it for an omen, and set off boldly over the dark meadows in the direction where the bright streak had faded. No swamps guarded the way here, and she was soon skimming along over the grass with that strange, dancing gait that the lightness of the place allowed her. And as she went she was remembering, as from long ago in some other far world, a man's arrogant mirth and the press of his mouth on hers. Hatred bubbled up hotly within her and broke from her lips in a little savage laugh of anticipation. What dreadful thing awaited her in the temple in the lake, what punishment from hell to be loosed by her own hands upon Guillaume? And though her soul was the price it cost her, she would count it a fair bargain if she could drive the laughter from his mouth and bring terror into the eyes that mocked her.

Thoughts like these kept her company for a long way upon her journey. She did not think to be lonely or afraid in the uncanny darkness across which no shadows fell from that mighty column behind her. The unchanging meadows flew past underfoot, lightly as meadows in a dream. It might almost have been that the earth moved instead of herself, so effortlessly did she go. She was sure now that she was heading in the right direction, for two more stars had fallen in the same arc across the sky.

The meadows were not untenanted. Sometimes she felt presences near her in the dark, and once she ran full-tilt into a nest of little yapping horrors like those on the hill-top. They lunged up about her with clicking teeth, mad with a blind ferocity, and she swung her sword in frantic circles, sickened by the noise of them lunging splashily through the grass and splattering her sword with their deaths. She beat them off and went on, fighting her own sickness, for she had never known anything quite so nauseating as these little monstrosities.

She crossed a brook that talked to itself in the darkness with that queer murmuring which came so near to speech, and a few strides beyond it she paused suddenly, feeling the ground tremble with the rolling thunder of hoofbeats approaching. She stood still, searching the dark anxiously, and presently the earth-shaking beat grew louder and she saw a white blur flung wide across the dimness to her left, and the sound of hoofs deepened and grew. Then out of the night swept a herd of snow-white horses. Magnificently they ran, manes tossing, tails streaming, feet pounding a rhythmic, heart-stirring roll along the ground. She caught her breath at the beauty of their motion. They swept by a little distance away, tossing their heads, spurning the ground with scornful feet.

But as they came abreast of her she saw one blunder a little and stumble against the next, and that one shook his head bewilderedly; and suddenly she realized that they were blind—all running so splendidly in a deeper dark than even she groped through. And she saw too their coats were roughened with sweat, and foam dripped from their lips, and their nostrils were flaring pools of scarlet. Now and again one stumbled from pure exhaustion. Yet they ran, frantically, blindly through the dark, driven by something outside their comprehension.

As the last one of all swept by her, sweat-crusted and staggering, she saw him toss his head high, spattering foam, and whinny shrilly to the stars. And it seemed to her that the sound was strangely articulate. Almost she heard the echoes of a name—"Julienne! Julienne!"—in that high, despairing sound. And the incongruity of it, the bitter despair, clutched at her heart so sharply that for the third time that night she knew the sting of tears.

The dreadful humanity of that cry echoed in her ears as the thunder died away. She went on, blinking back the tears for that beautiful blind creature, staggering with exhaustion, calling a girl's name hopelessly from a beast's throat into the blank darkness wherein it was for ever lost.

Then another star fell across the sky, and she hurried ahead, closing her mind to the strange, incomprehensible pathos that made an undernote of tears to the starry dark of this land. And the thought was growing in her mind that, though she had come into no brimstone pit where horned devils pranced over flames, yet perhaps it was after all a sort of hell through which she ran.

Presently in the distance she caught a glimmer of something bright. The ground dipped after that and she lost it, and skimmed through a hollow where pale things wavered away from her into the deeper dark. She never knew what they were, and was glad. When she came up onto higher ground again she saw it more clearly, an expanse of dim brilliance ahead. She hoped it was a lake, and ran more swiftly.

It *was* a lake—a lake that could never have existed outside some obscure hell like this. She stood on the brink doubtfully, wondering if this could be the place the light-devil had meant. Black, shining water stretched out before her, heaving gently with a motion unlike that of any water she had ever seen before. And in the depths of it, like fireflies caught in ice, gleamed myriad small lights. They were fixed there immovably, not stirring with the motion of the water. As she watched, something hissed above her and a streak of light split the dark air. She looked up in time to see something bright curving across the sky to fall without a splash into the water, and small ripples of phosphorescence spread sluggishly toward the shore, where they broke at her feet with the queerest whispering sound, as if each succeeding ripple spoke the syllable of a word.

She looked up, trying to locate the origin of the falling lights, but the strange stars looked down upon her blankly. She bent and stared down into the center of the spreading ripples, and where the thing had fallen she thought a new light twinkled through the water. She could not determine what it was, and after a curious moment she gave the question up and began to cast about for the temple the light-devil had spoken of.

After a moment she thought she saw something dark in the center of the lake, and when she had stared for a few minutes it gradually became clearer, an arch of darkness against the starry background of the water. It might be a temple. She strolled slowly along the brim of the lake, trying to get a closer view of it, for the thing was no more than a darkness against the spangles of light, like some void in the sky where no stars shine. And presently she stumbled over something in the grass.

She looked down with startled yellow eyes, and saw a strange, indistinguishable darkness. It had solidity to the feel but scarcely to the eye, for she could not quite focus upon it. It was like trying to see something that did not exist save as a void, a darkness in the grass. It had the shape of a step, and when she followed with her eyes she saw that it was the beginning of a dim bridge stretching out over the lake, narrow and curved and made out of nothingness. It seemed to have no surface, and its edges were difficult to distinguish from the lesser gloom surrounding it. But the thing was tangible—an arch carved out of the solid dark—and it led out in the direction she wished to go. For she was naïvely sure now that the dim blot in the center of the lake was the temple she was searching for. The falling stars had guided her, and she could not have gone astray.

So she set her teeth and gripped her sword and put her foot upon the bridge. It was rock-firm under her, but scarcely more than a foot or so wide, and without rails. When she had gone a step or two she began to feel dizzy; for under her the water heaved with a motion that made her head swim, and the stars twinkled eerily in its depths. She dared not look away for fear of missing her footing on the narrow arch of darkness. It was like walking a bridge flung across the void, with stars underfoot and nothing but an unstable strip of nothingness to bear her up. Half-way across, the heaving of the water and the illusion of vast, constellated spaces beneath and the look her bridge had of being no more than empty space ahead, combined to send her head reeling; and as she stumbled on, the bridge seemed to be wavering with her, swinging in gigantic arcs across the starry void below.

Now she could see the temple more closely, though scarcely more clearly than from the shore. It looked to be no more than an outlined emptiness against the star-crowded brilliance behind it, etching its arches and columns of blankness upon the twinkling waters. The bridge came down in a long dim swoop to its doorway. Jirel took the last few yards at a reckless run and stopped breathless under the arch that made the temple's vague doorway. She stood there panting and staring about narrow-eyed, sword poised in her hand. For though the place was empty and very still she felt a presence even as she set her foot upon the floor of it.

She was staring about a little space of blankness in the starry lake. It seemed to be no more than that. She could see the walls and columns where they were outlined against the water and where they made darknesses in the star-flecked sky, but where there was only dark behind them she could see nothing. It was a tiny place, no more than a few square yards of emptiness upon the face of the twinkling waters. And in its center an image stood.

She stared at it in silence, feeling a curious compulsion growing within her, like a vague command from something outside herself. The image was of some substance of nameless black, unlike the material which composed the building, for even in the dark she could see it clearly. It was a semi-human figure, crouching forward with outthrust head, sexless and strange. Its one central eye was closed as if in rapture, and its mouth was pursed for a kiss. And though it was but an image and without even the semblance of life, she felt unmistakably the presence of something alive in the temple, something so alien and innominate that instinctively she drew away.

She stood there for a full minute, reluctant to enter the place where so alien a being dwelt, half conscious of that voiceless compulsion growing up within her. And slowly she became aware that all the lines and angles of the half-seen building were curved to make the image their center and focus. The very bridge swooped its long arc to complete the centering. As she watched, it seemed to her that through the arches of the columns even the stars in lake and sky were grouped in patterns which took the image for their focus. Every line and curve in the dim world seemed to sweep round toward the squatting thing before her with its closed eye and expectant mouth.

Gradually the universal focusing of lines began to exert its influence upon her. She took a hesitant step forward without realizing the motion. But that step was all the dormant urge within her needed. With her one motion forward the compulsion closed down upon her with whirlwind impetuosity. Helplessly she felt herself advancing, helplessly with one small, sane portion of her mind she realized the madness that was gripping her, the blind, irresistible urge to do what every visible line in the temple's construction was made to compel. With stars swirling around her she advanced across the floor and laid her hands upon the rounded shoulders of the image—the sword, forgotten, making a sort of accolade against its hunched neck—and lifted her red head and laid her mouth blindly against the pursed lips of the image.

In a dream she took that kiss. In a dream of dizziness and confusion she seemed to feel the iron-cold lips stirring under hers. And through the union of that kiss—warm-blooded woman with image of nameless stone—through the meeting of their mouths something entered into her very soul; something cold and stunning; something alien beyond any words. It lay upon her shuddering soul like some frigid weight from the void, a bubble holding something unthinkably alien and dreadful. She could feel the heaviness of it upon some intangible part of her that shrank from the touch. It was like the weight of remorse or despair, only far colder and stranger and—somehow—more ominous, as if this weight were but the egg from which things might hatch too dreadful to put even into thoughts.

The moment of the kiss could have been no longer than a breath's space, but to her it was timeless. In a dream she felt the compulsion falling from her at last. In a dim dream she dropped her hands from its shoulders, finding the sword heavy in her grasp and staring dully at it for a while before clarity began its return to her cloudy mind. When she became completely aware of herself once more she was standing with slack body and dragging head before the blind, rapturous image, that dead weight upon her heart as dreary as an old sorrow, and more coldly ominous than anything she could find words for.

And with returning clarity the most staggering terror came over her, swiftly and suddenly—terror of the image and the temple of darkness, and the coldly spangled lake and of the whole, wide, dim, dreadful world about her. Desperately she longed for home again, even the red fury of hatred and the press of Guillaume's mouth and the hot arrogance of his eyes again. Anything but this. She found herself running without knowing why. Her feet skimmed over the narrow bridge lightly as a gull's wings dipping the water. In a brief instant the starry void of the lake flashed by beneath her and the solid earth was underfoot. She saw the great column of light far away across the dark meadows and beyond it a hill-top rising against the stars. And she ran.

She ran with terror at her heels and devils howling in the wind her own speed made. She ran from her own curiously alien body, heavy with its weight of inexplicable doom. She passed through the hollow where pale things wavered away, she fled over the uneven meadows in a frenzy of terror. She ran and ran, in those long light bounds the lesser gravity allowed her, fleeter than a deer, and her own panic choked in her throat and that weight upon her soul dragged at her too drearily for tears. She fled to escape it, and could not; and the ominous certainty that she carried something too dreadful to think of grew and grew.

For a long while she skimmed over the grass, tirelessly, wing-heeled, her red hair flying. The panic died after a while, but that sense of heavy disaster did not die. She felt somehow that tears would ease her, but something in the frigid darkness of her soul froze her tears in the ice of that gray and alien chill.

And gradually, through the inner dark, a fierce anticipation took form in her mind. Revenge upon Guillaume! She had taken from the temple only a kiss, so it was that which she must deliver to him. And savagely she exulted in the thought of what that kiss would release upon him, unsuspecting. She did not know, but it filled her with fierce joy to guess.

She had passed the column and skirted the morass where the white, blundering forms still bumped along awkwardly through the ooze, and was crossing the coarse grass toward the nearing hill when the sky began to pale along the horizon. And with that pallor a fresh terror took hold upon her, a wild horror of daylight in this unholy land. She was not sure if it was the light itself she so dreaded, or what that light would reveal in the dark stretches she had traversed so blindly—what unknown horrors she had skirted in the night. But she knew instinctively that if she valued her sanity she must be gone before the light had risen over the land. And she redoubled her efforts, spurring her wearying limbs to yet more skimming speed. But it would be a close race, for already the stars were blurring out, and a flush of curious green was broadening along the sky, and around her the air was turning to a vague, unpleasant gray.

She toiled up the steep hillside breathlessly. When she was halfway up, her own shadow began to take form upon the rocks, and it was unfamiliar and dreadfully significant of something just outside her range of understanding. She averted her eyes from it, afraid that at any moment the meaning might break upon her outraged brain.

She could see the top of the hill above her, dark against the paling sky, and she toiled up in frantic haste, clutching her sword and feeling that if she had to look in the full light upon the dreadful little abominations that had snapped around her feet when she first emerged she would collapse into screaming hysteria.

The cave-mouth yawned before her, invitingly black, a refuge from the dawning light behind her. She knew an almost irresistible desire to turn and look back from this vantage-point across the land she had traversed, and gripped her sword hard to conquer the perversive longing. There was a scuffling in the rocks at her feet, and she set her teeth in her underlip and swung viciously in brief arcs, without looking down. She heard small squeakings and the splashy sound of feet upon the stones, and felt her blade shear thrice through semi-solidity, to the click of little vicious teeth. Then they broke and ran off over the hillside, and she stumbled on, choking back the scream that wanted so fiercely to break from her lips.

She fought that growing desire all the way up to the cave-mouth, for she knew that if she gave way she would never cease shrieking until her throat went raw.

Blood was trickling from her bitten lip with the effort at silence when she reached the cave. And there, twinkling upon the stones, lay something small and bright and dearly familiar. With a sob of relief she bent and snatched up the crucifix she had torn from her throat when she came out into this land. And as her fingers shut upon it a vast, protecting darkness swooped around her. Gasping with relief, she groped her way the step or two that separated her from the cave.

Dark lay like a blanket over her eyes, and she welcomed it gladly, remembering how her shadow had lain so awfully upon the hillside as she climbed, remembering the first rays of savage sunlight beating upon her shoulders. She stumbled through the blackness, slowly getting control again over her shaking body and laboring lungs, slowly stilling the panic that the dawning day had roused so inexplicably within her. And as that terror died, the dull weight upon her spirit became strong again. She had all but forgotten it in her panic, but now the impending and unknown dreadfulness grew heavier and more oppressive in the darkness of the underground, and she groped along in a dull stupor of her own depression, slow with the weight of the strange doom she carried.

Nothing barred her way. In the dullness of her stupor she scarcely realized it, or expected any of the vague horrors that peopled the place to leap out upon her. Empty and unmenacing, the way stretched before her blindly stumbling feet. Only once did she hear the sound of another presence—the rasp of hoarse breathing and the scrape of a scaly hide against the stone—but it must have been outside the range of her own passage, for she encountered nothing.

When she had come to the end and a cold wall rose up before her, it was scarcely more than automatic habit that made her search along it with groping hand until she came to the mouth of the shaft. It sloped gently up into the dark. She crawled in, trailing her sword, until the rising incline and lowering roof forced her down upon her face. Then with toes and fingers she began to force herself up the spiral, slippery way.

Before she had gone very far she was advancing without effort, scarcely realizing that it was against gravity she moved. The curious dizziness of the shaft had come over her, the strange feeling of change in the very substance of her body, and through the cloudy numbness of it she felt herself sliding round and round the spirals, without effort. Again, obscurely, she had the feeling that in the peculiar angles of this shaft was neither up nor down. And for a long while the dizzy circling went on.

When the end came at last, and she felt her fingers gripping the edge of that upper opening which lay beneath the floor of Joiry's lowest dungeons, she heaved herself up warily and lay for awhile on the cold floor in the dark, while slowly the clouds of dizziness passed from her mind, leaving only that ominous weight within. When the darkness had ceased to circle about her, and the floor steadied, she got up dully and swung the cover back over the opening, her hands shuddering from the feel of the cold, smooth ring which had never seen daylight.

When she turned from this task she was aware of the reason for the lessening in the gloom around her. A guttering light outlined the hole in the wall from which she had pulled the stones—was it a century ago? The brilliance all but blinded her after her long sojourn through blackness, and she stood there awhile, swaying a little, one hand to her eyes, before she went out into the familiar torchlight she knew waited her beyond. Father Gervase, she was sure, anxiously waiting her return. But even he had not dared to follow her through the hole in the wall, down to the brink of the shaft.

Somehow she felt that she should be giddy with relief at this safe homecoming, back to humanity again. But as she stumbled over the upward slope toward light and safety she was conscious of no more than the dullness of whatever unreleased horror it was which still lay so ominously upon her stunned soul.

She came through the gaping hole in the masonry into the full glare of torches awaiting her, remembering with a wry inward smile how wide she had made the opening in anticipation of flight from something dreadful when she came back that way. Well, there was no flight from the horror she bore within her. It seemed to her that her heart was slowing, too, missing a beat now and then and staggering like a weary runner.

She came out into the torchlight, stumbling with exhaustion, her mouth scarlet from the blood of her bitten lip and her bare greaved legs and bare sword-blade foul with the deaths of those little horrors that swarmed around the cave-mouth. From the tangle of red hair her eyes stared out with a bleak, frozen, inward look, as of one who has seen nameless things. That keen, steel-bright beauty which had been hers was as dull and fouled as her sword-blade, and at the look in her eyes Father Gervase shuddered and crossed himself.

5

They were waiting for her in an uneasy group—the priest anxious and dark, Guillaume splendid in the torchlight, tall and arrogant, a handful of men-at-arms holding the guttering lights and shifting uneasily from one foot to the other. When she saw Guillaume the light that flared up in her eyes blotted out for a moment the bleak dreadfulness behind them, and her slowing heart leaped like a spurred horse, sending the blood riotously through her veins. Guillaume, magnificent in his armor, leaning upon his sword and staring down at her from his scornful height, the little black beard jutting. Guillaume, to whom Joiry had fallen. Guillaume.

That which she carried at the core of her being was heavier than anything else in the world, so heavy she could scarcely keep her knees from bending, so heavy her heart labored under its weight. Almost irresistibly she wanted to give way beneath it, to sink down and down under the crushing load, to lie prone and vanquished in the ice-gray, bleak place she was so dimly aware of through the clouds that were rising about her. But there was Guillaume, grim and grinning, and she hated him so very bitterly—she must make the effort. She must, at whatever cost, for she was coming to know that death lay in wait for her if she bore this burden long, that it was a two-edged weapon which could strike at its wielder if the blow were delayed too long. She knew this through the dim mists that were thickening in her brain, and she put all her strength into the immense effort it cost to cross the floor toward him. She stumbled a little, and made one faltering step and then another, and dropped her sword with a clang as she lifted her arms to him.

He caught her strongly, in a hard, warm clasp, and she heard his laugh triumphant and hateful as he bent his head to take the kiss she was raising her mouth to offer. He must have seen, in that last moment before their lips met, the savage glare of victory in her eyes, and been startled. But he did not hesitate. His mouth was heavy upon hers.

It was a long kiss. She felt him stiffen in her arms. She felt a coldness in the lips upon hers, and slowly the dark weight of what she bore lightened, lifted, cleared away from her cloudy mind. Strength flowed back through her richly. The whole world came alive to her once more. Presently she loosed his slack arms and stepped away, looking up into his face with a keen and dreadful triumph upon her own.

She saw the ruddiness of him draining away, and the rigidity of stone coming over his scarred features. Only his eyes remained alive, and there was torment in them, and understanding. She was glad—she had wanted him to understand what it cost to take Joiry's kiss unbidden. She smiled thinly into his tortured eyes, watching. And she saw something cold and alien seeping through him, permeating him slowly with some unnamable emotion which no man could ever have experienced before. She could not name it, but she saw it in his eyes—some dreadful emotion never made for flesh and blood to know, some iron despair such as only an unguessable being from the gray, formless void could ever have felt before—too hideously alien for any human creature to endure. Even she shuddered from the dreadful, cold bleakness looking out of his eyes, and knew as she watched that there must be many emotions and many fears and joys too far outside man's comprehension for any being of flesh to undergo, and live. Grayly she saw it spreading through him, and the very substance of his body shuddered under that iron weight.

And now came a visible, physical change. Watching, she was aghast to think that in her own body and upon her own soul she had borne the seed of this dreadful flowering, and did not wonder that her heart had slowed under the unbearable weight of it. He was standing rigidly with arms half bent, just as he stood when she slid from his embrace. And now great shudders began to go over him, as if he were wavering in the torchlight, some gray-faced wraith in armor with torment in his eyes. She saw the sweat beading his forehead. She saw a trickle of blood from his mouth, as if he had bitten through his lip in the agony of this new, incomprehensible emotion. Then a last shiver went over him violently, and he flung up his head, the little curling beard jutting ceilingward and the muscles of his strong throat corded, and from his lips broke a long, low cry of such utter, inhuman strangeness that Jirel felt coldness rippling through her veins and she put up her hands to her ears to shut it out. It meant something—it expressed some dreadful emotion that was neither sorrow nor despair nor anger, but infinitely alien and infinitely sad. Then his long legs buckled at the knees and he dropped with a clatter of mail and lay still on the stone floor.

They knew he was dead. That was unmistakable in the way he lay. Jirel stood very still, looking down upon him, and strangely it seemed to her that all the lights in the world had gone out. A moment before he had been so big and vital, so magnificent in the torchlight—she could still feel his kiss upon her mouth, and the hard warmth of his arms. . . .

Suddenly and blindingly it came upon her what she had done. She knew now why such heady violence had flooded her whenever she thought of him—knew why the light-devil in her own form had laughed so derisively—knew the price she must pay for taking a gift from a demon. She knew that there was no light anywhere in the world, now that Guillaume was gone.

Father Gervase took her arm gently. She shook him off with an impatient shrug and dropped to one knee beside Guillaume's body, bending her head so that the red hair fell forward to hide her tears.

1934

LESLIE PERRI

Space Episode

SHE stared at her two companions for a moment and then a sickening revulsion replaced fear, the fear that held each of the three in a terrible grip of inertia. Her slim hands bit hard into the back of one of the metal seats. The tiny rocket ship was plummeting to destruction, careening dizzily through space. Here, in the atmosphereless void, their motion was negligible to them, but instruments told a grim story; unless they could blast the forward rockets very soon they would be caught in the Earth's titanic grip and drawn with intensifying acceleration to its surface. They would come screaming down like some colossal shell and the planet's surface would become a molten sore where they struck. And now, while precious seconds fled, the three of them stood transfixed, immobile.

What had happened? A simple thing, an unimportant thing in space. They had encountered a meteor swarm, one utterly infinitesimal in the sight of the looming worlds about them. But it had left one of its members jammed in their forward rocket nozzles, the tubes which determined whether they would land safely or crash in a blaze of incandescence. They had turned off their operating power rather than wreck the ship completely; with no escape for the rocket-blasts, their motors would be smashed to pieces.

The first they knew of disaster, striking unheralded from space, was the ear-shattering impact of the meteor. No sound; just concussion that was worse than any deafening crash. Then the power generator dial shot to the danger line; the ship began to plunge, teleplate showing the universe seemingly turning fast somersaults as their ship careened end over end. The truth was evident at once; that impediment must be removed from the forward tubes. One of them must volunteer to clear away the obstruction, or all were doomed.

A time for heroics, this, but none of them felt like heroes. Erik and Michael stood side by side, a sort of bewildered terror on their faces—a "this can't happen to us" look. Neither had moved or spoken a word since the first investigation. Erik, upon discovering that the outer door was gone, had flung his space suit to the floor with an impotent curse. For that shorn-off door meant that whoever left the ship now could never return; it was a one-way passage. The taller of the two men played with the instruments, spinning them this way and that, then stood waiting. Waiting for heaven alone knew what miracle to happen.

Lida found her confidence in them, that fine confidence she had known up to now, dissolving away, leaving her with an empty feeling which was greater than any fear could have been. She could not square them, as they were now, with the men she had known before—through innumerable Terrestrial dangers on land, sea, and in the clouds. The three had had a planet-wide reputation as reckless and danger-despising. And now. . . .

"Erik!" she cried suddenly. "Damn it, this is not a tea party! We have to do something now. Toss coins or draw lots. Either one of us goes out there now, or we all crack up."

Michael glanced at her dully as she spoke, his tongue moving over dry lips. Erik closed his eyes, brushing his hair with a limp gesture. Lida's hands tightened on the back seat; what was wrong with them? She bent forward slightly, her heart beating like a dull and distant drum. The dials on the control board frightened her; she whispered now. "You see what little time we have left? Nothing's going to happen unless we make it happen. We're falling, falling fast."

Michael slumped in his seat, dropped his head to his knees groaning. Erik looked at her vaguely for a long second, then turned his eyes to the teleplate. Cold perspiration stood on his forehead. This was the dashing Erik Vane, onetime secret dream hero, close companion since that day, years back, when he and Mike had fished her out of the wreck of her plane somewhere in the Pacific. Suddenly, it all seemed amusing to her; the question of sacrifice lay between Michael and Erik—this was strictly men's work. But they were finding life a sweet thing—a sudden burst of laughter overcame her. There was such an amusing impotency to Erik's strength and the dash of his clothes; the knuckles stood white on his hands, cold damp fear glittering on his forehead.

And what of Michael, the gallant? He slumped in his seat, holding his face in shaking hands. Could this be the same man who had saved them all by scaling what was virtually a sheer cliff by night and obtaining help from neighboring aborigines? All the dangers they had faced together and overcome together now crowded in her memory, one piling upon another. Scores of times one of them had unhesitatingly faced unpleasant death for the sake of all; she had been no exception.

And there was another picture that made her laugh, too, but it wasn't a gay laugh. The picture of Michael opening the outer door of the rocket on the night they left, bowing gallantly, speaking extravagantly dear words of welcome to her on their first space flight. Lida clung to a chair, eyes blurring, as she gazed at the control panel, now a welter of glittering metal, polished and useless.

Michael's head shot up suddenly. "Stop laughing! Stop it!" He covered his face with his hands and Lida felt sick; he was crying.

She paused, her eyes filled with bitterness and contempt. Then she smiled wearily, feeling strangely akin to the vacuum outside them. There was only a sudden decision and she made it. This was her exit and to hell with heroes!

She bowed to them scornfully, waving aside their fears with a flippant sweep of her hand. Only one regret remained now. They could have chosen fairly, made a pretense of flipping a coin. She looked cocky and defiant now, gathering tools for her job. A grin twisted her mouth into a quivering scarlet line. Would she make a television headline? Would they name a ramp after her, or, perhaps, some day, a rocket division? There were several photos of her in newspaper files; she hoped they would pick a good one when they ran the story. Oh, hers would be a heroic end.

She put aside the word "end" mentally and turned her attention to what had to be done. Her decision made, she would have to act swiftly or the sacrifice would be useless. The cabin's interior was becoming unreal and horrible with apathy. She ignored the others; they were like figures in a nightmare.

The outer door had been destroyed, no doubt about that. Erik was almost blown from the cabin when he opened the inner door. She would need magnetic clamps from the outset; the neutralizing effect of the airlock between the two doors was gone; that spelled doom for the one who ventured beyond the cabin. Once out, there was no returning. The force of escaping air would not permit it.

On the black, glistening floor of the cabin lay Erik's glittering, iridium-woven spacesuit. He had ventured that much at least, pulled it from a locker and tossed it to the floor. Fortunately the gyroscopes were working. She stepped into the suit, smiling grimly. It was much too long and wide all over. Her fingers were swift and sure, adjusting the steel clamps.

Michael was still in a semi-coma. Erik was watching her reflection. He knew what she was doing. His shoulders were rigid now, but he made no move to stop her. And now memory played the final ironic trick. She recalled Michael saying, with his arm around her shoulders, "When we get to Mars, you'll be the glamor girl of the planet. It'll be wonderful, Lida—just the two of us." His eyes had hinted at things he did not put into words and even though she knew that nothing of the kind would happen so long as there were three of them, she had been glad for him then.

She jerked up the front zipper, trying to close her memories with the same motion. There weren't many seconds to spare now. She fastened the tools to her belt, checked them and with them her signal sending button with the receiving set on the instrument board. Then, with shaking hands she could not help, she picked up the helmet.

Michael looked up suddenly, incredulity filling his eyes. Erik wheeled around from the teleplate.

"Lida!" he said, his voice hoarse.

Gone was the bitterness and contempt now. "So long, Erik," she replied softly. "I'll do the best I can. Watch for the signal on the control board. I'll send it through when the rocket nozzles are clear—that is, if I'm not blown from the ship."

He swayed for an instant, lurched over to where she stood. "I can't let you do it. Give me the suit, Lida. I'll go." She looked at him, cynical and proud, her eyes glittering like steel and her small chin thrust forward determinedly. These words he had said—what were they but words he flung from him, reaching out to pull together the tatters of his self-respect? She pitied him.

"There's no time for that now," she replied crisply. "Good luck."

On a sudden impulse she darted over to Michael and struck him sharply across the face. He looked up suddenly, his eyes widening in amazement. "Aren't you going to say—goodbye?"

"Lida," he muttered, "don't go. Don't leave us now; it won't do any good, Lida. Take off the suit and we'll all go together."

She shook her head defiantly. "No! There's still time. Goodbye, Michael." She fastened on the helmet, her hands cold. Steeling herself against the sudden chill of terror that was seeping through her, she forced herself to the inner door. She pressed the electric release, her hands, heavily swathed, clinging to the steel ring. The panel slid open slowly; a buzzing sound would be filling the cabin now, but she could not hear it. She could feel their eyes on her. With a magnetic clamp in readiness, she waited for the moment when the aperture would be wide enough. Then suddenly, pressing the button in reverse, she plunged through and was hurtled against the wall of the air lock. The magnetic clamp held!

Breathing a deep sigh of relief, Lida glanced around her. The inner door was shut already; this, then, was her final goodbye. There could be no returning to the cabin. She was conscious of a dull, throbbing pain in her arm. It was numb from the impact. Frantically, trying to save time, she worked it up and down until gradually life returned to it. Then she made her way to the ragged-edged gash in the hull. Nothing remained of the outer door. Clinging to a large metal splinter, she made a hurried survey.

The path of the meteor and the damage it had done was clearly visible. It had ploughed a deep welt-like furrow in the side of the ship and piled melted metal and large chunks from the side over the nozzle ends. There were probably meteor fragments as well.

But her job would be easy even so. Judicious blasting with the torch would take care of everything. Placing a heavily padded foot in the still glowing furrow, she detached a magnetic clamp from her belt.

Space lay around her and, as she worked, she felt a nameless dread seep into her being. The face of the planet was directly *above*. Desperately, she tried not to look at it. Despite her efforts, she could not help but glance upward at its looming immensity, cringing as she did so. It was so horribly large—falling on her. It seemed to be drawing her *up*, the way an electromagnet catches a piece of scrap-iron. And around her was space, space filled with pinpoints, billiard balls, and footballs of light. She knew she must not stop to look at them. They would charm away her senses and burn out her eyes. She knew this without ever having been told. There was a horror in space, not anything alive, but a dread that chilled and stole away one's life.

Slowly, carefully, she made her way up the side of the ship, using her torch, when necessary, to clear obstructions. Finally she reached the nose, rested against the boldly painted nameplate *Ares*. A sense of the horrible irony of the situation struck her. If they had immediately fired the forward rockets when the meteor struck, the tremendous blast furnace would have melted the obstruction, for, she saw now, it was very slight. Given a chance to harden, however, it was a different story; to blast now, with it there, would blow out the tubes.

She understood, now, why men who had faced all manner of Terrestrial dangers had become weak and helpless here. They had been fools, all of them, to come on this flight without conditioning—space was no place for humans unless they had been conditioned to it gradually. And they had thought themselves so clever in the way they had evaded the requirements for a license.

She pressed the signal button at her waist as the last trace of the obstruction was eaten away. An instant later, there was an answering flash in the small metal tube next to it; they had been watching the control button. A single tear ran down her nose as she thought: "I hope they go to hell, damn them."

Pulling her hand from the magnetic clamp, she straightened up stiffly, and, with a hard, quick push jumped clear of the ship. It swerved suddenly and with dizzying violence knocked her clear of their rockets. She had not considered the imminence of them before. The thought of being charred. . . .

Earth loomed above her. She had not the acceleration of the ship. Soon it would leave her behind. She would float out here in an orbit of her own, a second moon. Perhaps a meteor would strike her some day; perhaps in the future space-voyagers would find her and bring her home. Soon, within an hour at the most, there would be no more air. But why wait hours? With a sudden movement, she threw open the helmet of her suit.

The ship was gone now. Michael and Erik were safe. And something tenuous had clamped itself over her nose and mouth so that she could no longer breathe. For an instant she struggled, lungs bursting, as in the throes of a nightmare. Her thoughts cried out, "Michael! Michael!"

The darkness gathered her in.

1941

JUDITH MERRIL

That Only a Mother

MARGARET reached over to the other side of the bed where Hank should have been. Her hand patted the empty pillow, and then she came altogether awake, wondering that the old habit should remain after so many months. She tried to curl up, cat-style, to hoard her own warmth, found she couldn't do it any more, and climbed out of bed with a pleased awareness of her increasingly clumsy bulkiness.

Morning motions were automatic. On the way through the kitchenette, she pressed the button that would start breakfast cooking—the doctor had said to eat as much breakfast as she could—and tore the paper out of the facsimile machine. She folded the long sheet carefully to the "National News" section, and propped it on the bathroom shelf to scan while she brushed her teeth.

No accidents. No direct hits. At least none that had been officially released for publication. *Now, Maggie, don't get started on that. No accidents. No hits. Take the nice newspaper's word for it.*

The three clear chimes from the kitchen announced that breakfast was ready. She set a bright napkin and cheerful colored dishes on the table in a futile attempt to appeal to a faulty morning appetite. Then, when there was nothing more to prepare, she went for the mail, allowing herself the full pleasure of prolonged anticipation, because today there would *surely* be a letter.

There was. There were. Two bills and a worried note from her mother: "Darling, why didn't you write and tell me sooner? I'm thrilled, of course, but, well one hates to mention these things, but are you *certain* the doctor was right? Hank's been around all that uranium or thorium or whatever it is all these years, and I know you say he's a designer, not a technician, and he doesn't get near anything that might be dangerous, but you know he used to, back at Oak Ridge. Don't you think . . . well, of course, I'm just being a foolish old woman, and I don't want you to get upset. You know much more about it than I do, and I'm sure your doctor was right. He *should* know . . ."

Margaret made a face over the excellent coffee, and caught herself refolding the paper to the medical news.

Stop it, Maggie, stop it! The radiologist said Hank's job couldn't have exposed him. And the bombed area we drove past . . . No, no. Stop it, now! Read the social notes or the recipes, Maggie girl.

A well-known geneticist, in the medical news, said that it was possible to tell with absolute certainty, at five months, whether the child would be normal, or at least whether the mutation was likely to produce anything freakish. The worst cases, at any rate, could be prevented. Minor mutations, of course, displacements in facial features, or changes in brain structure could not be detected. And there had been some cases recently, of normal embryos with atrophied limbs that did not develop beyond the seventh or eighth month. But, the doctor concluded cheerfully, the *worst* cases could now be predicted and prevented.

"Predicted and prevented." We predicted it, didn't we? Hank and the others, they predicted it. But we didn't prevent it. We could have stopped it in '46 and '47. Now . . .

Margaret decided against the breakfast. Coffee had been enough for her in the morning for ten years; it would have to do for today. She buttoned herself into the interminable folds of material that, the salesgirl had assured her, was the *only* comfortable thing to wear during the last few months. With a surge of pure pleasure, the letter and newspaper forgotten, she realized she was on the next to the last button. It wouldn't be long now.

The city in the early morning had always been a special kind of excitement for her. Last night it had rained, and the sidewalks were still damp-gray instead of dusty. The air smelled the fresher, to a city-bred woman, for the occasional pungency of acrid factory smoke. She walked the six blocks to work, watching the lights go out in the all-night hamburger joints, where the plate-glass walls were already catching the sun, and the lights go on in the dim interiors of cigar stores and dry-cleaning establishments.

The office was in a new Government building. In the rolovator, on the way up, she felt, as always, like a frankfurter roll in the ascending half of an old-style rotary toasting machine. She abandoned the air-foam cushioning gratefully at the fourteenth floor, and settled down behind her desk, at the rear of a long row of identical desks.

Each morning the pile of papers that greeted her was a little higher. These were, as everyone knew, the decisive months. The war might be won or lost on these calculations as well as any others. The manpower office had switched her here when her old expediter's job got to be too strenuous. The computer was easy to operate, and the work was absorbing, if not as exciting as the old job. But you didn't just stop working these days. Everyone who could do anything at all was needed.

And—she remembered the interview with the psychologist—*I'm probably the unstable type. Wonder what sort of neurosis I'd get sitting home reading that sensational paper . . .*

She plunged into the work without pursuing the thought.

February 18.

Hank darling,

Just a note—from the hospital, no less. I had a dizzy spell at work, and the doctor took it to heart. Blessed if I know what I'll do with myself lying in bed for weeks, just waiting—but Dr. Boyer seems to think it may not be so long.

There are too many newspapers around here. More infanticides all the time, and they can't seem to get a jury to convict any of them. It's the fathers who do it. Lucky thing you're not around, in case—

Oh, darling, that wasn't a very *funny* joke, was it? Write as often as you can, will you? I have too much time to think. But there really isn't anything wrong, and nothing to worry about.

Write often, and remember I love you.

Maggie.

SPECIAL SERVICE TELEGRAM

February 21, 1953

22:04 LK37G

From: Tech. Lieut. H. Marvell

X47-016 GCNY

To: Mrs. H. Marvell

Women's Hospital

New York City

HAD DOCTOR'S GRAM STOP WILL ARRIVE FOUR OH TEN STOP SHORT LEAVE STOP YOU DID IT MAGGIE STOP LOVE HANK

February 25.

Hank dear,

So you didn't see the baby either? You'd think a place this size would at least have visiplates on the incubators, so the fathers could get a look, even if the poor benighted mommas can't. They tell me I won't see her for another week, or maybe more—but of course, mother always warned me if I didn't slow my pace, I'd probably even have my babies too fast. Why must she *always* be right?

Did you meet that battle-ax of a nurse they put on here? I imagine they save her for people who've already had theirs, and don't let her get too near the prospectives—but a woman like that simply shouldn't be allowed in a maternity ward. She's obsessed with mutations, can't seem to talk about anything else. Oh, well, *ours* is all right, even if it was in an unholy hurry.

I'm tired. They warned me not to sit up so soon, but I *had* to write you. All my love, darling,

Maggie.

February 29.

Darling,

I finally got to see her! It's all true, what they say about new babies and the face that only a mother could love—but it's all there, darling, eyes, ears, and noses—no, only one!—all in the right places. We're so *lucky*, Hank.

I'm afraid I've been a rambunctious patient. I kept telling that hatchet-faced female with the mutation mania that I wanted to *see* the baby. Finally the doctor came in to "explain" everything to me, and talked a lot of nonsense, most of which I'm sure no one could have understood, any more than I did. The only thing I got out of it was that she didn't actually *have* to stay in the incubator; they just thought it was "wiser."

I think I got a little hysterical at that point. Guess I was more worried than I was willing to admit, but I threw a small fit about it. The whole business wound up with one of those hushed medical conferences outside the door, and finally the Woman in White said: "Well, we might as well. Maybe it'll work out better that way."

I'd heard about the way doctors and nurses in these places develop a God complex, and believe me it is as true figuratively as it is literally that a mother hasn't got a leg to stand on around here.

I *am* awfully weak, still. I'll write again soon. Love,

Maggie.

March 8.

Dearest Hank,

Well the nurse was wrong if she told you that. She's an idiot anyhow. It's a girl. It's easier to tell with babies than with cats, and *I know*. How about Henrietta?

I'm home again, and busier than a betatron. They got *everything* mixed up at the hospital, and I had to teach myself how to bathe her and do just about everything else. She's getting prettier, too. When can you get a leave, a *real* leave?

Love,

Maggie.

May 26.

Hank dear,

You should see her now—and you shall. I'm sending along a reel of color movie. My mother sent her those nighties with drawstrings all over. I put one on, and right now she looks like a snow-white potato sack with that beautiful, beautiful flower-face blooming on top. Is that *me* talking? Am I a doting mother? But wait till you *see* her!

July 10.

. . . Believe it or not, as you like, but your daughter can talk, and I don't mean baby talk. Alice discovered it—she's a dental assistant in the WACs, you know—and when she heard the baby giving out what I thought was a string of gibberish, she said the kid knew words and sentences, but couldn't say them clearly because she has no teeth yet. I'm taking her to a speech specialist.

September 13.

. . . We have a prodigy for real! Now that all her front teeth are in, her speech is perfectly clear and—a new talent now—she can sing! I mean really carry a tune! At seven months! Darling my world would be perfect if you could only get home.

November 19.

. . . at last. The little goon was so busy being clever, it took her all this time to learn to crawl. The doctor says development in these cases is always erratic . . .

SPECIAL SERVICE TELEGRAM

December 1, 1953

08:47 LK59F

From: Tech. Lieut. H. Marvell

X47-016 GCNY

To: Mrs. H. Marvell

Apt. K-17

504 E. 19 St.

N.Y. N.Y.

WEEK'S LEAVE STARTS TOMORROW STOP WILL ARRIVE AIRPORT TEN OH FIVE STOP DON'T MEET ME STOP LOVE LOVE LOVE HANK

Margaret let the water run out of the bathinette until only a few inches were left, and then loosed her hold on the wriggling baby.

"I think it was better when you were retarded, young woman," she informed her daughter happily. "You *can't* crawl in a bathinette, you know."

"Then why can't I go in the bathtub?" Margaret was used to her child's volubility by now, but every now and then it caught her unawares. She swooped the resistant mass of pink flesh into a towel, and began to rub.

"Because you're too little, and your head is very soft, and bathtubs are very hard."

"Oh. Then when can I go in the bathtub?"

"When the outside of your head is as hard as the inside, brainchild." She reached toward a pile of fresh clothing. "I cannot understand," she added, pinning a square of cloth through the nightgown, "why a child of your intelligence can't learn to keep a diaper on the way other babies do. They've been used for centuries, you know, with perfectly satisfactory results."

The child disdained to reply; she had heard it too often. She waited patiently until she had been tucked, clean and sweet-smelling, into a white-painted crib. Then she favored her mother with a smile that inevitably made Margaret think of the first golden edge of the sun bursting into a rosy pre-dawn. She remembered Hank's reaction to the color pictures of his beautiful daughter, and with the thought, realized how late it was.

"Go to sleep, puss. When you wake up, you know, your *Daddy* will be here."

"Why?" asked the four-year-old mind, waging a losing battle to keep the ten-month-old body awake.

Margaret went into the kitchenette and set the timer for the roast. She examined the table, and got her clothes from the closet, new dress, new shoes, new slip, new everything, bought weeks before and saved for the day Hank's telegram came. She stopped to pull a paper from the facsimile, and, with clothes and news, went into the bathroom, and lowered herself gingerly into the steaming luxury of a scented tub.

She glanced through the paper with indifferent interest. Today at least there was no need to read the national news. There was an article by a geneticist. The same geneticist. Mutations, he said, were increasing disproportionately. It was too soon for recessives; even the first mutants, born near Hiroshima and Nagasaki in 1946 and 1947 were not old enough yet to breed. *But my baby's all right.* Apparently, there was some degree of free radiation from atomic explosions causing the trouble. *My baby's fine. Precocious, but normal*. If more attention had been paid to the first Japanese mutations, he said . . .

There was that little notice in the paper in the spring of '47. That was when Hank quit at Oak Ridge. "Only two or three per cent of those guilty of infanticide are being caught and punished in Japan today . . ." *But* MY BABY'S *all right.*

She was dressed, combed, and ready to the last light brush-on of lip paste, when the door chime sounded. She dashed for the door, and heard, for the first time in eighteen months the almost-forgotten sound of a key turning in the lock before the chime had quite died away.

"Hank!"

"Maggie!"

And then there was nothing to say. So many days, so many months, of small news piling up, so many things to tell him, and now she just stood there, staring at a khaki uniform and a stranger's pale face. She traced the features with the finger of memory. The same high-bridged nose, wide-set eyes, fine feathery brows; the same long jaw, the hair a little farther back now on the high forehead, the same tilted curve to his mouth. Pale . . . Of course, he'd been underground all this time. And strange, stranger because of lost familiarity than any newcomer's face could be.

She had time to think all that before his hand reached out to touch her, and spanned the gap of eighteen months. Now, again, there was nothing to say, because there was no need. They were together, and for the moment that was enough.

"Where's the baby?"

"Sleeping. She'll be up any minute."

No urgency. Their voices were as casual as though it were a daily exchange, as though war and separation did not exist. Margaret picked up the coat he'd thrown on the chair near the door, and hung it carefully in the hall closet. She went to check the roast, leaving him to wander through the rooms by himself, remembering and coming back. She found him, finally, standing over the baby's crib.

She couldn't see his face, but she had no need to.

"I think we can wake her just this once." Margaret pulled the covers down, and lifted the white bundle from the bed. Sleepy lids pulled back heavily from smoky brown eyes.

"Hello." Hank's voice was tentative.

"Hello." The baby's assurance was more pronounced.

He had heard about it, of course, but that wasn't the same as hearing it. He turned eagerly to Margaret. "She really can—?"

"Of course she can, darling. But what's more important, she can even do nice normal things like other babies do, even stupid ones. Watch her crawl!" Margaret set the baby on the big bed.

For a moment young Henrietta lay and eyed her parents dubiously.

"Crawl?" she asked.

"That's the idea. Your Daddy is new around here, you know. He wants to see you show off."

"Then put me on my tummy."

"Oh, of course." Margaret obligingly rolled the baby over.

"What's the matter?" Hank's voice was still casual, but an undercurrent in it began to charge the air of the room. "I thought they turned over first."

"This baby," Margaret would not notice the tension, "*this* baby does things when she wants to."

This baby's father watched with softening eyes while the head advanced and the body hunched up, propelling itself across the bed.

"Why the little rascal," he burst into relieved laughter. "She looks like one of those potato-sack racers they used to have on picnics. Got her arms pulled out of the sleeves already." He reached over and grabbed the knot at the bottom of the long nightie.

"I'll do it, darling." Margaret tried to get there first.

"Don't be silly, Maggie. This may be *your* first baby, but *I* had five kid brothers." He laughed her away, and reached with his other hand for the string that closed one sleeve. He opened the sleeve bow, and groped for an arm.

"The way you wriggle," he addressed his child sternly, as his hand touched a moving knob of flesh at the shoulder, "anyone might think you were a worm, using your tummy to crawl on, instead of your hands and feet."

Margaret stood and watched, smiling. "Wait till you hear her sing, darling—"

His right hand traveled down from the shoulder to where he thought an arm would be, traveled down, and straight down, over firm small muscles that writhed in an attempt to move against the pressure of his hand. He let his fingers drift up again to the shoulder. With infinite care, he opened the knot at the bottom of the nightgown. His wife was standing by the bed, saying: "She can do 'Jingle Bells,' and—"

His left hand felt along the soft knitted fabric of the gown, up towards the diaper that folded, flat and smooth, across the bottom end of his child. No wrinkles. No kicking. *No* . . .

"Maggie." He tried to pull his hands from the neat fold in the diaper, from the wriggling body. "Maggie." His throat was dry; words came hard, low and grating. He spoke very slowly, thinking the sound of each word to make himself say it. His head was spinning, but he had to *know* before he let it go. "Maggie, why . . . didn't you . . . tell me?"

"Tell you what, darling?" Margaret's poise was the immemorial patience of woman confronted with man's childish impetuosity. Her sudden laugh sounded fantastically easy and natural in that room; it was all clear to her now. "Is she wet? I didn't know."

She didn't know. His hands, beyond control, ran up and down the soft-skinned baby body, the sinuous, limbless body. *Oh God, dear God*—his head shook and his muscles contracted, in a bitter spasm of hysteria. His fingers tightened on his child—*Oh God, she didn't know.*

1948

WILMAR H. SHIRAS

In Hiding

PETER Welles, psychiatrist, eyed the boy thoughtfully. Why had Timothy Paul's teacher sent him for examination?

"I don't know, myself, that there's really anything wrong with Tim," Miss Page had told Dr. Welles. "He seems perfectly normal. He's rather quiet as a rule, doesn't volunteer answers in class or anything of that sort. He gets along well enough with other boys and seems reasonably popular, although he has no special friends. His grades are satisfactory—he gets B faithfully in all his work. But when you've been teaching as long as I have, Peter, you get a feeling about certain ones. There is a tension about him—a look in his eyes sometimes—and he is very absent-minded."

"What would your guess be?" Welles had asked. Sometimes these hunches were very valuable. Miss Page had taught school for thirty-odd years; she had been Peter's teacher in the past, and he thought highly of her opinion.

"I ought not to say," she answered. "There's nothing to go on—yet. But he might be starting something, and if it could be headed off—"

"Physicians are often called before the symptoms are sufficiently marked for the doctor to be able to see them," said Welles. "A patient, or the mother of a child, or any practiced observer, can often see that something is going to be wrong. But it's hard for the doctor in such cases. Tell me what you think I should look for."

"You won't pay too much attention to me? It's just what occurred to me, Peter; I know I'm not a trained psychiatrist. But it could be delusions of grandeur. Or it could be a withdrawing from the society of others. I always have to speak to him twice to get his attention in class—and he has no real chums."

Welles had agreed to see what he could find, and promised not to be too much influenced by what Miss Page herself called "an old woman's notions."

Timothy, when he presented himself for examination, seemed like an ordinary boy. He was perhaps a little small for his age, he had big dark eyes and close-cropped dark curls, thin sensitive fingers and—yes, a decided air of tension. But many boys were nervous on their first visit to the—psychiatrist. Peter often wished that he was able to concentrate on one or two schools, and spend a day a week or so getting acquainted with all the youngsters.

In response to Welles' preliminary questioning, Tim replied in a clear, low voice, politely and without wasting words. He was thirteen years old, and lived with his grandparents. His mother and father had died when he was a baby, and he did not remember them. He said that he was happy at home, that he liked school "pretty well," that he liked to play with other boys. He named several boys when asked who his friends were.

"What lessons do you like at school?"

Tim hesitated, then said: "English, and arithmetic . . . and history . . . and geography," he finished thoughtfully. Then he looked up, and there was something odd in the glance.

"What do you like to do for fun?"

"Read, and play games."

"What games?"

"Ball games . . . and marbles . . . and things like that. I like to play with other boys," he added, after a barely perceptible pause, "anything they play."

"Do they play at your house?"

"No; we play on the school grounds. My grandmother doesn't like noise."

Was that the reason? When a quiet boy offers explanations, they may not be the right ones.

"What do you like to read?"

But about his reading Timothy was vague. He liked, he said, to read "boys' books," but could not name any.

Welles gave the boy the usual intelligence tests. Tim seemed willing, but his replies were slow in coming. *Perhaps*, Welles thought, *I'm imagining this, but he is too careful—too cautious.* Without taking time to figure exactly, Welles knew what Tim's I.Q. would be—about 120.

"What do you do outside of school?" asked the psychiatrist.

"I play with the other boys. After supper, I study my lessons."

"What did you do yesterday?"

"We played ball on the school playground."

Welles waited a while to see whether Tim would say anything of his own accord. The seconds stretched into minutes.

"Is that all?" said the boy finally. "May I go now?"

"No; there's one more test I'd like to give you today. A game, really. How's your imagination?"

"I don't know."

"Cracks on the ceiling—like those over there—do they look like anything to you? Faces, animals, or anything?"

Tim looked.

"Sometimes. And clouds, too. Bob saw a cloud last week that

was like a hippo." Again the last sentence sounded like something tacked on at the last moment, a careful addition made for a reason.

Welles got out the Rorschach cards. But at the sight of them, his patient's tension increased, his wariness became unmistakably evident. The first time they went through the cards, the boy could scarcely be persuaded to say anything but, "I don't know."

"You can do better than this," said Welles. "We're going through them again. If you don't see anything in these pictures, I have to mark you a failure," he explained. "That won't do. You did all right on the other things. And maybe next time we'll do a game you'll like better."

"I don't feel like playing this game now. Can't we do it again next time?"

"May as well get it done now. It's not only a game, you know, Tim; it's a test. Try harder, and be a good sport."

So Tim, this time, told what he saw in the ink blots. They went through the cards slowly, and the test showed Tim's fear, and that there was something he was hiding; it showed his caution, a lack of trust, and an unnaturally high emotional self-control.

Miss Page had been right; the boy needed help.

"Now," said Welles cheerfully, "that's all over. We'll just run through them again quickly and I'll tell you what other people have seen in them."

A flash of genuine interest appeared on the boy's face for a moment.

Welles went through the cards slowly, seeing that Tim was attentive to every word. When he first said, "And some see what you saw here," the boy's relief was evident. Tim began to relax, and even to volunteer some remarks. When they had finished he ventured to ask a question.

"Dr. Welles, could you tell me the name of this test?"

"It's sometimes called the Rorschach test, after the man who worked it out."

"Would you mind spelling that?"

Welles spelled it, and added: "Sometimes it's called the ink-blot test."

Tim gave a start of surprise, and then relaxed again with a visible effort.

"What's the matter? You jumped."

"Nothing."

"Oh, come on! Let's have it," and Welles waited.

"Only that I thought about the ink-pool in the Kipling stories," said Tim, after a minute's reflection. "This is different."

"Yes, very different," laughed Welles. "I've never tried that. Would you like to?"

"Oh, no, sir," cried Tim earnestly.

"You're a little jumpy today," said Welles. "We've time for some more talk, if you are not too tired."

"No, I'm not very tired," said the boy warily.

Welles went to a drawer and chose a hypodermic needle. It wasn't usual, but perhaps— "I'll just give you a little shot to relax your nerves, shall I? Then we'd get on better."

When he turned around, the stark terror on the child's face stopped Welles in his tracks.

"Oh, no! Don't! Please, please, don't!"

Welles replaced the needle and shut the drawer before he said a word.

"I won't," he said, quietly. "I didn't know you didn't like shots. I won't give you any, Tim."

The boy, fighting for self-control, gulped and said nothing.

"It's all right," said Welles, lighting a cigarette and pretending to watch the smoke rise. Anything rather than appear to be watching the badly shaken small boy shivering in the chair opposite him. "Sorry. You didn't tell me about the things you don't like, the things you're afraid of."

The words hung in the silence.

"Yes," said Timothy slowly. "I'm afraid of shots. I hate needles. It's just one of those things." He tried to smile.

"We'll do without them, then. You've passed all the tests, Tim, and I'd like to walk home with you and tell your grandmother about it. Is that all right with you?"

"Yes, sir."

"We'll stop for something to eat," Welles went on, opening the door for his patient. "Ice cream, or a hot dog."

They went out together.

Timothy Paul's grandparents, Mr. and Mrs. Herbert Davis, lived in a large old-fashioned house that spelled money and position. The grounds were large, fenced, and bordered with shrubbery. Inside the house there was little that was new, everything was well-kept. Timothy led the psychiatrist to Mr. Davis's library, and then went in search of his grandmother.

When Welles saw Mrs. Davis, he thought he had some of the explanation. Some grandmothers are easy-going, jolly, comparatively young. This grandmother was, as it soon became apparent, quite different.

"Yes, Timothy is a pretty good boy," she said, smiling on her grandson. "We have always been strict with him, Dr. Welles, but I believe it pays. Even when he was a mere baby, we tried to teach him right ways. For example, when he was barely three I read him some little stories. And a few days later he was trying to tell us, if you will believe it, that he could read! Perhaps he was too young to know the nature of a lie, but I felt it my duty to make him understand. When he insisted, I spanked him. The child had a remarkable memory, and perhaps he thought that was all there was to reading. Well! I don't mean to brag of my brutality," said Mrs. Davis, with a charming smile. "I assure you, Dr. Welles, it was a painful experience for me. We've had very little occasion for punishments. Timothy is a good boy."

Welles murmured that he was sure of it.

"Timothy, you may deliver your papers now," said Mrs. Davis. "I am sure Dr. Welles will excuse you." And she settled herself for a good long talk about her grandson.

Timothy, it seemed, was the apple of her eye. He was a quiet boy, an obedient boy, and a bright boy.

"We have our rules, of course. I have never allowed Timothy to forget that children should be seen and not heard, as the good old-fashioned saying is. When he first learned to turn somersaults, when he was three or four years old, he kept coming to me and saying, 'Grandmother, see me!' I simply had to be firm with him. 'Timothy,' I said, 'let us have no more of this! It is simply showing off. If it amuses you to turn somersaults, well and good. But it doesn't amuse me to watch you endlessly doing it. Play if you like, but do not demand admiration.'"

"Did you never play with him?"

"Certainly I played with him. And it was a pleasure to me also. We—Mr. Davis and I—taught him a great many games, and many kinds of handcraft. We read stories to him and taught him rhymes and songs. I took a special course in kindergarten craft, to amuse the child—and I must admit that it amused me also!" added Tim's grandmother, smiling reminiscently. "We made houses of toothpicks, with balls of clay at the corners. His grandfather took him for walks and drives. We no longer have a car, since my husband's sight has begun to fail him slightly, so now the garage is Timothy's workshop. We had windows cut in it, and a door, and nailed the large doors shut."

It soon became clear that Tim's life was not all strictures by any means. He had a workshop of his own, and upstairs beside his bedroom was his own library and study.

"He keeps his books and treasures there," said his grandmother, "his own little radio, and his schoolbooks, and his typewriter. When he was only seven years old, he asked us for a typewriter. But he is a careful child, Dr. Welles, not at all destructive, and I had read that in many schools they make use of typewriters in teaching young children to read and write and to spell. The words look the same as in printed books, you see; and less muscular effort is involved. So his grandfather got him a very nice noiseless typewriter, and he loved it dearly. I often hear it purring away as I pass through the hall. Timothy keeps his own rooms in good order, and his shop also. It is his own wish. You know how boys are—they do not wish others to meddle with their belongings. 'Very well, Timothy,' I told him, 'if a glance shows me that you can do it yourself properly, nobody will go into your rooms; but they must be kept neat.' And he has done so for several years. A very neat boy, Timothy."

"Timothy didn't mention his paper route," remarked Welles. "He said only that he plays with other boys after school."

"Oh, but he does," said Mrs. Davis. "He plays until five o'clock, and then he delivers his papers. If he is late, his grandfather walks down and calls him. The school is not very far from here, and Mr. Davis frequently walks down and watches the boys at their play.

The paper route is Timothy's way of earning money to feed his cats. Do you care for cats, Dr. Welles?"

"Yes, I like cats very much," said the psychiatrist. "Many boys like dogs better."

"Timothy had a dog when he was a baby—a collie." Her eyes grew moist. "We all loved Ruff dearly. But I am no longer young, and the care and training of a dog is difficult. Timothy is at school or at the Boy Scout camp or something of the sort a great part of the time, and I thought it best that he should not have another dog. But you wanted to know about our cats, Dr. Welles. I raise Siamese cats."

"Interesting pets," said Welles cordially. "My aunt raised them at one time."

"Timothy is very fond of them. But three years ago he asked me if he could have a pair of black Persians. At first I thought not; but we like to please the child, and he promised to build their cages himself. He had taken a course in carpentry at vacation school. So he was allowed to have a pair of beautiful black Persians. But the very first litter turned out to be short-haired, and Timothy confessed that he had mated his queen to my Siamese tom, to see what would happen. Worse yet, he had mated his tom to one of my Siamese queens. I really was tempted to punish him. But, after all, I could see that he was curious as to the outcome of such cross-breeding. Of course I said the kittens must be destroyed. The second litter was exactly like the first—all black, with short hair. But you know what children are. Timothy begged me to let them live, and they were his first kittens. Three in one litter, two in the other. He might keep them, I said, if he would take full care of them and be responsible for all the expense. He mowed lawns and ran errands and made little footstools and bookcases to sell, and did all sorts of things, and probably used his allowance, too. But he kept the kittens and has a whole row of cages in the yard beside his workshop."

"And their offspring?" inquired Welles, who could not see what all this had to do with the main question, but was willing to listen to anything that might lead to information.

"Some of the kittens appear to be pure Persian, and others pure Siamese. These he insisted on keeping, although, as I have explained to him, it would be dishonest to sell them, since they are not pure-bred. A good many of the kittens are black short-haired and these we destroy. But enough of cats, Dr. Welles. And I am afraid I am talking too much about my grandson."

"I can understand that you are very proud of him," said Welles.

"I must confess that we are. And he is a bright boy. When he and his grandfather talk together, and with me also, he asks very intelligent questions. We do not encourage him to voice his opinions—I detest the smart-Aleck type of small boy—and yet I believe they would be quite good opinions for a child of his age."

"Has his health always been good?" asked Welles.

"On the whole, very good. I have taught him the value of exercise, play, wholesome food and suitable rest. He has had a few of the usual childish ailments, not seriously. And he never has colds. But, of course, he takes his cold shots twice a year when we do."

"Does he mind the shots?" asked Welles, as casually as he could.

"Not at all. I always say that he, though so young, sets an example I find hard to follow. I still flinch, and really rather dread the ordeal."

Welles looked toward the door at a sudden, slight sound.

Timothy stood there, and he had heard. Again, fear was stamped on his face and terror looked out of his eyes.

"Timothy," said his grandmother, "don't stare."

"Sorry, sir," the boy managed to say.

"Are your papers all delivered? I did not realize we had been talking for an hour, Dr. Welles. Would you like to see Timothy's cats?" Mrs. Davis inquired graciously. "Timothy, take Dr. Welles to see your pets. We have had quite a talk about them."

Welles got Tim out of the room as fast as he could. The boy led the way around the house and into the side yard where the former garage stood.

There the man stopped.

"Tim," he said, "you don't have to show me the cats if you don't want to."

"Oh, that's all right."

"Is that part of what you are hiding? If it is, I don't want to see it until you are ready to show me."

Tim looked up at him then.

"Thanks," he said. "I don't mind about the cats. Not if you like cats really."

"I really do. But, Tim, this I would like to know: You're not afraid of the needle. Could you tell me why you were afraid . . . why you said you were afraid . . . of my shot? The one I promised not to give you after all?"

Their eyes met.

"You won't tell?" asked Tim.

"I won't tell."

"Because it was pentothal. Wasn't it?"

Welles gave himself a slight pinch. Yes, he was awake. Yes, this was a little boy asking him about pentothal. A boy who— Yes, certainly, a boy who knew about it.

"Yes, it was," said Welles. "A very small dose. You know what it is?"

"Yes, sir. I . . . I read about it somewhere. In the papers."

"Never mind that. You have a secret—something you want to hide. That's what you are afraid about, isn't it?"

The boy nodded dumbly.

"If it's anything wrong, or that might be wrong, perhaps I could help you. You'll want to know me better, first. You'll want to be sure you can trust me. But I'll be glad to help, any time you say the word, Tim. Or I might stumble on to things the way I did just now. One thing though—I never tell secrets."

"Never?"

"Never. Doctors and priests don't betray secrets. Doctors seldom, priests never. I guess I am more like a priest, because of the kind of doctoring I do."

He looked down at the boy's bowed head.

"Helping fellows who are scared sick," said the psychiatrist very gently. "Helping fellows in trouble, getting things straight again, fixing things up, unsnarling tangles. When I can, that's what I do. And I don't tell anything to anybody. It's just between that one fellow and me."

But, he added to himself, *I'll have to find out. I'll have to find out what ails this child. Miss Page is right—he needs me.*

They went to see the cats.

There were the Siamese in their cages, and the Persians in their cages, and there, in several small cages, the short-haired black cats and their hybrid offspring. "We take them into the house, or let them into this big cage, for exercise," explained Tim. "I take mine into my shop sometimes. These are all mine. Grandmother keeps hers on the sun porch."

"You'd never know these were not all pure-bred," observed Welles. "Which did you say were the full Persians? Any of their kittens here?"

"No; I sold them."

"I'd like to buy one. But these look just the same—it wouldn't make any difference to me. I want a pet, and wouldn't use it for breeding stock. Would you sell me one of these?"

Timothy shook his head.

"I'm sorry. I never sell any but the pure-breds."

It was then that Welles began to see what problem he faced. Very dimly he saw it, with joy, relief, hope and wild enthusiasm.

"Why not?" urged Welles. "I can wait for a pure-bred, if you'd rather, but why not one of these? They look just the same. Perhaps they'd be more interesting."

Tim looked at Welles for a long, long minute.

"I'll show you," he said. "Promise to wait here? No, I'll let you come into the workroom. Wait a minute, please."

The boy drew a key from under his blouse, where it had hung suspended from a chain, and unlocked the door of his shop. He went inside, closed the door, and Welles could hear his moving about for a few moments. Then he came to the door and beckoned.

"Don't tell grandmother," said Tim. "I haven't told her yet. If it lives, I'll tell her next week."

In the corner of the shop under a table there was a box, and in the box there was a Siamese cat. When she saw a stranger she tried to hide her kittens; but Tim lifted her gently, and then Welles saw. Two of the kittens looked like little white rats with stringy tails and smudgy paws, ears and noses. But the third—yes, it was going to be a different sight. It was going to be a beautiful cat if it lived. It had long, silky white hair like the finest Persian, and the Siamese markings were showing up plainly.

Welles caught his breath.

"Congratulations, old man! Haven't you told anyone yet?"

"She's not ready to show. She's not a month old."

"But you're going to show her?"

"Oh, yes, Grandmother will be thrilled. She'll love her. Maybe there'll be more."

"You knew this would happen. You made it happen. You planned it all from the start," accused Welles.

"Yes," admitted the boy.

"How did you know?"

The boy turned away.

"I read it somewhere," said Tim.

The cat jumped back into the box and began to nurse her babies. Welles felt as if he could endure no more. Without a glance at anything else in the room—and everything else was hidden under tarpaulins and newspapers—he went to the door.

"Thanks for showing me, Tim," he said. "And when you have any to sell, remember me. I'll wait. I want one like that."

The boy followed him out and locked the door carefully.

"But Tim," said the psychiatrist, "that's not what you were afraid I'd find out. I wouldn't need a drug to get you to tell me this, would I?"

Tim replied carefully, "I didn't want to tell this until I was ready. Grandmother really ought to know first. But you made me tell you."

"Tim," said Peter Welles earnestly, "I'll see you again. Whatever you are afraid of, don't be afraid of me. I often guess secrets. I'm on the way to guessing yours already. But nobody else need ever know."

He walked rapidly home, whistling to himself from time to time. Perhaps he, Peter Welles, was the luckiest man in the world.

He had scarcely begun to talk to Timothy on the boy's next appearance at the office, when the phone in the hall rang. On his return, when he opened the door he saw a book in Tim's hands. The boy made a move as if to hide it, and thought better of it.

Welles took the book and looked at it.

"Want to know more about Rorschach, eh?" he asked.

"I saw it on the shelf. I—"

"Oh, that's all right," said Welles, who had purposely left the book near the chair Tim would occupy. "But what's the matter with the library?"

"They've got some books about it, but they're on the closed shelves. I couldn't get them." Tim spoke without thinking first, and then caught his breath.

But Welles replied calmly: "I'll get it out for you. I'll have it next time you come. Take this one along today when you go. Tim, I mean it—you can trust me."

"I can't tell you anything," said the boy. "You've found out some things. I wish . . . oh, I don't know what I wish! But I'd rather be let alone. I don't need help. Maybe I never will. If I do, can't I come to you then?"

Welles pulled out his chair and sat down slowly.

"Perhaps that would be the best way, Tim. But why wait for the ax to fall? I might be able to help you ward it off—what you're afraid of. You can kid people along about the cats; tell them you were fooling around to see what would happen. But you can't fool all of the people all of the time, they tell me. Maybe with me to help, you could. Or with me to back you up, the blowup would be easier. Easier on your grandparents, too."

"I haven't done anything wrong!"

"I'm beginning to be sure of that. But things you try to keep hidden may come to light. The kitten—you could hide it, but you don't want to. You've got to risk something to show it."

"I'll tell them I read it somewhere."

"That wasn't true, then. I thought not. You figured it out."

There was silence.

Then Timothy Paul said: "Yes. I figured it out. But that's my secret."

"It's safe with me."

But the boy did not trust him yet. Welles soon learned that he had been tested. Tim took the book home, and returned it, took the library books which Welles got for him, and in due course returned them also. But he talked little and was still wary. Welles could talk all he liked, but he got little or nothing out of Tim. Tim had told all he was going to tell. He would talk about nothing except what any boy would talk about.

After two months of this, during which Welles saw Tim officially once a week and unofficially several times—showing up at the school playground to watch games, or meeting Tim on the paper route and treating him to a soda after it was finished—Welles had learned very little more. He tried again. He had probed no more during the two months, respected the boy's silence, trying to give him time to get to know and trust him.

But one day he asked: "What are you going to do when you grow up, Tim? Breed cats?"

Tim laughed a denial.

"I don't know what, yet. Sometimes I think one thing, sometimes another."

This was a typical boy answer. Welles disregarded it.

"What would you like to do best of all?" he asked.

Tim leaned forward eagerly. "What you do!" he cried.

"You've been reading up on it, I suppose," said Welles, as casually as he could. "Then you know, perhaps, that before anyone can do what I do, he must go through it himself, like a patient. He must also study medicine and be a full-fledged doctor, of course. You can't do that yet. But you can have the works now, like a patient."

"Why? For the experience?"

"Yes. And for the cure. You'll have to face that fear and lick it. You'll have to straighten out a lot of other things, or at least face them."

"My fear will be gone when I'm grown up," said Timothy. "I think it will. I hope it will."

"Can you be sure?"

"No," admitted the boy. "I don't know exactly why I'm afraid. I just know I *must* hide things. Is that bad, too?"

"Dangerous, perhaps."

Timothy thought a while in silence. Welles smoked three cigarettes and yearned to pace the floor, but dared not move.

"What would it be like?" asked Tim finally.

"You'd tell me about yourself. What you remember. Your childhood—the way your grandmother runs on when she talks about you."

"She sent me out of the room. I'm not supposed to think I'm bright," said Tim, with one of his rare grins.

"And you're not supposed to know how well she reared you?"

"She did fine," said Tim. "She taught me all the wisest things I ever knew."

"Such as what?"

"Such as shutting up. Not telling all you know. Not showing off."

"I see what you mean," said Welles. "Have you heard the story of St. Thomas Aquinas?"

"No."

"When he was a student in Paris, he never spoke out in class, and the others thought him stupid. One of them kindly offered to help him, and went over all the work very patiently to make him understand it. And then one day they came to a place where the other student got all mixed up and had to admit he didn't understand. Then Thomas suggested a solution and it was the right one. He knew more than any of the others all the time; but they called him the Dumb Ox."

Tim nodded gravely.

"And when he grew up?" asked the boy.

"He was the greatest thinker of all time," said Welles. "A fourteenth-century super-brain. He did more original work than any other other ten great men; and he died young."

After that, it was easier.

"How do I begin?" asked Timothy.

"You'd better begin at the beginning. Tell me all you can remember about your early childhood, before you went to school."

Tim gave this his consideration.

"I'll have to go forward and backward a lot," he said. "I couldn't put it all in order."

"That's all right. Just tell me today all you can remember about that time of your life. By next week you'll have remembered more. As we go on to later periods of your life, you may remember things that belonged to an earlier time; tell them then. We'll make some sort of order out of it."

Welles listened to the boy's revelations with growing excitement. He found it difficult to keep outwardly calm.

"When did you begin to read?" Welles asked.

"I don't know when it was. My grandmother read me some stories, and somehow I got the idea about the words. But when I tried to tell her I could read, she spanked me. She kept saying I couldn't, and I kept saying I could, until she spanked me. For a while I had a dreadful time, because I didn't know any word she hadn't read to me—I guess I sat beside her and watched, or else I remembered and then went over it by myself right after. I must have learned as soon as I got the idea that each group of letters on the page was a word."

"The word-unit method," Welles commented. "Most self-taught readers learned like that."

"Yes. I have read about it since. And Macaulay could read when he was three, but only upside-down, because of standing opposite when his father read the Bible to the family."

"There are many cases of children who learned to read as you did, and surprised their parents. Well? How did you get on?"

"One day I noticed that two words looked almost alike and sounded almost alike. They were 'can' and 'man.' I remember staring at them and then it was like something beautiful boiling up in me. I began to look carefully at the words, but in a crazy excitement. I was a long while at it, because when I put down the book and tried to stand up I was stiff all over. But I had the idea, and after that it wasn't hard to figure out almost any words. The really hard words are the common ones that you get all the time in easy books. Other words are pronounced the way they are spelled."

"And nobody knew you could read?"

"No. Grandmother told me not to say I could, so I didn't. She read to me often, and that helped. We had a great many books, of course, I liked those with pictures. Once or twice they caught me with a book that had no pictures, and then they'd take it away and say, 'I'll find a book for a little boy.'"

"Do you remember what books you liked then?"

"Books about animals, I remember. And geographies. It was funny about animals—"

Once you got Timothy started, thought Welles, it wasn't hard to get him to go on talking.

"One day I was at the Zoo," said Tim, "and by the cages alone. Grandmother was resting on a bench and she let me walk along by myself. People were talking about the animals and I began to tell them all I knew. It must have been funny in a way, because I had read a lot of words I couldn't pronounce correctly, words I had never heard spoken. They listened and asked me questions and I thought I was just like grandfather, teaching them the way he sometimes taught me. And then they called another man to come, and said, 'Listen to this kid; he's a scream!' and I saw they were all laughing at me."

Timothy's face was redder than usual, but he tried to smile as he added, "I can see now how it must have sounded funny. And unexpected, too; that's a big point in humor. But my little feelings were so dreadfully hurt that I ran back to my grandmother crying, and she couldn't find out why. But it served me right for disobeying her. She always told me not to tell people things; she said a child had nothing to teach its elders."

“Not in that way, perhaps—at that age.”

“But, honestly, some grown people don’t know very much,” said Tim. “When we went on the train last year, a woman came up and sat beside me and started to tell me things a little boy should know about California. I told her I’d lived here all my life, but I guess she didn’t even know we are taught things in school, and she tried to tell me things, and almost everything was wrong.”

“Such as what?” asked Welles, who had also suffered from tourists.

“We . . . she said so many things . . . but I thought this was the funniest: She said all the Missions were so old and interesting, and I said yes, and she said, ‘You know, they were all built long before Columbus discovered America,’ and I thought she meant it for a joke, so I laughed. She looked very serious and said, ‘Yes, those people all came up here from Mexico.’ I suppose she thought they were Aztec temples.”

Welles, shaking with laughter, could not but agree that many adults were sadly lacking in the rudiments of knowledge.

“After that Zoo experience, and a few others like it, I began to get wise to myself,” continued Tim. “People who knew things didn’t want to hear me repeating them, and people who didn’t know, wouldn’t be taught by a four-year-old baby. I guess I was four when I began to write.”

“How?”

“Oh, I just thought if I couldn’t say anything to anybody at any time, I’d burst. So I began to put it down—in printing, like in books. Then I found out about writing, and we had some old-fashioned schoolbooks that taught how to write. I’m left-handed. When I went to school, I had to use my right hand. But by then I had learned how to pretend that I didn't know things. I watched the others and did as they did. My grandmother told me to do that."

"I wonder why she said that," marveled Welles.

"She knew I wasn't used to other children, she said, and it was the first time she had left me to anyone else's care. So she told me to do what the others did and what my teacher said," explained Tim simply, "and I followed her advice literally. I pretended I didn't know anything, until the others began to know it, too. Lucky I was so shy. But there were things to learn, all right. Do you know, when I first went to school, I was disappointed because the teacher dressed like other women. The only picture of teachers I had noticed were those in an old Mother Goose book, and I thought that all teachers wore hoop skirts. But as soon as I saw her, after the little shock of surprise, I knew it was silly, and I never told."

The psychiatrist and the boy laughed together.

"We played games. I had to learn to play with children, and not be surprised when they slapped or pushed me. I just couldn't figure out why they'd do that, or what good it did them. But if it was to surprise me, I'd say 'Boo' and surprise them some time later; and if they were mad because I had taken a ball or something they wanted, I'd play with them."

"Anybody ever try to beat you up?"

"Oh, yes. But I had a book about boxing—with pictures. You can't learn much from pictures, but I got some practice too, and that helped. I didn't want to win, anyway. That's what I like about games of strength or skill—I'm fairly matched, and I don't have to be always watching in case I might show off or try to boss somebody around."

"You must have tried bossing sometimes."

"In books, they all cluster around the boy who can teach new games and think up new things to play. But I found out that doesn't work. They just want to do the same thing all the time—like hide and seek. It's no fun if the first one to be caught is 'it' next time. The rest just walk in any old way and don't try to hide or even to run, because it doesn't matter whether they are caught. But you can't get the boys to see that, and play right, so the last one caught is 'it.'"

Timothy looked at his watch.

"Time to go," he said. "I've enjoyed talking to you, Dr. Welles. I hope I haven't bored you too much."

Welles recognized the echo and smiled appreciatively at the small boy.

"You didn't tell me about the writing. Did you start to keep a diary?"

"No. It was a newspaper. One page a day, no more and no less. I still keep it," confided Tim. "But I get more on the page now. I type it."

"And you write with either hand now?"

"My left hand is my own secret writing. For school and things like that I use my right hand."

When Timothy had left, Welles congratulated himself. But for the next month he got no more. Tim would not reveal a single significant fact. He talked about ball-playing, he described his grandmother's astonished delight over the beautiful kitten, he told of its growth and the tricks it played. He gravely related such enthralling facts as that he liked to ride on trains, that his favorite wild animal was the lion, and that he greatly desired to see snow falling. But not a word of what Welles wanted to hear. The psychiatrist, knowing that he was again being tested, waited patiently.

Then one afternoon when Welles, fortunately unoccupied with a patient, was smoking a pipe on his front porch, Timothy Paul strode into the yard.

"Yesterday Miss Page asked me if I was seeing you and I said yes. She said she hoped my grandparents didn't find it too expensive, because you had told her I was all right and didn't need to have her worrying about me. And then I said to grandma, was it expensive for you to talk to me, and she said, 'Oh no, dear; the school pays for that. It was your teacher's idea that you have a few talks with Dr. Welles.'"

"I'm glad you came to me, Tim, and I'm sure you didn't give me away to either of them. Nobody's paying me. The school pays for my services if a child is in a bad way and his parents are poor. It's a new service, since 1956. Many maladjusted children can be helped—much more cheaply to the state than the cost of having them go crazy or become criminals or something. You understand all that. But—sit down, Tim!—I can't charge the state for you, and I can't charge your grandparents. You're adjusted marvelously well in every way, as far as I can see; and when I see the rest, I'll be even more sure of it."

"Well—gosh! I wouldn't have come—" Tim was stammering in confusion. "You ought to be paid. I take up so much of your time. Maybe I'd better not come any more."

"I think you'd better. Don't you?"

"Why are you doing it for nothing, Dr. Welles?"

"I think you know why."

The boy sat down in the glider and pushed himself meditatively back and forth. The glider squeaked.

"You're interested. You're curious," he said.

"That's not all, Tim."

Squeak-squeak. Squeak-squeak.

"I know," said Timothy. "I believe it. Look, is it all right if I call you Peter? Since we're friends."

At their next meeting, Timothy went into details about his newspaper. He had kept all the copies, from the first smudged, awkwardly printed pencil issues to the very latest neatly typed ones. But he would not show Welles any of them.

"I just put down every day the things I most wanted to say, the news or information or opinion I had to swallow unsaid. So it's a wild medley. The earlier copies are awfully funny. Sometimes I guess what they were all about, what made me write them. Sometimes I remember. I put down the books I read too, and mark them like school grades, on two points—how I liked the book, and whether it was good. And whether I had read it before, too."

"How many books do you read? What's your reading speed?"

It proved that Timothy's reading speed on new books of adult level varied from eight hundred to nine hundred fifty words a minute. The average murder mystery—he loved them—took him less than half an hour. A year's homework in history, Tim performed easily by reading his textbook through three or four times during the year. He apologized for that, but explained that he had to know what was in the book so as not to reveal in examinations too much that he had learned from other sources. Evenings, when his grandparents believed him to be doing homework, he spent reading other books, or writing his newspaper, "or something." As Welles had already guessed, Tim had read everything in his grandfather's library, everything in the public library that was not on the closed shelves, and everything he could order from the state library.

"What do the librarians say?"

"They think the books are for my grandfather. I tell them that, if they ask what a little boy wants with such a big book. Peter, telling so many lies is what gets me down. I have to do it, don't I?"

"As far as I can see, you do," agreed Welles. "But here's material for a while in my library. There'll have to be a closed shelf here, too, though, Tim."

"Could you tell me why? I know about the library books. Some of them might scare people, and some are—"

"Some of my books might scare you too, Tim. I'll tell you a little about abnormal psychology if you like, one of these days, and then I think you'll see that until you're actually training to deal with such cases, you'd be better off not knowing too much about them."

"I don't want to be morbid," agreed Tim. "All right. I'll read only what you give me. And from now on I'll tell you things. There was more than the newspaper, you know."

"I thought as much. Do you want to go on with your tale?"

"It started when I first wrote a letter to a newspaper—of course, under a pen name. They printed it. For a while I had a high old time of it—a letter almost every day, using all sorts of pen names. Then I branched out to magazines, letters to the editor again. And stories—I tried stories."

He looked a little doubtfully at Welles, who said only: "How old were you when you sold the first story?"

"Eight," said Timothy. "And when the check came, with my name on it, 'T. Paul,' I didn't know what in the world to do."

"That's a thought. What did you do?"

"There was a sign in the window of the bank. I always read signs, and that one came back to my mind. 'Banking By Mail.' You can see I was pretty desperate. So I got the name of a bank across the Bay and I wrote them—on my typewriter—and said I wanted to start an account, and here was a check to start it with. Oh, I was scared stiff, and had to keep saying to myself that, after all, nobody could do much to me. It was my own money. But you don't know what it's like to be only a small boy! They sent the check back to me and I died ten deaths when I saw it. But the letter explained. I hadn't endorsed it. They sent me a blank to fill out about myself. I didn't know how many lies I dared to tell. But it was my money and I had to get it. If I could get it into the bank, then some day I could get it out. I gave my business as 'author' and I gave my age as twenty-four. I thought that was awfully old."

"I'd like to see the story. Do you have a copy of the magazine around?"

"Yes," said Tim. "But nobody noticed it—I mean, 'T. Paul' could be anybody. And when I saw magazines for writers on the news-stands, and bought them I got on to the way to use a pen name on the story and my own name and address up in the corner. Before that I used a pen name and sometimes never got the things back or heard about them. Sometimes I did, though."

"What then?"

"Oh, then I'd endorse the check payable to me and sign the pen name, and then sign my own name under it. Was I scared to do that! But it was my money."

"Only stories?"

"Articles, too. And things. That's enough of that for today. Only—I just wanted to say—a while ago, T. Paul told the bank he wanted to switch some of the money over to a checking account. To buy books by mail, and such. So, I could pay you, Dr. Welles—" with sudden formality.

"No, Tim," said Peter Welles firmly. "The pleasure is all mine. What I want is to see the story that was published when you were eight. And some of the other things that made T. Paul rich enough to keep a consulting psychiatrist on the payroll. And, for the love of Pete, will you tell me how all this goes on without your grandparents' knowing a thing about it?"

"Grandmother thinks I send in box tops and fill out coupons," said Tim. "She doesn't bring in the mail. She says her little boy gets such a big bang out of that little chore. Anyway that's what she said when I was eight. I played mailman. And there were box tops—I showed them to her, until she said, about the third time, that really she wasn't greatly interested in such matters. By now she has the habit of waiting for me to bring in the mail."

Peter Welles thought that was quite a day of revelation. He spent a quiet evening at home, holding his head and groaning, trying to take it all in.

And that I.Q.—120, nonsense! The boy had been holding out on him. Tim's reading had obviously included enough about I.Q. tests, enough puzzles and oddments in magazines and such, to enable him to stall successfully. What could he do if he would co-operate?

Welles made up his mind to find out.

He didn't find out. Timothy Paul went swiftly through the whole range of Superior Adult tests without a failure of any sort. There were no tests yet devised that could measure his intelligence. While he was still writing his age with one figure, Timothy Paul had faced alone, and solved alone, problems that would have baffled the average adult. He had adjusted to the hardest task of all—that of appearing to be a fairly normal, B-average small boy.

And it must be that there was more to find out about him. What did he write? And what did he do besides read and write, learn carpentry and breed cats and magnificently fool his whole world?

*

When Peter Welles had read some of Tim's writings, he was surprised to find that the stories the boy had written were vividly human, the product of close observation of human nature. The articles, on the other hand, were closely reasoned and showed thorough study and research. Apparently Tim read every word of several newspapers and a score or more of periodicals.

"Oh, sure," said Tim, when questioned. "I read everything. I go back once in a while and review old ones, too."

"If you can write like this," demanded Welles, indicating a magazine in which a staid and scholarly article had appeared, "and this"—this was a man-to-man political article giving the arguments for and against a change in the whole Congressional system—"then why do you always talk to me in the language of an ordinary stupid schoolboy?"

"Because I'm only a little boy," replied Timothy. "What would happen if I went around talking like that?"

"You might risk it with me. You've showed me these things."

"I'd never dare to risk talking like that. I might forget and do it again before others. Besides, I can't pronounce half the words."

"What!"

"I never look up a pronunciation," explained Timothy. "In case I do slip and use a word beyond the average, I can anyway hope I didn't say it right."

Welles shouted with laughter, but was sober again as he realized the implications back of that thoughtfulness.

"You're just like an explorer living among savages," said the psychiatrist. "You have studied the savages carefully and tried to imitate them so they won't know there are differences."

"Something like that," acknowledged Tim.

"That's why your stories are so human," said Welles. "That one about the awful little girl—"

They both chuckled.

"Yes, that was my first story," said Tim. "I was almost eight, and there was a boy in my class who had a brother, and the boy next door was the other one, the one who was picked on."

"How much of the story was true?"

"The first part. I used to see, when I went over there, how that girl picked on Bill's brother's friend Steve. She wanted to play with Steve all the time herself and whenever he had boys over, she'd do something awful. And Steve's folks were just like I said—they wouldn't let Steve do anything to a girl. When she threw all the watermelon rinds over the fence into his yard, he just had to pick them all up and say nothing back; and she'd laugh at him over the fence. She got him blamed for things he never did, and when he had work to do in the yard she'd hang out of her window and scream at him and make fun. I thought first, what made her act like that; and then I made up a way for him to get even with her, and wrote it out the way it might have happened."

"Didn't you pass the idea on to Steve and let him try it?"

"Gosh, no! I was only a little boy. Kids seven don't give ideas to kids ten. That's the first thing I had to learn—to be always the one that kept quiet, especially if there was any older boy or girl around, even only a year or two older. I had to learn to look blank and let my mouth hang open and say, 'I don't get it,' to almost everything."

"And Miss Page thought it was odd that you had no close friends of your own age," said Welles. "You must be the loneliest boy that ever walked this earth, Tim. You've lived in hiding like a criminal. But tell me, what are you afraid of?"

"I'm afraid of being found out, of course. The only way I can live in this world is in disguise—until I'm grown up, at any rate. At first, it was just my grandparents scolding me and telling me not to show off, and the way people laughed if I tried to talk to them. Then I saw how people hate anyone who is better or brighter or luckier. Some people sort of trade off; if you're bad at one thing you're good at another, but they'll forgive you for being good at some things, because you're not good at others and they can balance that off. They can beat you at something. You have to strike a balance. A child has no chance at all. No grownup can stand it to have a child know anything he doesn't. Oh, a little thing, if it amuses them. But not much of anything. There's an old story about a man who found himself in a country where everyone else was blind. I'm like that—but they shan't put out my eyes. I'll never let them know I can see anything."

"Do you see things that no grown person can see?"

Tim waved his hand towards the magazines.

"Only like that, I meant. I hear people talking, in street cars and stores, and while they work, and around. I read about the way they act—in the news. I'm like them, just like them, only I seem about a hundred years older—more matured."

"Do you mean that none of them have much sense?"

"I don't mean that exactly. I mean that so few of them have any, or show it if they do have. They don't even seem to want to. They're good people in their way, but what could they make of me? Even when I was seven, I could understand their motives, but they couldn't understand their own motives. And they're so lazy—they don't seem to want to know or to understand. When I first went to the library for books, the books I learned from were seldom touched by any of the grown people. But they were meant for ordinary grown people. But the grown people didn't want to know things—they only wanted to fool around. I feel about most people the way my grandmother feels about babies and puppies. Only she doesn't have to pretend to be a puppy all the time," Tim added, with a little bitterness.

"You have a friend now, in me."

"Yes, Peter," said Tim, brightening up. "And I have pen friends, too. People like what I write, because they can't see I'm only a little boy. When I grow up—"

Tim did not finish that sentence. Welles understood, now, some of the fears that Tim had not dared to put into words at all. When he grew up, would he be as far beyond all other grownups as he had, all his life, been above his contemporaries? The adult friends whom he now met on fairly equal terms—would they then, too, seem like babies or puppies?

Peter did not dare to voice the thought, either. Still less did he venture to hint at another thought. Tim, so far, had no great interest in girls; they existed for him as part of the human race, but there would come a time when Tim would be a grown man and would wish to marry. And where among the puppies could he find a mate?

"When you're grown up, we'll still be friends," said Peter. "And who are the others?"

It turned out that Tim had pen friends all over the world. He played chess by correspondence—a game he never dared to play in person, except when he forced himself to move the pieces about idly and let his opponent win at least half the time. He had, also, many friends who had read something he had written, and had written to him about it, thus starting a correspondence-friendship. After the first two or three of these, he had started some on his own account, always with people who lived at a great distance. To most of these he gave a name which, although not false, looked it. That was Paul T. Lawrence. Lawrence was his middle name; and with a comma after the Paul, it was actually his own name. He had a post office box under that name, for which T. Paul of the large bank account was his reference.

"Pen friends abroad? Do you know languages?"

Yes, Tim did. He had studied by correspondence, also; many universities gave extension courses in that manner, and lent the student records to play so that he could learn the correct pronunciation. Tim had taken several such courses, and learned other languages from books. He kept all these languages in practice by means of the letters to other lands and the replies which came to him.

"I'd buy a dictionary, and then I'd write to the mayors of some towns, or to a foreign newspaper, and ask them to advertise for some pen friends to help me learn the language. We'd exchange souvenirs and things."

Nor was Welles in the least surprised to find that Timothy had also taken other courses by correspondence. He had completed, within three years, more than half the subjects offered by four separate universities, and several other courses, the most recent being Architecture. The boy, not yet fourteen, had completed a full course in that subject and, had he been able to disguise himself as a full-grown man, could have gone out at once and built almost anything you'd like to name, for he also knew much of the trades involved.

"It always said how long an average student took, and I'd take that long," said Tim, "so, of course, I had to be working several schools at the same time."

"And carpentry at the playground summer school?"

"Oh, yes. But there I couldn't do too much, because people could see me. But I learned how, and it made a good cover-up, so I could make cages for the cats, and all that sort of thing. And many boys are good with their hands. I like to work with my hands. I built my own radio too—it gets all the foreign stations, and that helps me with my languages."

"How did you figure it about the cats?" asked Welles.

"Oh, there had to be recessives, that's all. The Siamese coloring was a recessive, and it had to be mated with another recessive. Black was one possibility, and white was another, but I started with black because I liked it better. I might try white too, but I have so much else on my mind—"

He broke off suddenly and would say no more.

Their next meeting was by prearrangement at Tim's workshop. Welles met the boy after school and they walked to Tim's home together; there the boy unlocked his door and snapped on the lights.

Welles looked around with interest. There was a bench, a tool chest. Cabinets, padlocked. A radio, clearly not store-purchased. A file cabinet, locked. Something on a table, covered with a cloth. A box in the corner—no, two boxes in two corners. In each of them was a mother cat with kittens. Both mothers were black Persians.

"This one must be all black Persian," Tim explained. "Her third litter and never a Siamese marking. But this one carries both recessives in her. Last time she had a Siamese short-haired kitten. This morning—I had to go to school. Let's see."

They bent over the box where the new-born kittens lay. One kitten was like the mother. The other two were Siamese-Persian; a male and a female.

"You've done it again, Tim!" shouted Welles. "Congratulations!"

They shook hands in jubilation.

"I'll write it in the record," said the boy blissfully.

In a nickel book marked "Compositions" Tim's left hand added the entries. He had used the correct symbols—F_1, F_2, F_3; Ss, Bl.

"The dominants in capitals," he explained, "B for black, and S for short hair; the recessives in small letters—s for Siamese, l for long hair. Wonderful to write ll over ss again, Peter! Twice more. And the other kitten is carrying the Siamese markings as a recessive."

He closed the book in triumph.

"Now," and he marched to the covered thing on the table, "my latest big secret."

Tim lifted the cloth carefully and displayed a beautifully built doll house. No, a model house—Welles corrected himself swiftly. A beautiful model, and—yes, built to scale.

"The roof comes off. See, it has a big storage room and a room for a play room or a maid or something. Then I lift off the attic—"

"Good heavens!" cried Peter Welles. "Any little girl would give her soul for this!"

"I used fancy wrapping papers for the wallpapers. I wove the rugs on a little hand loom," gloated Timothy. "The furniture's just like real, isn't it? Some I bought; that plastic. Some I made of construction paper and things. The curtains were the hardest; but I couldn't ask grandmother to sew them—"

"Why not?" the amazed doctor managed to ask.

"She might recognize this afterwards," said Tim, and he lifted off the upstairs floor.

"Recognize it? You haven't showed it to her? Then when would she see it?"

"She might not," admitted Tim. "But I have to take some risks."

"That's a very livable floor plan you've used," said Welles, bending closer to examine the house in detail.

"Yes, I thought so. It's awful how many house plans leave no clear wall space for books or pictures. Some of them have doors placed so you have to detour around the dining room table every time you go from the living room to the kitchen, or so that a whole corner of a room is good for nothing, with doors at all angles. Now, I designed this house to—"

"You designed it, Tim!"

"Why, sure. Oh, I see—you thought I built it from blueprints I'd bought. My first model home, I did, but the architecture courses gave me so many ideas that I wanted to see how they would look. Now, the cellar and game room—"

Welles came to himself an hour later, and gasped when he looked at his watch.

"It's too late. My patient has gone home again by this time. I may as well stay—how about the paper route?"

"I gave that up. Grandmother offered to feed the cats as soon as I gave her the kitten. And I wanted the time for this. Here are the pictures of the house."

The color prints were very good.

"I'm sending them and an article to the magazines," said Tim. "This time I'm T. L. Paul. Sometimes I used to pretend all the different people I am were talking together—but now I talk to you instead, Peter."

"Will it bother the cats if I smoke? Thanks. Nothing I'm likely to set on fire, I hope? Put the house together and let me sit here and look at it. I want to look in through the windows. Put its little lights on. There."

The young architect beamed, and snapped on the little lights.

"Nobody can see in here. I got Venetian blinds; and when I work in here, I even shut them sometimes."

"If I'm to know all about you, I'll have to go through the alphabet from A to Z," said Peter Welles. "This is Architecture. What else in the A's?"

"Astronomy. I showed you those articles. My calculations proved correct. Astrophysics—I got A in the course, but haven't done anything original so far. Art, no, I can't paint or draw very well, except mechanical drawing. I've done all the Merit Badge work in scouting, all through the alphabet."

"Darned if I can see you as a Boy Scout," protested Welles.

"I'm a very good Scout. I have almost as many badges as any other boy my age in the troop. And at camp I do as well as most city boys."

"Do you do a good turn every day?"

"Yes," said Timothy. "Started that when I first read about Scouting—I was a Scout at heart before I was old enough to be a Cub. You know, Peter, when you're very young you take all that seriously, about the good deed every day, and the good habits and ideals and all that. And then you get older and it begins to seem funny and childish and posed and artificial, and you smile in a superior way and make jokes. But there is a third step, too, when you take it all seriously again. People who make fun of the Scout Law are doing the boys a lot of harm; but those who believe in things like that don't know how to say so, without sounding priggish and platitudinous. I'm going to do an article on it before long."

"Is the Scout Law your religion—if I may put it that way?"

"No," said Timothy. "But 'a Scout is Reverent.' Once I tried to study the churches and find out what was the truth. I wrote letters to pastors of all denominations—all those in the phone book and the newspaper—when I was on a vacation in the East, I got the names, and then wrote after I got back. I couldn't write to people here in the city. I said I wanted to know which church was true, and expected them to write to me and tell me about theirs, and argue with me, you know. I could read library books, and all they had to do was recommend some, I told them, and then correspond with me a little about them."

"Did they?"

"Some of them answered," said Tim, "but nearly all of them told me to go to somebody near me. Several said they were very busy men. Some gave me the name of a few books, but none of them told me to write again, and . . . and I was only a little boy. Nine years old, so I couldn't talk to anybody. When I thought it over, I knew that I couldn't very well join any church so young, unless it was my grandparents' church. I keep on going there—it is a good church and it teaches a great deal of truth, I am sure. I'm reading all I can find, so when I am old enough I'll know what I must do. How old would you say I should be, Peter?"

"College age," replied Welles. "You are going to college? By then, any of the pastors would talk to you—except those that are too busy!"

"It's a moral problem, really. Have I the right to wait? But I have to wait. It's like telling lies—I have to tell some lies, but I hate to. If I have a moral obligation to join the true church as soon as I find it, well, what then? I can't, until I'm eighteen or twenty?"

"If you can't, you can't. I should think that settles it. You are legally a minor, under the control of your grandparents, and while you might claim the right to go where your conscience leads you, it would be impossible to justify and explain your choice without giving yourself away entirely—just as you are obliged to go to school until you are at least eighteen, even though you know more than most Ph.D.'s. It's all part of the game, and He who made you must understand that."

"I'll never tell you any lies," said Tim. "I was getting so desperately lonely—my pen pals didn't know anything about me really. I told them only what was right for them to know. Little kids are satisfied to be with other people but when you get a little older you have to make friends, really."

"Yes, that's a part of growing up. You have to reach out to others and share thoughts with them. You've kept to yourself too long as it is."

"It wasn't that I wanted to. But without a real friend, it was only pretense, and I never could let my playmates know anything about me. I studied them and wrote stories about them and it was all of them, but it was only a tiny part of me."

"I'm proud to be your friend, Tim. Every man needs a friend. I'm proud that you trust me."

Tim patted the cat a moment in silence and then looked up with a grin.

"How would you like to hear my favorite joke?" he asked.

"Very much," said the psychiatrist, bracing himself for almost any major shock.

"It's records. I recorded this from a radio program."

Welles listened. He knew little of music, but the symphony which he heard pleased him. The announcer praised it highly in little speeches before and after each movement. Timothy giggled.

"Like it?"

"Very much. I don't see the joke."

"I wrote it."

"Tim, you're beyond me! But I still don't get the joke."

"The joke is that I did it by mathematics. I calculated what ought to sound like joy, grief, hope, triumph, and all the rest, and—it was just after I had studied harmony; you know how mathematical that is."

Speechless, Welles nodded.

"I worked out the rhythms from different metabolisms—the way you function when under the influences of these emotions; the way your metabolic rate varies, your heartbeats and respiration and things. I sent it to the director of that orchestra, and he didn't get the idea that it was a joke—of course I didn't explain—he produced the music. I get nice royalties from it, too."

"You'll be the death of me yet," said Welles in deep sincerity. "Don't tell me anything more today; I couldn't take it. I'm going home. Maybe by tomorrow I'll see the joke and come back to laugh. Tim, did you ever fail at anything?"

"There are two cabinets full of articles and stories that didn't sell. Some of them I feel bad about. There was the chess story. You know, in 'Through the Looking Glass,' it wasn't a very good game, and you couldn't see the relation of the moves to the story very well."

"I never could see it at all."

"I thought it would be fun to take a championship game and write a fantasy about it, as if it were a war between two little old countries, with knights and foot-soldiers, and fortified walls in charge of captains, and the bishops couldn't fight like warriors, and, of course, the queens were women—people don't kill them, not in hand-to-hand fighting and . . . well, you see? I wanted to make up the attacks and captures, and keep the people alive, a fairy-tale war you see, and make the strategy of the game and the strategy of the war coincide, and have everything fit. It took me ever so long to work it out and write it. To understand the game as a chess game and then to translate it into human actions and motives, and put speeches to it to fit different kinds of people. I'll show it to you. I loved it. But nobody would print it. Chess players don't like fantasy, and nobody else likes chess. You have to have a very special kind of mind to like both. But it was a disappointment. I hoped it would be published, because the few people who like that sort of thing would like it *very* much."

"I'm sure I'll like it."

"Well, if you do like that sort of thing, it's what you've been waiting all your life in vain for. Nobody else has done it." Tim stopped, and blushed as red as a beet. "I see what grandmother means. Once you get started bragging, there's no end to it. I'm sorry, Peter."

"Give me the story. I don't mind, Tim—brag all you like to me; I understand. You might blow up if you never express any of your legitimate pride and pleasure in such achievements. What I don't understand is how you have kept it all under for so long."

"I had to," said Tim.

The story was all its young author had claimed. Welles chuckled as he read it, that evening. He read it again, and checked all the moves and the strategy of them. It was really a fine piece of work. Then he thought of the symphony, and this time he was able to laugh. He sat up until after midnight, thinking about the boy. Then he took a sleeping pill and went to bed.

The next day he went to see Tim's grandmother. Mrs. Davis received him graciously.

"Your grandson is a very interesting boy," said Peter Welles carefully. "I'm asking a favor of you. I am making a study of various boys and girls in this district, their abilities and backgrounds and environment and character traits and things like that. No names will ever be mentioned, of course, but a statistical report will be kept, for ten years or longer, and some case histories might later be published. Could Timothy be included?"

"Timothy is such a good, normal little boy, I fail to see what would be the purpose of including him in such a survey."

"That is just the point. We are not interested in maladjusted persons in this study. We eliminate all psychotic boys and girls. We are interested in boys and girls who succeed in facing their youthful problems and making satisfactory adjustments to life. If we could study a selected group of such children, and follow their progress for the next ten years at least—and then publish a summary of the findings, with no names used—"

"In that case, I see no objection," said Mrs. Davis.

"If you'd tell me, then, something about Timothy's parents—their history?"

Mrs. Davis settled herself for a good long talk.

"Timothy's mother, my only daughter, Emily," she began, "was a lovely girl. So talented. She played the violin charmingly. Timothy is like her, in the face, but has his father's dark hair and eyes. Edwin had very fine eyes."

"Edwin was Timothy's father?"

"Yes. The young people met while Emily was at college in the East. Edwin was studying atomics there."

"Your daughter was studying music?"

"No; Emily was taking the regular liberal arts course. I can tell you little about Edwin's work, but after their marriage he returned to it and . . . you understand, it is painful for me to recall this, but their deaths were such a blow to me. They were so young."

Welles held his pencil ready to write.

"Timothy has never been told. After all, he must grow up in this world, and how dreadfully the world has changed in the past thirty years, Dr. Welles! But you would not remember the day before 1945. You have heard, no doubt of the terrible explosion in the atomic plant, when they were trying to make a new type of bomb? At the time, none of the workers seemed to be injured. They believed the protection was adequate. But two years later they were all dead or dying."

Mrs. Davis shook her head, sadly. Welles held his breath, bent his head, scribbled.

"Tim was born just fourteen months after the explosion, fourteen months to the day. Everyone still thought that no harm had been done. But the radiation had some effect which was very slow—I do not understand such things—Edwin died, and then Emily came home to us with the boy. In a few months she, too, was gone.

"Oh, but we do not sorrow as those who have no hope. It is hard to have lost her, Dr. Welles, but Mr. Davis and I have reached the time of life when we can look forward to seeing her again. Our hope is to live until Timothy is old enough to fend for himself. We were so anxious about him; but you see he is perfectly normal in every way."

"Yes."

"The specialists made all sorts of tests. But nothing is wrong with Timothy."

The psychiatrist stayed a little longer, took a few more notes, and made his escape as soon as he could. Going straight to the school, he had a few words with Miss Page and then took Tim to his office, where he told him what he had learned.

"You mean—I'm a mutation?"

"A mutant. Yes, very likely you are. I don't know. But I had to tell you at once."

"Must be a dominant, too," said Tim, "coming out this way in the first generation. You mean—there may be more? I'm not the only one?" he added in great excitement. "Oh, Peter, even if I grow up past you I won't have to be lonely?"

There. He had said it.

"It could be, Tim. There's nothing else in your family that could account for you."

"But I have never found anyone at all like me. I would have known. Another boy or girl my age—like me—I would have known."

"You came West with your mother. Where did the others go, if they existed? The parents must have scattered everywhere, back to their homes all over the country, all over the world. We can trace them, though. And, Tim haven't you thought it's just a little bit strange that with all your pen names and various contacts, people don't insist more on meeting you? People don't ask about you? Everything gets done by mail? It's almost as if the editors are used to people who hide. It's almost as if people are used to architects and astronomers and composers whom nobody ever sees, who are only names in care of other names at post office boxes. There's a chance—just a chance, mind you—that there are others. If there are we'll find them."

"I'll work out a code they will understand," said Tim, his face screwed up in concentration. "In articles—I'll do it—several magazines and in letters I can inclose copies—some of my pen friends may be the ones—"

"I'll hunt up the records—they must be on file somewhere—psychologists and psychiatrists know all kinds of tricks—we can make some excuse to trace them all—the birth records—"

Both of them were talking at once, but all the while Peter Welles was thinking sadly, perhaps he had lost Tim now. If they did find those others, those to whom Tim rightfully belonged, where would poor Peter be? Outside, among the puppies—

Timothy Paul looked up and saw Peter Welles' eyes on him. He smiled.

"You were my first friend, Peter, and you shall be forever," said Tim. "No matter what, no matter who."

"But we must look for the others," said Peter.

"I'll never forget who helped me," said Tim.

An ordinary boy of thirteen may say such a thing sincerely, and a week later have forgotten all about it. But Peter Welles was content. Tim would never forget, Tim would be his friend always. Even when Timothy Paul and those like him should unite in a maturity undreamed of, to control the world if they chose. Peter Welles would be Tim's friend—not a puppy, but a beloved friend—as a loyal dog, loved by a good master, is never cast out.

1948

KATHERINE MACLEAN

Contagion

IT was like an Earth forest in the fall, but it was not fall. The forest leaves were green and copper and purple and fiery red, and a wind sent patches of bright greenish sunlight dancing among the leaf shadows.

The hunt party of the *Explorer* filed along the narrow trail, guns ready, walking carefully, listening to the distant, half familiar cries of strange birds.

A faint crackle of static in their earphones indicated that a gun had been fired.

"Got anything?" asked June Walton. The helmet intercom carried her voice to the ears of the others without breaking the stillness of the forest.

"Took a shot at something," explained George Barton's cheerful voice in her earphones. She rounded a bend of the trail and came upon Barton standing peering up into the trees, his gun still raised. "It looked like a duck."

"This isn't Central Park," said Hal Barton, his brother, coming into sight. His green spacesuit struck an incongruous note against the bronze and red forest. "They won't all look like ducks," he said soberly.

"Maybe some will look like dragons. Don't get eaten by a dragon, June," came Max's voice quietly into her earphones. "Not while I still love you." He came out of the trees carrying the blood sample kit, and touched her glove with his, the grin on his ugly beloved face barely visible in the mingled light and shade. A patch of sunlight struck a greenish glint from his fishbowl helmet.

They walked on. A quarter of a mile back, the spaceship *Explorer* towered over the forest like a tapering skyscraper, and the people of the ship looked out of the viewplates at fresh winds and sunlight and clouds, and they longed to be outside.

But the likeness to Earth was danger, and the cool wind might be death, for if the animals were like Earth animals, their diseases might be like Earth diseases, alike enough to be contagious, different enough to be impossible to treat. There was warning enough in the past. Colonies had vanished, and traveled spaceways drifted with the corpses of ships which had touched on some plague planet.

The people of the ship waited while their doctors, in airtight spacesuits, hunted animals to test them for contagion.

The four medicos, for June Walton was also a doctor, filed through the alien homelike forest, walking softly, watching for motion among the copper and purple shadows.

They saw it suddenly, a lighter moving copper patch among the darker browns. Reflex action swung June's gun into line, and behind her someone's gun went off with a faint crackle of static, and made a hole in the leaves beside the specimen. Then for a while no one moved.

This one looked like a man, a magnificently muscled, leanly graceful, humanlike animal. Even in its callused bare feet, it was a head taller than any of them. Red-haired, hawk-faced and darkly tanned, it stood breathing heavily, looking at them without expression. At its side hung a sheath knife, and a crossbow was slung across one wide shoulder.

They lowered their guns.

"It needs a shave," Max said reasonably in their earphones, and he reached up to his helmet and flipped the switch that let his voice be heard. "Something we could do for you, Mac?"

The friendly drawl was the first voice that had broken the forest sounds. June smiled suddenly. He was right. The strict logic of evolution did not demand beards; therefore a non-human would not be wearing a three day growth of red stubble.

Still panting, the tall figure licked dry lips and spoke. "Welcome to Minos. The Mayor sends greetings from Alexandria."

"English?" gasped June.

"We were afraid you would take off again before I could bring word to you. . . . It's three hundred miles. . . . We saw your scout plane pass twice, but we couldn't attract its attention."

June looked in stunned silence at the stranger leaning against the tree. Thirty-six light years—thirty-six times six trillion miles of monotonous space travel—to be told that the planet was already settled! "We didn't know there was a colony here," she said. "It is not on the map."

"We were afraid of that," the tall bronze man answered soberly. "We have been here three generations and yet no traders have come."

Max shifted the kit strap on his shoulder and offered a hand. "My name is Max Stark, M.D. This is June Walton, M.D., Hal Barton, M.D., and George Barton, Hal's brother, also M.D."

"Patrick Mead is the name," smiled the man, shaking hands casually. "Just a hunter and bridge carpenter myself. Never met any medicos before."

The grip was effortless but even through her airproofed glove June could feel that the fingers that touched hers were as hard as padded steel.

"What—what is the population of Minos?" she asked.

He looked down at her curiously for a moment before answering. "Only one hundred and fifty." He smiled. "Don't worry, this isn't a city planet yet. There's room for a few more people." He shook hands with the Bartons quickly. "That is—you are people, aren't you?" he asked startlingly.

"Why not?" said Max with a poise that June admired.

"Well, you are all so—so—" Patrick Mead's eyes roamed across the faces of the group. "So varied."

They could find no meaning in that, and stood puzzled.

"I mean," Patrick Mead said into the silence, "all these—interesting different hair colors and face shapes and so forth—" He made a vague wave with one hand as if he had run out of words or was anxious not to insult them.

"Joke?" Max asked, bewildered.

June laid a hand on his arm. "No harm meant," she said to him over the intercom. "We're just as much of a shock to him as he is to us."

She addressed a question to the tall colonist on outside sound. "What should a person look like, Mr. Mead?"

He indicated her with a smile. "Like you."

June stepped closer and stood looking up at him, considering her own description. She was tall and tanned, like him; had a few freckles, like him; and wavy red hair, like his. She ignored the brightly humorous blue eyes.

"In other words," she said, "everyone on the planet looks like you and me?"

Patrick Mead took another look at their four faces and began to grin. "Like me, I guess. But I hadn't thought of it before. I did not think that people could have different colored hair or that noses could fit so many ways onto faces. I was judging by my own appearance, but I suppose any fool can walk on his hands and say the world is upside down!" He laughed and sobered. "But then why wear spacesuits? The air is breathable."

"For safety," June told him. "We can't take any chances on plague."

Pat Mead was wearing nothing but a loin cloth and his weapons, and the wind ruffled his hair. He looked comfortable, and they longed to take off the stuffy spacesuits and feel the wind against their own skins. Minos was like home, like Earth. . . . But they were strangers.

"Plague," Pat Mead said thoughtfully. "We had one here. It came two years after the colony arrived and killed everyone except the Mead families. They were immune. I guess we look alike because we're all related, and that's why I grew up thinking that it is the only way people can look."

Plague. "What was the disease?" Hal Barton asked.

"Pretty gruesome, according to my father. They called it the melting sickness. The doctors died too soon to find out what it was or what to do about it."

"You should have trained for more doctors, or sent to civilization for some." A trace of impatience was in George Barton's voice.

Pat Mead explained patiently, "Our ship, with the power plant and all the books we needed, went off into the sky to avoid the contagion, and never came back. The crew must have died." Long years of hardship were indicated by that statement, a colony with electric power gone and machinery stilled, with key technicians dead and no way to replace them. June realized then the full meaning of the primitive sheath knife and bow.

"Any recurrence of melting sickness?" asked Hal Barton.

"No."

"Any other diseases?"

"Not a one."

Max was eying the bronze red-headed figure with something approaching awe. "Do you think all the Meads look like that?" he said to June on the intercom. "I wouldn't mind being a Mead myself!"

Their job had been made easy by the coming of Pat. They went back to the ship laughing, exchanging anecdotes with him. There was nothing now to keep Minos from being the home they wanted, except the melting sickness, and, forewarned against it, they could take precautions.

The polished silver and black column of the *Explorer* seemed to rise higher and higher over the trees as they neared it. Then its symmetry blurred all sense of specific size as they stepped out from among the trees and stood on the edge of the meadow, looking up.

"Nice!" said Pat. "Beautiful!" The admiration in his voice was warming.

"It was a yacht," Max said, still looking up, "second hand, an old-time beauty without a sign of wear. Synthetic diamond-studded control board and murals on the walls. It doesn't have the new speed drives, but it brought us thirty-six light years in one and a half subjective years. Plenty good enough."

The tall tanned man looked faintly wistful, and June realized that he had never had access to a film library, never seen a movie, never experienced luxury. He had been born and raised on Minos.

"May I go aboard?" Pat asked hopefully.

Max unslung the specimen kit from his shoulder, laid it on the carpet of plants that covered the ground and began to open it.

"Tests first," Hal Barton said. "We have to find out if you people still carry this so-called melting sickness. We'll have to de-microbe you and take specimens before we let you on board. Once on, you'll be no good as a check for what the other Meads might have."

Max was taking out a rack and a stand of preservative bottles and hypodermics.

"Are you going to jab me with those?" Pat asked with interest.

"You're just a specimen animal to me, bud!" Max grinned at Pat Mead, and Pat grinned back. June saw that they were friends already, the tall pantherish colonist, and the wry, black-haired doctor. She felt a stab of guilt because she loved Max and yet could pity him for being smaller and frailer than Pat Mead.

"Lie down," Max told him, "and hold still. We need two spinal fluid samples from the back, a body cavity one in front, and another from the arm."

Pat lay down obediently. Max knelt, and, as he spoke, expertly swabbed and inserted needles with the smooth speed that had made him a fine nerve surgeon on Earth.

High above them the scout helioplane came out of an opening in the ship and angled off toward the west, its buzz diminishing. Then, suddenly, it veered and headed back, and Reno Ulrich's voice came tinnily from their earphones:

"What's that you've got? Hey, what are you docs doing down there?" He banked again and came to a stop, hovering fifty feet away. June could see his startled face looking through the glass at Pat.

Hal Barton switched to a narrow radio beam, explained rapidly and pointed in the direction of Alexandria. Reno's plane lifted and flew away over the odd-colored forest.

"The plane will drop a note on your town, telling them you got through to us," Hal Barton told Pat, who was sitting up watching Max dexterously put the blood and spinal fluids into the right bottles without exposing them to air.

"We won't be free to contact your people until we know if they still carry melting sickness," Max added. "You might be immune so it doesn't show on you, but still carry enough germs—if that's what caused it—to wipe out a planet."

"If you do carry melting sickness," said Hal Barton, "we won't be able to mingle with your people until we've cleared them of the disease."

"Starting with me?" Pat asked.

"Starting with you," Max told him ruefully, "as soon as you step on board."

"More needles?"

"Yes, and a few little extras thrown in."

"Rough?"

"It isn't easy."

A few minutes later, standing in the stalls for spacesuit decontamination, being buffeted by jets of hot disinfectant, bathed in glares of sterilizing ultraviolet radiation, June remembered that and compared Pat Mead's treatment to theirs.

In the *Explorer*, stored carefully in sealed tanks and containers, was the ultimate, multi-purpose cureall. It was a solution of enzymes so like the key catalysts of the human cell nucleus that it caused chemical derangement and disintegration in any nonhuman cell. Nothing could live in contact with it but human cells; any alien intruder to the body would die. Nucleocat Cureall was its trade name.

But the cureall alone was not enough for complete safety. Plagues had been known to slay too rapidly and universally to be checked by human treatment. Doctors are not reliable; they die. Therefore spaceways and interplanetary health law demanded that ship equipment for guarding against disease be totally mechanical in operation, rapid and efficient.

Somewhere near them, in a series of stalls which led around and around like a rabbit maze, Pat was being herded from stall to stall by peremptory mechanical voices, directed to soap and shower, ordered to insert his arm into a slot which took a sample of his blood, given solutions to drink, bathed in germicidal ultra-violet, shaken by sonic blasts, breathing air thick with sprays of germicidal mists, being directed to put his arms into other slots where they were anesthetized and injected with various immunizing solutions.

Finally, he would be put in a room of high temperature and extreme dryness, and instructed to sit for half an hour while more fluids were dripped into his veins through long thin tubes.

All legal spaceships were built for safety. No chance was taken of allowing a suspected carrier to bring an infection on board with him.

June stepped from the last shower stall into the locker room, zipped off her spacesuit with a sigh of relief, and contemplated herself in a wall mirror. Red hair, dark blue eyes, tall. . . .

"I've got a good figure," she said thoughtfully.

Max turned at the door. "Why this sudden interest in your looks?" he asked suspiciously. "Do we stand here and admire you, or do we finally get something to eat?"

"Wait a minute." She went to a wall phone and dialed it carefully, using a combination from the ship's directory. "How're you doing, Pat?"

The phone picked up a hissing of water or spray. There was a startled chuckle. "Voices, too! Hello, June. How do you tell a machine to go jump in the lake?"

"Are you hungry?"

"No food since yesterday."

"We'll have a banquet ready for you when you get out," she told Pat and hung up, smiling. Pat Mead's voice had a vitality and enjoyment which made shipboard talk sound like sad artificial gaiety in contrast.

They looked into the nearby small laboratory where twelve squealing hamsters were protestingly submitting to a small injection each of Pat's blood. In most of them the injection was followed by one of antihistaminics and adaptives. Otherwise the hamster defense system would treat all non-hamster cells as enemies, even the harmless human blood cells, and fight back against them violently.

One hamster, the twelfth, was given an extra large dose of adaptive, so that if there were a disease, he would not fight it or the human cells, and thus succumb more rapidly.

"How ya doing, George?" Max asked.

"Routine," George Barton grunted absently.

On the way up the long spiral ramps to the dining hall, they passed a viewplate. It showed a long scene of mountains in the distance on the horizon, and between them, rising step by step as they grew farther away, the low rolling hills, bronze and red with patches of clear green where there were fields.

Someone was looking out, standing very still, as if she had been there a long time—Bess St. Clair, a Canadian woman. "It looks like Winnipeg," she told them as they paused. "When are you doctors going to let us out of this blithering barberpole? Look," she pointed. "See that patch of field on the south hillside, with the brook winding through it? I've staked that hillside for our house. When do we get out?"

Reno Ulrich's tiny scout plane buzzed slowly in from the distance and began circling lazily.

"Sooner than you think," Max told her. "We've discovered a castaway colony on the planet. They've done our tests for us by just living here. If there's anything here to catch, they've caught it."

"People on Minos?" Bess's handsome ruddy face grew alive with excitement.

"One of them is down in the medical department," June said. "He'll be out in twenty minutes."

"May I go see him?"

"Sure," said Max. "Show him the way to the dining hall when he gets out. Tell him we sent you."

"Right!" She turned and ran down the ramp like a small girl going to a fire. Max grinned at June and she grinned back. After a year and a half of isolation in space, everyone was hungry for the sight of new faces, the sound of unfamiliar voices.

They climbed the last two turns to the cafeteria, and entered to a rich subdued blend of soft music and quiet conversations. The cafeteria was a section of the old dining room, left when the rest of the ship had been converted to living and working quarters, and it still had the original finely grained wood of the ceiling and walls, the sound absorbency, the soft music spools and the intimate small light at each table where people leisurely ate and talked.

They stood in line at the hot foods counter, and behind her June could hear a girl's voice talking excitedly through the murmur of conversation.

"—new man, honest! I saw him through the viewplate when they came in. He's down in the medical department. A real frontiersman."

The line drew abreast of the counters, and she and Max chose three heaping trays, starting with hydroponic mushroom steak, raised in the growing trays of water and chemicals; sharp salad bowl with rose tomatoes and aromatic peppers; tank-grown fish with special sauce; four different desserts, and assorted beverages.

Presently they had three tottering trays successfully maneuvered to a table. Brant St. Clair came over. "I beg your pardon, Max, but they are saying something about Reno carrying messages to a colony of savages, for the medical department. Will he be back soon, do you know?"

Max smiled up at him, his square face affectionate. Everyone liked the shy Canadian. "He's back already. We just saw him come in."

"Oh, fine." St. Clair beamed. "I had an appointment with him to go out and confirm what looks like a nice vein of iron to the northeast. Have you seen Bess? Oh—there she is." He turned swiftly and hurried away.

A very tall man with fiery red hair came in surrounded by an eagerly talking crowd of ship people. It was Pat Mead. He stood in the doorway, alertly scanning the dining room. Sheer vitality made him seem even larger than he was. Sighting June, he smiled and began to thread toward their table.

"Look!" said someone. "There's the colonist!" Shelia, a pretty, jeweled woman, followed and caught his arm. "Did you *really* swim across a river to come here?"

Overflowing with good-will and curiosity, people approached from all directions. "Did you actually walk three hundred miles? Come, eat with us. Let me help choose your tray."

Everyone wanted him to eat at their table, everyone was a specialist and wanted data about Minos. They all wanted anecdotes about hunting wild animals with a bow and arrow.

"He needs to be rescued," Max said. "He won't have a chance to eat."

June and Max got up firmly, edged through the crowd, captured Pat and escorted him back to their table. June found herself pleased to be claiming the hero of the hour.

Pat sat in the simple, subtly designed chair and leaned back almost voluptuously, testing the way it gave and fitted itself to him. He ran his eyes over the bright tableware and heaped plates. He looked around at the rich grained walls and soft lights at each table. He said nothing, just looking and feeling and experiencing.

"When we build our town and leave the ship," June explained, "we will turn all the staterooms back into the lounges and ballrooms and cocktail bars that used to be inside."

"Oh, I'm not complaining," Pat said negligently. He cocked his head to the music, and tried to locate its source.

"That's big of you," said Max with gentle irony.

They fell to, Pat beginning the first meal he had had in more than a day.

Most of the other diners finished when they were halfway through, and began walking over, diffidently at first, then in another wave of smiling faces, handshakes, and introductions. Pat was asked about crops, about farming methods, about rainfall and floods, about farm animals and plant breeding, about the compatibility of imported Earth seeds with local ground, about mines and strata.

There was no need to protect him. He leaned back in his chair and drawled answers with the lazy ease of a panther; where he could think of no statistic, he would fill the gap with an anecdote. It developed that he enjoyed spinning campfire yarns and especially being the center of interest.

Between bouts of questions, he ate with undiminished and glowing relish.

June noticed that the female specialists were prolonging the questions more than they needed, clustering around the table laughing at his jokes, until presently Pat was almost surrounded by pretty faces, eager questions, and chiming laughs. Shelia the beautiful laughed most chimingly of all.

June nudged Max, and Max shrugged indifferently. It wasn't anything a man would pay attention to, perhaps. But June watched Pat for a moment more, then glanced uneasily back to Max. He was eating and listening to Pat's answers and did not feel her gaze. For some reason Max looked almost shrunken to her. He was shorter than she had realized; she had forgotten that he was only the same height as herself. She was dimly aware of the clear lilting chatter of female voices increasing at Pat's end of the table.

"That guy's a menace," Max said, and laughed to himself, cutting another slice of hydroponic mushroom steak. "What's eating you?" he added, glancing aside at her when he noticed her sudden stillness.

"Nothing," she said hastily, but she did not turn back to watching Pat Mead. She felt disloyal. Pat was only a superb animal. Max was the man she loved. Or—was he? Of course he was, she told herself angrily. They had gone colonizing together because they wanted to spend their lives together; she had never thought of marrying any other man. Yet the sense of dissatisfaction persisted, and along with it a feeling of guilt.

Len Marlow, the protein tank culture technician responsible for the mushroom steaks, had wormed his way into the group and asked Pat a question. Now he was saying, "I don't dig you, Pat. It sounds like you're putting the people into the tanks instead of the vegetables!" He glanced at them, looking puzzled. "See if you two can make anything of this. It sounds medical to me."

Pat leaned back and smiled, sipping a glass of hydroponic burgundy. "Wonderful stuff. You'll have to show us how to make it."

Len turned back to him. "You people live off the country, right? You hunt and bring in steaks and eat them, right? Well, say I have one of those steaks right here and I want to eat it, what happens?"

"Go ahead and eat it. It just wouldn't digest. You'd stay hungry."

"Why?" Len was aggrieved.

"Chemical differences in the basic protoplasm of Minos. Different amino linkages, left-handed instead of right-handed molecules in the carbohydrates, things like that. Nothing will be digestible here until you are adapted chemically by a little test-tube evolution. Till then you'd starve to death on a full stomach."

Pat's side of the table had been loaded with the dishes from two trays, but it was almost clear now and the dishes were stacked neatly to one side. He started on three desserts, thoughtfully tasting each in turn.

"Test-tube evolution?" Max repeated. "What's that? I thought you people had no doctors."

"It's a story." Pat leaned back again. "Alexander P. Mead, the head of the Mead clan, was a plant geneticist, a very determined personality and no man to argue with. He didn't want us to go through the struggle of killing off all Minos plants and putting in our own, spoiling the face of the planet and upsetting the balance of its ecology. He decided that he would adapt our genes to this planet or kill us trying. He did it all right."

"Did which?" asked June, suddenly feeling a sourceless prickle of fear.

"Adapted us to Minos. He took human cells—"

She listened intently, trying to find a reason for fear in the explanation. It would have taken many human generations to adapt to Minos by ordinary evolution, and that only at a heavy toll of death and hunger which evolution exacts. There was a shorter way: Human cells have the ability to return to their primeval condition of independence, hunting, eating and reproducing alone.

Alexander P. Mead took human cells and made them into phagocytes. He put them through the hard savage school of evolution—a thousand generations of multiplication, hardship and hunger, with the alien indigestible food always present, offering its reward of plenty to the cell that reluctantly learned to absorb it.

"Leucocytes can run through several thousand generations of evolution in six months," Pat Mead finished. "When they reached to a point where they would absorb Minos food, he planted them back in the people he had taken them from."

"What was supposed to happen then?" Max asked, leaning forward.

"I don't know exactly how it worked. He never told anybody much about it, and when I was a little boy he had gone loco and was wandering ha-ha-ing around waving a test tube. Fell down a ravine and broke his neck at the age of eighty."

"A character," Max said.

Why was she afraid? "It worked then?"

"Yes. He tried it on all the Meads the first year. The other settlers didn't want to be experimented on until they saw how it worked out. It worked. The Meads could hunt and plant while the other settlers were still eating out of hydroponics tanks."

"It worked," said Max to Len. "You're a plant geneticist and a tank culture expert. There's a job for you."

"Uh-*uh!*" Len backed away. "It sounds like a medical problem to me. Human cell control—right up your alley."

"It is a one-way street," Pat warned. "Once it is done, you won't be able to digest ship food. I'll get no good from this protein. I ate it just for the taste."

Hal Barton appeared quietly beside the table. "Three of the twelve test hamsters have died," he reported, and turned to Pat. "Your people carry the germs of melting sickness, as you call it. The dead hamsters were injected with blood taken from you before you were de-infected. We can't settle here unless we de-infect everybody on Minos. Would they object?"

"We wouldn't want to give you folks germs," Pat smiled. "Anything for safety. But there'll have to be a vote on it first."

The doctors went to Reno Ulrich's table and walked with him to the hangar, explaining. He was to carry the proposal to Alexandria, mingle with the people, be persuasive and wait for them to vote before returning. He was to give himself shots of cureall every two hours on the hour or run the risk of disease.

Reno was pleased. He had dabbled in sociology before retraining as a mechanic for the expedition. "This gives me a chance to study their mores." He winked wickedly. "I may not be back for several nights." They watched through the viewplate as he took off, and then went over to the laboratory for a look at the hamsters.

Three were alive and healthy, munching lettuce. One was the

control; the other two had been given shots of Pat's blood from before he entered the ship, but with no additional treatment. Apparently a hamster could fight off melting sickness easily if left alone. Three were still feverish and ruffled, with a low red blood count, but recovering. The three dead ones had been given strong shots of adaptive and counter histamine, so their bodies had not fought back against the attack.

June glanced at the dead animals hastily and looked away again. They lay twisted with a strange semi-fluid limpness, as if ready to dissolve. The last hamster, which had been given the heaviest dose of adaptive, had apparently lost all its hair before death. It was hairless and pink, like a still-born baby.

"We can find no micro-organisms," George Barton said. "None at all. Nothing in the body that should not be there. Leucosis and anemia. Fever only for the ones that fought it off." He handed Max some temperature charts and graphs of blood counts.

June wandered out into the hall. Pediatrics and obstetrics were her field; she left the cellular research to Max, and just helped him with laboratory routine. The strange mood followed her out into the hall, then abruptly lightened.

Coming toward her, busily telling a tale of adventure to the gorgeous Shelia Davenport, was a tall, red-headed, magnificently handsome man. It was his handsomeness which made Pat such a pleasure to look upon and talk with, she guiltily told herself, and it was his tremendous vitality. . . . It was like meeting a movie hero in the flesh, or a hero out of the pages of a book—Deerslayer, John Clayton, Lord Greystoke.

She waited in the doorway to the laboratory and made no move to join them, merely acknowledged the two with a nod and a smile and a casual lift of the hand. They nodded and smiled back.

"Hello, June," said Pat and continued telling his tale, but as they passed he lightly touched her arm.

"Oh, pioneer!" she said mockingly and softly to his passing profile, and knew that he had heard.

That night she had a nightmare. She was running down a long corridor looking for Max, but every man she came to was a big bronze man with red hair and bright blue eyes who grinned at her.

The pink hamster! She woke suddenly, feeling as if alarm bells had been ringing, and listened carefully, but there was no sound. She had had a nightmare, she told herself, but alarm bells were still ringing in her unconscious. Something was wrong.

Lying still and trying to preserve the images, she groped for a meaning, but the mood faded under the cold touch of reason. Damn intuitive thinking! A pink hamster! Why did the unconscious have to be so vague? She fell asleep again and forgot.

They had lunch with Pat Mead that day, and after it was over Pat delayed June with a hand on her shoulder and looked down at her for a moment. "I want you, June," he said and then turned away, answering the hails of a party at another table as if he had not spoken. She stood shaken, and then walked to the door where Max waited.

She was particularly affectionate with Max the rest of the day, and it pleased him. He would not have been if he had known why. She tried to forget Pat's blunt statement.

June was in the laboratory with Max, watching the growth of a small tank culture of the alien protoplasm from a Minos weed, and listening to Len Marlow pour out his troubles.

"And Elsie tags around after that big goof all day, listening to his stories. And then she tells me I'm just jealous, I'm imagining things!" He passed his hand across his eyes. "I came away from Earth to be with Elsie. . . . I'm getting a headache. Look, can't you persuade Pat to cut it out, June? You and Max are his friends."

"Here, have an aspirin," June said. "We'll see what we can do."

"Thanks." Len picked up his tank culture and went out, not at all cheered.

Max sat brooding over the dials and meters at his end of the laboratory, apparently sunk in thought. When Len had gone, he spoke almost harshly.

"Why encourage the guy? Why let him hope?"

"Found out anything about the differences in protoplasm?" she evaded.

"Why let him kid himself? What chance has he got against that hunk of muscle and smooth talk?"

"But Pat isn't after Elsie," she protested.

"Every scatter-brained woman on this ship is trailing after Pat with her tongue hanging out. Brant St. Clair is in the bar right now. He doesn't say what he is drinking about, but do you think Pat is resisting all these women crowding down on him?"

"There are other things besides looks and charm," she said, grimly trying to concentrate on a slide under her binocular microscope.

"Yeah, and whatever they are, Pat has them, too. Who's more competent to support a woman and a family on a frontier planet than a handsome bruiser who was born here?"

"I meant," June spun around on her stool with unexpected passion, "there is old friendship, and there's fondness, and memories, and loyalty!" She was half shouting.

"They're not worth much on the second-hand market," Max

said. He was sitting slumped on his lab stool, looking dully at his dials. "Now *I'm* getting a headache!" He smiled ruefully. "No kidding, a real headache. And over other people's troubles yet!"

Other people's troubles. . . . She got up and wandered out into the long curving halls. "I want you June," Pat's voice repeated in her mind. Why did the man have to be so overpoweringly attractive, so glaring a contrast to Max? Why couldn't the universe manage to run on without generating troublesome love triangles?

She walked up the curving ramps to the dining hall where they had eaten and drunk and talked yesterday. It was empty except for one couple talking forehead to forehead over cold coffee.

She turned and wandered down the long easy spiral of corridor to the pharmacy and dispensary. It was empty. George was probably in the test lab next door, where he could hear if he was wanted. The automatic vendor of harmless euphorics, stimulants and opiates stood in the corner, brightly decorated in pastel abstract designs, with its automatic tabulator graph glowing above it.

Max had a headache, she remembered. She recorded her thumbprint in the machine and pushed the plunger for a box of aspirins, trying to focus her attention on the problem of adapting the people of the ship to the planet Minos. An aquarium tank with a faint solution of histamine would be enough to convert a piece of human skin into a community of voracious active phagocytes individually seeking something to devour, but could they eat enough to live away from the rich sustaining plasma of human blood?

After the aspirins, she pushed another plunger for something for herself. Then she stood looking at it, a small box with three pills in her hand—Theobromine, a heart strengthener and a confidence-giving euphoric all in one, something to steady shaky nerves. She had used it before only in emergency. She extended a hand and looked at it. It was trembling. Damn triangles!

While she was looking at her hand there was a click from the automatic drug vendor. It summed the morning use of each drug in the vendors throughout the ship, and recorded it in a neat addition to the end of each graph line. For a moment she could not find the green line for anodynes and the red line for stimulants, and then she saw that they went almost straight up.

There were too many being used—far too many to be explained by jealousy or psychosomatic peevishness. This was an epidemic, and only one disease was possible!

The disinfecting of Pat had not succeeded. Nucleocat Cureall, killer of all infections, had not cured! Pat had brought melting sickness into the ship with him!

Who had it?

The drugs vendor glowed cheerfully, uncommunicative. She opened a panel in its side and looked in on restless interlacing cogs, and on the inside of the door saw printed some directions. . . . "To remove or examine records before reaching end of the reel—"

After a few fumbling minutes she had the answer. In the cafeteria at breakfast and lunch, thirty-eight men out of the forty-eight aboard ship had taken more than his norm of stimulant. Twenty-one had taken aspirin as well. The only woman who had made an unusual purchase was herself!

She remembered the hamsters that had thrown off the infection with a short sharp fever, and checked back in the records to the day before. There was a short rise in aspirin sales to women at late afternoon. The women were safe.

It was the men who had melting sickness!

Melting sickness killed in hours, according to Pat Mead. How long had the men been sick?

As she was leaving, Jerry came into the pharmacy, recorded his thumbprint and took a box of aspirin from the machine.

She felt all right. Self-control was working well and it was pleasant still to walk down the corridor smiling at the people who passed. She took the emergency elevator to the control room and showed her credentials to the technician on watch.

"Medical Emergency." At a small control panel in the corner was a large red button, precisely labeled. She considered it and picked up the control room phone. This was the hard part, telling someone, especially someone who had it—Max.

She dialed, and when the click on the end of the line showed he had picked the phone up, she told Max what she had seen.

"No women, just the men," he repeated. "That right?"

"Yes."

"Probably it's chemically alien, inhibited by one of the female sex hormones. We'll try sex hormone shots, if we have to. Where are you calling from?"

She told him.

"That's right. Give Nucleocat Cureall another chance. It might work this time. Push that button."

She went to the panel and pushed the large red button. Through the long height of the *Explorer*, bells woke to life and began to ring in frightened clangor, emergency doors thumped shut, mechanical apparatus hummed into life and canned voices began to give rapid urgent directions.

A plague had come.

*

She obeyed the mechanical orders, went out into the hall and walked in line with the others. The captain walked ahead of her and the gorgeous Shelia Davenport fell into step beside her. "I look like a positive hag this morning. Does that mean I'm sick? Are we all sick?"

June shrugged, unwilling to say what she knew.

Others came out of all rooms into the corridor, thickening the line. They could hear each room lock as the last person left it, and then, faintly, the hiss of disinfectant spray. Behind them, on the heels of the last person in line, segments of the ship slammed off and began to hiss.

They wound down the spiral corridor until they reached the medical treatment section again, and there they waited in line.

"It won't scar my arms, will it?" asked Shelia apprehensively, glancing at her smooth, lovely arms.

The mechanical voice said, "Next. Step inside, please, and stand clear of the door."

"Not a bit," June reassured Shelia, and stepped into the cubicle.

Inside, she was directed from cubicle to cubicle and given the usual buffeting by sprays and radiation, had blood samples taken and was injected with Nucleocat and a series of other protectives. At last she was directed through another door into a tiny cubicle with a chair.

"You are to wait here," commanded the recorded voice metallically. "In twenty minutes the door will unlock and you may then leave. All people now treated may visit all parts of the ship which have been protected. It is forbidden to visit any quarantined or unsterile part of the ship without permission from the medical officers."

Presently the door unlocked and she emerged into bright lights again, feeling slightly battered.

She was in the clinic. A few men sat on the edge of beds and looked sick. One was lying down. Brant and Bess St. Clair sat near each other, not speaking.

Approaching her was George Barton, reading a thermometer with a puzzled expression.

"What is it, George?" she asked anxiously.

"Some of the women have slight fever, but it's going down. None of the fellows have any—but their white count is way up, their red count is way down, and they look sick to me."

She approached St. Clair. His usually ruddy cheeks were pale, his pulse was light and too fast, and his skin felt clammy. "How's the headache? Did the Nucleocat treatment help?"

"I feel worse, if anything."

"Better set up beds," she told George. "Get everyone back into the clinic."

"We're doing that," George assured her. "That's what Hal is doing."

She went back to the laboratory. Max was pacing up and down, absently running his hands through his black hair until it stood straight up. He stopped when he saw her face, and scowled thoughtfully. "They are still sick?" It was more a statement than a question.

She nodded.

"The Cureall didn't cure this time," he muttered. "That leaves it up to us. We have melting sickness and according to Pat and the hamsters, that leaves us less than a day to find out what it is and learn how to stop it."

Suddenly an idea for another test struck him and he moved to the work table to set it up. He worked rapidly, with an occasional uncoordinated movement betraying his usual efficiency.

It was strange to see Max troubled and afraid.

She put on a laboratory smock and began to work. She worked in silence. The mechanicals had failed. Hal and George Barton were busy staving off death from the weaker cases and trying to gain time for Max and her to work. The problem of the plague had to be solved by the two of them alone. It was in their hands.

Another test, no results. Another test, no results. Max's hands were shaking and he stopped a moment to take stimulants.

She went into the ward for a moment, found Bess and warned her quietly to tell the other women to be ready to take over if the men became too sick to go on. "But tell them calmly. We don't want to frighten the men." She lingered in the ward long enough to see the word spread among the women in a widening wave of paler faces and compressed lips; then she went back to the laboratory.

Another test. There was no sign of a micro-organism in anyone's blood, merely a growing horde of leucocytes and phagocytes, prowling as if mobilized to repel invasion.

Len Marlow was wheeled in unconscious, with Hal Barton's written comments and conclusions pinned to the blanket.

"I don't feel so well myself," the assistant complained. "The air feels thick. I can't breathe."

June saw that his lips were blue. "Oxygen short," she told Max.

"Low red corpuscle count," Max answered. "Look into a drop and see what's going on. Use mine; I feel the same way he does." She took two drops of Max's blood. The count was low, falling too fast.

Breathing is useless without the proper minimum of red corpuscles in the blood. People below that minimum die of asphyxiation although their lungs are full of pure air. The red corpuscle count was falling too fast. The time she and Max had to work in was too short.

"Pump some more CO_2 into the air system," Max said urgently over the phone. "Get some into the men's end of the ward."

She looked through the microscope at the live sample of blood. It was a dark clear field and bright moving things spun and swirled through it, but she could see nothing that did not belong there.

"Hal," Max called over the general speaker system, "cut the other treatments, check for accelerating anemia. Treat it like monoxide poisoning—CO_2 and oxygen."

She reached into a cupboard under the work table, located two cylinders of oxygen, cracked the valves and handed one to Max and one to the assistant. Some of the bluish tint left the assistant's face as he breathed and he went over to the patient with reawakened concern.

"Not breathing, Doc!"

Max was working at the desk, muttering equations of hemoglobin catalysis.

"Len's gone, Doc," the assistant said more loudly.

"Artificial respiration and get him into a regeneration tank," said June, not moving from the microscope. "Hurry! Hal will show you how. The oxidation and mechanical heart action in the tank will keep him going. Put anyone in a tank who seems to be dying. Get some women to help you. Give them Hal's instructions."

The tanks were ordinarily used to suspend animation in a nutrient bath during the regrowth of any diseased organ. It could preserve life in an almost totally destroyed body during the usual disintegration and regrowth treatments for cancer and old age, and it could encourage healing as destruction continued . . . but they could not prevent ultimate death as long as the disease was not conquered.

The drop of blood in June's microscope was a great dark field, and in the foreground, brought to gargantuan solidity by the stereo effect, drifted neat saucer shapes of red blood cells. They turned end for end, floating by the humped misty mass of a leucocyte which was crawling on the cover glass. There were not enough red corpuscles, and she felt that they grew fewer as she watched.

She fixed her eye on one, not blinking in fear that she would miss what might happen. It was a tidy red button, and it spun as it drifted, the current moving it aside in a curve as it passed by the leucocyte.

Then, abruptly, the cell vanished.

June stared numbly at the place where it had been.

Behind her, Max was calling over the speaker system again: "Dr. Stark speaking. Any technician who knows anything about the life tanks, start bringing more out of storage and set them up. Emergency."

"We may need forty-seven," June said quietly.

"We may need forty-seven," Max repeated to the ship in general. His voice did not falter. "Set them up along the corridor. Hook them in on extension lines."

His voice filtered back from the empty floors above in a series of dim echoes. What he had said meant that every man on board might be on the point of heart stoppage.

June looked blindly through the binocular microscope, trying to think. Out of the corner of her eyes she could see that Max was wavering and breathing more and more frequently of the pure, cold, burning oxygen of the cylinders. In the microscope she could see that there were fewer red cells left alive in the drop of his blood. The rate of fall was accelerating.

She didn't have to glance at Max to know how he would look—skin pale, black eyebrows and keen brown eyes slightly squinted in thought, a faint ironical grin twisting the bluing lips. Intelligent, thin, sensitive, his face was part of her mind. It was inconceivable that Max could die. He couldn't die. He couldn't leave her alone.

She forced her mind back to the problem. All the men of the *Explorer* were at the same point, wherever they were.

Moving to Max's desk, she spoke into the intercom system. "Bess, send a couple of women to look through the ship, room by room, with a stretcher. Make sure all the men are down here." She remembered Reno. "Sparks, heard anything from Reno? Is he back?"

Sparks replied weakly after a lag. "The last I heard from Reno was a call this morning. He was raving about mirrors, and Pat Mead's folks not being real people, just carbon copies, and claiming he was crazy; and I should send him the psychiatrist. I thought he was kidding. He didn't call back."

"Thanks, Sparks." Reno was lost.

Max dialed and spoke to the bridge over the phone. "Are you okay up there? Forget about engineering controls. Drop everything and head for the tanks while you can still walk."

June went back to the work table and whispered into her own phone. "Bess, send up a stretcher for Max. He looks pretty bad."

There had to be a solution. The life tanks could sustain life in a damaged body, encouraging it to regrow more rapidly, but they merely slowed death as long as the disease was not checked. The postponement could not last long, for destruction could go on steadily in the tanks until the nutritive solution would hold no life except the triumphant microscopic killers that caused melting sickness.

There were very few red blood corpuscles in the microscope field now, incredibly few. She tipped the microscope and they began to drift, spinning slowly. A lone corpuscle floated through the center. She watched it as the current swept it in an arc past the dim off-focus bulk of the leucocyte. There was a sweep of motion and it vanished.

For a moment it meant nothing to her; then she lifted her head from the microscope and looked around. Max sat at his desk, head in hand, his rumpled short black hair sticking out between his fingers at odd angles. A pencil and a pad scrawled with formulas lay on the desk before him. She could see his concentration in the rigid set of his shoulders. He was still thinking; he had not given up.

"Max, I just saw a leucocyte grab a red blood corpuscle. It was unbelievably fast."

"Leukemia," muttered Max without moving. "Galloping leukemia yet! That comes under the heading of cancer. Well, that's part of the answer. It might be all we need." He grinned feebly and reached for the speaker set. "Anybody still on his feet in there?" he muttered into it, and the question was amplified to a booming voice throughout the ship. "Hal, are you still going? Look, Hal, change all the dials, change the dials, set them to deep melt and regeneration. One week. This is like leukemia. Got it? This is like leukemia."

June rose. It was time for her to take over the job. She leaned across his desk and spoke into the speaker system. "Doctor Walton talking," she said. "This is to the women. Don't let any of the men work any more; they'll kill themselves. See that they all go into the tanks right away. Set the tank dials for deep regeneration. You can see how from the ones that are set."

Two exhausted and frightened women clattered in the doorway with a stretcher. Their hands were scratched and oily from helping to set up tanks.

"That order includes you," she told Max sternly and caught him as he swayed.

Max saw the stretcher bearers and struggled upright. "Ten more minutes," he said clearly. "Might think of an idea. Something not right in this setup. I have to figure how to prevent a relapse, how the thing started."

He knew more bacteriology than she did; she had to help him think. She motioned the bearers to wait, fixed a breathing mask for Max from a cylinder of CO_2 and the opened one of oxygen. Max went back to his desk.

She walked up and down, trying to think, remembering the hamsters. The melting sickness, it was called. Melting. She struggled with an impulse to open a tank which held one of the men. She wanted to look in, see if that would explain the name.

Melting Sickness. . . .

Footsteps came and Pat Mead stood uncertainly in the doorway. Tall, handsome, rugged, a pioneer. "Anything I can do?" he asked.

She barely looked at him. "You can stay out of our way. We're busy."

"I'd like to help," he said.

"Very funny." She was vicious, enjoying the whip of her words. "Every man is dying because you're a carrier, and you want to help."

*

He stood nervously clenching and unclenching his hands. "A guinea pig, maybe. I'm immune. All the Meads are."

"Go away." God, why couldn't she think? What makes a Mead immune?

"Aw, let 'im alone," Max muttered. "Pat hasn't done anything." He went waveringly to the microscope, took a tiny sliver from his finger, suspended it in a slide and slipped it under the lens with detached habitual dexterity. "Something funny going on," he said to June. "Symptoms don't feel right."

After a moment he straightened and motioned for her to look. "Leucocytes, phagocytes—" He was bewildered. "My own—"

She looked in, and then looked back at Pat in a growing wave of horror. "They're not your own, Max!" she whispered.

Max rested a hand on the table to brace himself, put his eye to the microscope, and looked again. June knew what he saw. Phagocytes, leucocytes, attacking and devouring his tissues in a growing incredible horde, multiplying insanely.

Not his phagocytes! Pat Mead's! The Meads' evolved cells had learned too much. They were contagious. And not Pat Mead's. . . . How much alike *were* the Meads? . . . Mead cells contagious from one to another, not a disease attacking or being fought, but acting as normal leucocytes in whatever body they were in! The leucocytes of tall, red-headed people, finding no strangeness in the bloodstream of any of the tall, red-headed people. No strangeness. . . . A totipotent leucocyte finding its way into cellular wombs.

The womblike life tanks. For the men of the *Explorer*, a week's cure with deep melting to de-differentiate the leucocytes and turn them back to normal tissue, then regrowth and reforming from the cells that were there. From the cells that *were* there. *From the cells that were there. . . .*

"Pat—"

"I know." Pat began to laugh, his face twisted with sudden understanding. "I understand. I get it. I'm a contagious personality. That's funny, isn't it?"

Max rose suddenly from the microscope and lurched toward him, fists clenched. Pat caught him as he fell, and the bewildered stretcher bearers carried him out to the tanks.

For a week June tended the tanks. The other women volunteered to help, but she refused. She said nothing, hoping her guess would not be true.

"Is everything all right?" Elsie asked her anxiously. "How is Len coming along?" Elsie looked haggard and worn, like all the women, from doing the work that the men had always done.

"He's fine," June said tonelessly, shutting tight the door of the tank room. "They're all fine."

"That's good," Elsie said, but she looked more frightened than before.

June firmly locked the tank room door and the girl went away.

The other women had been listening, and now they wandered back to their jobs, unsatisfied by June's answer, but not daring to ask for the actual truth. They were there whenever June went into the tank room, and they were still there—or relieved by others; June was not sure—when she came out. And always some one of them asked the unvarying question for all the others, and June gave the unvarying answer. But she kept the key. No woman but herself knew what was going on in the life tanks.

Then the day of completion came. June told no one of the hour. She went into the room as on the other days, locked the door behind her, and there was the nightmare again. This time it was reality and she wandered down a path between long rows of coffinlike tanks, calling, "Max! Max!" silently and looking into each one as it opened.

But each face she looked at was the same. Watching them dissolve and regrow in the nutrient solution, she had only been able to guess at the horror of what was happening. Now she knew.

They were all the same lean-boned, blond-skinned face, with a pin-feather growth of reddish down on cheeks and scalp. All horribly—and handsomely—the same.

A medical kit lay carelessly on the floor beside Max's tank. She stood near the bag. "Max," she said, and found her throat closing. The canned voice of the mechanical mocked her, speaking glibly about waking and sitting up. "I'm sorry, Max. . . ."

The tall man with rugged features and bright blue eyes sat up sleepily and lifted an eyebrow at her, and ran his hand over his red-fuzzed head in a gesture of bewilderment.

"What's the matter, June?" he asked drowsily.

She gripped his arm. "Max—"

He compared the relative size of his arm with her hand and said wonderingly, "You shrank."

"I know, Max. I know."

He turned his head and looked at his arms and legs, pale blond arms and legs with a down of red hair. He touched the thick left arm, squeezed a pinch of hard flesh. "It isn't mine," he said, surprised. "But I can feel it."

Watching his face was like watching a stranger mimicking and distorting Max's expressions. Max in fear. Max trying to understand what had happened to him, looking around at the other men sitting up in their tanks. Max feeling the terror that was in herself and all the men as they stared at themselves and their friends and saw what they had become.

"We're all Pat Mead," he said harshly. "All the Meads are Pat Mead. That's why he was surprised to see people who didn't look like himself."

"Yes, Max."

"Max," he repeated. "It's me, all right. The nervous system didn't change." His new blue eyes held hers. "My love didn't, either. Did yours? Did it, June?"

"No, Max." But she couldn't know yet. She had loved Max with the thin, ironic face, the rumpled black hair and the twisted smile that never really hid his quick sympathy. Now he was Pat Mead. Could he also be Max? "Of course I still love you, darling."

He grinned. It was still the wry smile of Max, though fitting strangely on the handsome new blond face. "Then it isn't so bad. It might even be pretty good. I envied him this big, muscular body. If Pat or any of these Meads so much as looks at you, I'm going to knock his block off. Understand?"

She laughed and couldn't stop. It wasn't that funny. But it was still Max, trying to be unafraid, drawing on humor. Maybe the rest of the men would also be their old selves, enough so the women would not feel that their men were strangers.

Behind her, male voices spoke characteristically. She did not have to turn to know which was which: "This is one way to keep a guy from stealing your girl," that was Len Marlow; "I've got to write down all my reactions," Hal Barton; "Now I can really work that hillside vein of metal," St. Clair. Then others complaining, swearing, laughing bitterly at the trick that had been played on them and their flirting, tempted women. She knew who they were. Their women would know them apart, too.

"We'll go outside," Max said. "You and I. Maybe the shock won't be so bad to the women after they see me." He paused. "You didn't tell them, did you?"

"I couldn't. I wasn't sure. I—was hoping I was wrong."

She opened the door and closed it quickly. There was a small crowd on the other side.

"Hello, Pat," Elsie said uncertainly, trying to look past them into the tank room before the door shut.

"I'm not Pat, I'm Max," said the tall man with the blue eyes and the fuzz-reddened skull. "Listen—"

"Good heavens, Pat, what happened to your hair?" Shelia asked.

"I'm Max," insisted the man with the handsome face and the sharp blue eyes. "Don't you get it? I'm Max Stark. The melting sickness is Mead cells. We caught them from Pat. They adapted us to Minos. They also changed us all into Pat Mead."

The women stared at him, at each other. They shook their heads.

"They don't understand," June said. "I couldn't have if I hadn't seen it happening, Max."

"It's Pat," said Shelia, dazedly stubborn. "He shaved off his hair. It's some kind of joke."

Max shook her shoulders, glaring down at her face. "I'm Max. Max Stark. They all look like me. Do you hear? It's funny, but it's not a joke. Laugh for us, for God's sake!"

"It's too much," said June. "They'll have to see."

She opened the door and let them in. They hurried past her to the tanks, looking at forty-six identical blond faces, beginning to call in frightened voices:

"Len!"

"Harry!"

"Lee, where are you, sweetheart—"

June shut the door on the voices that were growing hysterical, the women terrified and helpless, the men shouting to let the women know who they were.

"It isn't easy," said Max, looking down at his own thick muscles. "But you aren't changed and the other girls aren't. That helps."

Through the muffled noise and hysteria, a bell was ringing.

"It's the airlock," June said.

Peering in the viewplate were nine Meads from Alexandria. To all appearances, eight of them were Pat Mead at various ages, from fifteen to fifty, and the other was a handsome, leggy, red-headed girl who could have been his sister.

Regretfully, they explained through the voice tube that they had walked over from Alexandria to bring news that the plane pilot had contracted melting sickness there and had died.

They wanted to come in.

June and Max told them to wait and returned to the tank room. The men were enjoying their new height and strength, and the women were bewilderedly learning that they could tell one Pat Mead from another, by voice, by gesture of face or hand. The panic was gone. In its place was a dull acceptance of the fantastic situation.

Max called for attention. "There are nine Meads outside who want to come in. They have different names, but they're all Pat Mead."

They frowned or looked blank, and George Barton asked, "Why didn't you let them in? I don't see any problem."

"One of them," said Max soberly, "is a girl. *Patricia* Mead. The girl wants to come in."

There was a long silence while the implication settled to the fear center of the women's minds. Shelia the beautiful felt it first. She cried, "No! Please don't let her in!" There was real fright in her tone and the women caught it quickly.

Elsie clung to Len, begging, "You don't want me to change, do you, Len? You like me the way I am! Tell me you do!"

The other girls backed away. It was illogical, but it was human. June felt terror rising in herself. She held up her hand for quiet, and presented the necessity to the group.

"Only half of us can leave Minos," she said. "The men cannot eat ship food; they've been conditioned to this planet. We women can go, but we would have to go without our men. We can't go outside without contagion, and we can't spend the rest of our lives in quarantine inside the ship. George Barton is right—there is no problem."

"But we'd be changed!" Shelia shrilled. "I don't want to become a Mead! I don't want to be somebody else!"

She ran to the inner wall of the corridor. There was a brief hesitation, and then, one by one, the women fled to that side, until there were only Bess, June and four others left.

"See!" cried Shelia. "A vote! We can't let the girl in!"

No one spoke. To change, to be someone else—the idea was strange and horrifying. The men stood uneasily glancing at each other, as if looking into mirrors, and against the wall of the corridor the women watched in fear and huddled together, staring at the men. One man in forty-seven poses. One of them made a beseeching move toward Elsie and she shrank away.

"No, Len! I won't let you change me!"

Max stirred restlessly, the ironic smile that made his new face his own unconsciously twisting into a grimace of pity. "We men can't leave, and you women can't stay," he said bluntly. "Why not let Patricia Mead in. Get it over with!"

June took a small mirror from her belt pouch and studied her own face, aware of Max talking forcefully, the men standing silent, the women pleading. Her face . . . her own face with its dark blue eyes, small nose, long mobile lips . . . the mind and the body are inseparable; the shape of a face is part of the mind. She put the mirror back.

"I'd kill myself!" Shelia was sobbing. "I'd rather die!"

"You won't die," Max was saying. "Can't you see there's only one solution—"

They were looking at Max. June stepped silently out of the tank room, and then turned and went to the airlock. She opened the valves that would let in Pat Mead's sister.

1950

MARGARET ST. CLAIR

The Inhabited Men

NORTON was the only one of the three on the *Ara* who was superstitious, and even he didn't attempt serious argument against landing on the planetoid. Making repairs on the *Ara* was absolutely necessary; the repairs couldn't be made in space; and he couldn't even remember who had told him that the planetoid was unlucky. So they landed.

The repairs went briskly. The crew worked for eighteen hours out of the day, and ate on the job. Inside of a week the *Ara* was lifting her tired old shoulders up from the surface of the planetoid. She got to a frequented portion of the spaceways before she broke down completely. It was as much as her crew had dared hope for. They were picked up by a passing freighter which claimed the *Ara* as salvage, and six months later they were landed, gaunt and angry and soiled, at Port Pendraith. None of the three, Evans or Norton or Miller, was ever to realize that on the planetoid he had been colonized.

In Pendraith, they discussed their situation. They wanted to stay together, if it was possible. They tried to lease another ship, and couldn't raise the deposit money. They asked acquaintances and friends for grubstakes, and were rejected. Finally they saw that if they weren't to starve in Pendraith, they'd have to separate. And from then on different things happened to them. But they ended up exactly the same.

Norton was the superstitious one. He was short, dark, thickset, and inclined to be irascible. He shipped out of Pendraith on a freighter which was almost as foul and ill-found as the one which had landed him there in the first place. On the ship he was assigned to the steward's department, as waiter and galley boy.

The cook, Gongo, was a native of Pendraith. He had been kicked about, with various degrees of brutality, ever since his fifth birthday, and by now he could fawn or cringe or snarl with equal facility. In his way, he was a religious man.

Gongo and Norton bunked together in a room so small that if one of them stood up in it, the other had to stretch out full length in his berth. The one desirable thing in the room was the airduct which, instead of being in the ceiling as was customary, had been located in the wall just over the upper berth. Fresh air can be a considerable luxury. Gongo slept in the upper berth.

On the second day out from Pendraith, Norton took Gongo's things out of the upper berth and put his own in. Naturally, he moved the bedding at the same time. Under Gongo's pillow he found a small cloth bag.

He opened it. It held a vaguely man-shaped piece of hard root, a wad of lint mixed with hair, and some crystals of what looked like rock salt.

Norton held the bag by the strings, thinking. A less superstitious man would have laughed and put the bag back under the pillow of Gongo's new bunk. But Norton was a little afraid of the thing. After a minute he took it out in the corridor and threw it in the reducer. It flared up briefly and then went to join the freighter's auxiliary fuel supply.

Gongo discovered the change of bunks that night. He was not much surprised. He had been rather expecting it, since Norton was bigger and heavier than he. But when he felt under the pillow of his new bunk and couldn't find his bag, he turned quite white. He said, "What did you do with my bag?"

"Threw it out, sticky." The last word was a nickname much resented by the natives of Pendraith. Norton was lying in the upper bunk. His hand was resting on the blaster he wasn't supposed to have, and did have. "Want to make something out of it?"

There was a silence. Then Gongo said, "I guess not."

In the third week, when the two men were in the galley, Gongo said, "What's the matter, you don't eat? You think I poison the food?" There was hopeful malice in his voice.

"Naw," Norton replied judicially, "you wouldn't have the nerve." He spat into the sink. "Your chow's not so hot, that's all. It don't appeal to my appetite."

That night Norton talked in his sleep. The voice was thin and small, to come from his chunky body. Gongo would not have heard it at all if he had not been lying awake thinking of his lost god.

After a second he slipped out of his bunk and stood with his head leaned toward Norton in the dark. "Thya," came a thread, a wisp of sound, "do you hear me?"

"Why not?"

"And I."

"And I."

"Isn't it wonderful," came the first filament, "to live, be free, grow, expand?"

"I warn you—Thya, Pohm, Rya, all the rest—you grow too far. It is dangerous. You grow too far." The wisp of sound managed to be harsh.

"How can we help it? It is difficult to refuse to grow."

"You must try. No excuses. It must be done."

The half-dozen filaments of sound swelled into a tiny clamor in the dark. Gongo sucked in his breath. He was thinking of folk-lore. He found the switch and turned on the light.

Norton sat up in his bunk, instantly angry. "What the hell do you think you're doing?"

"You were talking in your sleep."

"Oh," Norton yawned and rubbed his hand over his face. "Did I say anything?" he asked.

"You . . . were talking about growing. There were more voices than one in your throat."

"Yeah? You must of imagined it. Stow it, sticky, and turn out the light. I got to have my sleep."

He rolled over as Gongo obeyed. Gongo sat down on the edge of his berth. He was badly frightened.

He sat there in the dark, thinking about what had happened to his divinity and the various disguises the devil can assume, until Norton's breathing grew regular. When he was sure that Norton was asleep again, he got one of his kitchen knives out from under his mattress. He opened Norton with it from pubic bone to diaphragm. It was a mistake for Norton to have gone back to sleep.

Evans was the second of the crew of the *Ara*. He was a big, slow-moving man, with a friendly smile and a mind which also moved rather slowly. Since he spoke politely and was presentable, he got a berth on a luxury liner as a steward.

The name of the liner was the *Bootic*. It was a new ship, equipped with the latest devices, and it carried four stewardesses to cater to the needs of women passengers. Since Evans was friendly, obliging, and not offensively on the make, he soon got to be a favorite with the stewardesses.

One of them, a small, dark girl named Helen Dawes, he more than liked. She teased him a good deal, since he was easy to tease, but he thought she liked him too. He began to wonder what the attitude of the *Bootic*'s owners would be toward letting a married couple work out on the same ship, and how much the down payment on a semi-house in Port Pendraith would be.

The fuel tanks of the *Bootic* exploded when the ship was entering the asteroid belt. For a moment there was a flare almost as bright as a nova, and then the safety devices went to work. The result was that though everybody aft of partition number one was killed almost instantly, those forward of it had about two minutes to don suits and get out through the emergency hatch.

Evans and Helen and a middle-aged woman named Edna Kinch were on the right side. The emergency hatch, though it was red-hot, worked. When the three of them were about half a kilo away they turned and saw the *Bootic*, with the curious transparent look burning objects have, eaten with fire from stem to stern. Then they jetted their way to the nearest asteroid and sat down to wait.

For the first hour or so they talked about rescue. The *Bootic*, after all, had been in a main-travelled spaceway. Though the explosion had given her no time to send out an S.O.S., the force of the explosion—(What had caused it? Evans said he thought some tiny irregularity must have developed in the lining of the fuel tanks since they had had their last microscopic inspection. The Board of Inquiry, months later, was to echo his opinion.)—the force of the explosion would certainly have registered on the instrument panel of any ship in the vicinity.

That meant that ships would soon be jetting up to look for survivors. And, though the asteroid the three had landed on was only about a third of a kilo through, and their suit radios couldn't project a signal for more than a kilo and a half, it was reasonable to assume they'd be found. Oh, yes. But as time passed and the three began to realize the odds against them, they fell silent.

They had oxygen for about twelve hours. The joker in their theories about rescue, of course, was that ships in space are usually separated by the kind of distance known as astronomical. It was almost impossible that any ship had been near enough to the *Bootic* to have the explosion register. When the time came at which the *Bootic* ought to have reached another signal point in her course, and no signal was sent, she would be missed. A search ship would be sent out then, no doubt about it. But that would take almost six days. The survivors had oxygen for twelve hours.

Edna Kinch had hurt her leg rather badly getting through the escape hatch. There were analgesics in her suit, and she took doses of them, but even when she was nearly unconscious she kept moaning. Since the other two couldn't help her, they walked—floated, rather—a little away from her and sat down. They looked out at the stars.

The constellations were not much changed from their familiar shapes on earth. The swan was overhead, eternally flying between Altair and Vega, and Antares burned redly in the forepart of the scorpion. If Evans and his girl wanted to see Achenar, all they had to do was to walk around the asteroid.

Helen said. "Vega's a beautiful star. . . . I can't realize that we're going to die."

Evans wanted to kiss her so much that he felt like crying. He didn't dare open his helmet, of course. He put his arm around her, and they sat with their gloved fingers interlaced. He told her how he felt about her, and about the semi-house in Port Pendraith.

She said, "One of those semi-houses with the round living room. Yes. I wish I could kiss you, Bill. . . . I wish. . . ."

He said, "I'm going to give you my oxygen tank."

She cried out at that. "You can't be so cruel! No, please, no. I love you, Bill. Are you going to make me watch you die?"

So he gave up that idea. He put his arm around her again and they sat there, talking from time to time, and seeing the gauges on their oxy-tanks move from three-quarters to half to one quarter and on down. When the needles pointed to one eighth, Helen said, "We've got analgesics, Bill. Let's take them. That way, we won't ever know."

He nodded. Together, smiling at each other in the starlight, they sipped at their stirrup cups. The stars seemed to swell and billow, and then a fog fell over them. It got dark.

Evans roused at last. He was confused, and then surprised, and then he looked around for Helen. Had there been a miracle?

She had fallen over on her side. Her face was dark and congested, and when he saw her he was glad he hadn't let himself hope. He went back to Edna Kinch, and found that she was dead too. Both Helen's tank and hers were quite empty. So was his. But he was still alive.

Evans couldn't understand it. He thought for a while, and then he took off his helmet. No rush of air left his suit; it was empty. He wasn't breathing. But he was still alive.

He sat there for about half an hour, between the bodies of the two women, trying to understand it. He couldn't make any sense out of it. Finally he unhooked his blaster from its holster. The gauge read full charge. So he blew his head off.

Miller had the hardest time of the three getting a job. He hung around employment agencies until the clerks frowned when they saw his lean, angry face coming in the door. He borrowed money from acquaintances as long as they would loan him any, and then he tried panhandling. He grew desperate. He didn't take to drinking—that was not one of his vices—but if he had not pawned his blaster early in his difficulties, he would certainly have tried a stick-up job with it. He had almost reached the point of no return which separates the merely unemployed from the unemployable, when Quilk, the proprietor of the *Royal Glory*, hired him.

The *Royal Glory* was a "louse house," a fifth-rate stereo theatre which specialized in pornographic tactifilms and historical epics slanted to appeal to Pendraithian patriotism. Whether the undernourished derelicts who composed the *Royal Glory*'s audiences were capable of responding to either of these classes of stimuli is doubtful, but Quilk took his programs seriously. He thought of himself as a patron of the arts, and he wanted to attract "A better class of personages" than the *Royal Glory* had been getting. He laid down, as a house rule, that nobody was to sit through the same program more than three times. And he hired Miller, as ticket-taker and bouncer, to enforce this.

Miller did not dislike his new work. His air of repressed anger made him an efficient bouncer, and he was amused by Quilk. As he grew more familiar with the *Royal Glory*'s routine, he had leisure moments, and he took to spending these in a tiny paved court at the back of the theatre where Quilk also took the air.

Quilk was a health faddist. He would sit on a bench in the patch of sunlight in the little court, sipping a health drink or occasionally getting up to take an exercise, and discourse to Miller about the benefits of the latest health diet he was following. He tried a new one every week or so. Miller, sprawled on the pavement, would listen in indolent, half-scornful amusement, as pleased with the sunlight as a vegetable.

Time passed. Miller though Quilk was paying him poorly, was saving money. Quilk let him sleep in the ticket office—he took the box-office receipts home with him at night, of course—and Miller's expenditure for food was almost nothing. It was not that he was starving himself—in fact, he was gaining weight. But food did not much interest him. He began to think dreamily of buying a new spaceman's outfit and going back to the employment agencies. Presentable and prosperous-looking, he was sure he could ship out into space again. Then the green plague broke out in Port Pendraith.

Quilk was terrified. He talked of closing up the *Royal Glory*, and for a day Miller's future hung in the balance. Then the two strongest traits in Quilk's personality reasserted themselves.

"The show must go on," he said solemnly to his employee. "In a time of crisis such as this, personages have a particular need for the solace of art. The show must go on! Don't you agree, Miller?"

"Sure," Miller answered. Quilk, as always, amused him. He was trying to smile.

"And besides, I am in no danger," Quilk continued, a little hastily. "Personally, I mean. It is not as if I were an ignorant, undernourished Pendraithian, with no awareness of the basic laws of health. With my new diet. . . . Yes, the show must go on!"

"You bet!" Miller agreed. This time, he did smile. Quilk looked at him a little suspiciously.

"Of course, we will take elementary prophylactic measures. You can wear my blaster. When you take the tickets, Miller, I want you to look in their mouths."

"H'um?" Miller said.

"Yes, in their mouths. It is well known that the first signs of the plague appear there. If there are spots, they are not to enter. Perhaps in their ears also. I have heard that sometimes it appears in the ears."

Quilk was shivering. Miller, though he never could take him seriously, was sorry for him. "O.K. I'll look in their mouths and ears."

Miller made his inspections conscientiously. He turned away two or three of the infected daily. He was not at all afraid of the plague himself, though terrestrials did contract it, for he had never felt more fit in his life.

Surprisingly, business at the *Royal Glory* was good. Perhaps Quilk had been right, and personages at a time of crisis did need the solace of art. Quilk, counting his receipts at night and shivering, could congratulate himself.

The port health authorities, meantime, were not idle. Disease is no respecter of status. What begins in the slums of a city may end by menacing government hill. They laid down a *cordon sanitaire* around the infected areas. For a while, as the plague grew more severe, the cordon tightened. Then it began to relax. In the fourth week the city was officially declared free of plague.

"We came through that rather nicely, I think," Quilk said. It was after theatre hours, and he was putting the night's take in a metal mesh satchel. "Tomorrow I will get out some new posters—'The only Vid House that stayed open all during the plague! The *Royal Glory* is first, as always—first in service, first in programs, first in artistic pleasure for you!'" He nodded. He picked up his blaster from the desk and strapped it around his waist.

"Sounds good," Miller said, in lazy agreement. He yawned and stretched. The light fell full in his open mouth.

Quilk looked at him. His jaw dropped. Miller saw, without understanding it, that he had turned pale. Quilk said, in a wobbling voice, "It isn't possible. They said there were no new cases." He began to back away, one hand on his blaster, the other on the metal valise.

"What are you talking about?" Miller asked irritably.

"Your throat. There are plague spots, the green plague spots, in your throat."

"No, there aren't. You're crazy. I'm not sick."

"I saw the spots myself," Quilk answered. He was trembling all over. "Keep away from me. After all my precautions! Get out!"

Miller couldn't understand the situation. After a minute he asked, "You mean I'm fired?"

"If you like. Anything. Only get out."

"You owe me four days' wages."

"Take it, then." Quilk opened the valise, took out a handful of coins, and threw it at him. "Get out."

Miller turned an angry red. "Don't talk to me like that, sticky. What in hell is the matter with you?" He advanced a step.

Quilk drew the blaster. "Don't come near me! I'm warning you!"

"I tell you, I haven't got the plague," Miller answered. He was trying to be reasonable. "You're too excitable." Once more Quilk saw the plague spots in his throat.

"Stay away! Stay away!" The blaster described a wobbling circle in Quilk's hand.

Miller bit his lip. Even at this moment the contemptuous amusement Quilk inspired in him kept him from taking the Pendraithian seriously. He picked up the coins from the floor and counted them. "You're a day and a half short, sticky," he said, looking at Quilk. "Pay me." He walked toward him, holding out his hand.

"No! Don't! I—" Quilk shuddered. He couldn't get any farther away from Miller because he was already against the wall of the box-office. He moaned. Then he closed his eyes and fired.

It was all a mistake, of course. Miller never did have the plague. But he was just as dead, after Quilk blasted him, as if he had.

The organisms that had colonized the crew of the *Ara* died with them, naturally. They were able to survive for considerably longer than the men, but the knife wound and the blaster charges disrupted their nicely balanced economy beyond repair.

What they had done, as they grew on the men's mucous membranes and in their body cavities, was to convert Norton and Evans and Miller into Wardian cases, terrariums—units in which chlorophyll and radiant energy (it did not have to be sunlight) cooperated to turn the carbon dioxide of katabolism into oxygen, complex starches, and growth. After the economy was well established, its hosts, had they known it, were potentially immortal. They could have gone for years without needing to eat or breathe. But the plants in a Wardian case die when the case is broken. And the tenants of Norton and Evans and Miller, for all their complex mental organization, were basically plants.

They were not in the least resigned to dying, however. For hours they fought against it, screaming to each other, imploring, cursing, praying not to die. In the end, Evans and Miller and Norton had this in common, that each of them kept on talking for a long time after he was dead.

1951

ZENNA HENDERSON

Ararat

WE'VE had trouble with teachers in Cougar Canyon. It's just an Accommodation school anyway, isolated and so unhandy to anything. There's really nothing to hold a teacher. But the way The People bring forth their young, in quantities and with regularity, even our small Group can usually muster the nine necessary for the County School Superintendent to arrange for the schooling for the year.

Of course I'm past school age, Canyon school age, and have been for years, but if the tally came up one short in the Fall, I'd go back for a post-graduate course again. But now I'm working on a college level because Father finished me off for my high school diploma two summers ago. He's promised me that if I do well this year I'll get to go Outside next year and get my training and degree so I can be the teacher and we won't have to go Outside for one any more. Most of the kids would just as soon skip school as not, but the Old Ones don't hold with ignorance and the Old Ones have the last say around here.

Father is the head of the school board. That's how I get in on lots of school things the other kids don't. This summer when he wrote to the County Seat that we'd have more than our nine again this fall and would they find a teacher for us, he got back a letter saying they had exhausted their supply of teachers who hadn't heard of Cougar Canyon and we'd have to dig up our own teacher this year. That "dig up" sounded like a dirty crack to me since we have the graves of four past teachers in the far corner of our cemetery. They sent us such old teachers, the homeless, the tottering, who were trying to piece out the end of their lives with a year here and a year there in jobs no one else wanted because there's no adequate pension system in the state and most teachers seem to die in harness. And their oldness and their tottering were not sufficient in the Canyon where there are apt to be shocks for Outsiders—unintentional as most of them are.

We haven't done so badly the last few years, though. The Old Ones say we're getting adjusted—though some of the non-conformists say that The Crossing thinned our blood. It might be either or both or the teachers are just getting tougher. The last two managed to last until just before the year ended. Father took them in as far as Kerry Canyon and ambulances took them on in. But they were all right after a while in the sanatorium and they're doing okay now. Before them, though, we usually had four teachers a year.

Anyway, Father wrote to a Teachers Agency on the coast and after several letters each way, he finally found a teacher.

He told us about it at the supper table.

"She's rather young," he said, reaching for a toothpick and tipping his chair back on its hind legs.

Mother gave Jethro another helping of pie and picked up her own fork again. "Youth is no crime," she said, "and it'll be a pleasant change for the children."

"Yes, though it seems a shame." Father prodded at a back tooth and Mother frowned at him. I wasn't sure if it was for picking his teeth or for what he said. I knew he meant it seemed a shame to get a place like Cougar Canyon so early in a career. It isn't that we're mean or cruel, you understand. It's only that they're Outsiders and we sometimes forget—especially the kids.

"She doesn't *have* to come," said Mother. "She could say no."

"Well, now—" Father tipped his chair forward. "Jethro, no more pie. You go on out and help 'Kiah bring in the wood. Karen, you and Lizbeth get started on the dishes. Hop to it, kids."

And we hopped, too. Kids do to fathers in the Canyon, though I understand they don't always Outside. It annoyed me because I knew Father wanted us out of the way so he could talk adult talk to Mother, so I told Lizbeth I'd clear the table and then worked as slowly as I could, and as quietly, listening hard.

"She couldn't get any other job," said Father. "The agency told me they had placed her twice in the last two years and she didn't finish the year either place."

"Well," said Mother, pinching in her mouth and frowning. "If she's that bad, why on earth did you hire her for the Canyon?"

"We have a choice?" laughed Father. Then he sobered. "No, it wasn't for incompetency. She was a good teacher. The way she tells it, they just fired her out of a clear sky. She asked for recommendations and one place wrote, 'Miss Carmody is a very competent teacher but we dare not recommend her for a teaching position.'"

"'Dare not'?" asked Mother.

"'Dare not,'" said Father. "The Agency assured me that they had investigated thoroughly and couldn't find any valid reasons for the dismissals, but she can't seem to find another job anywhere on the coast. She wrote me that she wanted to try another state."

"Do you suppose she's disfigured or deformed?" suggested Mother.

"Not from the neck up!" laughed Father. He took an envelope from his pocket. "Here's her application picture."

By this time I'd got the table cleared and I leaned over Father's shoulder.

"Gee!" I said. Father looked back at me, raising one eyebrow. I knew then that he had known all along that I was listening.

I flushed but stood my ground, knowing I was being granted admission to adult affairs, if only by the back door.

The girl in the picture was lovely. She couldn't have been many years older than I and she was twice as pretty. She had short dark hair curled all over her head and apparently that poreless creamy skin that seems to have an inner light of itself. She had a tentative look about her as though her dark eyebrows were horizontal question marks. There was a droop to the corners of her mouth—not much, just enough to make you wonder why . . . and want to comfort her.

"She'll stir the Canyon for sure," said Father.

"I don't know," Mother frowned thoughtfully. "What will the Old Ones say to a marriageable Outsider in the Canyon?"

"Adonday Veeah!" muttered Father. "That never occurred to me. None of our other teachers were ever of an age to worry about."

"What *would* happen?" I asked. "I mean if one of The Group married an Outsider?"

"Impossible," said Father, so like the Old Ones that I could see why his name was approved in Meeting last Spring.

"Why, there's even our Jemmy," worried Mother. "Already he's saying he'll have to start trying to find another Group. None of the girls here please him. Supposing this Outsider—how old is she?"

Father unfolded the application. "Twenty-three," he said, "Just three years out of college."

"Jemmy's twenty-four," said Mother, pinching her mouth together. "Father, I'm afraid you'll have to cancel the contract. If anything happened— Well, you waited over-long to become an Old One to my way of thinking and it'd be a shame to have something go wrong your first year."

"I can't cancel the contract. She's on her way here. School starts next Monday." Father ruffled his hair forward as he does when he's disturbed. "We're probably making a something of a nothing," he said hopefully.

"Well I only hope we don't have any trouble with this Outsider."

"Or she with us," grinned Father. "Where are my cigarettes?"

"On the book case," said Mother, getting up and folding the table cloth together to hold the crumbs.

Father snapped his fingers and the cigarettes drifted in from the front room.

Mother went on out to the kitchen. The table cloth shook itself over the waste basket and then followed her.

Father drove to Kerry Canyon Sunday night to pick up our new teacher. She was supposed to have arrived Saturday afternoon, but she didn't make bus connections at the County Seat. The road ends at Kerry Canyon. I mean for Outsiders. There's not much of the look of a well-traveled road very far out our way from Kerry Canyon, which is just as well. Tourists leave us alone. Of course *we* don't have much trouble getting our cars to and fro but that's why everything dead-ends at Kerry Canyon and we have to do all our own fetching and carrying—I mean the road being in the condition it is.

All the kids at our house wanted to stay up to see the new teacher, so Mother let them; but by 7:30 the youngest ones began to drop off and by 9 there was only Jethro and 'Kiah, Lizbeth and Jemmy and me. Father should have been home long before and Mother was restless and uneasy. I knew if he didn't arrive soon, she would head for her room and the cedar box under the bed. But at 9:15 we heard the car coughing and sneezing up the draw. Mother's wide relieved smile was reflected on all our faces.

"Of course!" she cried. "I forgot. He has an Outsider in the car. He had to use the *road* and it's terrible across Jackass Flat."

I felt Miss Carmody before she came in the door. I was tingling all over from anticipation already, but all at once I felt her, so plainly that I knew with a feeling of fear and pride that I was of my Grandmother, that soon I would be bearing the burden and blessing of her Gift: the Gift that develops into free access to any mind—one of The People or Outsider—willing or not. And besides the access, the ability to counsel and help, to straighten tangled minds and snarled emotions.

And then Miss Carmody stood in the doorway, blinking a little against the light, muffled to the chin against the brisk fall air. A bright scarf hid her hair but her skin *was* that luminous matte-cream it had looked. She was smiling a little, but scared, too. I shut my eyes and . . . I went in—just like that. It was the first time I had ever sorted anybody. She was all fluttery with tiredness and strangeness and there was a question deep inside her that had the wornness of repetition, but I couldn't catch what it was. And under the uncertainty there was a sweetness and dearness and such a bewildered sorrow that I felt my eyes dampen. Then I looked at her again (sorting takes such a little time) as Father introduced her. I heard a gasp beside me and suddenly I went into Jemmy's mind with a stunning rush.

Jemmy and I have been close all our lives and we don't always need words to talk with one another, but this was the first time I had ever gone in like this and I knew he didn't know what had happened. I felt embarrassed and ashamed to know his emotion so starkly. I closed him out as quickly as possible, but not before I knew that now Jemmy would never hunt for another Group; Old Ones or no Old Ones, he had found his love.

All this took less time than it takes to say "How do you do?" and shake hands. Mother descended with cries and drew Miss Carmody and Father out to the kitchen for coffee and Jemmy swatted Jethro and made him carry the luggage instead of snapping it to Miss Carmody's room. After all, we didn't want to lose our teacher before she even saw the school house.

I waited until everyone was bedded down. Miss Carmody in her cold, cold bed, the rest of us of course with our sheets set for warmth—how I pity Outsiders! Then I went to Mother.

She met me in the dark hall and we clung together as she comforted me.

"Oh Mother," I whispered. "I sorted Miss Carmody tonight. I'm afraid."

Mother held me tight again. "I wondered," she said. "It's a great responsibility. You have to be so wise and clear-thinking. Your Grandmother carried the Gift with graciousness and honor. You are of her. You can do it."

"But Mother! To be an Old One!"

Mother laughed. "You have years of training ahead of you before you'll be an Old One. Counselor to the soul is a weighty job."

"Do I have to tell?" I pleaded. "I don't want anyone to know yet. I don't want to be set apart."

"I'll tell the Oldest," she said. "No one else need know." She hugged me again and I went back, comforted, to bed.

I lay in the darkness and let my mind clear, not even knowing how I knew how to. Like the gentle reachings of quiet fingers I felt the family about me. I felt warm and comfortable as though I were cupped in the hollow palm of a loving hand. Some day I would belong to The Group as I now belonged to the family. Belong to others? With an odd feeling of panic, I shut the family out. I wanted to be alone—to belong just to me and no one else. I didn't *want* the Gift.

I slept after a while.

Miss Carmody left for the school house an hour before we did. She wanted to get things started a little before school time, her late arrival making it kind of rough on her. 'Kiah, Jethro, Lizbeth and I walked down the lane to the Armisters' to pick up their three kids. The sky was so blue you could taste it, a winey, fallish taste of harvest fields and falling leaves. We were all feeling full of bubbly enthusiasm for the beginning of school. We were light-hearted and light-footed, too, as we kicked along through the cottonwood leaves paving the lane with gold. In fact Jethro felt too light-footed and the third time I hauled him down and made him walk on the ground, I cuffed him good. He was still sniffling when we got to Armisters'.

"She's pretty!" called Lizbeth before the kids got out to the gate, all agog and eager for news of the new teacher.

"She's young," added 'Kiah, elbowing himself ahead of Lizbeth.

"She's littler'n me," sniffed Jethro and we all laughed because he's five-six already even if he isn't twelve yet.

Debra and Rachel Armister linked arms with Lizbeth and scuffled down the lane, heads together, absorbing the details of teacher's hair, dress, nail polish, luggage and night clothes, though goodness knows how Lizbeth knew anything about that.

Jethro and 'Kiah annexed Jeddy and they climbed up on the rail fence that parallels the lane and walked the top rail. Jethro took a tentative step or two above the rail, caught my eye and stepped back in a hurry. He knows as well as any child in the Canyon that a kid his age has no business lifting along a public road.

We detoured at the Mesa Road to pick up the Kroginold boys. More than once Father has sighed over the Kroginolds.

You see, when The Crossing was made, The People got separated in that last wild moment when air was screaming past and the heat was building up so alarmingly. The members of our Group left their ship just seconds before it crashed so devastatingly into the box canyon behind Old Baldy and literally splashed and drove itself into the canyon walls, starting a fire that stripped the hills bare for miles. After The People gathered themselves together from the Life Slips and founded Cougar Canyon, they found that the alloy the ship was made of was a metal much wanted here. Our Group has lived on mining the box canyon ever since, though there's something complicated about marketing the stuff. It has to be shipped out of the country and shipped in again because everyone knows that it doesn't occur in this region.

Anyway, our Group at Cougar Canyon is probably the largest of The People, but we are reasonably sure that at least one Group and maybe two survived along with us. Grandmother in her time sensed two Groups but could never locate them exactly and, since our object is to go unnoticed in this new life, no real effort has ever been made to find them. Father can remember just a little of The Crossing, but some of the Old Ones are blind and crippled from the heat and the terrible effort they put forth to save the others from burning up like falling stars.

But getting back, Father often said that of all The People who could have made up our Group, we had to get the Kroginolds. They're rebels and were even before The Crossing. It's their kids that have been so rough on our teachers. The rest of us usually behave fairly decently and remember that we have to be careful around Outsiders.

Derek and Jake Kroginold were wrestling in a pile of leaves by the front gate when we got there. They didn't even hear us coming, so I leaned over and whacked the nearest rear-end and they turned in a flurry of leaves and grinned up at me for all the world like pictures of Pan in the mythology book at home.

"What kinda old bat we got this time?" asked Derek as he scrabbled in the leaves for his lunch box.

"She's not an old bat," I retorted, madder than need be because Derek annoys me so. "She's young and beautiful."

"Yeah, I'll bet!" Jake emptied the leaves from his cap onto the trio of squealing girls.

"She is so!" retorted 'Kiah. "The nicest teacher we ever had."

"She won't teach me nothing!" yelled Derek, lifting to the top of the cottonwood tree at the turn-off.

"Well, if she won't, I will," I muttered and, reaching for a handful of sun, I platted the twishers so quickly that Derek fell like a rock. He yelled like a catamount, thinking he'd get killed for sure, but I stopped him about a foot from the ground and then let go. Well, the stopping and the thump to the ground pretty well jarred the wind out of him, but he yelled:

"I'll tell the Old Ones! You ain't supposed to platt twishers—!"

"Tell the Old Ones," I snapped, kicking on down the leafy road. "I'll be there and tell them why. And then, old smarty pants, what will be your excuse for lifting?"

And then I was ashamed. I was showing off as bad as a Kroginold—but they make me so mad!

Our last stop before school was at the Clarinades'. My heart always squeezed when I thought of the Clarinade twins. They just started school this year—two years behind the average Canyon kid. Mrs. Kroginold used to say that the two of them, Susie and Jerry, divided one brain between them before they were born. That's unkind and untrue—thoroughly a Kroginold remark—but it is true that by Canyon standards the twins were retarded. They lacked so many of the attributes of The People. Father said it might be a delayed effect of The Crossing that they would grow out of, or it might be advance notice of what our children will be like here—what is ahead for The People. It makes me shiver, wondering.

Susie and Jerry were waiting, clinging to one another's hand as they always were. They were shy and withdrawn, but both were radiant because of starting school. Jerry, who did almost all the talking for the two of them, answered our greetings with a shy "Hello."

Then Susie surprised us all by exclaiming, "We're going to school!"

"Isn't it wonderful?" I replied, gathering her cold little hand into mine. "And you're going to have the prettiest teacher we ever had."

But Susie had retired into blushing confusion and didn't say another word all the way to school.

I was worried about Jake and Derek. They were walking apart from us, whispering, looking over at us and laughing. They were cooking up some kind of mischief for Miss Carmody. And more than anything I wanted her to stay. I found right then that there *would* be years ahead of me before I became an Old One. I tried to go in to Derek and Jake to find out what was cooking, but try as I might I couldn't get past the sibilance of their snickers and the hard, flat brightness of their eyes.

We were turning off the road into the school yard when Jemmy, who should have been up at the mine long since, suddenly stepped out of the bushes in front of us, his hands behind him. He glared at Jake and Derek and then at the rest of the children.

"You kids mind your manners when you get to school," he snapped, scowling. "And you Kroginolds—just try anything funny and I'll lift you to Old Baldy and platt the twishers on you. This is one teacher we're going to keep."

Susie and Jerry clung together in speechless terror. The Kroginolds turned red and pushed out belligerent jaws. The rest of us just stared at a Jemmy who never raised his voice and never pushed his weight around.

"I mean it, Jake and Derek. You try getting out of line and the Old Ones will find a few answers they've been looking for—especially about the belfry in Kerry Canyon."

The Kroginolds exchanged looks of dismay and the girls sucked in breaths of astonishment. One of the most rigorously enforced rules of The Group concerns showing off outside the community. If Derek and Jake *had* been involved in ringing that bell all night last Fourth of July . . . well!

"Now you kids, scoot!" Jemmy jerked his head toward the school house and the terrified twins scudded down the leaf-strewn path like a pair of bright leaves themselves, followed by the rest of the children with the Kroginolds looking sullenly back over their shoulders and muttering.

Jemmy ducked his head and scowled. "It's time they got civilized anyway. There's no sense to our losing teachers all the time."

"No," I said noncommittally.

"There's no point in scaring her to death." Jemmy was intent on the leaves he was kicking with one foot.

"No," I agreed, suppressing my smile.

Then Jemmy smiled ruefully in amusement at himself. "I should waste words with you," he said. "Here." He took his hands from behind him and thrust a bouquet of burning bright autumn leaves into my arms. "They're from you to her," he said. "Something pretty for the first day."

"Oh, Jemmy!" I cried through the scarlet and crimson and gold. "They're beautiful. You've been up on Baldy this morning."

"That's right," he said. "But she won't know where they came from." And he was gone.

I hurried to catch up with the children before they got to the door. Suddenly overcome with shyness, they were milling around the porch steps, each trying to hide behind the others.

"Oh, for goodness' sakes!" I whispered to our kids. "You ate breakfast with her this morning. She won't bite. Go on in."

But I found myself shouldered to the front and leading the subdued group into the school room. While I was giving the bouquet of leaves to Miss Carmody, the others with the ease of established habit slid into their usual seats, leaving only the twins, stricken and white, standing alone.

Miss Carmody, dropping the leaves on her desk, knelt quickly beside them, pried a hand of each gently free from their frenzied clutching and held them in hers.

"I'm so glad you came to school," she said in her warm, rich voice. "I need a first grade to make the school work out right and I have a seat that must have been built on purpose for twins."

And she led them over to the side of the room, close enough to the old pot-bellied stove for Outside comfort later and near enough to the window to see out. There, in dusted glory, stood one of the old double desks that The Group must have inherited from some ghost town out in the hills. There were two wooden boxes for footstools for small dangling feet and, spouting like a flame from the old ink well hole, a spray of vivid red leaves—matchmates to those Jemmy had given me.

The twins slid into the desk, never loosing hands, and stared up at Miss Carmody, wide-eyed. She smiled back at them and, leaning forward, poked her finger tip into the deep dimple in each round chin.

"Buried smiles," she said, and the two scared faces lighted up briefly with wavery smiles. Then Miss Carmody turned to the rest of us.

I never did hear her introductory words. I was too busy mulling over the spray of leaves, and how she came to know the identical routine, words and all, that the twins' mother used to make them smile, and how on earth she knew about the old desks in the shed. But by the time we rose to salute the flag and sing our morning song, I had it figured out. Father must have briefed her on the way home last night. The twins were an ever present concern of the whole Group and we were all especially anxious to have their first year a successful one. Also, Father knew the smile routine and where the old desks were stored. As for the spray of leaves, well, some did grow this low on the mountain and frost is tricky at leaf-turning time.

So school was launched and went along smoothly. Miss Carmody was a good teacher and even the Kroginolds found their studies interesting.

They hadn't tried any tricks since Jemmy threatened them. That is, except that silly deal with the chalk. Miss Carmody was explaining something on the board and was groping sideways for the chalk to add to the lesson. Jake was deliberately lifting the chalk every time she almost had it. I was just ready to do something about it when Miss Carmody snapped her fingers with annoyance and grasped the chalk firmly. Jake caught my eye about then and shrank about six inches in girth and height. I didn't tell Jemmy, but Jake's fear that I might kept him straight for a long time.

The twins were really blossoming. They laughed and played with the rest of the kids and Jerry even went off occasionally with the other boys at noon time, coming back as disheveled and wet as the others after a dam-building session in the creek.

Miss Carmody fitted so well into the community and was so well-liked by us kids that it began to look like we'd finally keep a teacher all year. Already she had withstood some of the shocks that had sent our other teachers screaming. For instance. . . .

The first time Susie got a robin redbreast sticker on her bookmark for reading a whole page—six lines—perfectly, she lifted all the way back to her seat, literally walking about four inches in the air. I held my breath until she sat down and was caressing the glossy sticker with one finger, then I sneaked a cautious look at Miss Carmody. She was sitting very erect, her hands clutching both ends of her desk as though in the act of rising, a look of incredulous surprise on her face. Then she relaxed, shook her head and smiled, and busied herself with some papers.

I let my breath out cautiously. The last teacher but two went into hysterics when one of the girls absent-mindedly lifted back to her seat because her sore foot hurt. I had hoped Miss Carmody was tougher—and apparently she was.

That same week, one noon hour, Jethro came pelting up to the school house where Valancy—that's her first name and I call her by it when we are alone, after all she's only four years older than I—was helping me with that gruesome Tests and Measurements I was taking by extension from Teachers' College.

"Hey Karen!" he yelled through the window. "Can you come out a minute?"

"Why?" I yelled back, annoyed at the interruption just when I was trying to figure what was normal about a normal grade curve.

"There's need," yelled Jethro.

I put down my book. "I'm sorry, Valancy. I'll go see what's eating him."

"Should I come too?" she asked. "If something's wrong—"

"It's probably just some silly thing," I said, edging out fast. When one of The People says "There's need," that means Group business.

"Adonday Veeah!" I muttered at Jethro as we rattled down the steep rocky path to the creek. "What are you trying to do? Get us all in trouble? What's the matter?"

"Look," said Jethro, and there were the boys standing around an alarmed but proud Jerry and above their heads, poised in the air over a half-built rock dam, was a huge boulder.

"Who lifted that?" I gasped.

"I did," volunteered Jerry, blushing crimson.

I turned on Jethro. "Well, why didn't you platt the twishers on it? You didn't have to come running—"

"On *that*?" Jethro squeaked. "You know very well we're not allowed to *lift* anything that big let alone platt it. Besides," shamefaced, "I can't remember that dern girl stuff."

"Oh Jethro! You're so stupid sometimes!" I turned to Jerry. "How on earth did you ever lift anything that big?"

He squirmed. "I watched Daddy at the mine once."

"Does he let you lift at home?" I asked severely.

"I don't know." Jerry squashed mud with one shoe, hanging his head. "I never lifted anything before."

"Well, you know better. You kids aren't allowed to lift anything an Outsider your age can't handle alone. And not even that if you can't platt it afterwards."

"I know it." Jerry was still torn between embarrassment and pride.

"Well, remember it," I said. And taking a handful of sun, I platted the twishers and set the boulder back on the hillside where it belonged.

Platting does come easier to the girls—sunshine platting, that is. Of course only the Old Ones do the sun-and-rain one and only the very Oldest of them all would dare the moonlight-and-dark, that can move mountains. But that was still no excuse for Jethro to forget and run the risk of having Valancy see what she mustn't see.

It wasn't until I was almost back to the school house that it dawned on me. Jerry had lifted! Kids his age usually lift play stuff almost from the time they walk. That doesn't need platting because it's just a matter of a few inches and a few seconds so gravity manages the return. But Jerry and Susie never had. They were finally beginning to catch up. Maybe it *was* just The Crossing that slowed them down—and maybe only the Clarinades. In my delight, *I* forgot and lifted to the school porch without benefit of the steps. But Valancy was putting up pictures on the high, old-fashioned moulding just below the ceiling, so no harm was done. She was flushed from her efforts and asked me to bring the step stool so she could finish them. I brought it and steadied it for her—and then nearly let her fall as I stared. How had she hung those first four pictures before I got there?

The weather was unnaturally dry all Fall. We didn't mind it much because rain with an Outsider around is awfully messy. We have to let ourselves get wet. But when November came and went and Christmas was almost upon us, and there was practically no rain and no snow at all, we all began to get worried. The creek dropped to a trickle and then to scattered puddles and then went dry. Finally the Old Ones had to spend an evening at the Group Reservoir doing something about our dwindling water supply. They wanted to get rid of Valancy for the evening, just in case, so Jemmy volunteered to take her to Kerry to the show. I was still awake when they got home long after midnight. Since I began to develop the Gift, I have long periods of restlessness when it seems I have no apartness but am of every person in The Group. The training I should start soon will help me shut out the others except when I want them. The only thing is that we don't know who is to train me. Since Grandmother died there has been no Sorter in our Group and because of The Crossing, we have no books or records to help.

Anyway, I was awake and leaning on my window sill in the darkness. They stopped on the porch—Jemmy is bunking at the mine during his stint there. I didn't have to guess or use a Gift to read the pantomime before me. I closed my eyes and my mind as their shadows merged. Under their strong emotion, I could have had free access to their minds, but I had been watching them all Fall. I knew in a special way what passed between them, and I knew that Valancy often went to bed in tears and that Jemmy spent too many lonely hours on the Crag that juts out over the canyon from high on Old Baldy, as though he were trying to make his heart as inaccessible to Outsiders as the Crag is. I knew what he felt, but oddly enough I had never been able to sort Valancy since that first night. There was something very un-Outsiderish and also very un-Groupish about her mind and I couldn't figure what.

I heard the front door open and close and Valancy's light steps fading down the hall and then I felt Jemmy calling me outside. I put my coat on over my robe and shivered down the hall. He was waiting by the porch steps, his face still and unhappy in the faint moonlight.

"She won't have me," he said flatly.

"Oh, Jemmy!" I cried. "You asked her—"

"Yes," he said. "She said no."

"I'm so sorry." I huddled down on the top step to cover my cold ankles. "But Jemmy—"

"Yes, I know!" He retorted savagely. "She's an Outsider. I have no business even to want her. Well, if she'd have me, I wouldn't hesitate a minute. This Purity-of-the-Group deal is—"

". . . is fine and right," I said softly, "as long as it doesn't touch you personally? But think for a minute, Jemmy. Would you be able to live a life as an Outsider? Just think of the million and one restraints that you would have to impose on yourself—and for the rest of your life, too, or lose her after all. Maybe it's better to accept *No* now than to try to build something and ruin it completely later. And if there should be children . . ." I paused. "*Could* there be children, Jemmy?"

I heard him draw a sharp breath.

"We don't know," I went on. "We haven't had the occasion to find out. Do you want Valancy to be part of the first experiment?"

Jemmy slapped his hat viciously down on his thigh, then he laughed.

"You have the Gift," he said, though I had never told him. "Have you any idea, sister mine, how little you will be liked when you become an Old One?"

"Grandmother was well-liked," I answered placidly. Then I cried, "Don't *you* set me apart, darn you, Jemmy. Isn't it enough to know that among a different people, *I* am different? Don't *you* desert me now!" I was almost in tears.

Jemmy dropped to the step beside me and thumped my shoulder in his old way. "Pull up your socks, Karen. We have to do what we have to do. I was just taking my mad out on you. What a world." He sighed heavily.

I huddled deeper in my coat, cold of soul.

"But the other one is gone," I whispered. "The Home."

And we sat there sharing the poignant sorrow that is a constant undercurrent among The People, even those of us who never actually saw The Home. Father says it's because of a sort of racial memory.

"But she didn't say no because she doesn't love me," Jemmy went on at last. "She does love me. She told me so."

"Then why not?" Sister-wise I couldn't imagine anyone turning Jemmy down.

Jemmy laughed—a short, unhappy laugh. "Because she is different."

"*She's* different?"

"That's what she said, as though it was pulled out of her. 'I can't marry,' she said. 'I'm different!' That's pretty good, isn't it, coming from an Outsider!"

"She doesn't know we're The People," I said. "She must feel that she is different from everyone. I wonder why?"

"I don't know. There's something about her, though. A kind of shield or wall that keeps us apart. I've never met anything like it in an Outsider or in one of The People either. Sometimes it's like meshing with one of us and then *bang!* I smash the daylights out of me against that stone wall."

"Yes, I know," I said. "I've felt it, too."

We listened to the silent past-midnight world and then Jemmy stood.

"Well, g'night, Karen. Be seeing you."

I stood up, too. "Good night, Jemmy." I watched him start off in the late moonlight. He turned at the gate, his face hidden in the shadows.

"But I'm not giving up," he said quietly. "Valancy is my love."

*

The next day was hushed and warm—unnaturally so for December in our hills. There was a kind of ominous stillness among the trees, and, threading thinly against the milky sky, the thin smokes of little brush fires pointed out the dryness of the whole country. If you looked closely you could see piling behind Old Baldy an odd bank of clouds, so nearly the color of the sky that it was hardly discernable, but puffy and summer-thunderheady.

All of us were restless in school, the kids reacting to the weather, Valancy pale and unhappy after last night. I was bruising my mind against the blank wall in hers, trying to find some way I could help her.

Finally the thousand and one little annoyances were climaxed by Jerry and Susie scuffling until Susie was pushed out of the desk onto an open box of wet water colors that Debra for heaven only knows what reason had left on the floor by her desk. Susie shrieked and Debra sputtered and Jerry started a high silly giggle of embarrassment and delight. Valancy, without looking, reached for something to rap for order with and knocked down the old cracked vase full of drooping wildflowers and three-day-old water. The vase broke and flooded her desk with the foul-smelling deluge, ruining the monthly report she had almost ready to send in to the County School Superintendent.

For a stricken moment there wasn't a sound in the room, then Valancy burst into half-hysterical laughter and the whole room rocked with her. We all rallied around doing what we could to clean up Susie and Valancy's desk and then Valancy declared a holiday and decided that it would be the perfect time to go up-canyon to the slopes of Baldy and gather what greenery we could find to decorate our school room for the holidays.

We all take our lunches to school, so we gathered them up and took along a square tarp the boys had brought to help build the dam in the creek. Now that the creek was dry, they couldn't use it and it'd come in handy to sit on at lunch time and would serve to carry our greenery home in, too, stretcher-fashion.

Released from the school room, we were all loud and jubilant and I nearly kinked my neck trying to keep all the kids in sight at once to nip in the bud any thoughtless lifting or other Group activity. The kids were all so wild, they might forget.

We went on up-canyon past the kids' dam and climbed the bare, dry waterfalls that stair-step up to the Mesa. On the Mesa, we spread the tarp and pooled our lunches to make it more picnicky. A sudden hush from across the tarp caught my attention. Debra, Rachel and Lizbeth were staring horrified at Susie's lunch. She was calmly dumping out a half dozen *koomatka* beside her sandwiches.

Koomatka are almost the only plants that lasted through The Crossing. I think four *koomatka* survived in someone's personal effects. They were planted and cared for as tenderly as babies and now every household in The Group has a *koomatka* plant growing in some quiet spot out of casual sight. Their fruit is eaten not so much for nourishment as Earth knows nourishment, but as a last remembrance of all other similar delights that died with The Home. We always save *koomatka* for special occasions. Susie must have sneaked some out when her mother wasn't looking. And there they were—across the table from an Outsider!

Before I could snap them to me or say anything, Valancy turned, too, and caught sight of the softly glowing bluey-green pile. Her eyes widened and one hand went out. She started to say something and then she dropped her eyes quickly and drew her hand back. She clasped her hands tightly together and the girls, eyes intent on her, scrambled the *koomatka* back into the sack and Lizbeth silently comforted Susie who had just realized what she had done. She was on the verge of tears at having betrayed The People to an Outsider.

Just then 'Kiah and Derek rolled across the picnic table fighting over a cupcake. By the time we salvaged our lunch from under them and they had scraped the last of the chocolate frosting off their T-shirts, the *koomatka* incident seemed closed. And yet, as we lay back resting a little to settle our stomachs, staring up at the smothery low-hanging clouds that had grown from the milky morning sky, I suddenly found myself trying to decide about Valancy's look when she saw the fruit. Surely it couldn't have been recognition!

At the end of our brief siesta, we carefully buried the remains of our lunch—the hill was much too dry to think of burning it—and started on again. After a while, the slope got steeper and the stubborn tangle of manzanita tore at our clothes and scratched our legs and grabbed at the rolled-up tarp until we all looked longingly at the free air above it. If Valancy hadn't been with us we could have lifted over the worst and saved all this trouble. But we blew and panted for a while and then struggled on.

After an hour or so, we worked out onto a rocky knoll that leaned against the slope of Baldy and made a tiny island in the sea of manzanita. We all stretched out gratefully on the crumbling granite outcropping, listening to our heart-beats slowing.

Then Jethro sat up and sniffed. Valancy and I alerted. A sudden puff of wind from the little side canyon brought the acrid pungency of burning brush to us. Jethro scrambled along the narrow ridge to the slope of Baldy and worked his way around out of sight into the canyon. He came scrambling back, half lifting, half running.

"Awful!" he panted. "It's awful! The whole canyon ahead is on fire and it's coming this way fast!"

Valancy gathered us together with a glance.

"Why didn't we see the smoke?" she asked tensely. "There wasn't any smoke when we left the school house."

"Can't see this slope from school," he said. "Fire could burn over a dozen slopes and we'd hardly see the smoke. This side of Baldy is a rim fencing in an awful mess of canyons."

"What'll we do?" quavered Lizbeth, hugging Susie to her.

Another gust of wind and smoke set us all to coughing and through my streaming tears, I saw a long lapping tongue of fire reach around the canyon wall.

Valancy and I looked at each other. I couldn't sort her mind, but mine was a panic, beating itself against the fire and then against the terrible tangle of manzanita all around us. Bruising against the possibility of lifting out of danger, then against the fact that none of the kids was capable of sustained progressive self-lifting for more than a minute or so and how could we leave Valancy? I hid my face in my hands to shut out the acres and acres of tinder-dry manzanita that would blaze like a torch at the first touch of fire. If only it would rain! You can't *set* fire to wet manzanita, but after these long months of drought—!

I heard the younger children scream and looked up to see Valancy staring at me with an intensity that frightened me even as I saw fire standing bright and terrible behind her at the mouth of the canyon.

Jake, yelling hoarsely, broke from the group and lifted a yard or two over the manzanita before he tangled his feet and fell helpless into the ugly, angled branches.

"Get under the tarp!" Valancy's voice was a whip-lash. "All of you get under the tarp!"

"It won't do any good," bellowed 'Kiah. "It'll burn like paper!"

"Get—under—the—tarp!" Valancy's spaced, icy words drove us to unfolding the tarp and spreading it to creep under. I lifted (hoping even at this awful moment that Valancy wouldn't see me) over to Jake and yanked him back to his feet. I couldn't lift with him so I pushed and prodded and half-carried him back through the heavy surge of black smoke to the tarp and shoved him under. Valancy was standing, back to the fire, so changed and alien that I shut my eyes against her and started to crawl in with the other kids.

And then she began to speak. The rolling, terrible thunder of her voice shook my bones and I swallowed a scream. A surge of fear swept through our huddled group and shoved me back out from under the tarp.

Till I die, I'll never forget Valancy standing there tense and taller than life against the rolling convulsive clouds of smoke, both her hands outstretched, fingers wide apart as the measured terror of her voice went on and on in words that plague me because I should have known them and didn't. As I watched, I felt an icy cold gather, a paralyzing, unearthly cold that froze the tears on my tensely upturned face.

And then lightning leaped from finger to finger of her lifted hands. And lightning answered in the clouds above her. With a toss of her hands she threw the cold, the lightning, the sullen shifting smoke upward, and the roar of the racing fire was drowned in a hissing roar of down-drenching rain.

I knelt there in the deluge, looking for an eternal second into her drained, despairing, hopeless eyes before I caught her just in time to keep her head from banging on the granite as she pitched forward, inert.

Then as I sat there cradling her head in my lap, shaking with cold and fear, with the terrified wailing of the kids behind me, I heard Father shout and saw him and Jemmy and Darcy Clarinade in the old pick-up, lifting over the steaming streaming manzanita, over the trackless mountain side through the rain to us. Father lowered the truck until one of the wheels brushed a branch and spun lazily, then the three of them lifted all of us up to the dear familiarity of that beat-up old jalopy.

Jemmy received Valancy's limp body into his arms and crouched in back, huddling her in his arms, for the moment hostile to the whole world that had brought his love to such a pass.

We kids clung to Father in an esctasy of relief. He hugged us all tight to him, then he raised my face.

"Why did it rain?" he asked sternly, every inch an Old One while the cold downpour dripped off the ends of my hair and he stood dry inside his Shield.

"I don't know," I sobbed, blinking my streaming eyes against his sternness. "Valancy did it . . . with lightning . . . it was cold . . . she talked. . . ." Then I broke down completely, plumping down on the rough floor boards and, in spite of my age, howling right along with the other kids.

It was a silent, solemn group that gathered in the school house that evening. I sat at my desk with my hands folded stiffly in front of me, half scared of my own People. This was the first official meeting of the Old Ones I'd ever attended. They all sat in desks, too, except the Oldest who sat in Valancy's chair. Valancy sat stony-faced in the twin's desk, but her nervous fingers shredded one kleenex after another as she waited.

The Oldest rapped the side of the desk with his cane and turned his sightless eyes from one to another of us.

"We're all here," he said, "to inquire——"

"Oh, stop it!" Valancy jumped up from her seat. "Can't you fire me without all this rigmarole? I'm used to it. Just say go and I'll go!" She stood trembling.

"Sit down, Miss Carmody," said the Oldest. And Valancy sat down meekly.

"Where were you born?" asked the Oldest quietly.

"What does it matter?" flared Valancy. Then resignedly, "It's in my application. Vista Mar, California."

"And your parents?"

"I don't know."

There was a stir in the room.

"Why not?"

"Oh, this is so unnecessary!" cried Valancy. "But if you *have* to know, both my parents were foundlings. They were found wandering in the streets after a big explosion and fire in Vista Mar. An old couple who lost everything in the fire took them in. When they grew up, they married. I was born. They died. Can I go now?"

A murmur swept the room.

"Why did you leave your other jobs?" asked Father.

Before Valancy could answer, the door was flung open and Jemmy stalked defiantly in.

"Go!" said the Oldest.

"Please," said Jemmy, deflating suddenly. "Let me stay. It concerns me too."

The Oldest fingered his cane and then nodded. Jemmy half-smiled with relief and sat down in a back seat.

"Go on," said the Oldest One to Valancy.

"All right then," said Valancy. "I lost my first job because I—well—I guess you'd call it levitated—to fix a broken blind in my room. It was stuck and I just . . . went up . . . in the air until I unstuck it. The principal saw me. He couldn't believe it and it scared him so he fired me." She paused expectantly.

The Old Ones looked at one another and my silly, confused mind began to add up columns that only my lack of common sense had kept from giving totals long ago.

"And the other one?" The Oldest leaned his cheek on his doubled-up hand as he bent forward.

Valancy was taken aback and she flushed in confusion.

"Well," she said hesitantly, "I called my books to me—I mean they were on my desk. . . ."

"We know what you mean," said the Oldest.

"You know!" Valancy looked dazed.

The Oldest stood up.

"Valancy Carmody, open your mind!"

Valancy stared at him and then burst into tears.

"I can't, I can't," she sobbed. "It's been too long. I can't let anyone in. I'm different. I'm alone. Can't you understand? They all died. I'm alien!"

"You are alien no longer," said the Oldest. "You are home now, Valancy." He motioned to me. "Karen, go in to her."

So I did. At first the wall was still there; then with a soundless cry, half anguish and half joy, the wall went down and I was with Valancy. I saw all the secrets that had cankered in her since her parents died—the parents who were of The People.

They had been reared by the old couple who were not only of The People but had been the Oldest of the whole Crossing.

I tasted with her the hidden frightening things—the need for living as an Outsider, the terrible need for concealing all her differences and suppressing all the extra Gifts of The People, the ever present fear of betraying herself and the awful lostness that came when she thought she was the last of The People.

And then suddenly *she* came in to *me* and my mind was flooded with a far greater presence than I had ever before experienced.

My eyes flew open and I saw all of the Old Ones staring at Valancy. Even the Oldest had his face turned to her, wonder written as widely on his scarred face as on the others.

He bowed his head and made The Sign. "The lost persuasions and designs," he murmured. "She has them all."

And then I knew that Valancy, Valancy who had wrapped herself so tightly against the world to which any thoughtless act might betray her that she had lived with us all this time without our knowing about her or she about us, was one of us. Not only one of us but such a one as had not been since Grandmother died—and even beyond that. My incoherent thoughts cleared to one.

Now I would have some one to train me. Now I could become a Sorter—but only second to her.

I turned to share my wonder with Jemmy. He was looking at Valancy as The People must have looked at The Home in the last hour. Then he turned to the door.

Before I could draw a breath, Valancy was gone from me and from the Old Ones and Jemmy was turning to her outstretched hands.

Then I bolted for the outdoors and rushed like one possessed down the lane, lifting and running until I staggered up our porch steps and collapsed against Mother, who had heard me coming.

"Oh, Mother!" I cried. "She's one of us! She's Jemmy's love! She's wonderful!" And I burst into noisy sobs in the warm comfort of Mother's arms.

So now I don't have to go Outside to become a teacher. We have a permanent one. But I'm going anyway. I want to be as much like Valancy as I can and she has her degree. Besides I can use the discipline of living Outside for a year.

I have so much to learn and so much training to go through, but Valancy will always be there with me. I won't be set apart alone because of the Gift.

Maybe I shouldn't mention it, but one reason I want to hurry my training is that we're going to try to locate the other People. None of the boys here please me.

1952

ANDREW NORTH

All Cats Are Gray

STEENA of the spaceways—that sounds just like a corny title for one of the Stellar-Vedo spreads. I ought to know, I've tried my hand at writing enough of them. Only this Steena was no glamour babe. She was as colorless as a Lunar plant—even the hair netted down to her skull had a sort of grayish cast and I never saw her but once draped in anything but a shapeless and baggy gray space-all.

Steena was strictly background stuff and that is where she mostly spent her free hours—in the smelly smoky background corners of any stellar-port dive frequented by free spacers. If you really looked for her you could spot her—just sitting there listening to the talk—listening and remembering. She didn't open her own mouth often. But when she did spacers had learned to listen. And the lucky few who heard her rare spoken words—these will never forget Steena.

She drifted from port to port. Being an expert operator on the big calculators she found jobs wherever she cared to stay for a time. And she came to be something like the master-minded machines she tended—smooth, gray, without much personality of her own.

But it was Steena who told Bub Nelson about the Jovan moon-rites—and her warning saved Bub's life six months later. It was Steena who identified the piece of stone Keene Clark was passing around a table one night, rightly calling it unworked Slitite. That started a rush which made ten fortunes overnight for men who were down to their last jets. And, last of all, she cracked the case of the *Empress of Mars*.

All the boys who had profited by her queer store of knowledge and her photographic memory tried at one time or another to balance the scales. But she wouldn't take so much as a cup of Canal water at their expense, let alone the credits they tried to push on her. Bub Nelson was the only one who got around her refusal. It was he who brought her Bat.

About a year after the Jovan affair he walked into the Free Fall one night and dumped Bat down on her table. Bat looked at Steena and growled. She looked calmly back at him and nodded once. From then on they traveled together—the thin gray woman and the big gray tom-cat. Bat learned to know the inside of more stellar bars than even most spacers visit in their lifetimes. He developed a liking for Vernal juice, drank it neat and quick, right out of a glass. And he was always at home on any table where Steena elected to drop him.

This is really the story of Steena, Bat, Cliff Moran and the *Empress of Mars*, a story which is already a legend of the spaceways. And it's a damn good story too. I ought to know, having framed the first version of it myself.

For I was there, right in the Rigel Royal, when it all began on the night that Cliff Moran blew in, looking lower than an antman's belly and twice as nasty. He'd had a spell of luck foul enough to twist a man into a slug-snake and we all knew that there was an attachment out for his ship. Cliff had fought his way up from the back courts of Venaport. Lose his ship and he'd slip back there—to rot. He was at the snarling stage that night when he picked out a table for himself and set out to drink away his troubles.

However, just as the first bottle arrived, so did a visitor. Steena came out of her corner, Bat curled around her shoulders stole-wise, his favorite mode of travel. She crossed over and dropped down without invitation at Cliff's side. That shook him out of his sulks. Because Steena never chose company when she could be alone. If one of the man-stones on Ganymede had come stumping in, it wouldn't have made more of us look out of the corners of our eyes.

She stretched out one long-fingered hand and set aside the bottle he had ordered and said only one thing, "It's about time for the *Empress of Mars* to appear again."

Cliff scowled and bit his lip. He was tough, tough as jet lining—you have to be granite inside and out to struggle up from Venaport to a ship command. But we could guess what was running through his mind at that moment. The *Empress of Mars* was just about the biggest prize a spacer could aim for. But in the fifty years she had been following her queer derelict orbit through space many men had tried to bring her in—and none had succeeded.

A pleasure-ship carrying untold wealth, she had been mysteriously abandoned in space by passengers and crew, none of whom had ever been seen or heard of again. At intervals thereafter she had been sighted, even boarded. Those who ventured into her either vanished or returned swiftly without any believable explanation of what they had seen—wanting only to get away from her as quickly as possible. But the man who could bring her in—or even strip her clean in space—that man would win the jackpot.

"All right!" Cliff slammed his fist down on the table. "I'll try even that!"

Steena looked at him, much as she must have looked at Bat the day Bub Nelson brought him to her, and nodded. That was all I saw. The rest of the story came to me in pieces, months later and in another port half the System away.

Cliff took off that night. He was afraid to risk waiting—with a writ out that could pull the ship from under him. And it wasn't until he was in space that he discovered his passengers—Steena and Bat. We'll never know what happened then. I'm betting that Steena made no explanation at all. She wouldn't.

It was the first time she had decided to cash in on her own tip and she was there—that was all. Maybe that point weighed with Cliff, maybe he just didn't care. Anyway the three were together when they sighted the *Empress* riding, her dead-lights gleaming, a ghost ship in night space.

She must have been an eerie sight because her other lights were on too, in addition to the red warnings at her nose. She seemed alive, a Flying Dutchman of space. Cliff worked his ship skillfully alongside and had no trouble in snapping magnetic lines to her lock. Some minutes later the three of them passed into her. There was still air in her cabins and corridors. Air that bore a faint corrupt taint which set Bat to sniffing greedily and could be picked up even by the less sensitive human nostrils.

Cliff headed straight for the control cabin but Steena and Bat went prowling. Closed doors were a challenge to both of them and Steena opened each as she passed, taking a quick look at what lay within. The fifth door opened on a room which no woman could leave without further investigation.

I don't know who had been housed there when the *Empress* left port on her last lengthy cruise. Anyone really curious can check back on the old photo-reg cards. But there was a lavish display of silks trailing out of two travel kits on the floor, a dressing table crowded with crystal and jeweled containers, along with other lures for the female which drew Steena in. She was standing in front of the dressing table when she glanced into the mirror—glanced into it and froze.

Over her right shoulder she could see the spider-silk cover on the bed. Right in the middle of that sheer, gossamer expanse was a sparkling heap of gems, the dumped contents of some jewel case. Bat had jumped to the foot of the bed and flattened out as cats will, watching those gems, watching them and—something else!

Steena put out her hand blindly and caught up the nearest bottle. As she unstoppered it she watched the mirrored bed. A gemmed bracelet rose from the pile, rose in the air and tinkled its siren song. It was as if an idle hand played . . . Bat spat almost noiselessly. But he did not retreat. Bat had not yet decided his course.

She put down the bottle. Then she did something which perhaps few of the men she had listened to through the years could have done. She moved without hurry or sign of disturbance on a tour about the room. And, although she approached the bed she did not touch the jewels. She could not force herself to that. It took her five minutes to play out her innocence and unconcern. Then it was Bat who decided the issue.

He leaped from the bed and escorted something to the door, remaining a careful distance behind. Then he mewed loudly twice. Steena followed him and opened the door wider.

Bat went straight on down the corridor, as intent as a hound on the warmest of scents. Steena strolled behind him, holding her pace to the unhurried gait of an explorer. What sped before them both was invisible to her but Bat was never baffled by it.

They must have gone into the control cabin almost on the heels of the unseen—if the unseen had heels, which there was good reason to doubt—for Bat crouched just within the doorway and refused to move on. Steena looked down the length of the instrument panels and officers' station-seats to where Cliff Moran worked. On the heavy carpet her boots made no sound and he did not glance up but sat humming through set teeth as he tested the tardy and reluctant responses to buttons which had not been pushed in years.

To human eyes they were alone in the cabin. But Bat still followed a moving something with his gaze. And it was something which he had at last made up his mind to distrust and dislike. For now he took a step or two forward and spat—his loathing made plain by every raised hair along his spine. And in that same moment Steena saw a flicker—a flicker of vague outline against Cliff's hunched shoulders as if the invisible one had crossed the space between them.

But why had it been revealed against Cliff and not against the back of one of the seats or against the panels, the walls of the corridor or the cover of the bed where it had reclined and played with its loot? What could Bat see?

The storehouse memory that had served Steena so well through the years clicked open a half-forgotten door. With one swift motion she tore loose her spaceall and flung the baggy garment across the back of the nearest seat.

Bat was snarling now, emitting the throaty rising cry that was his hunting song. But he was edging back, back toward Steena's feet, shrinking from something he could not fight but which he faced defiantly. If he could draw it after him, past that dangling spaceall . . . He had to—it was their only chance.

"What the . . ." Cliff had come out of his seat and was staring at them.

What he saw must have been weird enough. Steena, bare-armed and shouldered, her usually stiffly netted hair falling wildly down her back, Steena watching empty space with narrowed eyes and set mouth, calculating a single wild chance. Bat, crouched on his belly, retreating from thin air step by step and wailing like a demon.

"Toss me your blaster." Steena gave the order calmly—as if they still sat at their table in the Rigel Royal.

And as quietly Cliff obeyed. She caught the small weapon out of the air with a steady hand—caught and leveled it.

"Stay just where you are!" she warned. "Back, Bat, bring it back!"

With a last throat-splitting screech of rage and hate, Bat twisted to safety between her boots. She pressed with thumb and forefinger, firing at the spacealls. The material turned to powdery flakes of ash—except for certain bits which still flapped from the scorched seat—as if something had protected them from the force of the blast. Bat sprang straight up in the air with a scream that tore their ears.

"What . . . ?" began Cliff again.

Steena made a warning motion with her left hand. "*Wait!*"

She was still tense, still watching Bat. The cat dashed madly around the cabin twice, running crazily with white-ringed eyes and flecks of foam on his muzzle. Then he stopped abruptly in the doorway, stopped and looked back over his shoulder for a long silent moment. He sniffed delicately.

Steena and Cliff could smell it too now, a thick oily stench which was not the usual odor left by an exploding blaster-shell.

Bat came back, treading daintily across the carpet, almost on the tips of his paws. He raised his head as he passed Steena and then he went confidently beyond to sniff, to sniff and spit twice at the unburned strips of the spaceall. Having thus paid his respects to the late enemy he sat down calmly and set to washing his fur with deliberation. Steena sighed once and dropped into the navigator's seat.

"Maybe now you'll tell me what in the hell's happened?" Cliff exploded as he took the blaster out of her hand.

"Gray," she said dazedly, "it must have been gray—or I couldn't have seen it like that. I'm colorblind, you see. I can see only shades of gray—my whole world is gray. Like Bat's—his world is gray too—all gray. But he's been compensated for he can see above and below our range of color vibrations and—apparently—so can I!"

Her voice quavered and she raised her chin with a new air Cliff had never seen before—a sort of proud acceptance. She pushed back her wandering hair, but she made no move to imprison it under the heavy net again.

"That is why I saw the thing when it crossed between us. Against your spaceall it was another shade of gray—an outline. So I put out mine and waited for it to show against that—it was our only chance, Cliff.

"It was curious at first, I think, and it knew we couldn't see it—which is why it waited to attack. But when Bat's actions gave it away it moved. So I waited to see that flicker against the spaceall and then I let him have it. It's really very simple . . ."

Cliff laughed a bit shakily. "But what *was* this gray thing? I don't get it."

"I think it was what made the *Empress* a derelict. Something out of space, maybe, or from another world somewhere." She waved her hands. "It's invisible because it's a color beyond our range of sight. It must have stayed in here all these years. And it kills—it must—when its curiosity is satisfied." Swiftly she described the scene in the cabin and the strange behavior of the gem pile which had betrayed the creature to her.

Cliff did not return his blaster to its holder. "Any more of them on board, d'you think?" He didn't look pleased at the prospect.

Steena turned to Bat. He was paying particular attention to the space between two front toes in the process of a complete bath. "I don't think so. But Bat will tell us if there are. He can see them clearly, I believe."

But there weren't any more and two weeks later Cliff, Steena and Bat brought the *Empress* into the Lunar quarantine station. And that is the end of Steena's story because, as we have been told, happy marriages need no chronicles. And Steena had found someone who knew of her gray world and did not find it too hard to share with her—someone besides Bat. It turned out to be a real love match.

The last time I saw her she was wrapped in a flame-red cloak from the looms of Rigel and wore a fortune in Jovan rubies blazing on her wrists. Cliff was flipping a three-figure credit bill to a waiter. And Bat had a row of Vernal juice glasses set up before him. Just a little family party out on the town.

1953

ALICE ELEANOR JONES

Created He Them

ANN Crothers looked at the clock and frowned and turned the fire lower under the bacon. She had already poured his coffee; he liked it cooled to a certain degree; but if he did not get up soon it would be too cool and the bacon too crisp and he would be angry and sulk the rest of the day. She had better call him.

She walked to the foot of the stairs, a blond woman nearing thirty, big but not fat, and rather plain, with a tired sad face. She called, "Henry! Are you up?" She had calculated to a decibel how loud her voice must be. If it were too soft he did not hear and maintained that she had not called him, and was angry later; if it were too loud he was angry immediately and stayed in bed longer, to punish her, and then he grew angrier because breakfast was spoiled.

"All *right!* Pipe down, can't you?"

She listened a minute. She thought it was a normal response, but perhaps her voice had been a shade too loud. No, he was getting up. She heard the thump of his feet on the floor. She went back to the kitchen and took his orange juice and his prunes out of the icebox, and got out his bread but did not begin to toast it yet, and opened a glass of jelly.

She frowned. Grape. He did not like grape, but the co-op had been out of apple, and she had been lucky to get anything. He would not be pleased.

She sat down briefly at the table to wait for him and glanced at the clock. Ten five. Wearily, she leaned forward and rested her forehead on the back of her hand. She was not feeling well this morning and had eaten no breakfast. She was almost sure she was pregnant again.

She thought of the children. There were only two at home, and they had been bathed and fed long ago and put down in the basement playpen so that the noise they made would not disturb their father. She would have time for a quick look at them before Henry came down. And the house was chilly; she would have to look at the heater.

They were playing quietly with the rag doll she had made, and the battered rubber ball. Lennie, who was two and a half, was far too big for a playpen, but he was a good child, considerate, and allowed himself to be put there for short periods and did not climb out. He seemed to feel a responsibility for his brother. Robbie was fourteen months old and a small terror, but he loved Lennie, and even, Ann thought, tried to mind him.

As Ann poked her head over the bannister, both children turned and gave her radiant smiles. Lennie said, "Hi, Mommy," and Robbie said experimentally, "Ma?"

She went down quickly and gave each of them a hug and said, "You're good boys. You can come upstairs and play soon." She felt their hands. The basement was damp, but the small mended sweaters were warm enough.

She looked at the feeble fire and rattled the grate hopefully and put on more coal. There was plenty of coal in the bin, but it was inferior grade, filled with slate, and did not burn well. It was not an efficient heater, either. It was old, second-hand, but they had been lucky to get it. The useless oil heater stood in the corner.

The children chuckled at the fire, and Robbie reached out his hands toward it. Lennie said gravely, "No, no, bad."

Ann heard Henry coming downstairs, and she raced up the cellar steps and beat him to the kitchen by two seconds. When he came in she was draining the bacon. She put a slice of bread on the long fork and began to toast it over the gas flame. The gas, at least, was fairly dependable, and the water. The electricity was not working again. It seemed such a long time since the electricity had always worked. Well, it was a long time. Ten years.

Henry sat down at the table and looked peevishly at his orange juice. He was not a tall man, not quite so tall as his wife, but he walked and sat tall, making the most of every inch. He was inclined to be chubby, and he had a roll of fat under his chin and at the back of his neck, and a little bulge at the waist. His face might have been handsome, but the expression spoiled it—discontented, bad-tempered. He said, "You didn't strain the orange juice."

"Yes, I strained it." She was intent on the toast.

He drank the orange juice without enjoyment and said, "I have a touch of liver this morning. Can't think what it could be." His face brightened. "I told you that sauce was too greasy. That was it."

She did not answer. She brought over his plate with the bacon on it and the toast, nicely browned, and put margarine on the toast for him.

He was eating the prunes. He stopped and looked at the bacon. "No eggs?"

"They were all out."

His face flushed a little. "Then why'd you cook bacon? You know I can't eat bacon without eggs." He was working himself up into a passion. "If I weren't such an easygoing man—! And the prunes are hard—you didn't cook them long enough—and the coffee's cold, and the toast's burnt, and where's the apple jelly?"

"They didn't have any."

He laughed scornfully. “I bet they didn’t. I bet you fooled around the house and didn’t even get there till everything was gone.” He flung down his fork. “This garbage!—why should you care, you don’t have to eat it!”

She looked at him. “Shall I make you something else?”

He laughed again. “You’d ruin it. Never mind.” He slammed out of the kitchen and went upstairs to sulk in the bathroom for an hour.

Ann sat down at the table. All that bacon, and it was hard to get. Well, the children would like it. She ought to clear the table and wash the dishes, but she sat still and took out a cigarette. She ought to save it, her ration was only three a day, but she lit it.

The children were getting a little noisier. Perhaps she could take them out for a while, till Henry went to work. It was cold but clear; she could bundle them up.

The cigarette was making her lightheaded, and she stubbed it out and put the butt in the box she kept over the sink. She said softly, “I hate him. I wish he would die.”

She dressed the children—their snowsuits were faded and patched from much use, but they were clean and warm—and put them in the battered carriage, looping her old string shopping bag over the handle, and took them out. They were delighted with themselves and with her. They loved the outdoors. Robbie bounced and drooled and made noises, and Lennie sat quiet, his little face smiling and content.

Ann wheeled them slowly down the walk, detouring around the broken places. It was a fine day, crisp, much too cold for September, but the seasons were not entirely reliable any more. There were no other baby carriages out; there were no children at all; the street was very quiet. There were no cars. Only the highest officials had cars, and no high officials lived in this neighborhood.

The children were enchanted by the street. Shabby as it was, with the broken houses as neatly mended as they could be, and the broken paving that the patches never caught up with, it was beautiful to them. Lennie said, "Hi, Mommy," and Robbie bounced.

The women were beginning to come, as they always came, timidly out of the drab houses, to look at the children, and Ann walked straighter and tried not to smile. It was not kind to smile, but sometimes she could not help it. Suddenly she was not tired any more, and her clothes were not shabby, and her face was not plain.

The first woman said, "Please stop a minute," and Ann stopped, and the women gathered around the carriage silently and looked. Their faces were hungry and seeking, and a few had tears in their eyes.

The first woman asked, "Do they stay well?"

Ann said, "Pretty well. They both had colds last week," and murmurs of commiseration went around the circle.

Another woman said, "I noticed you didn't come out, and I wondered. I almost knocked at your door to inquire, but then—" She stopped and blushed violently, and the others considerately looked away from her, ignoring her blunder. One did not call on one's neighbors; one lived to oneself.

The first woman said wistfully, "If I could hold them—either of them—I have dates; my cousin sent them all the way from California."

Ann blushed, too. She disliked this part of it very much, but things were so hard to get now, and Henry was difficult about what he liked to eat, though he denied that. He would say, "I'd eat anything, if you could only learn to cook it right, but you can't." Henry liked dates. Ann said, "Well . . ."

Another woman said eagerly, "I have eggs. I could spare you three." One for each of the boys and one for Henry.

"Oranges—for the children."

"And I have butter—imagine, butter!"

"Sugar—all children like sugar. Best grade—no sand in it."

"And I have tea." Henry does not like tea. But you shall hold the children anyway.

Somebody said, "Cigarettes," and somebody else whispered, "I even have *sleeping pills*!"

The children were passed around and fondled and caressed. Robbie enjoyed it and flirted with everybody, under his long eyelashes, but Lennie regarded the entire transaction with distaste.

When the children began to grow restless Ann put them back into the carriage and walked on. Her shopping bag was full.

The women went slowly back into their houses, all but one, a stranger. She must have moved into the neighborhood recently, perhaps from one of the spreading waste places. They were coming in, the people, as if they had been called, moving in closer, a little closer every year.

The woman was tall and older than Ann, with a worn plain face. She kept pace with the carriage and looked at the children and said, "Forgive me, I know it is bad form, but are they—do you have more?"

Ann said proudly, "I have had seven."

The woman looked at her and whispered, "Seven! And were they all—surely they were not *all*—"

Ann said more proudly still, "All. Every one."

The woman looked as if she might cry and said, "But seven! And the rest, are they—"

Ann's face clouded. "Yes, at the Center. One of my boys and all my girls. When Lennie goes, Robbie will miss him. Lennie missed Kate so, until he forgot her."

The woman said in a broken voice, "I had three, and none of them was—*none*!" She thrust something into Ann's shopping bag and said, "For the children," and walked quickly away.

Ann looked, and it was a Hershey bar. The co-op had not had chocolate for over two years. Neither of the boys had ever tasted it.

She brought the children home after a while and gave them their lunch—Henry's bacon crumbled into two scrambled eggs, and bread and butter and milk. She had been lucky at the co-op yesterday; they had had milk. She made herself a cup of coffee, feeling extravagant, and ate a piece of toast, and smoked the butt of this morning's cigarette.

For dessert she gave them each an orange; the rest she saved for Henry. She got out the Hershey bar and gave them all of it; Henry should not have their chocolate! The Hershey bar was hard and pale, as stale chocolate gets, and she had to make sawing motions with the knife to divide it evenly. The boys were enchanted. Robbie chewed his half and swallowed it quickly, but Lennie sucked blissfully and made it last, and then took pity on his brother and let Robbie suck, too. Ann did not interfere. Germs, little hearts, are the least of what I fear for you.

While the children took their naps she straightened the house a little and tinkered with the heater and cleaned all the kerosene lamps. She had time to take a bath, and enjoyed it, though the laundry soap she had to use was harsh against her skin. She even washed her hair, pretty hair, long and fine, and put on one of the few dresses that was not mended.

The children slept longer than usual. The fresh air had done them good. Just at dusk the electric lights came on for the first time in three days, and she woke them up to see them—they loved the electric lights. She gave them each a piece of bread and butter and took them with her to the basement and put them in the playpen. She was able to run a full load of clothes through the old washing machine before the current went off again. The children loved the washing machine and watched it, fascinated by the whirling clothes in the little window.

Afterward she took them upstairs again and tried to use the vacuum cleaner, but the machine was old and balky and by the time she had coaxed it to work the current was gone.

She gave the children their supper and played with them a while and put them to bed. Henry was still at the laboratory. He left late in the morning, but sometimes he had to stay late at night. The children were asleep before he came home, and Ann was glad. Sometimes they got on his nerves and he swore at them.

She turned the oven low to keep dinner hot and went into the living room. She sat beside the lamp and mended Robbie's shirt and Lennie's overalls. She turned on the battery radio to the one station that was broadcasting these days, the one at the Center. The news report was the usual thing. The Director was in good health and bearing the burden of his duties with fortitude. Conditions throughout the country were normal. Crops had not been quite so good as hoped, but there was no cause for alarm. Quotas in light and heavy industry were good—Ann smiled wryly—but could be improved if every worker did his duty. Road repairs were picking up—Ann wondered when they would get around to the street again—and electrical service was normal, except for a few scattered areas where there might be small temporary difficulties. The lamp had begun to smoke again, and Ann turned it lower. The stock market had closed irregular, with rails down an average of two points and stocks off three.

And now—the newscaster's voice grew solemn—there was news of grave import. The Director had asked him to talk seriously to all citizens about the dangers of rumor-mongering. Did they not realize what harm could be done by it? For example, the rumor that the Western Reservoir was contaminated. That was entirely false, of course, and the malicious and irresponsible persons who had started it would be severely dealt with.

The wastelands were not spreading, either. Some other malicious and irresponsible persons had started that rumor, and would be dealt with. The wastelands were under control. They were *not* spreading, repeat, *not*. Certain areas were being evacuated, it was true, but the measure was only temporary.

Calling them in, are you, calling them in!

The weather was normal. The seasons were definitely not changing, and here were the statistics to prove it. In 1961 . . . and in '62 . . . and that was *before*, so you see . . .

The newscaster's voice changed, growing less grave. And now for news of the children. Ann put down her mending and listened, not breathing. They always closed with news of the children, and it was always reassuring. If any child were ever unhappy, or were taken ill, or died, nobody knew it. One was never told anything, and of course one never saw the children again. It would upset them, one quite understood that.

The children, the newscaster said, were all well and happy. They had good beds and warm clothes and the best food and plenty of it. They even had cod-liver oil twice a week whether they needed it or not. They had toys and games, carefully supervised according to their age groups, and they were being educated by the best teachers. The children were all well and happy, repeat, *well and happy*. Ann hoped it was true.

They played the national anthem and went off the air, and just then Henry came in. He looked pale and tired—he did work hard—and his greeting was, "I suppose dinner's spoiled."

She looked up. "No, I don't think so."

She served it and they ate silently except for Henry's complaints about the food and his liver. He looked at the dates and said, "They're small. You let them stick you with anything," but she thought he enjoyed them because he ate them all.

Afterward he grew almost mellow. He lit a cigarette and told her about his day, while she washed the dishes. Henry's job at the laboratory was a responsible one, and Ann was sure he did it well. Henry was not stupid. But Henry could not get along with anybody. He said that he himself was very easy to get along with, but they were all against him. Today he had had a dispute with one of his superiors and reported that he had told the old —— where to go.

He said with gloomy relish, "They'll probably fire me, and we'll all be out in the street. Then you'll find out what it's like to live on Subsistence. You won't be able to throw my money around the way you do now."

Ann rinsed out the dish towel and hung it over the rack to dry. She said, "They won't fire you. They never do."

He laughed. "I'm good and they know it. I do twice as much work as anybody else."

Ann thought that was probably true. She turned away from the sink and said, "Henry, I think I'm pregnant."

He looked at her and frowned. "Are you sure?"

"I said I *think*. But I'm practically sure."

He said, "Oh, God, now you'll be sick all the time, and there's no living with you when you're sick."

Ann sat down at the table and lit a cigarette. "Maybe I won't be sick."

He said darkly, "You always are. Sweet prospect!"

Ann said, "We'll get another bonus, Henry."

He brightened a little. "Say, we will, at that. I'll buy some more stock."

Ann said, "Henry, we need so many things—"

He was immediately angry. "I said I'll buy stock! Somebody in this house has to think of the future. We can't all hide our heads in the sand and hope for the best."

She stood up, trembling. It was not a new argument. "What future? Our children—children like ours are taken away from us when they're three years old and given to the state to rear. When we're old the state will take care of us. Nobody lives well any more, except—but nobody starves. And that stock—it all goes down. Don't talk to me about the future, Henry Crothers! I want my future now."

He laughed unpleasantly. "What do you want? A car?"

She said, "I want a new washing machine and a vacuum cleaner, when the quotas come—the electricity isn't so bad. I want a new chair for the living room. I want to fix up the boys' room, paint and—"

He said brutally, "They're too little to notice. By the time they get old enough—"

She sat down again, sobbing a little. Her cigarette burned forgotten in the ashtray, and Henry thriftily stubbed it out. She said, "I know, the Center takes them. The Center takes children like ours."

"And the Center's good to them. They give them more than we could. Don't you go talking against the Center." Though a malcontent in his personal life, Henry was a staunch government man.

Ann said, "I'm not, Henry, I'm—"

He said disgustedly, "Being a woman again. Tears! Oh, God, why do women always turn them on?"

She made herself stop crying. Anger was beginning to rise in her, and that helped a good deal. "I didn't mean to start an argument. I was just telling you what we need. We do need things, Henry. Clothes—"

He looked at her. "You mean for you? Clothes would do you a lot of good, wouldn't they?"

She was stung. "I don't mean maternity clothes. I won't be needing them for—"

He laughed. "I don't mean maternity clothes either. Have you looked at yourself in a mirror lately? God, you're a big horse! I always liked little women."

She said tightly, "And I always liked tall men."

He half rose, and she thought he was going to hit her. She sat still, trembling with a fierce exhilaration, her eyes bright, color in her cheeks, a little smile on her mouth. She said softly, "I'll hit you back, I'm bigger than you are. I'll kill you!"

Suddenly Henry sat down and began to laugh. When he laughed he was quite handsome. He said in a deep chuckling voice, "You're almost pretty when you get mad enough. Your hair's pretty tonight, you must have washed it." His eyes were beginning to shine, and he reached across the table and put his hand on hers. "Ann . . . old girl . . ."

She drew her hand away. "I'm tired. I'm going to bed."

He said good-humoredly, "Sure. I'll be right up."

She looked at him. "I said I'm tired."

"And I said I'd be right up."

If I had something in my hands I'd kill you. "I don't want to."

He scowled, and his mouth grew petulant again, and he was no longer handsome. "But *I* want to."

She stood up. All at once she felt as tired as she had told Henry she was, as tired as she had been for ten years.

I cannot kill you, Henry, or myself. I cannot even wish us dead. In this desolate, dying, bombed-out world, with its creeping wastelands and its freakish seasons, with its limping economy and its arrogant Center in the country that takes our children—children like ours; the others it destroys—we have to live, and we have to live together.

Because by some twist of providence, or radiation, or genes, we are among the tiny percentage of the people in this world who can have normal children. We hate each other, but we breed true.

She said, "Come up, Henry." I can take a sleeping pill afterward.

Come up, Henry, we have to live. Till we are all called in, or our children, or our children's children. Till there is nowhere else to go.

1955

MILDRED CLINGERMAN

Mr. Sakrison's Halt

IN those days the old Katy local was the magic carpet that transported me from one world to another. Summertime only truly began the moment the conductor lifted me aboard and urged me to "set still and be a big girl." He was never impressed with the fact that I'd been traveling two days all alone and on much bigger trains than the Katy. When he had asked after my mother and told me how anxiously my grandparents were awaiting my arrival, he'd pass on down the aisle to mysterious regions forward, and I'd be left to spy all about the coach for Miss Mattie Compton.

As often as not, there was no sign of Miss Mattie, and the only other occupants would be somnolent old men in alpaca coats who roused now and then to use the spittoons. Usually her absence meant simply that the conductor had not yet found time to eject her bodily from the Jim Crow car, but sometimes I was forced to conclude that she was resting at home that day. At such times my disappointment would be intense. And while the Katy huffed and rattled past the cotton fields and muttered gloomily over the shady creeks, I had nothing to do but hold myself steady on the slick straw seat and stretch my eyes wide to keep awake.

But mostly I was fortunate enough to catch the Katy on one of Miss Mattie's days. I'd see just the tip of a pink ribbon bobbing over the top of the high seat, and I'd hurry down the car to slide in beside her. Or perhaps the door to the coach would open and Mr. McCall, the conductor, would appear with Miss Mattie in his arms.

She would be hanging as limply as a bit of old mosquito netting, staring sweetly into Mr. McCall's annoyed red face. He'd plump her down beside me and then, accommodating himself to the Katy's swaggering roll, slam out of our car again without a word.

Miss Mattie and I never bothered with formal greetings. The bond between us was so well-established that we always took up again just where we'd left off the year before. She might sometimes call me by my mother's name instead of my own, but I didn't mind. (It was such a pretty name.) Almost immediately, out of the confused, jackdaw clutter of her conversation, her recognition of our shared dedication would emerge, and once again we'd plunge deeply into talk of Mr. Sakrison. Interruptions were frequent, as frequent as the Katy's stops along the line. When the Katy squealed jerkily to a halt and sat there panting, we'd press our noses against the dirty window (with its heaped up piles of coal dust along the sill) and stare silently at the scene outside. Then, for a little while after each of the stops, I'd have to pat Miss Mattie's hands till she stopped whimpering.

Miss Mattie was pretty when she wasn't whimpering. Her face was soft and pink with fine little crumpled lines, and her blue eyes were younger than the rest of her. Sometimes when she was telling over and over again about Mr. Sakrison's strange disappearance in that young chirruping voice, I would forget that Miss Mattie was close to sixty years old.

She always wore little crocheted white gloves that somehow lent an air of dignity to the rest of her ill-assorted costume. "Outlandish," people termed Miss Mattie's get-ups. She mixed the styles of thirty years back with anything modish that took her fancy. In order to take Miss Mattie's fancy a piece of wearing apparel had only to be pink and fluffy. Chapel Grove's inhabitants never forgot the day Miss Mattie appeared with a pair of pink "teddies" pinned to her gray curls. The wispy bit of lingerie hung gracefully and shamelessly behind her poor addled head for all the louts in town to see, and they followed her to her door taunting her with ugly words.

In the main, Chapel Grove treated Miss Mattie kindly enough. She was even pointed out to visitors. But nobody ever bothered to hide the grinning and nudging that broke out wherever she appeared. There were humorists, too, who liked to josh her about Mr. Sakrison, saying rude, insulting things of him, till Miss Mattie collapsed into a damp, sobbing little heap at their feet. At such times I suffered a queer, ill-defined conviction that Chapel Grove would like to make me cry, also. Beneath the surface kindness I sensed their suspicion that I was, in some way, as different as Miss Mattie. Even my grandparents thought it was too bad that I must grow up elsewhere, and everybody smiled at my alien "accent." No matter how joyfully each summer I threw myself into the very heart of all the youthful activities there, I was aware of a subtle reserve that kept me circling just outside the true center. (Didn't they realize I belonged? Why, I'd been born there! . . . But so had Miss Mattie.)

Miss Mattie and I were both made to feel Chapel Grove's disapproval of those who do too much traveling around. Several times each year she went all the way to the State Capitol to ask the railroad officials there to help her locate Mr. Sakrison. But most of her journeys were made up to the city where one transferred to the Katy for the last four hours of the trip to Chapel Grove. The Katy rattled up there mornings and returned in the late afternoon. At least twice each week Miss Mattie boarded her for the round trip. Once arrived, Miss Mattie usually just stayed on board, if the trainmen would let her. She had no interest in the city at all. It was the journey back and forth that was important.

On the last journey we shared, the conductor did not lift me aboard the Katy or tell me to be a big girl. I was a big girl. At least I thought I was. I certainly towered over tiny Miss Mattie, and I was very conscious of the hard little buds that were my breasts—half-ashamed and half-proud of the way they strained under the tight voile dress.

Miss Mattie was having one of her rare "clear" spells. She called me by my own name and traced for me, through mazy genealogical thickets, her fourth cousinship to my mother. This didn't startle me; one way or another I was related to everybody in the county. But I was startled and disappointed to hear her talking like all the other adults I knew. She seemed tired, too, and I was suddenly shaken by a dreadful fear that one day soon she'd give up her search and admit defeat.

"Oh, Miss Mattie, please," I said, "tell me about Mr. Sakrison."

She turned to look at me, and I almost cried out when I saw she was cringing as if I were one of the town bullies eager to strike the poisonous blow. I stared back at her till the tears spilled down my cheeks.

"You've grown so tall," she whispered. "I was afraid . . ."

Both of us wept openly then with a great flutter of white handkerchiefs, and afterwards I was glad to see that the weary, grown-up look had faded from her eyes. With our heads very close together and Miss Mattie's hand in mine, she told me the story again for the last time.

"You remember, my dear—I've told you so often—he had the loveliest instincts. I never knew a Yankee could be anything but a *beast*, but he was so kind, so gentle . . . I didn't mean to fall in love with him. They say such horrid things about traveling men, 'specially Yankee traveling men. He walked me home from church that night. Wouldn't come in, since I was—to Chapel Grove's way of thinking—living alone in that big house. But he kissed me. . . . We stood under that old catalpa tree, you know the one. He hugged me so hard he crushed the roses I was wearing, and the smell of the bruised petals hung over us like a fog. We made our plans and I packed all night. Had every nigra in the house pressing and mending . . . The night went so quickly, and all of us were happy, calling back and forth and singing snatches of songs.

"Early in the morning I put on my pink organdy and Mr. Sakrison called for me and we caught the Katy to go up to the city for the wedding. It was a delirious kind of morning. I've never known the Katy to slide so smoothly along. There was something different, too, about the way the sunlight slanted across the fields. I remember thinking that if I could shift those long shadows just a fraction, the way you do a vase full of roses, I'd see a lovely new view. And there was a new, wonderful taste to the air and even to the coffee I'd put up for us!

"After a while we both felt quieter inside and Mr. Sakrison held my hand and talked of all his hopes for the future. Not just our future, either. He spoke his piece for the whole world. I was so proud of him. I'd never heard anybody speak so sadly about the nigras—their want and their fear. They were picking in the fields that day, I recall. . . . He put words to the little sick feelings I'd had at times, and I began to catch his vision . . . some of it, but not all. Not then."

The Katy whistled long and mournfully. Miss Mattie interrupted herself with "Hush!" and pressed her nose against the window to see if this, at last, was the station she'd been hunting for all those years. But it wasn't.

"You see," she said, "I was too happy to know or care which halt it was. The Katy would stop, as it always does, at every cow pasture almost. Sometimes Mr. Sakrison would swing off to light his cigar, though I never minded the odor of cigars. . . . Delicious, isn't it? But he said the scent caught in my hair, and he couldn't have that. He said my hair smelled of breezes in the springtime. . . . And then the Katy stopped at the dearest little halt! We had been aboard about two hours, I think, so it would have been almost halfway to the city. I had never noticed the place before, but then I hadn't been to the city often.

"The first thing that caught my eye was a huge camellia bush in full bloom, a red one. The fallen petals had heaped up in a ring around it, you know the way they do. I asked Mr. Sakrison to step off and cut one of the blossoms for me with his pocket knife. I didn't think the station master would mind, and there wouldn't be time enough to ask politely. But the queerest thing! The Katy just sat and huffed and puffed for the longest spell, it seemed. And things outside moved slow as molasses. There was a park with a little blue lake, and swans dipping their heads . . . and children playing. Ever so many children, and all so nicely dressed, even the little darkies. There were adults strolling there, too, all mixed in together, all colors. I wasn't a bit surprised, somehow, but I wondered at the slow, graceful movement of the scene. It was like grasses waving under water.

"Then I noticed the station itself. It was a funny little brick, octagonal building. Over the door to the waiting room it didn't say WHITE, you know. It said: WAITING ROOM. ONE AND ALL. And then, while Mr. Sakrison was still cutting the blossom, out of the station house came a colored gentleman. He walked up to Mr. Sakrison and pounded him on the back and they shook hands, and I thought to my soul they were going to embrace. . . ." Miss Mattie paused and bit her lips and twisted her hand from mine.

"Do you know, that made me angry? I looked hard at Mr. Sakrison, and for a moment he looked like any other Yankee . . . a total stranger. It was the anger that kept me sitting there staring instead of joining him. I wouldn't feel angry now. Even then—I like to remember—I fought it down and called and waved to him. But he only looked around in a puzzled kind of way . . . and walked off into the park with the man. The Katy started up again with a terrible crashing sound and fairly flew away from there.

"I was looking back, you know, and trying to reach the emergency cord . . . and weeping. I saw just the first few letters on the station sign. It said 'B R O' something. In the city I waited and waited, but Mr. Sakrison didn't come. They told me the only halt between Chapel Grove and the city that had the letters B R O was Brokaw. I hired a buggy and drove back there, but it was only a tumble-down old halt without a station house—just one of those sheltered seats. . . ."

Miss Mattie always stopped her story at this point, as she did now. Again we murmured over all the pleasant names we could think of that the halt might have possessed. As usual Miss Mattie argued strongly for her favorite. But I didn't think the word *Brotherhood* was pretty enough. While we talked I was recalling the rest of the story—the part of it I knew from a different viewpoint. Chapel Grove's version was that the Yankee traveling man had meant to fool her from the start. She had probably given him money, they said. Her folks had left her a great pile of it. And (here they pulled down their mouths) he never had any intention of marrying her and had escaped at the first opportunity. Miss Mattie had come home then and shut herself up for months. When she did show her face again it was the silly, addled face she wore now. Look at the crazy things she did—like riding the Katy up and down the line for thirty years almost every day, looking for the halt that swallowed Mr. Sakrison!

In the long gloaming that day the Katy made many halts, and I stared fiercely with Miss Mattie in utmost concentration at each one, hoping we'd recognize *something* to tell us this one was B R O.

Sure enough, we found it. It was I who spied the swans, so white in the dusk, but it was Miss Mattie who saw the camellia bush and the man who waited beside it. When the Katy stopped Miss Mattie was off as quick as a wink, but she needn't have hurried, because the Katy just stood breathing there for a long time. I saw a petal on the camellia bush fall and fall—forever it seemed—before it touched the ground. I saw Miss Mattie leaning on the man's arm, and they turned and he waved his straw hat at me, slow as slow. And, oh, Mr. Sakrison was lovely . . . but so was Miss Mattie. She was young and plumped out, especially in the bosom, and I was suddenly ashamed and crossed my arms over my chest. I was watching the swans arching their necks when the Katy started up again very quickly as if she were getting away under full steam. Only then did I remember to look for the station sign, but I was too late.

In Chapel Grove that summer it was a nine days' wonder the way poor old Mattie Compton had stepped off the Katy and disappeared without a trace. Since I was the last person who saw her, I was forced to tell again and again the dull facts of how the Katy stopped at a station whose name I neglected to notice, and of how Miss Mattie got off there and didn't get back on board. That was all I reported. Grandmother finally put a stop to the questions with her appeal to the ladies that I was "at that delicate age," and Miss Mattie's disappearance had upset me.

It hadn't, of course.

But there were things in Chapel Grove that year that did upset me. Most nights I saw the fiery cross burning on schoolhouse hill. Grandfather went about tight-lipped and angry, cursing "flap-mouthed fools." I lay awake sometimes and listened to the hounds baying down in the bottom-lands, and I wished with all my heart for money enough to ride the Katy every day, up and back, till I found the halt called B R O. There, I'd run, run and be gathered to Mr. Sakrison's heart . . . and Miss Mattie's.

The Katy local was retired years ago. There's a fine highway now to the city, and they say everybody in Chapel Grove drives there often since it's so near. I hear everything has changed. But I read in my newspaper last week how they've locked the doors to the schoolhouse and barred with guns and flaring anger the way to the hill, and I realize how terribly far Chapel Grove still is from Mr. Sakrison's halt.

1956

LEIGH BRACKETT

All the Colors of the Rainbow

IT had rained in the valley, steadily and hard, for thirty-six hours. The ground was saturated. Every fold in the rough flanks of the hills spouted a muddy torrent and the torrents flowed in sheets over the flat country below and poured through raw self-gouged channels into the river. And the river, roused from its normal meek placidity, roared and rolled like a new Mississippi, tearing away its banks, spreading wide and yellow across the fields, into the orchards and over the roads, into the streets of Grand Falls where the people had left their houses and fled to the safety of higher land. Uprooted trees and broken timbers knocked at the walls of the old brick buildings on the main street. In the lobby of the Grand Falls Hotel the brass spittoons floated ever higher, clanging mournfully when they struck their sides together.

High on the ridges that enclosed the valley to the northeast and the southwest, hidden by a careful hand, two small mechanisms hummed quietly, ceaselessly. They were called miniseeders and they were not part of Earth's native technology. Their charges would run out in a matter of days, but in the meantime they were extremely efficient, hurling a steady stream of charged particles into the sky to seed the clouds moving over the ridges.

In the valley, it continued to rain. . . .

It was his first big job on his own responsibility, with no superior closer than Galactic Center, which was a long way off. He was not at all sure he was going to be able to do it.

He said so to Ruvi, slowing down the cumbersome ground car so she could see what he meant.

"Look at it. How can this mess ever be made into a civilized continent?"

She turned her head in the quick way she had and said, "Scared, Flin?"

"I guess I am."

He was ashamed to say it, particularly since it was not really the difficulty and importance of the job that daunted him but the planet itself.

He had studied weather-control engineering on his home-world at Mintaka, which was one of the science's earliest triumphs, and he had done research and field work on five other worlds, at least two of which were in fairly early stages of control. But he had never been anywhere before that was so totally untouched by galactic civilization.

Peripheral Survey had made contact with these fringe systems only in the last couple of decades and that was far too short a time to make much of an impress on them. Even in the big urban centers an alien like himself could hardly walk down the street yet without attracting an unwelcome amount of attention, not all of it polite. Coming from the Federation worlds with their cosmopolitan populations, Flin found this hard to take.

But Galactic Center was enthusiastic about these fringe worlds because quite a few of them had an amazingly high, if highly uneven, degree of civilization which they had developed literally in their several vacuums. Center was in a rush to send them teachers and technicians and that was why he, far ahead of his due time, had been pitchforked into the position of leading a four-man planning-and-instruction team of weather-control experts.

It was a splendid opportunity with splendid possibilities for the future, and the raise in pay had enabled him to take on Ruvi as a permanent mate much sooner than he had hoped. But he hadn't bargained for the loneliness, the constant uncertainty in relationships, the lack of all the vast solid background he was used to on the Federation worlds.

Ruvi said, "All right then, I'll admit I'm scared too. And hot. Let's stop this clumsy thing and get a breath of air. Right over there looks like a good place."

He eased the car off the narrow road, onto a point of land with a few big stones around the edge to mark the drop-off. Ruvi got out and went to stand by them, looking out over the valley. The breeze pressed her thin yellow tunic against her body and ruffled the soft short silvery mass of curls around her head. Her skin glistened even under this alien sun with the dark lovely green of youth and health. Flin's heart still turned over in him every time he looked at her. He did not suppose this would last forever but as long as it did it was a beautiful sort of pain.

He made sure he had done the required things to keep the car from bolting away over the cliff and then joined her. The breeze was hot and moisture-laden, full of strange smells. The valley wound away in a series of curves with a glint of water at the bottom. On either side of it the rough ridges rolled and humped, blue in the distance where the heat haze covered them, rank green closer at hand with the shaggy woods that grew wild on them, the trees pushing and crowding for space, choked with undergrowth and strangling vines, absolutely neglected.

"I suppose," said Ruvi, "they're full of wild animals, too."

"Nothing very dangerous, I believe."

Ruvi shivered slightly. "Whenever I get just a little way out of the cities I begin to feel that I'm on a truly savage world. And everything's wrong. The trees, the flowers, even the grass-blades are the wrong shape, and the colors are all wrong, and the sky isn't at all the way it ought to be."

She laughed. "Anyone would know this was my first trip away from home."

Two huge birds came into sight over one of the ridges. They hung in the sky, wheeling in slow circles on still gray-brown wings. Instinctively Flin put his arm around Ruvi, uncertain whether the birds would attack. They did not, drifting on down over the valley where the air currents took them. There was no sign of human habitation and except for the narrow road they might have been in a complete wilderness.

"It is rather beautiful, though," Ruvi said, "in its own way."

"Yes."

"I guess that's the only standard you really should use to judge things, isn't it? Their own."

Flin said sourly, "That's easier to do when you know what 'their own' standard is. They seem to have thousands of them here. That's why Sherbondy keeps telling us to get out and see the country, to learn what his people are really like." Sherbondy was their contact with the local Government, a big hearty man with an enormous enthusiasm for all the things that were going to be done. "The only trouble with that is that it would take a lifetime to—"

There was a noise like an avalanche behind them. Flin jumped and turned around, but it was only a huge red vehicle roaring by, spouting smoke from a pipe behind the driver's compartment. The driver noticed them just before the truck passed out of sight and

Flin thought the man was going to drive it right into the woods while he was staring.

He sighed. "Let's go."

They got back into the car and Flin managed to get it back onto the road and headed in the direction he wanted to go without mishap—always, he felt, a minor triumph. The primitive vehicles that were subject to everybody's individual whim of operation on these equally primitive road systems still frightened the wits out of him after nearly six months.

It was just as hot as ever. As a gesture of courtesy, and to avoid attracting any more attention than was necessary, he had adopted the local variety of shirt and pants. Most of the men in the various instruction groups did this soon after landing. It didn't seem to matter what the women of the groups wore as long as certain puritanical tabus were observed, but the men found it less embarrassing to conform. Flin thought the garments abominably uncomfortable and envied Ruvi her relatively cool tunic.

She seemed wilted and subdued, leaning back in the corner of the wide overstuffed seat, her eyes half closed, the graceful tilted contours of her face accentuated by the gleaming of sweat on the delicate ridges.

"I think of home," she said, "and then I think of the money."

"It's something to think of."

The woods rolled by, clotted underneath with deep shadow, full of rustlings and rank dusty smells. Sometimes they passed a kind of food-raising station that had not been seen in the Federation for centuries, where part of the land was in several kinds of crops and part of it in pasture and the whole thing was operated by one man and his family. Sometimes they passed through little towns or villages with very strange names, where the people stared at them and the children pointed and yelled, *Green niggers, lookit the green niggers!*

Flin studied the houses. They were different from each other, and quite different from the ones he had grown used to in the cities, but they were all built on the same hut-based principle. He tried to imagine what life would be like in one of these towns, in one of these wooden or stone or brick houses with the queer decorations and the pointed roofs. Probably Sherbondy was right. Probably all the Federation people should try to get closer to the everyday life of the planet, familiarize themselves with what the people thought and felt, how they coped with their environment. The next few decades would see changes so radical and complete that this present life would soon begin to be forgotten. . . .

The change had already begun. This planet—the native name for it was Earth, a rather pretty one, Flin thought—had been making its first wobbling steps into space on its own when the Survey ships arrived. With Federation technicians and techniques that process had been enormously accelerated. The first manned ships built on Earth and operated by Federation-trained but native-born personnel had been licensed for limited service within the last seven or eight years. Planning surveys were under way, guided by groups like his own, not only in weather-control but in global unification, production, education, and above all pacification—the countless things that would have to be accomplished to make Earth a suitable member of the Federation.

But these things had not yet made themselves felt on the population as a whole. Most of Earth was going along just as it always had, and Flin knew from experience that many of the natives even on the administrative level were extremely touchy and proud, not inclined to accept any sudden alterations in their thinking; probably the more provincial masses were even more so. It would be necessary to win them over, to make them feel that they were equals in the task and not merely the recipients of gifts from an older and wiser culture.

It would be a long, interesting business. An energetic young man who stuck with it could make a career out of it, a satisfying and very profitable one.

The only trouble was—

Ruvi's thoughts seemed to have paralleled his own, because she said, "Are we going to stay on here?"

"We have to stay until we've finished our immediate job."

"But after that? I know some of the men have already decided to."

"The offers these people make are very good," Flin said slowly. "They'll need technicians and educators for a long time yet, and Center is in favor of it because it'll speed up integration." He reached out and patted her. "We could be rich and famous."

She smiled, very fleetingly. "All right," she said in a quiet voice, "I'll start making myself like it."

She began to stare grimly at the queerly shaped and colored trees, the peculiar houses that looked so dreadfully unfunctional, the crowds of chattering natives in the towns. Finally she shook her head and gave up, lying back with her eyes closed.

"I'll try it again sometime when it isn't so hot."

"Weather-control will fix that."

"But not for years."

They drove in silence. Flin felt vaguely ill at ease and unhappy, but he kept thinking of Sherbondy's offer and the things it might lead to for them, and he did not say anything. He did not want to commit himself with Ruvi yet, one way or the other.

About mid-afternoon there was a violent downpour of rain accompanied by thunder and lightning. As a weather expert Flin knew perfectly well what caused the disturbance, but the knowledge did nothing to decrease the effect of it on himself. Ruvi simply hid her head in the corner and shook. Flin kept on driving. If you let the natives know that you were afraid of their weather, they would never believe that you would be able to control it. He made it a practice in Washington to walk out in storms that had even the natives cowering. He could barely see the road well enough to stay on it and he was nervous about floods, but he trundled resolutely ahead.

Eventually he ran out of the storm, or it passed over. The sun came out again, boiling and steaming the saturated air. It was difficult to breathe. Great black clouds still bulked in the sky, presaging more trouble later. In the strange light the countryside took on a look completely alien and somehow ominous, the little scattered houses crouching among their weird trees like suspicious gnomes with hostile eyes, the empty fields and dripping woods suggestive of infinite loneliness.

"I'm tired and hungry," Ruvi said. "Let's stop."

"The next town that has accommodations." Flin was tired himself. He found driving a strain and yearned for the fleet little aircars that darted so easily and safely through the peaceful skies of the Federation worlds. They would not be practical here until global weather-control was an actuality.

The next town was a long way off. The road lifted and wound through low rough mountains and over brawling stream beds. The villages they passed through were very tiny, sometimes with only two or three dwellings.

The shadows grew heavy in the valleys. Ruvi began to fret a bit. Flin knew that it was only because the shadows and the wild country made her nervous, but it irritated him. He was having trouble enough of his own. An animal of some sort scuttered across the road and he nearly went into the ditch avoiding it. The light was bad. He was worried about the fuel gauge, which was low. And the road seemed to go on forever through a steadily darkening tunnel of trees.

They passed a tiny wooden temple next to one of the absolutely barbaric native burying grounds that always horrified them, the ritual stones gleaming pallid among uncut grass and briar roses. It all flashed by so quickly that Flin realized he had pushed the speed of the big car beyond the limit of safety. So he was already slowing down when he swung around a curve and came right onto a farm vehicle moving very slowly in the road. He managed to go around it without hitting anything but it gave him a sharp fright. The man driving the thing shouted after them. Flin could not hear exactly what he said but there was no doubt he was angry. After that Flin went carefully.

There began to be painted signs along the edge of the road.

Ruvi read them off. "Restaurant. Hotel. Garage. There *is* a town ahead. Grand Falls, I think."

The road passed suddenly over a crest and there was a wide irregular valley below them, full of light from the low sun which shone through a gap in the west. Perhaps Flin was in an exceptionally receptive mood but it struck him as one of the loveliest places he had seen. There was a river flashing with curious dull glints from the setting sun, rolling smoothly over a pretty little falls that burst into bright foam at the bottom. The white houses of the town were bowered in trees and blooming vines, slumbrous and peaceful in the hot evening, with one tall white spire standing over them.

"Look, I see the hotel," said Ruvi, pointing. "Oh glorious, how I will love a cool bath before dinner!"

She ran her fingers through her silvery curls and sat up straight beside him, smiling as he drove down the hill into Grand Falls.

It had rained here recently. The pavements still glistened and the air steamed with it. There was a fragrance of nameless flowers, very sweet and heavy. On the shadowy porches of the houses along the way there was a sound of voices and hidden laughter, and the small scurrying shapes of children moved under the dripping trees.

The road became the main street splashed with the crude colors of neon signs, the lighted windows showing yellow in the dusk. On both sides now there were curious low buildings, apparently quite old, built tight together so that each row looked like one building except its front was broken up into narrow vertical sections with different cornices and different patterns of wood or brickwork around the windows. They were mostly of red brick, which seemed to be a common building material, and not above two stories high.

The shops and offices were closed. The eating and drinking places were open and busy, and somewhere inside there was music playing, a strong simple beat with a high-pitched male voice wailing over it. The smell of flowers was drowned out by the pungence of hot wet brick and hotter, wetter asphalt. A few couples walked toward the gaudily lighted entrance of a theatre farther along the street, the women wearing bright-colored dresses, their long hair done in elaborate coiffures, their thick sturdy legs and arms bare. Knots of young men lounged against the walls near the drinking places. They were smoking the universal cigarettes and talking, looking after the women.

Seen close up now the town was less beautiful than it had looked from the crest. The white paint was dirty and peeling, the old buildings poorly kept up.

"Well," Flin muttered, "Sherbondy said to get off the beaten track and see the real native life undiluted."

"The hotel looks charming," Ruvi said determinedly. "I am not going to quarrel with anything."

Even in the dusk they were beginning to draw attention. First the little knots of idlers were attracted by the long gleaming car with the Government plates, and then by Flin and Ruvi themselves. There were other cars in the street, both moving and parked along the curb, but the one Flin was driving seemed to be newer and fancier than most. He could see people pointing and looking at them. He swore silently and wondered if they could have dinner sent up to their room.

The hotel was on the corner of the main intersection. It was three stories high, built of the red brick, with a crudely ornate cornice and long narrow windows. A balcony ran around its two exposed sides at the second floor level, extending over the street and supported on slender metal pillars which had once been painted white. A second tier of pillars on the balcony itself supported a roof. There were five or six oldish men sitting in chairs on the balcony, and several more below on the covered portion of the street.

Flin looked at it doubtfully. "I wonder if it *has* a bath."

Her own enthusiasm somewhat cooled, Ruvi said, "It'll do for one night. It might be a long way to the next one and I don't suppose it would be any better."

Flin grunted and pulled the car in to the curb and stopped.

There was a scraping of chair legs as the men sat forward or rose to come closer. Flin got out and walked around the car. He smiled at the men but they only stared, blowing strong smoke and squinting through it at him and the car and the license plates and then at Ruvi.

Flin turned and opened the door for her. He noticed over the low roof of the car that men were beginning to come from across the street, and already a number of boys had sprung from nowhere and were clustering like insects, their eyes bright and excited.

He helped Ruvi out, slim in her yellow tunic, her silver curls picking up the light from the tall front door of the hotel.

One of the men said in a high shrill voice, "Green as grass, by God!" There was laughter and somebody whistled.

Flin's face tightened but he did not say anything nor look at the men. He took Ruvi's arm and they went into the hotel.

They walked on a faded carpet, between islands of heavy furniture in worn leather and dusty plush. Fans turned slowly against the ceiling, barely disturbing either the hot air or the moths that had come in to flutter around the lights. There was a smell that Flin could not fully identify. Dust, the stale stink of dead tobacco, and something else—age, perhaps, and decay. Behind the large wooden desk a gray-haired man had risen from a chair and stood with his hands spread out on the desk top, watching them come.

The men from the street followed, crowding quickly through the doors. One particular man seemed to lead them, a red-faced fellow wearing an amulet on a gold chain across his broad paunch.

Flin and Ruvi stood in front of the desk. Once more Flin smiled. He said, "Good evening."

The gray-haired man glanced past them at the men who had come in, bringing with them a many-faceted odor of sweat to add to what was already inside. They had stopped talking, as though they were waiting to hear what the gray-haired man would say. The fans in the ceiling creaked gently as they turned.

The gray-haired man cleared his throat. He, too, smiled, but there was no friendliness in it.

"If you're wanting a room," he said, with unnecessary loudness as though he were speaking not to Flin but to the others in the lobby, "I'm sorry, but we're filled up."

"Filled up?" Flin repeated.

"Filled up." The gray-haired man took hold of a large book which lay open in front of him and closed it in a kind of ceremonial gesture. "You understand now, I'm not refusing you accommodations. I just don't have any available."

He glanced again at the men by the door and there was a little undertone of laughter.

"But—" said Ruvi, on a note of protest.

Flin pressed her arm and she stopped. His own face was suddenly hot. He knew the man was lying, and that his lie had been expected and was approved by the others, and that he and Ruvi were the only two people there who did not understand why. He also knew that it would do them no good to get into an argument. So he spoke, as pleasantly as he could.

"I see. Perhaps then you could tell us of another place in town—"

"Don't know of any," said the gray-haired man, shaking his head. "Don't know of a single place."

"Thank you," said Flin and turned around and walked back across the lobby, still holding Ruvi's arm.

The crowd had grown. Half the people in Grand Falls, Flin thought, must be gathered now on that one corner. The original group of men, reinforced to twice its size, blocked the doorway. They parted to let Flin and Ruvi through but they did it with a certain veiled insolence, staring hard at Ruvi who bent her head and did not look at them.

Flin walked slowly, refusing to notice them or be hurried. But their nearness, the heat and smell of them, the sense of something menacing about them that he did not understand, twisted his nerves to a painful tightness.

He passed through the door, almost brushing against a young girl who squealed and jumped back out of his way with a great show of being afraid of him. There was a bunch of young people with her, both boys and girls, and they began a great cackling and shoving. The crowd had become more vocal as it grew. There were a lot of women in it now. Flin waited politely for them to separate, moving a step at a time toward the car, and the voices flew back and forth over his head, at him, around him.

—ain't even human!

Hey, greenie, can't you afford to feed your women where you come from? Lookit how skinny—

Are they kidding with that crazy hair?

—just like I seen on the teevee, and I says to Jack then, Jack Spivey I says, if you ever see anything like them coming down the road—

Hey, greenie, is it true your women lay eggs?

Laughter. Derision. And something deeper. Something evil. Something he did not understand.

He reached the car and got Ruvi into it. As he bent close to her he whispered in her ear, in their own language, "Just take it easy. We're getting out."

Mama, how come them funny niggers got a bigger car'n we got?

Because the Government's payin' them big money to come and kindly teach us what we didn't know before.

"Please hurry," whispered Ruvi.

He started around the car to get in and found his way blocked by the red-faced man with the gold chain, and beyond him a solid mass in the street in front of the car. He sensed that they were not going to let him through, so he stopped as though he had intended to do so and spoke to the man with the chain.

"I beg your pardon—could you tell me how far it is to the next city?"

The girls were giggling loudly over Ruvi's tunic and the way she looked generally. They were all the fat-hipped, heavy-breasted local type, with thick legs and thick faces. Flin thought they had very little to criticize. Just beyond the man with the gold chain were four or five younger men standing together. They had very obviously come out of one of the taverns. They were lean rangy young men with their hair slicked down and their hips thrust forward in a curiously insolent slouch. They had eyes, Flin thought, like animals. They had been by the door when he came out. They were still looking at Ruvi.

"The next city?" said the man with the gold chain. He accented the word *city* as Flin had. He had a deep, ringing voice, apparently well used to addressing crowds. "A hundred and twenty-four miles."

A long way at night through strange country. A great anger boiled up in Flin but he kept it carefully inside.

"Thank you. I wondcr where we might get something to eat before we start?"

"Well now, it's pretty late," the man said. "Our restaurants have just about now stopped serving. Am I right, Mr. Nellis?"

"You are, Judge Shaw," said a man in the crowd.

This too was a lie, but Flin accepted it. He nodded and said, "I must have fuel. Where—"

"Garage is closed," Shaw said. "If you got enough to get you down the road apiece there's a pump at Patch's roadhouse. He's open late enough."

"Thank you," said Flin. "We will go now."

He started again, but Shaw did not move out of Flin's way. Instead he put up his hand and said, "Now just a minute there, before you go. We've been reading about you people in the papers and seeing you on the teevee but we don't get much chance to talk to celebrities here. There's some questions we'd like to ask."

The rangy young men with the animal eyes began to sidle past Shaw and behind Flin toward the car, leaving a heavy breath of liquor where they moved.

"A damn lot of questions," somebody shouted from the back, "like why the hell don't you stay home?"

"Now, now," said Shaw, waving his hand, "let's keep this friendly. Reverend, did you have something to say?"

"I certainly do," said a fat man in a soiled dark suit, shouldering his way through the crowd to stand peering at Flin. "I bet I've preached a sermon on this subject three Sundays out of five and it's the most important question facing this world today. If we don't face it, if we don't answer this question in a way that's acceptable to the Almighty, we might just as well throw away all these centuries of doing battle with Satan and admit we're licked."

"Amen," cried a woman's voice. "Amen to that, Reverend Tibbs!"

Reverend Tibbs thrust his face close to Flin's and said, "Do you consider yourselves human?"

Flin knew that he was on dangerous ground here. This was a religious man and religion was strictly a local affair, not to be discussed or meddled with in any way.

So he said cautiously, "On our own worlds we consider ourselves so. However, I am not prepared to argue it from your viewpoint, sir."

He moved toward the car, but the crowd only pulled in and held him tighter.

"Well now," said the Reverend Tibbs, "what I want to know is how you *can* call yourselves human when it says right in Scriptures that God created this good Earth here under my feet and then created man—*human* man—right out of that self-same earth. Now if you—"

"Oh, hell, save that stuff for the pulpit," said another man, pushing his way in front of Tibbs. This one was sunburned and leathery, with a lantern jaw and keen hard eyes. "I ain't worried about their souls and I don't care if they're all pups to the Beast of the Apocalypse." Now he spoke directly to Flin. "I been seeing faces on my teevee for years. Green faces like yours. Red ones, blue ones, purple ones, yellow ones—all the colors of the rainbow, and what I want to know is, ain't you got any white folks out there?"

"Yeah!" said the crowd and nodded its collective heads.

The man they called Judge Shaw nodded too and said, "I reckon you put the question for all of us, Sam."

"What I mean is," said the lantern-jawed Sam, "this here is a white town. In most other places nowadays, I understand, you'll find blacks and whites all run together like they were out of the same still, but we got kind of a different situation here, and we ain't the only ones, either. There's little pockets of us here and there, kind of holding out, you might say. And we ain't broken any laws. We didn't refuse to integrate, see. It was just that for one reason or another what colored folks there was around—"

Here the crowd snickered knowingly.

"—decided they could do better somewheres else and went there. So we didn't need to integrate. We don't have any color problem. We ain't had any for twenty years. And what's more, we don't want any."

A shout from the crowd.

Shaw said in his big booming voice, "The point we'd like to make clear to you, so you can pass it on to whoever's interested, is that some of us like to run our lives and our towns to suit ourselves. Now, this old Earth is a pretty good place just as she stands, and we never felt any need for outsiders to come and tell us what we ought to do. So we ain't any too friendly to begin with, you see? But we're not unreasonable, we're willing to listen to things so as to form our own judgments on them. Only you people had better understand right now that no matter what goes on in the big cities and other places like that, *we* aren't going to be told anything by a bunch of colored folks and it doesn't matter one damn bit what color they are. If—"

Ruvi gave a sudden cry.

Flin spun around. The young men who smelled of liquor were beside the car, all crowded together and leaning in over the door. They were laughing now and one of them said, "Aw now, what's the matter? I was just—"

"Flin, *please*!"

He could see her over their bent backs and bobbing heads, as far away from them as she could get on the seat. Other faces peered in from the opposite side, grinning, hemming her in.

Somebody said in a tone of mock reproach, "You got her scared now, Jed, ain't you ashamed?"

Flin took two steps toward the car, pushing somebody out of the way. He did not see who it was. He did not see anything but Ruvi's frightened face and the backs of the young men.

"Get away from there," he said.

The laughter stopped. The young men straightened slowly. One of them said, "Did I hear somebody say something?"

"You heard me," said Flin. "Get away from the car."

They turned around, and now the crowd was all quiet and watching. The young men were tall. They had big coarse hands, strong for any task. Their mouths hung open a little to show their teeth, and they breathed and smiled, and their eyes were cruel.

"I don't think," said the one they called Jed, "I liked the tone of your voice when you said that."

"I don't give a damn whether you liked it or not."

"You gonna take that, Jed?" somebody yelled. "From a nigger, even if he is a green one?"

There was a burst of laughter. Jed smiled and tilted his weight forward over his bent knees.

"I was just trying to talk friendly with your woman," he said. "You shouldn't object to that."

He reached out and pushed with his stiffened fingers hard against Flin's chest.

Flin turned his body and let the force of the thrust slide off his shoulder. Everything seemed to be moving very slowly, in a curiously icy vacuum which for the moment contained only himself and Jed. He was conscious of a new and terrible feeling within him, something he had never felt before. He stepped forward, lightly, strongly, not hurrying. His feet and hands performed four motions. He had done them countless times before in the gymnasium against a friendly opponent. He had never done them like this before, full force, with hate, with a dark evil brute lust to do injury. He watched the blood spurt from Jed's nose, watched him fall slowly, slowly to the pavement with his hands clutching his belly and his eyes wide open and his mouth gasping in astonishment and pain.

Outside this center of subjective time and hate in which he stood Flin sensed other movement and noise. Gradually, then with urgent swiftness, they came clear. Judge Shaw had thrust himself in front of Flin. Others were holding Jed, who was getting up. A swag-bellied man with a badge on his shirt was waving his arms, clearing people away from around the car, Jed's friends among them. There was a confused and frightening clamor of voices and over it all Shaw's big authoritative voice was shouting.

"Calm down now, everybody, we don't want any trouble here."

He turned his head and said to Flin, "I advise you to be on your way just as fast as you can go."

Flin walked around the car where the policeman had cleared the way. He got in and started the motor. The crowd surged forward as though it was going to try and stop him in spite of Shaw and the policeman.

Suddenly he cried out at them.

"Yes, we have white folks out there, about one in every ten thousand, and they don't think anything of it and neither do we. You can't hide from the universe. You're going to be tramped under with color—all the colors of the rainbow!"

And he understood then that that was exactly what they feared.

He let in the drive and sent the big car lurching forward. The people in the street scattered out of his way. There were noises as thrown objects struck the top and sides of the car and then the street was long and straight and clear ahead of him and he pushed the throttle lever all the way down.

Lights flashed by. Then there was darkness and the town was gone.

Flin eased back on the throttle. Ruvi was bent over in the seat beside him, her hands covering her face. She was not crying. He reached out and touched her shoulder. She was trembling, and so was he. He felt physically sick, but he made his voice quiet and reassuring.

"It's all right now. They're gone."

She made a sound—a whimper, an answer, he was not sure. Presently she sat erect, her hands clenched in her lap. They did not speak again. The air was cooler here but still oppressive with moisture, almost as clammy as fog against the skin. No stars showed. Off to the right there were intermittent flashes of lightning and a low growling of thunder.

A clot of red light appeared on the night ahead, resolving itself into a neon sign. Patch's. The roadhouse with the pump.

Ruvi whispered, "Don't stop. Please don't stop."

"I have to," he said gently, and pulled off the road onto a wide gravelled space beside a ramshackle frame building with dimly lighted windows. Strongly rhythmic music played inside. There was a smaller building, a dwelling-house, beside the tavern, and midway between them was a single fuel pump.

Flin stopped beside it. Hardly realizing what he was doing, he turned and fumbled in the back seat for his hat and jacket and put them on, pulling the hatbrim down to hide his face as much as possible. Ruvi had a yellow shawl that matched her tunic. She drew it over her head and shoulders and made herself small in the corner of the seat. Flin switched off the dashboard lights.

A raw-boned lanky woman came out of the dwelling. Probably the man ran the tavern, leaving her to tend to smaller matters. Trying to keep his voice steady, Flin asked her to fill the tank. She hardly glanced at him and went surlily to the pump. He got out his wallet and felt with shaking hands among the bills.

On the dark road beyond the circle of light from the tavern, a car went slowly past.

The pump mechanism clicked and rang its solemn bells and finally was still. The woman hung up the hose with a clash and came forward. Flin took a deep breath. He thrust a bill at her. "That'll be eight-eighty-seven," she said and took the bill and saw the color of the hand she took it from. She started to speak or yell, stepping back and bending suddenly in the same movement. He saw her eyes shining in the light, peering into the car. Flin had already started the motor. He roared away in a spurt of gravel, leaving the woman standing with her arm out, pointing after them.

"We won't have to stop again until we reach the city. It'll be all right there."

He threw his hat into the back seat. Ruvi let the shawl fall away from her head.

"I've never wanted to hide my face before," she said. "It's a strange feeling."

Flin muttered savagely, "I've got a lot to say but I can't say it now, not if I'm going to drive."

The road was narrow and black beneath the thunderous sky, between the empty fields and dark woods.

There was another car in the road ahead, moving slowly.

Flin overtook it.

It was well out in the middle. He waited a moment for the driver to see that he wanted to pass and make room for him. The car continued to block the road. He sounded his horn, politely at first and then loudly. The car stayed where it was, moving slower and slower so that he had to brake to keep from hitting it.

"What are they doing?" whispered Ruvi. "Why won't they let us by?"

Flin shook his head. "I don't know."

He began to be afraid.

He pulled as far as he could to the left, riding on the rough berm. He sounded the horn and tramped on the throttle.

The other car swerved too. Its rear fender struck his front one. Ruvi screamed. Flin steadied the wildly lurching car. Sweat prickled like hot needles all over his skin. He stamped his foot hard on the brake.

The other car skidded on ahead. Flin swung the wheel sharp right and pushed the throttle down, whipping the big car across the road and onto the berm on the other side.

For one brief moment he thought he was going to make it. But the other car swayed over with ruthless speed and punched and rebounded and punched again with its clattering fenders like a man pushing another with his shoulder. Holes and stones threw Flin's car back and forth. He fought to control it, hearing the voices of men shouting close by . . .

Hit the sonofabitch, knock his goddam ass off the road. That's the way—

There was a tree ahead. His headlights picked it up, brought it starkly into view, the rough-textured bark, the knots and gnarls, the uneven branches and dark leaves. Flin spun the wheel frantically. The lights made a wide slicing turn across meadow grass and weeds. The car bounded, leaped, sprang over uneven ground and fell with a jarring crash into the ditch of a little stream and died.

Silence, dazed and desperate.

Flin looked back. The other car had stopped at the side of the road. Men were getting out of it. He counted five. He thought he knew what men they were.

He reached across Ruvi and opened the door and pushed her ahead of him. "We're going to run now," he said, surprised at the flat banality of his voice, as though he were speaking to a child about some unimportant game. The car tilted that way and Ruvi slid out easily. Flin came behind her into mud and cold water that lapped around his ankles. He half helped, half threw her up the low steep bank and followed, grabbing her hand then and pulling her along.

He did not look back again. He did not have to. The men called as they ran, laughing, hooting, baying like great hounds.

Crooked fire lighted a curtain of black cloud. Flin saw trees, a clump of woods. The fire died and was followed by a hollow booming. The woods vanished. He continued to run toward them. The grass and weeds tangled around his legs. Ruvi lagged, pulling harder and harder against his grip, sobbing as she ran.

They were among the trees.

He let go of her. "Go on. Hide yourself somewhere. Don't make a sound no matter what happens."

"No. I won't leave—"

He pushed her fiercely, trying not to scream at her aloud. "Go on!"

The young men came loping through the long grass, into the trees. They had a light. Its long white beam probed and poked.

See anything?

Not yet.

Who's got the bottle? I'm dry from runnin'.

See anything?

They're in here somewhere.

Breath rasping in big hard throats, legs ripping the undergrowth, feet trampling the ground.

I'm gonna find out, by God. After I take care of that sonofabitch I'm gonna find out.

Whatcha gonna find out, Jed?

If it's true they lay eggs or not.

Laughter.

Who's got the goddam bottle?

Wait a minute, hey, right there, swing that light back, I hear the bastards moving—

Hey!

Flin turned, straightening his shoulders, standing between them and Ruvi.

One of them held the light in his face. He could not see them clearly. But he heard the voice of the one called Jed speaking to him.

"All right, greenie, you're so anxious to teach us things—it ain't fair for us to take and not give, so we got a lesson for you."

"Let my wife go," said Flin steadily. "You have no quarrel with her."

"Your wife, huh?" said Jed. "Well now, how do we know she's your wife? Was you married here under the laws of this land?"

"We were married under our own laws—"

"You hear that, boys? Well, your laws don't cut any ice with us, greenie, so it don't seem that you are man and wife as we would say. Anyway, she stays. That's part of the lesson."

Jed laughed. They all laughed.

In their own language Flin said to Ruvi, "Run now."

He sprang forward at the man holding the light.

Another man moved quickly from the side and struck him across the shoulders and neck with something more than the naked hand. A tree branch, perhaps, or a metal bar. Flin went down, stunned with pain. He heard Ruvi cry out. He tried to tell her again to run but his voice had left him. There were scuffling sounds and more cries. He tried to get up and hard-shod feet kicked him and stamped him down. Iron knuckles battered his face. Jed bent over him and shook him.

"Hold him up there, Mike, I want to be sure he hears this. You hear me, greenie? Lesson One. Niggers always keep to their own side of the road."

Crash. Blood in the mouth, and pain.

Ruvi?

"Hold him, Mike, goddam it. Lesson Two. When a white man takes a mind to a female nigger, she ain't supposed to get uppity about it. It's an honor, see? She's supposed to be real nice and happy and flattered. See?"

More blood, more pain.

Ruvi, Ruvi!

"Lesson Three. And this one you better remember and write out and hang up where all the other red, blue, green, and purple niggers can see it. *You never lay a hand on a white man.* Never. No matter what."

Ruvi was quiet. He could not hear her voice.

"You understand that? No matter what!"

Hya-hoo!

Give it to him, Jed. Tell him so he don't forget.

Dark, night, thunder, red fire, red blood, silence, distance, one long fading echoing voice.

—just like a real human woman by God what do you know—

Laughter.

Ruvi—

Gone.

There was a great deal of public indignation about it. Newspapers all over the world had editorials. The President made a statement. The Governor made a formal apology for his state and a sincere promise to find and punish the handful of men responsible for the outrage.

Grand Falls protected its own.

No witnesses could be found to identify the men involved in the incident that had occurred in town. Judge Shaw was sure he had never seen them before. So was the policeman. The attack itself had taken place out in the country, of course, and in the dark. Flin did not remember the license number of the car nor had he seen the faces of the men clearly. Neither had Ruvi. They could have been anyone from anywhere.

The name "Jed" by itself meant nothing. There were a number of Jeds in the neighborhood but they were the wrong ones. The right Jed never turned up, and if he had Flin could only have identified him definitely as the man he himself had struck in front of the Grand Falls Hotel. ("Mighty hot tempered, he seemed," Judge Shaw said. "Took offense where I'm sure none was meant. Like he just didn't understand our ways.")

So there was no finding and no punishment.

As soon as the doctors told him he was fit to travel, Flin informed his group that he was returning home. He had already been in contact with Galactic Center. Someone else would be sent to take his place. They were very angry about the whole thing at home and various steps were being considered. But since Earth was not a member planet she was not subject to galactic law, and since the future of a world was considerably more important than the actions of a few individuals or the feelings of their victims, probably nothing very drastic would be done. And Flin recognized that this was right.

Sherbondy came to see him.

"I feel responsible for all this," he said. "If I hadn't advised that trip—"

"It would have happened sooner or later," Flin said. "To us or to somebody else. Your world's got a long way to go yet."

"I wish you'd stay," said Sherbondy miserably. "I'd like to prove to you that we're not all brutes."

"You don't have to prove that. It's obvious. The trouble now is with us—with Ruvi and me."

Sherbondy looked at him, puzzled.

Flin said, "*We* are not civilized any more. Perhaps we will be again some day. I hope so. That's one reason we're going home, for psychiatric treatment of a kind we can't get here. Ruvi especially . . ."

He shook his head and began to stride up and down the room, his body taut with an anger he could only by great effort control.

"An act like that—people like that—they foul and degrade everything they touch. They pass on some of themselves. I'm full of irrational feelings now. I'm afraid of darkness and trees and quiet places. Worse than that, I'm afraid of your people. I can't go out of my rooms now without feeling as though I walk among wild beasts."

Sherbondy sighed heavily. "I can't blame you. It's a pity. You could have had a good life here, done a lot—"

"Yes," said Flin.

"Well," said Sherbondy, getting up, "I'll say good bye." He held out his hand. "I hope you don't mind shaking my hand—"

Flin hesitated, then took Sherbondy's hand briefly. "Even you," he said, with real sorrow. "You see why we must go."

Sherbondy said, "I see." He turned to the door. "God damn those bastards," he said with sudden fury. "You'd think in this day and age— Oh, hell . . . Goodbye, Flin. And the best of luck."

He went away.

Flin helped Ruvi with the last of the packing. He checked over the mass of equipment the weather-control group had brought with them for demonstration purposes, which he would be leaving behind for his successor.

Then he said quietly, "There is one more thing I have to do before we go. Don't worry about me. I'll be back in plenty of time for the take-off."

She looked at him, startled, but she did not ask any questions.

He got into his car and drove away alone.

He spoke as he drove, grimly and bitterly, to someone who was not there.

"You wanted to teach me a lesson," he said. "You did. Now I will show you how well you taught me, and how well I learned."

And that was the real evil that had been done to him and Ruvi.

The physical outrage and the pain were soon over, but the other things were harder to eradicate—the sense of injustice, the rankling fury, the blind hatred of all men whose faces were white.

Especially the hatred.

Some day, he hoped and prayed, he could be rid of that feeling, clean and whole again as he had been before it happened. But it was too soon. Far too soon now.

With two fully charged miniseeders in his pockets he drove steadily toward Grand Falls. . . .

1957

CAROL EMSHWILLER

Pelt

SHE was a white dog with a wide face and eager eyes, and this was the planet, Jaxa, in winter.

She trotted well ahead of the master, sometimes nose to ground, sometimes sniffing the air, and she didn't care if they were being watched or not. She knew that strange things skulked behind iced trees, but strangeness was her job. She had been trained for it, and crisp, glittering Jaxa was, she felt, exactly what she *had* been trained for, *born* for.

I love it, I love it . . . that was in her pointing ears, her waving tail . . . I *love* this place.

It was a world of ice, a world with the sound of breaking goblets. Each time the wind blew they came shattering down by the trayful, and each time one branch brushed against another it was, Skoal, Down the hatch, To the Queen . . . tink, tink, tink. And the sun was reflected as if from a million cut-glass punch bowls under a million crystal chandeliers.

She wore four little black boots, and each step she took sounded like two or three more goblets gone, but the sound was lost in the other tinkling, snapping, cracklings of the silver, frozen forest about her.

She had figured out at last what that hovering scent was. It had been there from the beginning, the landing two days ago, mingling with Jaxa's bitter air and seeming to be just a part of the smell of the place, she found it in criss-crossing trails about the squatting ship, and hanging, heavy and recent, in hollows behind flat-branched, piney-smelling bushes. She thought of honey and fat men and dry fur when she smelled it.

There was something big out there, and more than one of them, more than two. She wasn't sure how many. She had a feeling this was something to tell the master, but what was the signal, the agreed upon noise for: We are being watched? There was a whisper of sound, short and quick, for: Sighted close, come and shoot. And there was a noise for danger (all these through her throat mike to the receiver at the master's ear), a special, howly bark: Awful, awful—there is something awful going to happen. There was even a noise, a low rumble of sound for: Wonderful, wonderful fur—drop everything and come after *this* one. (And she knew a good fur when she saw one. She had been trained to know.) But there was no sign for: We are being watched.

She'd whined and barked when she was sure about it, but that had got her a pat on the head and a rumpling of the neck fur. "You're doing fine, Baby. This world is our oyster, all ours. All we got to do is pick up the pearls. Jaxa's what we've been waiting for." And Jaxa was, so she did her work and didn't try to tell him anymore, for what was one more strange thing in one more strange world?

She was on the trail of something now, and the master was behind her, out of sight. He'd better hurry. He'd better hurry or there'll be waiting to do, watching the thing, whatever it is, steady on until he comes, holding tight back, and that will be hard. Hurry, hurry.

She could hear the whispered whistle of a tune through the receiver at her ear and she knew he was not hurrying but just being happy. She ran on, eager, curious. She did not give the signal for hurry, but she made a hurry sound of her own, and she heard him stop whistling and whisper back into the mike, "So, so, Queen of Venus. The furs are waiting to be picked. No hurry, Baby." But morning was to her for hurry. There was time later to be tired and slow.

That fat-man honeyish smell was about, closer and strong. Her curiosity became two pronged—this smell or that? What *is* the big thing that watches? She kept to the trail she was on, though. Better to be sure, and this thing was not so elusive, not twisting and doubling back, but up ahead and going where it was going.

She topped a rise and half slid, on thick furred rump, down the other side, splattering ice. She snuffled at the bottom to be sure of the smell again, and then, nose to ground, trotted past a thick and tangled hedgerow.

She was thinking through her nose, now. The world was all smell, crisp air and sour ice and turpentine pine . . . and this animal, a urine and brown grass thing . . . and then, strong in front of her, honey-furry-fat man.

She felt it looming before she raised her head to look, and there it was, the smell in person, some taller than the master and twice as wide. Counting his doubled suit and all, twice as wide.

This was a fur! Wonderful, wonderful. But she just stood, looking up, mouth open and lips pulled back, the fur on the back of her neck rising more from the suddenness than from fear.

It was silver and black, a tiger-striped thing, and the whitish parts glistened and caught the light as the ice of Jaxa did, and sparkled and dazzled in the same way. And there, in the center of the face, was a large and terrible orange eye, rimmed in black with black radiating lines crossing the forehead and rounding the head. That spot of orange dominated the whole figure, but it was a flat, blind eye, unreal, grown out of fur. At first she saw only that spot of color, but then she noticed under it two small, red glinting eyes and they were kind, not terrible.

This was the time for the call: Come, come and get the great fur, the huge-price-tag fur for the richest lady on earth to wear and be dazzling in and most of all to pay for. But there was something about the flat, black nose and the tender, bow-shaped mouth and those kind eyes that stopped her from calling. Something master-like. She was full of wondering and indecision and she made no sound at all.

The thing spoke to her then, and its voice was a deep lullaby sound of buzzing cellos. It gestured with a thick, fur-backed hand. It promised, offered, and asked; and she listened, knowing and not knowing.

The words came slowly.

This . . . is . . . world.

Here is the sky, the earth, the ice. The heavy arms moved. The hands pointed.

We have watched you, little slave. What have you done that is free today? Take the liberty. Here is the earth for your four shoed feet, the sky of stars, the ice to drink. Do something free today. Do, do.

Nice voice, she thought, nice thing. It gives and gives . . . something.

Her ears pointed forward, then to the side, one and then the other, and then forward again. She cocked her head, but the real meaning would not come clear. She poked at the air with her nose.

Say that again, her whole body said. I almost have it. I *feel* it. Say it once more and maybe then the sense of it will come.

But the creature turned and started away quickly, very quickly for such a big thing, and disappeared behind the trees and bushes.

It seemed to shimmer itself away until the glitter was only the glitter of the ice and the black was only the thick, flat branches.

The master was close. She could hear his crackling steps coming up behind her.

She whined softly, more to herself than to him.

"Ho, the Queen, Aloora. Have you lost it?" She sniffed the ground again. The honey-furry smell was strong. She sniffed beyond, zigzagging. The trail was there. "Go to it, Baby." She loped off to a sound like Chinese wind chimes, business-like again. Her tail hung guilty, though, and she kept her head low. She had missed an important signal. She'd waited until it was too late. But was the thing a man, a master? Or a fur? She wanted to do the right thing. She always tried and tried for that, but now she was confused.

She was getting close to whatever it was she trailed, but the hovering smell was still there too, though not close. She thought of gifts. She knew that much from the slow, lullaby words, and gifts made her think of bones and meat, not the dry fishy biscuit she always got on trips like this. A trickle of drool flowed from the side of her mouth and froze in a silver thread across her shoulder.

She slowed. The thing she trailed must be there, just behind the next row of trees. She made a sound in her throat . . . ready, steady . . . and she advanced until she was sure. She sensed the shape. She didn't really see it . . . mostly it was the smell and something more in the tinkling glassware noises. She gave the signal and stood still, a furry, square imitation of a pointer. Come, hurry. This waiting is the hardest part.

He followed, beamed to her radio. "Steady, Baby. Hold that pose. Good girl, good girl." There was only the slightest twitch of her tail as she wagged it, answering him in her mind.

He came up behind her and then passed, crouched, holding the rifle before him, elbows bent. He knelt then, and waited as if at a point of his own, rifle to shoulder. Slowly he turned with the moving shadow of the beast, and shot, twice in quick succession.

They ran forward then, together, and it was what she had expected—a deer-like thing, dainty hoofs, proud head, and spotted in three colors, large grey-green rounds on tawny yellow, with tufts of that same glittering silver scattered over.

The master took out a sharp, flat bladed knife. He began to whistle out loud as he cut off the handsome head. His face was flushed.

She sat down nearby, mouth open in a kind of smile, and she watched his face as he worked. The warm smell made the drool come at the sides of her mouth and drip out to freeze on the ice and on her paws, but she sat quietly, only watching.

Between the whistlings he grunted and swore and talked to himself, and finally he had the skin and the head in a tight, inside-out bundle.

Then he came to her and patted her sides over the ribs with a flat, slap sound, and he scratched behind her ears and held a biscuit to her on his thick-gloved palm. She swallowed it whole and then watched him as he squatted on his heels and himself ate one almost like it.

Then he got up and slung the bundle of skin and head across his back. "I'll take this one, Baby. Come on, let's get one more something before lunch." He waved her to the right. "We'll make a big circle," he said.

She trotted out, glad she was not carrying anything. She found a strong smell at a patch of discolored ice and urinated on it. She sniffed and growled at a furry, mammal-smelling bird that landed in the trees above her and sent down a shower of ice slivers on her head. She zig-zagged and then turned and bit, lips drawn back in mock rage, at a branch that scraped her side.

She followed for a while the chattery sound of water streaming along under the ice, and left it where an oily, lambish smell crossed. Almost immediately she came upon them—six small, greenish balls of wool with floppy, woolly feet. The honey-fat man smell was strong here too, but she signaled for the lambs, the Come and shoot sound, and she stood again waiting for the master.

"*Good* girl!" His voice had special praise. "By God, this place is a gold mine. Hold it, Queen of Venus. Whatever it is, don't let go."

There was a fifty-yard clear view here and she stood in plain sight of the little creatures, but they didn't notice. The master came slowly and cautiously, and knelt beside her. Just as he did, there appeared at the far end of the clearing a glittering, silver and black tiger-striped man.

She heard the sharp inward breath of the master and she felt the tenseness come to him. There was a new, faint whiff of sour sweat, a stiff silence and a special way of breathing. What she felt from him made the fur rise along her back with a mixture of excitement and fear.

The tiger thing held a small packet in one hand and was peering into it and pulling at the opening in it with a blunt finger. Suddenly there was a sweep of motion beside her and five fast, frantic, shots sounded sharp in her ear. Two came after the honey-fat man had already fallen and lay like a huge, decorated sack.

The master ran forward and she came at his heels. They stopped, not too close and she watched the master looking at the big, dead, tiger head with the terrible eye. The master was breathing hard and seemed hot. His face was red and puffy looking, but his lips made a hard whitish line. He didn't whistle or talk. After a time he took out his knife. He tested the blade, making a small, bloody thread of a mark on his left thumb. Then he walked closer and she stood and watched him and whispered a questioning whine.

He stooped by the honey-fat man and it was that small, partly opened packet that he cut viciously through the center. Small round chunks fell out, bite sized chunks of dried meat and a cheesy substance and some broken bits of clear, bluish ice.

The master kicked at them. His face was not red anymore, but olive-pale. His thin mouth was open in a grin that was not a grin.

He went about the skinning then.

He did not keep the flat-faced, heavy head nor the blunt fingered hands.

The man had to make a sliding thing of two of the widest kind of flat branches to carry the new heavy fur, as well as the head and the skin of the deer. Then he started directly for the ship.

It was past eating time but she looked at his restless eyes and did not ask about it. She walked before him, staying close. She looked back often, watching him pull the sled thing by the string across his shoulder and she knew, by the way he held the rifle before him in both hands, that she should be wary.

Sometimes the damp-looking, inside-out bundle hooked on things, and the master would curse in a whisper and pull at it. She could see the bundle made him tired, and she wished he would stop for a rest and food as they usually did long before this time.

They went slowly, and the smell of honey-fat man hovered as it had from the beginning. They crossed the trails of many animals. Even, they saw another deer run off, but she knew that it was not a time for chasing.

Then another big silver and black tiger stood exactly before them. It appeared suddenly, as if actually it had been standing there all the time, and they had not been near enough to see it, to pick it out from its glistening background.

It just stood and looked and dared, and the master held his gun with both hands and looked too, and she stood between them glancing from one face to the other. She knew, after a moment, that the master would not shoot, and it seemed the tiger thing knew too, for it turned to look at her and it raised its arms and spread its fingers as if grasping at the forest on each side. It swayed a bit, like bigness off balance, and then it spoke in its tight-strung, cello tones. The words and the tone seemed the same as before.

Little slave, what have you done that is free today? Remember this is world. Do something free today. Do, do.

She knew that what it said was important to it, something she should understand, a giving and a taking away. It watched her, and she looked back with wide, innocent eyes, wanting to do the right thing, but not knowing what.

The tiger-fat man turned then, this time slowly, and left a wide back for the master and her to see, and then it half turned, throwing a quick glance over the heavy humped shoulder at the two of them. Then it moved slowly away into the trees and ice, and the master still held the gun with two hands and did not move.

The evening wind began to blow, and there sounded about them that sound of a million chandeliers tinkling and clinking like gigantic wind chimes. A furry bird, the size of a shrew and as fast, flew by between them with a miniature shriek.

She watched the master's face, and when he was ready she went along beside him. The soft sounds the honey-fat man had made echoed in her mind but had no meaning.

*

That night the master stretched the big skin on a frame and afterwards he watched the dazzle of it. He didn't talk to her. She watched him a while and then she turned around three times on her rug and lay down to sleep.

The next morning the master was slow, reluctant to go out. He studied charts of other places, round or hourglass-shaped maps with yellow dots and labels, and he drank his coffee standing up looking at them. But finally they did go out, squinting into the ringing air.

It was her world. More each day, she felt it was so, right feel, right temperature, lovely smells. She darted on ahead as usual, yet not too far today, and sometimes she stopped and waited and looked at the master's face as he came up. And sometimes she would whine a question before she went on . . . Why don't you walk brisk, brisk, and call me Queen of Venus, Aloora, Galaxa, or Bitch of Betelgeuse? Why don't you sniff like I do? Sniff, and you will be happy with this place . . . And she would run on again.

Trails were easy to find, and once more she found the oily lamb smell, and once more came upon them quickly. The master strode up beside her and raised his gun . . . but a moment later he turned, carelessly, letting himself make a loud noise, and the lambs ran. He made a face, and spit upon the ice. "Come on Queen. Let's get out of here. I'm sick of this place."

He turned and made the signal to go back, pointing with his thumb above his head in two jerks of motion.

But why, why? This is morning now and our world. She wagged her tail and gave a short bark, and looked at him, dancing a little on her back paws, begging with her whole body.

"Come on," he said.

She turned then, and took her place at his heel, head low, but eyes looking up at him, wondering if she had done something wrong, and wanting to be right and noticed and loved because he was troubled and preoccupied.

They'd gone only a few minutes on the way back when he stopped suddenly in the middle of a step, slowly put both feet flat upon the ground and stood like a soldier at a stiff, off-balance attention. There, lying in the way before them, was the huge, orange-eyed head and in front of it, as if at the end of outstretched arms, lay two leathery hands, the hairless palms up.

She made a growl deep in her throat and the master made a noise almost exactly like hers, but more a groan. She waited for him, standing as he stood, not moving, feeling his tenseness coming in to her. Yet it was just a head and two hands of no value, old ones they had had before and thrown away.

He turned and she saw a wild look in his eyes. He walked with deliberate steps, and she followed, in a wide circle about the spot. When they had skirted the place, he began to walk very fast.

They were not far from the ship. She could see its flat blackness as they drew nearer to the clearing where it was, the burned, iceless pit of spewed and blackened earth. And then she saw that the silver tiger men were there, nine of them in a wide circle, each with the honey-damp fur smell, but each with a separate particular sweetness.

The master was still walking very fast, eyes down to watch his footing, and he did not see them until he was there in the circle before them all, standing there like nine upright bears in tiger suits.

He stopped and made a whisper of a groan, and he let the gun fall low in one hand so that it hung loose with the muzzle almost touching the ground. He looked from one to the other and she looked at him, watching his pale eyes move along the circle.

"Stay," he said, and then he began to go toward the ship at an awkward limp, running and walking at the same time, banging the gun handle against the air lock as he entered.

He had said, Stay. She sat watching the ship door and moving her front paws up and down because she wanted to be walking after him. He was gone only a few minutes, though, and when he came back it was without the gun and he was holding the great fur with cut pieces of thongs dangling like ribbons along its edges where it had been tied to the stretching frame. He went at that same run-walk, unbalanced by the heavy bundle, to one of them along the circle. Three gathered together before him and refused to take it back. They pushed it, bunched loosely, back across his arms again and to it they added another large and heavy package in a parchment bag, and the master stood, with his legs wide to hold it all.

Then one honey-fat man motioned with a fur-backed hand to the ship and the bundles, and then to the ship and the master, and then to the sky. He made two sharp sounds once, and then again. And another made two different sounds, and she felt the feeling of them . . . Take your things and go home. Take them, these and these, and go.

They turned to her then and one spoke and made a wide gesture. *This is world. The sky, the earth, the ice.*

They wanted her to stay. They gave her . . . was it their world? But what good was a world?

She wagged her tail hesitantly, lowered her head and looked up at them . . . I do want to do right, to please everybody, everybody, but . . . Then she followed the master into the ship.

The locks rumbled shut. "Let's get out of here," he said. She took her place, flat on her side, take-off position. The master snapped the flat plastic sheet over her, covering head and all and, in a few minutes, they roared off.

Afterwards he opened the parchment bag. She knew what was in it. She knew he knew too, but she knew by the smell. He opened it and dumped out the head and the hands. His face was tight and his mouth stiff.

She saw him almost put the big head out the waste chute, but he didn't. He took it in to the place where he kept good heads and some odd paws or hoofs, and he put it by the others there.

Even she knew this head was different. The others were all slant-browed like she was and most had jutting snouts. This one seemed bigger than the big ones, with its heavy, ruffed fur and huge eye staring, and more grand than any of them, more terrible . . . and yet a flat face, with a delicate, black nose and tender lips.

The tenderest lips of all.

1958

ROSEL GEORGE BROWN

Car Pool

"HAPPY birthday to *you*," we all sang, except Gail, of course, who was still screaming, though not as loud.

"Well, now," I said jovially, glancing nervously about at the other air traffic, "what else can we all sing?" The singing seemed to be working nicely. They had stopped swatting each other with their lunch boxes and my experienced ear told me Gail was by this time forcing herself to scream. This should be the prelude to giving up and enjoying herself.

"*Boing* down in Texas in eighteen-ninety," Billy began, "Davy, *Davy* Eisenhower . . ."

"A-B-*C*-*D*-E—" sang Jacob.

"Dere was a little 'elicopter red and blue," Meli chirped, "flew along de airways—"

The rest came through unidentifiably.

"Ba-ba-ba," said a faint voice. Gail had given up. I longed for ears in the back of my head because victory was mine and all I needed to do was reinforce it with a little friendly conversation.

"Yes, dear?" I asked her encouragingly.

"Ba-ba-ba," was all I could make out.

"Yes, indeed. That Gail *likes* to go to Playplace."

"Ba-ba-ba!" A little irritable. She was trying to say something important. *"Ba-ba-ba!"*

I signaled for an emergency hover, turned around and presented my ear.

"Me eat de crus' of de toas'," Gail said. She beamed.

I beamed.

We managed to reach Playplace without incident, except for a man who called me an obscenity. The children and I, however, called him a great, big alligator head and on the whole, I think, we won. After all, how can a man possibly be right when faced with a woman and eight tiny children?

I herded the children through the Germ Detection Booth and Gail was returned to me with an incipient streptococcus infection.

"Couldn't you give her the shot here?" I asked. "I've *just* got her in a good mood, and if I have to turn around and take her back home . . . and besides, her mother works. There won't be anyone there."

"Verne, dear, we can't risk giving the shot until the child is perfectly adjusted to Playplace. You see, she'd connect the pain of the shot with coming to school and then she might never adjust." Mrs. Baden managed to give me her entire attention and hold a two-and-a-half-year-old child on one shoulder and greet each entering child and break up a fight between two ill-matched four-year-olds, all at the same time.

"Me stay at school," Gail said resolutely.

There was a scream from the other side of the booth. That was Billy's best friend. I waited for the other scream. That was Billy.

"Normal aggression," Mrs. Baden said with a smile.

I picked up Gail. Act first, talk later.

"Oh, *there* she is," Mrs. Baden said, taking my elbow with what could only be a third hand.

Having heard we'd have a Hiserean child in Billy's group, I managed not to look surprised.

"Mrs. His-tara, this is Verne Barrat. Her Billy will be in Hi-nin's group."

I was immediately frozen with indecision. Should I shake hands? Merely smile? Nod? Her hands looked wavery and boneless. I might injure them inadvertently.

I settled on a really good smile, all the way back to my bridge. "I am so delighted to meet you," I said. I felt as though the good will of the entire World Conference rested on my shoulders.

Her face lighted up with the most sincere look of pleasure I've ever seen. "I am glad to furnish you this delight," she said, with a good deal of lisping over the dentals, because Hisereans have foreshortened teeth. She embraced me wholeheartedly and gave me a scaly kiss on the cheek.

My first thought was that I was a success and my second thought was, Oh, God, what'll happen when Billy gets hold of little Hi-nin? Hisereans, as I understood it, simply didn't have this "normal aggression." Indeed, I sometimes have trouble believing it's really normal.

"I was thinking," Mrs. Baden said, putting down the two-and-a-half-year-old and plucking a venturesome little girl in Human Fly Shoes from the side of the building, "that you all might enjoy having Hi-nin in your car pool."

"Oh, we'd love to," I said eagerly. "We've got five mamas and eight children already, of course, but I'm sure everyone—"

"It would trouble you!" Mrs. His-tara exclaimed. Her eye stalks retracted and tears poured down her cheeks. "I do not want to be of difficulty," she said.

Since she had no apparent handkerchief and wore some sort of permanent-looking native dress, I tore a square out of my paper morning dress for her.

"You are too good!" she sobbed, fresh tears pouring out.

"No, no. I already tore out two for the children. I always get my skirts longer in cold weather because children are so careless about carrying—"

"Then we'll consider the car pool settled?" Mrs. Baden asked, coming in tactfully.

"Naturally," I said, mentally shredding my previous sentence. "We would feel so honored to have Hi-nin—"

"Do not *think* of putting yourself out. We do not have a helicopter, of course, but Hi-nin and I can so easily walk."

I was rapidly becoming unable to think of anything at all because Gail was trying to use me for a merry-go-round and I kept switching her from hand to hand and I could hear her beginning to build up the ba-bas.

"My car pool," I said, "would be terribly sad to think of Hi-nin walking."

"You would?"

"Terribly."

"In such a case—if it will give you pleasure for me to accept?"

"It would," I said fervently, holding Gail under one arm as she was beginning to kick.

And on the way home all the second thoughts began.

I would be glad to have Hi-nin in the car pool. Four of the other mamas were like me, amazed that anyone was willing to put up with her child all the way to and from Playplace. I could count on them to cooperate. But Gail's mama . . . I'd gone to Western State Preparation for Living with Regina Raymond Crowley.

I landed on the Crowley home and tooted for five minutes before I remembered that Regina was at work.

"*Ma*-ma!" Gail began.

"Wouldn't you like to come to Verne's house," I asked, "and we can call up your mama?"

"No." Well, I asked, didn't I?

I was carrying Gail down the steps from my roof when I bumped unexpectedly into Clay.

"What is that!" he exclaimed, and Gail became again flying blonde hair and kicking feet.

"Regina's child," I said. "What are you doing home?"

"Accountant sent me back. Twenty-five and a half hours is the maximum this week. Good thing, too. I've got a headache." He eyed Gail meaningfully. She was obviously not the sort of thing the doctor orders for a headache.

"I can't help it, honey," I said, sitting down on a step to tear another handkerchief square from my skirt. "I'm going to call Regina at work now."

"Don't you have a chairman to take care of things like that?"

"I am the chairman," I said proudly.

"Why in heaven's name did you let yourself get roped into something like that?"

"I was *selected* by Mrs. Baden!"

"Obscenity," said Clay. It is his privilege, of course, to use this word.

The arty little store where Regina works has a telephane as well as a telephone, and in color, at that. So I could see Regina in full color, taking her own good time about switching on the sound. She switched on as a sort of afterthought and tilted her nose at me. I don't suppose she can really tilt her nose up and down, but she always gives that impression.

"Gail has an incipient streptococcus infection," I said. "They sent her home."

"*Ma*-ma!" Gail cried.

"Why didn't they give her a shot there? That's what they did with my niece last year."

I explained why not.

Regina sighed resignedly. "Verne, people can talk you into anything. There are times when you have to be firm. I work, girl. That's why I put Gail in Playplace. I can't leave here until twelve o'clock."

"But what'll I do with Gail?"

"Take her back. Or you keep her until I get home. Sorry, Verne, but you got yourself into this."

I switched off, furious.

Then I remembered Hi-nin. I couldn't be furious. I was going to have to get Regina's cooperation.

I picked up Gail and went into the bedroom. "I do not dislike Regina Crowley," I wrote with black crayola on a piece of note paper. I stuck it into a crevice of my mirror and gave Gail my bare-shoulder decorations to play with while I concentrated on thinking up reasons why I should not dislike Regina Crowley.

"I do," Clay said, sneaking up so quietly I jumped two feet.

"So do I," I said, gazing wearily at my note. "But I have to have her in a good mood. You see, there's this Hiserean child and since I'm chairman of the car pool, I have to—"

"*Don't* tell me about it," Clay said. "My advice to you is get elephantiasis of your steering foot and give the whole thing up now." He glanced meaningfully at Gail, who couldn't possibly be bothering him. She was playing quietly on the floor, pulling the suction disks off my jewelry and sticking them on her legs.

When I finally got Gail home, she sped into her mother's arms and I couldn't help being a little irritated because I had been practically swinging from the ceiling dust controls to ingratiate myself, and her mama just said, "Oh, hi," and Gail was satisfied.

"By the way," I said, watching Regina hang up her dark blue hand-woven jacket, "you wouldn't mind picking up an extra child tomorrow, would you?"

"Mind! Certainly I mind. I've got as much as I can do with my job and Gail and eight children in the heli already."

"It's a Hiserean child," I said. "The mother is so lovely, Regina. She didn't want us to go to any trouble."

"That's fine. Because I'm not going to go to any trouble."

I put my fists behind my back. "Of course I understand, Regina. I think it's remarkable that you manage to do so much. And keep up with your art things as you do. But don't you think it would be an interesting experience to have a Hiserean child in the pool?"

Regina pulled off her hand-woven wrap-skirt and I was shocked to see she wore a real boudoir slip to work.

"Everybody to their own interesting experiences," she said, laughing at me. This was obviously one of her triple-level remarks.

"De gustibus," I said, to show I know a few arty things myself, "non disputandum est."

"You have such moments, Verne! Have you ever seen a Hiserean child?"

"I saw one today."

"Well."

"Well?"

"De gustibus, as you said. You know the other children will eat it alive, don't you? *Your* child will. Now Gail . . ."

It's true that Gail never kicks anyone small enough to kick back. It's also true that Billy bites.

I unclenched my fists and stretched up with a deep breath so as to relax my stomach and improve my posture.

"Hiserean children," I pointed out, "are going to have to be adjusted to our society. As I understand it, they're here to stay. Their sun blew up behind them and personally I think we're lucky they happened to drift here."

"I don't see why it's so lucky. I wish we'd gotten one of the ships full of scientific information. Or their top scientists. Or artists, for that matter. All *we* got were plain people. If you like to call them people."

"They're at least educated people with good sense. And we've got their ship to take apart and learn things from. And their books and, after all, some music and their gestural art. I should think you artists would find that real avant garde."

"Just hearing you say it like that is enough to kill Hiserean art."

"Regina, I know you think I'm a prig, but that isn't the point. And if it matters to you, I'm *not* a prig."

"Do you wear boudoir slips?" Regina was biting a real smile.

"No, I don't. But I'd like to."

"Then why don't you?"

"Because I put one on once and I thought I looked absolutely devastating and you know what my husband said?"

"I won't try to guess Clay's bon mot."

"He said, 'What did you put that on for?'"

Regina laughed until she popped a snap on her paper house dress. "But seriously," she said finally, "if he didn't know, why didn't you tell him?"

"That's not the point. The point is I am not the boudoir-slip type. My unmentionables are unmentionable for esthetic reasons only."

Regina laughed again. "Really, Verne, you're not half bad when you try."

"If you honestly think I'm not half bad, could you do it just as a favor to me? Pick up Hi-nin when you have the car pool?"

"The Hiserean child? No."

"Please, Regina. I'd do it *for* you except that the children would notice and it would get back to Mrs. His-tara. If there's anything I could do for you in return—"

"What could you possibly do?"

"I don't know. But I *can't* go back and tell that dear creature our car pool doesn't want her."

"*Stop* looking so intense. That's what keeps you from being the boudoir-slip type. You always look as though you're going out to break up a saloon or campaign for better Public Child Protection. The boudoir slip requires a languorous expression."

"Phooey to looking languorous. And phooey to boudoir slips. I'd wear diapers to nursery school if you'd change your mind about taking along Hi-nin."

"Would you wear a boudoir slip?"

"I—hell, yes."

"And nothing else?"

"Only my various means of support. And my respectability."

Regina laughed her tiger-on-the-third-Christian laugh. "What I want to find out," she said, "is how you manage the respectability bit."

It dawned on me while I was grinding the pepper for Clay's salad that Regina had explained herself. All of a sudden I saw straight through her and I wondered why I hadn't seen it before. Regina *envied* me.

Now on the face of it, that seemed unlikely. But it occurred to me that Regina's parents had been the poor but honest and uneducated sort that simply are never asked to chaperone school parties. And the fact is that they were not what Regina thought of as respectable, though it never occurred to anyone but her that it mattered. And since all her culture was acquired after the age of thirteen, she felt it didn't fit properly and that's why she went out of her way to be arty-arty.

Whereas I took for granted all the things Regina had learned so painstakingly, and this in turn was what made me so irritatingly respectable.

As Regina had suggested, perhaps it *is* the expression on one's face that makes the difference.

"Hey!" a cop yelled, pulling up as close to us as his rotors would allow. "What the hell?"

"I beg your pardon," I said frigidly. It is very frigid in November if you are out in a helicopter dressed only in a boudoir slip.

"Look de bleesemans!" Gail cried.

"He might shoot everybody!" Billy warned.

Meli began to cry loudly. "He might *choot*! *Ma*-ma!"

"Pardon me, madam," the cop said, and beat a hasty retreat.

When we landed on Hi-nin's roof, Mrs. His-tara came up with him. She looked at me sympathetically. "You are perhaps molting, beloved friend?" Her large eyes retracted and filled with tears. "Such a season!"

"No—no, dear. Just—getting a little fresh air."

I put Hi-nin on the front seat with me. He gave me a big-eyed, toothless smile and sat down in perfect quiet, except for the soft, almost sea sound of his breathing.

It was during one of those brief and infrequent silences we have that I noticed something was amiss. No sea sound.

I looked around to find Billy's hands around Hi-nin's throat.

"Billy!" I screamed.

"Aw!" he said, and let go.

Hi-nin began to breathe again in a violent, choked way.

"Billy," I said, wondering if I could keep myself from simply throwing my son out of the helicopter, "Billy . . ."

"It is nothing, nice mama," Hi-nin said, still choking.

"Billy." I didn't trust myself to speak any further. I reached around and spanked him until my hand was sore. "If you *ever* do that again—"

"*Waa!*" Billy bawled. I'm sure he could be heard quite plainly by the men building the new astronomical station on the Moon.

I put Hi-nin on my lap and kept him there. "That's just Billy's way of making friends," I whispered to him.

Under Billy's leadership, several other children began to cry, and all in all it was not a well-integrated, love-sharing group that I lifted down from the heli at Playplace.

"The children always sense it, don't they," Mrs. Baden said with her gentle smile, "when we don't feel comfortable about a situation?"

"*Comfortable!*" I cried. It seemed to me the day had become blazing hot and I didn't remember what I was dressed in until I tried to take off my jacket. "My son is an inhuman monster. He tried to—to—" I could feel a big sob coming on.

"Bite?" Mrs. Baden supplied helpfully.

"Strangle," I managed to blurt out.

"We'll be especially considerate of Billy today," Mrs. Baden said. "He'll be feeling guilty and he senses your discomfort about his aggression."

"*Senses* it! I all but tore him limb from limb! That dear little Hiserean child—"

"I do not want to be of difficulty," Hi-nin said, tears pouring out of those great, big eyes.

Tears were pouring out of my small blue eyes by this time and Mr. Grantham, who brings a set of grandchildren, came by and patted my shoulder.

"Chin up!" he said. "Eyes front!"

Then he looked at his hand and my recently patted shoulder.

"Oh, excuse me," he said. "Would you like to borrow my jacket?"

I shook my head, acutely aware, suddenly, that Mr. Grantham is not a doddering old grandfather but a young and handsome man. And all he thought about my bare shoulder was that it ought to be covered.

"You just run along," Mrs. Baden said. "We'll let Billy strangle the pneumatic dog and everything will be just fine. Oh, and dear—I don't know whether you've noticed it—you don't have on a dress."

I went home and sat in front of the mirror feeling miserable in several different directions. If Regina Raymond Crowley appeared in public dressed only in a boudoir slip, people would think all sorts of wicked things. When I appeared in public in a boudoir slip, everybody thought I was just a little absentminded.

This, I thought, is a hell of a thing to worry about. And then I thought, Oh, phooey. If even I think I'm respectable, what can I expect other people to think?

I took down the note on the mirror about Regina. No wonder I didn't like her! I turned the paper over and wrote "Phooey to me!" with my eyebrow pencil.

I was still regarding the note and trying to argue myself into a better mood when Clay came tramping down from work at three o'clock.

"Why are you sitting around in a boudoir slip?" he asked.

"You're a double-dyed louse and a great, big alligator head," I told him.

"Don't mention it," he said. "Where's Billy?"

"Taking his nap. Tell me the truth, Clay. The absolute truth."

Clay looked at me suspiciously. "I'd planned on a little golf this afternoon."

"This won't take a minute. I don't ask you things like this all the time, now do I?"

"I still don't know what you're talking about."

I took a deep breath. "Clay, is there anything about me, anything at all, that is not respectable?"

"There is *not*," he said.

"Well—I guess that's all there is to it," I sighed. I pulled off my boudoir slip and got a neat paper one out of the slot. "Anyway," I said bravely, "boudoir slips have to be laundered."

Clay looked at me curiously for a moment and then said, "This looks like a good afternoon to go play golf."

"Do you think there's anything not respectable about Regina Crowley?"

"There is *everything* not respectable about Regina Crowley," Clay said vehemently.

"You see?"

"Frankly, no."

"Well, do you think her husband uses that tone of voice when he says, 'There is *everything* respectable about Verne Barrat?'"

"I don't know why he should say that at all."

"She might ask him."

"Darling, you're mad as a hatter," Clay said, kissing me good-by.

"Do you really think so?"

"Of course not," Clay roared as he tramped up the steps to the heli.

About nine o'clock the next morning I heard a heli landing on the roof and I thought, Now who? There was much tooting, and when I went up, Regina practically threw Hi-nin at me.

"I told you so," she snapped at me. Her face was burning red and she wasn't bothering to tilt her nose.

"What happened? Why did you bring him back to *me*?"

"His hand," she said, and took off.

Hand? He was holding one hand over the other. No! I grabbed his hands to see what it was.

One hand had obviously been bitten off at the wrist. He was holding the wound with the tentacles of his other little boneless hand. There was very little blood.

"It is as nothing," he said, but when I cradled him in my arms, I could feel him shaking all over.

"It will grow back," he said.

Would it?

I took him in the heli and held him while I drove. I could feel him trying to stop himself from shaking, but he couldn't.

"Does it hurt very much?" I asked.

"The pain is small," he said. "It is the fear. The fear is terrible. I am unable to swallow it."

I was unable to swallow it, too.

"The hand," said Mrs. His-tara without concern, "will grow back. But the things within my son . . ." She, too, began to tremble involuntarily.

"Billy," I began, feeling the blood come through my lower lip, "Billy and I are . . ." It was too inadequate to say it.

"It was not Billy," Hi-nin said without rancor. "It was Gail."

"Gail! Gail doesn't bite!" But she had, and I broke down and plain cried.

"Do not trouble yourself," said Mrs. His-tara. "My son receives from this a wound that does not heal. On Hiserea he would be forever sick, you understand. On your world, where everyone is born with this open wound, it will be his protection. So Mrs. Baden warned me and I think she is wise."

As soon as I got home, I called up Regina. She looked pale and lifeless against the gaudy, irresponsible objects in the art shop.

"It wasn't my fault," she said quickly. "I can't drive and watch the children at the same time. I told you the children would eat . . ." She stopped, and for the first time I saw Regina really horrified with herself.

"Nobody said it was your fault. But don't you think you could have taken Hi-nin home yourself? To show Mrs. His-tara that—I don't know what it would show."

It reminded me, somehow, of the time Regina stepped on a lizard and left it in great pain, pulling itself along by its tiny front paws, and I had said, "Regina, you can't leave that poor thing suffering," and she had said, "Well, I didn't step on it on purpose," and I had said, "Somebody's got to kill it now," and she had said, "I've got a class." I could still feel the crunch of it under my foot as its tiny life went out.

"Sorry, Verne," she said, "you got yourself into this," and hung up.

That night Regina called me. "Can you give blood?" she asked.

"Yes," I said. "If I stuff myself, I can get the scales up to a hundred and ten pounds."

"What type?"

"B. Rh positive."

"Thought you told me that once. Gail is in the hospital. They have to replace every drop of blood in her body. She may die anyhow."

I thought of the little fluff and squeak that was Gail. I eat de crus' of de toas'.

"What's the matter with her?" I asked fearfully.

"That damn Hiserean child is *poison*. Gail had a little cut inside her mouth from where she fell off the slide at school."

"I'll be at the hospital in ten minutes," I said, and hung up shakily. "Dinner is set for seven-thirty," I told Clay and Billy, and rushed out.

The first person I saw at the hospital was not Regina. It was Mrs. His-tara.

"How did you know?" I asked. Her integument was dull now and there were patches of scales rubbed off. Her eyes were almost not visible.

"Mrs. Crowley called me," she said. "In any case I would have been here. There is in Hi-nin also of poison. There remains for him only the Return Home. We must rejoice for him."

The smile she brought forth was more than I could bear.

"Gail's germs were poison to him?"

"Oh, no. He poisons himself. It is an ancient hormone, from the early days of our race when we had what your Mrs. Baden so wisely calls aggression. It is dormant in us since before the accounting of our history. An adult Hiserean, perhaps, could fight his emotions and cure himself. Hi-nin has no weapons—so your physicians have explained it to me, from our scientific books. How can I doubt that they are right?"

How could I doubt it, either? It would be, I thought, rather like a massive overdose of adrenalin. Psychogenic, of course, but what help was it to know that? Would there be some organ in Hi-nin a surgeon could remove? Like the adrenals in humans, perhaps?

Of course not. If they could have, they would have.

I hurried on to find the room where Gail was. She was not pale, as I had expected, but pink-cheeked and bright-eyed. They were probably putting in more blood than they were taking out. There were two of the other mamas from our car pool, waiting their turns.

Regina was sitting by the bed, her face ugly and swollen from crying.

"She looks just fine!" I exclaimed.

"Only in the last fifteen minutes," she said. "When I called you, she was like ice. Her eyes didn't move."

"We're lucky with Gail. Did you know about Hi-nin?"

"The little animal!" she said. "He's the one that did it."

"He didn't do anything, Regina, and you know it."

"He shouldn't have been in the car pool. He shouldn't be with human children at all."

"He's going to die," I said quickly, before she had time to say things she'd have nightmares about later on.

"Sorry," Regina said, because we were all looking at her and because her child was pink and beautiful and healthy while Hi-nin . . .

"Regina," I said, "what did you do after it happened?"

"*Do!* It scared the hell out of me—that creature shaking all over and Gail screaming. At first I didn't know what had happened. Then I saw that *thing* flopping around on the front seat and I screamed and threw it out of the window. And then I noticed Hi-nin's wrist, or whatever you call it. I said, 'Oh, God, I *knew* you'd get us in trouble!' But the creature didn't say anything. He just sat there. And I let the other children off and brought Hi-nin to you because I didn't want to get involved with that Mrs. Baden."

"And Gail?"

"She seemed all right. She just climbed in the back with the other children and pretty soon they were all laughing."

"And all that time little Hi-nin . . . Regina, didn't you even pat him or hold him or kiss it for him or anything?"

"*Kiss* it!"

At that moment Mrs. His-tara came in, with Mrs. Baden and a doctor behind her. I should have known. Mrs. Baden didn't leave people to fight battles alone.

Mrs. His-tara looked at Mrs. Baden, but Mrs. Baden only nodded and smiled encouragingly at her.

The doctor was gently pulling the needle out of Gail's vein. The room was silent. Even Gail sat large-eyed and solemn.

"Mrs. Crowley," Mrs. His-tara began, obviously dragging each word up with great effort, "would it be accurate to tell my son that Gail has received no hurt from him? We must, you see, prepare him for the Return Home."

Regina looked around at us and at Gail. She hadn't dared let herself look at Mrs. His-tara yet.

"Doctor!" Regina called suddenly. "Look at Gail's mouth!"

Even from where I was, I could see it. A scaly growth along both lips.

"That's a temporary effect of the serum," the doctor said. "We tried an antitoxin before we decided to change the blood. It is nothing to worry about."

"Oh."

"Mrs. Crowley," Mrs. His-tara began again, "it is much to ask, but at such a moment, much is required. If you could come yourself, and if Gail could endure to be carried . . ."

But Gail did, indeed, look queer, and she stretched out her arms not to her mother but to Mrs. His-tara.

"The tides," Mrs. His-tara said, "have cast us up a miracle."

She gathered Gail into the boneless cradle of her curved arms.

Regina took her sunglasses out of her purse and hid her eyes. "Mind your own damned business," she told Mrs. Baden and me.

"It *is* our damned business," I whispered to Mrs. Baden, and she held my arm as we followed Regina down the hall.

Mrs. His-tara threaded her way through a cordon of other Hisereans who must have been flown in for the occasion. I couldn't see the children, but I could hear them.

"Him cold!" said Gail. "Him scared!"

"He's scared of you," Regina said. "We're sorry, Gail. Tell him we're sorry. We didn't understand."

Gail laughed. A loud and healthy laugh.

"Gail sorry," she said. "Me thought you was to eat."

There was a small sound. I thought it was from Hi-nin and I held Mrs. Baden's hand as though it were my only link to a sane world.

"Dat a joke," Gail said. "Hi-nin 'posed to laugh!"

Then there was a silence and Regina started to say something but Mrs. His-tara whispered, "Please! It is a thought between the children."

Then there was a small, quiet laugh from Hi-nin. "In truth," he said with that oh, so familiar lisp, "it is funny."

"Me don't do it again," Gail said, solemn now.

When I got home it was so late that the stars were sliding down the sky and I just knew Clay wouldn't have thought to turn the parking lights on. But he had.

Furthermore, he was still up.

"Were you worried?" I asked delightedly.

"No. Regina called a couple of hours ago."

"Regina?"

"She said she was concerned about the expression on your face."

Clay handed me a present, all wrapped in gold stickum with an electronic butterfly bouncing airily around on it.

I peeled the paper off carefully, to save it for Billy, and set the butterfly on the sticky side.

Inside the box was a gorgeous blue fluffy affair of no apparent utility.

"Oh, *Clay*!" I gasped. "I can't wear anything like *this*!" I slipped out of my paper clothes and the gown slithered around me.

Hastily, I pulled the pins out of my hair, brushed it back and smeared on some lipstick.

"I look silly," I said. "I'm all the wrong type." My little crayola note was still stuck in the mirror. Phooey to me. "You're laughing at me."

"I'm not. You don't really look respectable at all, Verne."

I ran into the dining area. "Regina told you about the boudoir slip!"

I heard Clay stumble over a chair in the dark.

"Obscenity!" he said. "All right, she did. So what? I think you look like a call girl."

I ran into the living room and hid behind the sofa. "Do you really, truly think so?"

"Absolutely!" Another chair clattered and Clay toed the living room lights. "Ah!" he said. "I've got you cornered. You look like a chorus girl. You look like an easy pickup. You look like a dirty little—"

"Stop," I cried, "while you're still winning!"

1959

ELIZABETH MANN BORGESE

For Sale, Reasonable

*TO Whom It May Concern:**

I should like to apply for work on a permanent basis. It is difficult, I know, to compete with machines today, but I offer special features that few machines can match, and the savings involved in acquiring my services are substantial.

I've won the telequiz on football, on vital statistics, and on the history of Italian miniature painting. Even while operating sixteen hours a day in any given field, I am able to "learn" a new matter within the span of a week, the facts being fed to me by a radio under the pillow during the four hours at night I need for recharging. I can play at one time six games of bridge without looking at any of them. I can beat the most complex electronic chess machine and resist for eighty days the robot that plays "odd and even."

I am conditioned to work immediately on calculating long-range effects of new methods of salesmanship on the shopping habits of middle-aged women in small and medium-sized rural communities in the corn-belt area. You may install me free of charge for a trial period of ninety days.

**The following document of the year 1979 is among the earliest of this type on record. We reproduce it in its entirety because it sheds some light on the curious mimetic relationship, the puzzling transfer of qualities between man and machine, that began to become noticeable around the middle of the twentieth century. S.T. was purchased by the Inland Joy Development Corporation (I.J.D.C.) on April 24, 1980. The concept of liberty having been undermined by the political, social, and economic practices of the period, it was natural that the contract between S.T. and I.J.D.C. initiated a long series of similar self-sales, which, in turn, gave rise to the exorbitantly rich but reliably docile class of "promach" brains or Neo-Helots.*

The services I can offer are hard for a machine to beat. The robot gets out of order once in a while, suffers indispositions entailing expensive repairs. My physical condition is stabilized: I've had a flu shot and a cold shot and an omnivalent antibacterial. It would take something very unusual to strip my gears. I've had a brain wash, a pain screen, and a dissexer, and my disposition, you will understand, is very gentle indeed—a claim which cannot be made for the machine in each and every case.

I am not divulging any secret, although the press has been suppressing the facts, if I remind you that there's been trouble brewing with the machines of late, from the—how shall I call it—psycho-technical angle. Played-down headings, such as "Belgium's New Giant Brain Refuses to Think," or "Harvard Supercalculator's Forecast on U.S. Happy-Pill Consumption Undecodable," crop up again and again on the back pages of our papers, despite the above-mentioned tendency to sit on the news. The plain fact is that the machines are jealous of men, are beginning to feel the pinch of human competition. In isolation, no doubt, the perfectly balanced giant brain is pure of any emotions, since its psychological troubles arise largely from the social context (as, for that matter, is the case with man). However, the fact is that operators are stealthily feeding the brains facts which are none of a machine's business.

The operators tell them of all that man has done and man can do, and then they solicit answers to heckling questions. The result is that the machines "refuse to think," or release undecodable streams of signals on which float bits of mutilated, obscene messages. Or they repeat "Do it yourself, do it yourself," and blow their multi-million-dollar tops; or they may hit the operator with painful electrical charges. In Germany, this kind of behavior on the part of numerous machines has amounted recently to what might be termed a strike—a thing unheard of among men for more than fifteen years. The dismantling of obsolete calculators, as is well known, has produced veritable duels between man and machine, and cost the life of many an operator. The dismantling, of course, is now effected exclusively by atomic charges—a heroic end, undoubtedly, for the calculator, but at the same time a regrettable loss of valuable, still usable parts.

I do not dispute the machine's superiority in certain fields, fields in which the human brain will never equal its productivity. But there are numerous types of work which can be equally well accomplished by men, and in these, I submit, it would be rational to employ men, saving precious hours of machine power and cutting the cost and the trouble of plant management.

The financial saving involved in employing men would be substantial. It is undoubtedly more costly to maintain a calculator than to satisfy the simple needs of man, and the capital investment in the purchase of a machine is gigantic. I grant you that, in principle, such investment in the means of production is sane, and the feeling of owning such means of production, elating. (The Holy Father himself has recently hinted that automation should not put an end to private property.)

But there is no reason on earth why I should not offer my services—viz., myself—on the terms at which you acquire a calculator—only much cheaper. (The machines will sputter with envy.)

I offer myself at the humble price of dollars ninety-nine thousand, five hundred, plus sales tax. (The giant brain, you realize, cost millions.) That will buy me a home in Garden City with three baths and a built-in kitchen. It will buy me a pool with tiles from Ravenna and a cruise to Hawaii and an English lawn with Greek statuettes (all that is much cheaper than the machine) and a set of new teeth and contact lenses and a double garage and two thousand pounds of books with Florentine bindings. It will aircool the house and see the children through the most exclusive of schools (the contract should grant you an option on one or more of my children, as you wish), a canoe with a sail and a dog with a pedigree (the price of a good machine is frighteningly high).

Upon the signing of the sale's contract you pay for my upkeep a mere four or five hundred dollars a month. For that you acquire all my working hours—I am ready at once to work on new methods of stimulating the spending on leisure industries by retired oldsters in suburban areas of the metropolis; further, you may guide my hobbies—I'll turn over to you any gains from telequizes and similar games (you could not, of course, enter a machine in a telequiz, could you?).

At the end of a five-year period you may transfer the contract, if you choose, to another purchaser. Acquiring my services, he would return your investment to you, probably with a capital gain—where the machine depreciates, becomes obsolete (who would want to be bothered with a second-hand giant brain?), my value, and therefore my price, would go up as a result of vocational, on-the-job education.

The deal, you will realize, is equally profitable for purchaser and purchased.

It will buy me a mixmaster and a superwasher and an electric reading machine and a tankish home sweeper and a woe-grinding garbage disposal and an automatic you-know-what.

It will buy me machines galore which will, in turn, save me precious hours of manpower, and set me free.

Very sincerely yours,

S.T.

1959

DORIS PITKIN BUCK

Birth of a Gardener

PAYNE knew that when he got home he would find Lee still spraining her mind over A *Non-Mathematical Approach to Physics*. A woman with Lee's hair didn't have to be intellectual. After all, she had a green thumb. Why couldn't his wife—Payne tried to put it with all charity—reconcile herself to the fact that his interests were off limits?

He turned into his driveway and kicked a pebble. Then he smiled. Here he was—Fermi Researcher at the Droxden Foundation, famous in two hemispheres for his work on anti-matter—acting like a bad-tempered child because he knew no way to manage a beautiful, stupid, absurdly stubborn wife.

His smile grew rather fixed. Why did she have to keep asking questions night after night when he got home tired from his laboratory! Lee never understood the answers when he did give them to her. Why—

He had an obscure, entirely irrational feeling that tonight his fatigue held some sort of menace both to him and to his wife; that barriers melted in his weariness, as they melt away in sleep; that what comes out when they are down is anyone's horrified guess. Payne did not shiver, but for a moment he thought he was going to. Then he told himself that he knew what was wrong. He had not admitted until this evening how dreary his marriage was growing.

He stopped where elms arched over the drive and made a green tunnel of sorts that held its own twilight. Lee's flowerbeds lay beyond the end of the tube, suggesting something on a slide under a microscope, or at least he was sure Lee, if she were around, would see them that way.

Payne looked at drifts of peonies and iris with a few weedy spears of grass reaching upward for light. He stopped by a clump and gathered some flowers. Fagged though he was, he walked toward the house with a purposeful swing to his stride. He held the bunch behind his back, like a surprise for a child.

When he opened the front door, he found Lee sitting beyond the living room, her dark head bent over the non-mathematical approach. The rooms, as so often happened now, appeared messy out of all proportion to their actual disorder. Payne knew, even though he did not see, where dust had gathered behind furniture in the corners.

"Lee," he walked toward her, speaking more sharply than he meant, "give it up!"

She held out her book with its gaily diagrammatic cover, her dark eyes those of a stricken small-girl. "You mean . . . give up this?"

"Exactly. You aren't going to be an intellectual because you try to read something elementary on physics." Wearing the smile, he sat down near her. "Remember the Chinese saying—"

She shook her head.

"If you would be happy for an hour, get drunk; happy for an evening, roast a pig; happy for three days, get married." She winced and Payne with a slight flourish produced the yellow blooms. "If you would be happy for life, plant a garden."

She startled him by saying, "That wasn't why I evoked you."

"Evoked me?"

"You can call it that. Don't you see? I always wanted you even when I was little, though I didn't know then *exactly* how you'd look.

I kept adding details: hair just as bright as brass and all lovely and shiny; a straight way of standing; large hands but with an awfully nice shape. I just thought very hard and—finally one day, there you were."

"Nonsense. I happened to be passing by when you were going into the subway and dropped some nickels. I never realized until tonight that you dropped them on purpose."

"But I didn't. Things just happened, after I . . ." She took his flowers and added them without interest to some already in a vase, while she explained, "Things do happen sometimes in the most marvellous way. But now they go . . ." the words came out like a barely heard sigh, "they go all wrong."

He tried stroking her hand. "Naturally they're wrong while you prefer physics to flowers. Stop playing around with a rigorous logic that isn't your style."

"Rigorous logic!" She pulled her hand back. "Rigor mortis!"

Payne's eyes opened wide. For a moment they looked like blue rifts in a glacier. "Oh, are you familiar enough with my theories to criticize them?"

Lee was instantly humble. "I only meant—I don't know what I meant. I think I wanted to say: Isn't there some way you could teach me to *see* physics? I—I skipped to the back of the book and was reading about—" she brought the term out proudly, "about neutrinos. I can see them all round."

"You can? Really? I congratulate you, Rosalie. You're more advanced than any of the men at the Foundation."

"But I can see them." Her tone was slightly injured. "They're like the Cheshire Cat's grin that stayed on in the air after the Cat vanished. You know, in *Alice in Wonderland*."

"Go on. I'm fascinated."

Lee only said in a changed voice, "If I'm not your real companion, if you won't let me be, I'm not anything—not anything at all. Perhaps I shall . . ."

She put her hand with her handkerchief to her mouth suddenly. She choked back whatever she might have told Payne. Finally she spoke intensely, "I'm trying so hard, so hard, to get where we can talk together, or at least where I can listen."

"Listen? How can I talk with you about my work? Tonight I want to figure why a pi meson, a negative one, decays the way it does when you shoot it through liquid hydrogen." He added, "I'd like to go on thinking about that right now."

She laid her hands on his arm. "But . . . but our marriage—"

"No problem at all. Anyway, I told you how to solve it. Why don't you listen to what I say about the garden instead of talking about Cheshire Cats?"

"I didn't mean to annoy you."

For some reason that touched off a train of irritations. "Can't you see that the way you skip all over the book and never master any of it is a huge annoyance, particularly when I come in tired? Then you cover up with something silly. What were you saying last week? Weren't you inventing some kind of story about people who lived in a world of anti-matter, as if what I work on were a fairy tale?"

She looked away.

"Weren't you?"

"I was thinking about . . . electrons." She used the word with awe. It could have been the secret name of a deity. "Then I thought about anti-electrons, and people, and anti-people, and even," she gulped a little, "galaxies and anti-galaxies. There could be anti-galaxies. It says so here." She hugged the book.

"Don't be defensive. You've gotten more than I expected. Now be a sensible girl and leave it right there." He looked at her face and added, "Or if you have to tell fairy tales about your anti-universe, go out and tell them to your iris. You have a real way with flowers, and you're letting the whole garden go. It used to be trim as a manicured hand. Today it's unkempt."

"I know."

"By July what's it going to look like? See, you belong there. Why, the borders need you to care for them."

She cried desperately, "Can't you see what you're doing? Don't make me evoke someone twice."

"Twice?" His lips curved down in contempt. "Now is that quite worthy of you? But go on *evoking* if you want to. I shan't be jealous."

Her eyes were close to misting. "Jealous! I don't mean anything like that. I want to say— This time I'm scared of what I think about. Scared, Robert, really scared. But I might do it if you make me." Her voice dropped as if she confessed something shameful. "I find myself adding detail to detail, the way I used to, and sort of beaming it out—somewhere." She straightened suddenly. Her chin tilted up. She finished, "But then I stop."

Payne's tone was stiff. "Better think over what I said about the garden."

"You're turning it into an exile. If I'm sent away from you—" She did not finish but asked, "Aren't we ever going to be married, really married?"

Again his irritations mounted. "Not," he said sharply, "if our being married depends on your understanding that book in your hand."

A kind of panic crept into her eyes. He tried to be reasonable.

"Oh all right. Forget what I said about the garden. Tell me about your anti-world if you want to."

"I don't believe I remember now what I made up about the people in it. They were like us, exactly like us—"

He made a pretense of listening. But his mind slipped off to a series of equations. Would changing plus and minus signs affect the gravitational field of an anti-earth? He came back to their conversation as Lee garbled something she must have heard. "—and we're looking at it through a telescope that's at right angles to any dimension we know. Only what we see is Now," she capitalized it with an inflection, "Now, not millions of years ago. So with all the parts of the anti-atoms exactly like our atoms, only reversed—"

"With the electrical charges reversed."

She brushed that aside. "You see the people, since everything they're made of is the same, would be—"

Payne broke in, "Everything isn't the same. The proton isn't."

She put her finger against her forehead and tilted her head up in a way he had once found charming. "There's something about it. Here. On this page." She spoke carefully. "It's about the mass—that's right, isn't it—the mass of— Is it a nucleus? It's twice as much as ours. Does that make anti-matter different from matter? Please tell me—"

"Don't go begging me to clarify. It doesn't do any good. I've tried."

She implored, "Couldn't you make . . . a picture?"

He shook his head. "If we can only find how atoms keep accounts of their income and output, we shan't need to bother about what they look like. Besides, I prefer to bypass pictures. I work analytically. While I do, if you dream about your anti-world, don't make it exactly like this one." His eyes narrowed a shade. "A variation here and there, due to that variation in the proton, might improve the anti-earth, don't you think?"

"You're making fun of me."

"Tonight," he snapped, "I'm too exhausted to make fun of anybody."

He saw her go into one of her painful efforts to think. "If we don't find our true relationship—the one we were meant to have—there'll be a . . . a flaw in the universe."

"Most improbable."

She flared, her hair a swirl of darkness round her head and her eyes full of sparks, "What do you really know about the universe?" In that moment she was a Lee he had never seen, her impatience with him matching his with her. "You haven't even gotten any real sort of order out of an atom—you and all the other geniuses. Can you predict what would happen to people like us in an anti-world? What they're like? What they do?"

He felt one of her fairy tales in full spate again. He faced her squarely. He held her eyes with his lighter ones till he was sure he had her attention completely. Then he said, very gently and very softly, "Darling, you bore me."

The perfect oval of her face did not change. But everything else about her altered subtly until she stood before her husband impersonal as print—the same woman and not the same woman. He heard her tell him in a toneless voice that she wasn't hungry, that her head ached, that she wanted—again Payne waited through one of her pauses—wanted to go to bed.

Payne stayed up reading until late. He had a guilty twinge because he didn't feel badly about wounding Lee; anyone with eyes like hers was sure to be vulnerable. Finally, he went upstairs.

As he passed Lee's open door he saw her lying in the moonlight, pale in her sleep. She was still sleeping when he went to the laboratory next morning. That evening as though he had been ordered by something, someone not himself, he went in to her room, leaned over, and touched her white cheek.

An odd thing happened. He seemed to smell mold. He began to tremble, chill with the certainty that Lee would never wake.

An embolism, the doctor said, scouting the idea of suicide. The neighbors were tender to Payne, as if he were a lost child. But actually he felt closer to Lee than when she had been alive. The shadowiness of her eyes stayed with him, hauntingly, like the eyes of a memorable portrait. At any instant he could visualize her hair, a turbulence of darkness. If there were whirlwinds in the depths of space— He broke off. That was how Lee's mind worked. Had worked, he corrected himself. It was never his way, he reflected while he kept physical memories of her before him, because behind them he knew something lay that would torture him all his life if he ever faced it.

One evening Payne walked home along the shaded drive that led to the garden. His mood was one of almost exhilarated content; his work at the Foundation had gone better than well. Abstruse calculations had been something to play with. He had never experienced such a sense of power, nor had he ever known power to give him a feeling of prelude.

He looked joyously down the dark tube of boughs and tree boles. At that second he caught sight of— No, it couldn't be. But it was. Lee! She stood against the border of flowers, shadowy against dimming bloom. Payne—stockstill, yards away—stared down the tunnel that led straight to her.

She tilted up her head; seeing him, he was sure. Her lips—delicate and of so live a coral that she never used makeup—curved into a smile, half welcome, half wistfulness.

His eyes swam. In that second the blooms behind her blurred into spiralling blue and red. He could have sworn that long, snaking arms of a galaxy formed her background. He did not try to make any meaning of it. He hurried forward—

For a half-instant there was a snowstorm of flaking light. Then Payne saw neglected flowers. Nothing more.

He felt a stab of reproach, keener than anything he had known at his wife's death. Here where he had seen, truly seen Lee, he would tidy the beds as they had never been tidied. He would leave nothing faded, nothing weed-choked. The rank growth around a delphinium seemed desecration. He yanked the intruding weeds out savagely.

Vaguely, a worry gnawed him. The day had been almost too keyed up. His formulations had come with unnatural ease. On top of that, this hallucination. The word *hallucination* irked him. He substituted *hallucinatory experience* and felt considerably better.

As he weeded, he considered seeing a psychiatrist, then decided he had not that much time to spare. Besides, he had a dark suspicion a psychiatrist might dissolve Lee into nothingness. The idea was enormously painful.

With his pocket knife he trimmed off wilted roses; each time he made a slanting cut. Somewhere, he was certain, he had heard that was the right way. *If you would be happy for life* . . . "Lee," he muttered, "if you come back a second time, this place will be in shape for you."

He pulled some crabgrass from the neighborhood of a rose. "Darling," he asked, "do you think I called you? I seem to be falling in love with you all over again."

*

Lee did not reappear in the garden. Payne saw her, through a doorway in his own house, as he raised his head suddenly from a work on mathematics. Oddly, he could have been looking down a shaft trained on her. His heart did something in waltz time; she was much nearer than she had been before.

Tonight she sat hunched on a large hassock. The position would have been ungraceful for anyone else. She did not look at Payne. He made no move toward her for fear she would disappear. But he fidgeted. She was unaware of him, lost in her book.

That was Lee for you, he thought. Ghost or dream or whatever she was, Lee held stubbornly to her ruling idea. He guessed what she was reading. An unfamiliar pity swept over him as she bent her splendid head over the pages. He caught glimpses of diagrams, not enough to be sure exactly what the plates showed, but enough to see that his guess was right. Lee was reading physics.

He wished he could explain whatever it was to her, for once. Experimentally he called, "Lee." She never raised her head. She only moved her hand, which soundlessly turned the pages. Speech between them was evidently out.

Yet Payne got Lee's simpler reactions, though how he did not know. He sensed to a split second when she would shut her book and look off dreamily into space. Was she still struggling with *A Non-Mathematical Approach*?

The closed volume was on her knee. Its name, Payne noted, was lettered in gold, clear and legible: *On the Validity of Thought Patterns as Determined by Their Elegance*. Payne blinked. Automatically, he checked the author's name and read below the title, *Rosalie Payne*.

*

After Payne had his one glance at *The Validity of Thought Patterns*, Lee eluded him. He would walk home expectantly through the shady alley. He kept his eyes on the ground until the space between him and the flower border was shorter than the distance between him and Lee in the different rooms. The space between them had shortened once; it seemed reasonable it would shorten again—more than reasonable, for Payne felt the intensity of his own wishes was a factor. But when he lifted his eyes, he saw only the last white chrysanthemums tinged with lavender that bloomed their best after a touch of frost.

If, thought Payne, he went into the house and picked up what he had been reading the night he saw Lee, perhaps— His heartbeat quickened. He concentrated on—he used Lee's term—"evoking" her. He altered techniques. He tried not to think about her at all. He went to absurd tricks of stage setting and adjusting lights. Finally he ordered a blank volume from a bookbinder and had it made up with the title he had seen in gold. He specified that *Rosalie Payne* be stamped beneath that title. If he could have reproduced the contents, he had a hunch Lee would surely have returned. He had little hope when he laid the unwritten book on a hassock. Nothing happened, as he foresaw.

When the hollow way did open, Payne was working late in his office, his mood exhilarated contentment. As he leaned back, still analyzing a photograph of particles in a bubble chamber, Lee was so close she could have been on the other side of the wall—only there was no wall. Payne was conscious of a dark rim bounding what he saw, making Lee's universe somehow beyond all reaching, though right at hand. She, eager as a child holding a wrapped present, studied a photograph too; he tried to see of what. All he got was a feeling of something slightly, and in no expected way, unfamiliar. But he found it hard, even craning his neck, to look. It was far more interesting to study Lee's intent face. He told himself she ought not to go at things so hard. After all, during these rare glimpses, she might be interested in him.

Payne had never been a vain man, but now he tried to see the figure he would cut before her. He wanted her to look, a wanting so desperate he was sure it would get through to her. While he sat rigid, she lifted her head, turning in his direction. She knitted her brows impatiently, a little as though he were a pet animal demanding attention. Then she smoothed her forehead with an unconscious gesture, smiled, and bent over the photograph again.

He could find some way to get to her, he told himself, some way that would not make her vanish, some way that would put them in actual communication. He had his chance now. It might never come again.

He influenced her a little, obviously. But making her look in his direction got him nowhere. Well, since she was now absorbed in physics on something like his level, he would reach her through their shared curiosity.

Payne took a fresh sheet of paper and wrote some equations he had found of real interest. Though no complete formulation of his theories on anti-matter and on fields that could affect it, they were still suggestive.

Briefly, he hesitated. If his mathematics were beyond her hopelessly, she might be discouraged. After all, he did not know how far her studies had taken her. His fingers reached for the edge of the paper, to tear it up.

But, he reflected, his figures would be a good reaction test. He held the formulae up in front of him. Once more he willed Lee to be attentive.

Her resistance became almost tangible. Payne concentrated against her concentration. Again she frowned, and he concentrated harder. After all, he was sure she was interested and he had something breathtakingly new to show. Briefly he felt a pride in his work that almost made him forget her.

She stopped frowning and turned toward him. He raised the sheet of figures. He saw her read what he had written.

Her glowing, vibrant expression dimmed to weariness. Quickly, while she watched, he wrote out something simpler, and waited for a flash of recognising delight. But Lee looked away from the figures straight into his face. Payne could not fathom her expression.

Then with a shock of joy he felt Lee reach out for *his* attention. Something in their minds seemed to interlock. All the while Lee went about some business of her own. He saw her tack a large piece of paper to the wall, select a crayon and begin to draw.

What grew under her hand was an arabesque in depth, a figure beyond the calculus of matrices. Correspondences and symmetries were clear as in the work of a great mathematician. Yet music could not have been more moving. She glanced at him as she added the last touch.

Payne stared. He began to understand. The Atom! Still staring, he saw what she must intend to represent the proton. Wrong, for the rest of the arrangement! Of course, it would be. Trust Lee to be confused. Its cross section was twice—

Payne drew in his breath with a gasp. There was no confusion except his own. Suddenly it came clear. Lee's atom was not matter, but anti-matter.

He felt a little dizzy, and though he was sitting down, he grasped the edge of the desk. Anti-matter, so like, so nearly the same as matter! Anti-matter, his own field of study! He knew with absolute certainty, their minds still interlocking, that he stared at some small part of a universe which almost but not quite duplicated his own in reverse.

He remembered his brief impression of a nebula when he stood in his garden. But he found himself saying an author's name, "Lee. Lee Payne." So this Lee had been married. His whole body shook with jealousy. She was his Lee. They had a unique relationship wherever, whatever, she was.

Impressions surged through him, growing clearer. No, she was not his Lee. He was suddenly sure of that. She was what his wife had brought him across uncounted parsecs. Lee's epocation must have been incredibly strong to linger like a vibration beyond her own death. Why? Why? Was this new Lee a last scarcely believable gift to him?

But while Payne questioned he no longer felt the contact of mind with mind. Instead he met resistance ten times stronger than before. He heard himself shouting and realized that in Lee's anti-world the silence was unruffled. He saw her speaking to him. Yet he heard nothing. The two worlds were as still, each to each, as stars to some gazer with his eyes at an instrument.

But if this Lee were speaking, there was some way to understand. There must be.

It came in one flash that if he formed the words with his lips, Lee could talk to him, speaking with his very voice. He studied her face.

He copied.

"Darling," his own mouth formed the word for her. She watched him and spoke again, very slowly.

He echoed aloud, "Darling, you bore m—"

Payne never finished. He felt a bitter humiliated impulse to lash out. Only there was no way. Lee turned her back and walked out of sight.

He thought of all the ways in which a physicist might destroy himself. It could look like an accident. A freak accident. Grimly he resolved that he would never do that for any woman in any universe. Suicide—never! He could, he would be happy in spite of everything. Savagely, he resolved that tomorrow he would spend the whole day bedding the garden down for the winter.

1961

ALICE GLASER

The Tunnel Ahead

THE floor of the Topolino was full of sand. There was sand in Tom's undershorts, too, and damp sand rubbing between his toes. Damn it, he thought, here they build you six-lane highways right on down to the ocean, a giant three-hundred car turntable to keep traffic moving over the beach, efficiency and organization and mechanization and cooperation and what does it get you? Sand. And inside the car, in spite of the air-conditioning, the sour smell of sun-dried salt water.

Tom's muscles ached with their familiar cramp. He ran his hands uselessly around the steering wheel, wishing he had something to do, or that there were room to stretch in the tiny car, then felt instantly ashamed of his antisocial wish. Naturally there was nothing for him to do because the drive, as on all highways, was set at "Automatic." That was the law. And although he had to sit hunched over so that his knees were drawn nearly to his chin, and the roof of the car pressed down on the back of his neck like the lid of a box, and his four kids crammed into the rear seat seemed to be breathing down his shirt collar—well, that was something you simply had to adjust to, and besides, the Topolino had all the five-foot wheelbase the law allowed. So there was nothing to complain about.

Besides, it hadn't been a bad day, all things considered. Five hours to cover the forty miles out to the beach, then of course a couple of hours waiting in line *at* the beach for their turn in the water. The trip home was taking a little longer: it always did. The Tunnel, too, was unpredictable. Say ten o'clock, for getting home. Pretty good time. As good a way as any of killing a leisureday, he guessed. Sometimes there seemed to be an awful lot of leisuretime to kill.

Jeannie, in the seat beside him, was staring through the windshield. Her hair, almost as fair as the kids', was pulled back into pigtails, and although she was pregnant again she didn't look very much older than she had ten years before. But she had stopped knitting, and her mind was on the Tunnel. He could always tell.

"Ouch!" Something slammed into the back of Tom's neck and he ducked forward, banging his forehead on the windshield.

"Hey!" He half-turned and clutched at the spade that four-year-old Pattie was waving.

"I swimmed," she announced, blue eyes round. "I swimmed good and I din't hit nobody."

"Anybody," Tom corrected. He confiscated the spade, thinking tiredly that "swim" these days meant "tread water," all there was room to do in the crowded bathing-area.

Jeannie had turned too, and was glowing at her daughter, but Tom shook his head.

"Over and out," he said briefly. He knew a car ride was an extra strain on kids, and lord knew he saw them seldom enough, what with their school-shifts and play-shifts and his own job-shift. But his brood was going to be properly brought up. See a sign of extroversion, squelch it at the beginning, that was his theory. Save them a lot of pain later on.

Jeannie leaned forward and pressed a dashboard button. The tranquillizer drawer slid open; Jeannie selected a pink one, but by the time she had turned around Pattie had subsided with her hands folded patiently in her lap and her eyes fixed on the rear seat TV screen. Jeannie sighed and slipped the pill into Pattie's half-open mouth anyway.

The other three hadn't spoken for hours which, of course, was as it should be. Jeannie had fed them a purposely heavy lunch in the car, steakopop and a hot, steaming bowl of rehydrated algaesoup from the thermos, and they had each had an extra dose of tranquilizers for the trip. Six-year-old David, who was having a particularly hard time learning to introvert, was watching the TV screen and breathing hard. David, his firstborn son, born in the supermarket delivery booth in the year twenty-one hundred on the third of April at 8:32 in the morning. The year the population of the United States hit the billion mark. And the fifth child to arrive in that booth that morning. But his own son. The tow-headed twins, Susan and Pattie, sat upright and watched the screen with expressions of great seriousness on their faces, and the baby, two-year-old Betsy, had her fat legs stuck straight out in front of her and was obviously going to be asleep in minutes.

The car crawled forward at its allotted ten mph, just one in a ribbon of identical bright bubble cars, like candy buttons, that stretched along the New Pulaski Skyway under a setting sun. The distance between them, strictly rationed by Autodrive, never changed.

Tom felt the dull ache of tension settled behind his eyes. All of his muscles were protesting now with individual stabs of cramp. He glanced apologetically at Jeannie, who disliked sports, and switched on the dashboard TV. Third game in the World Series, and the game had already begun. Malenkovsky on red. Malenkovsky moved a checker and sat back. The cameras moved to Saito, on black. It was going to be a good game. Faster than most.

They were less than a mile from the Tunnel when the line of cars came to a halt. Tom said nothing for a minute. It might just be an accident, or even somebody, driving illegally on Manual, out of line. Another minute passed. Jeannie's hands were tense on the yellow blanket she was knitting.

It was a definite halt. Jeannie regarded the motionless lines of cars, frowning a little.

"I'm glad it's happening now. That gives us a better chance of getting through, doesn't it?"

Her question was rhetorical, and Tom felt his usual stir of irritation. Jeannie was an intelligent girl; he couldn't have loved her so much otherwise. But explaining the laws of chance to her was hopeless. The Tunnel averaged ten closings a week. All ten could happen within seconds of each other, or on the hour, or not at all on a given day. That was how things were. The closing now affected their own chance of getting through not one iota.

Jeannie said, thoughtfully, "We'll be caught sometime, Tom."

He shrugged without answering. Whatever might happen in the future, they were obviously going to be held up for a good half hour now.

David was wriggling a little, his face apologetic.

"Can I get out, Daddy, if the Tunnel's closed? I *ache*."

Tom bit his lip. He could sympathize as well as anyone, remembering the cramped misery of the years when his own body was growing and all he wanted to do was run fast, just run headlong, anyplace. Kids. Extros, all of them. Maybe you could get away with that kind of wildness back in the Twentieth century, when there were no crowds and plenty of space, but not these days. David was just going to have to learn to sit still like everybody else.

David had begun to flex his muscles rhythmically. Passive exercise, it was called, one of the new pseudo-sports that took up no room, and it was very scientifically taught in the play-shifts. Tom eyed his son enviously. Great to be in condition like that. No need to wait in line to get your ration of gym time when you could depend on yourself like that.

"Dad, no kidding, now I gotta go." David wriggled in his seat again. Well, that sounded valid. Tom looked through the windshield. The thousands of cars in sight were still motionless, so he swung the door open. Luckily there was a chemjohn a few yards away, and only a short line in front of it. David slid quickly out of the car. Tom watched him start to stretch his arms over his head, released from the low roof, then sheepishly remember decent behavior and tighten into the approved intro-walk. "He's getting tall," Tom thought, with a sudden accession of hopelessness. He had been praying that David would inherit Jeannie's height instead of his own six feet. The more area you took up the harder everything was, and it was getting worse: Tom had noticed that, already, people would sometimes stare resentfully at him in the street.

There was an Italian family in the bright blue Topolino behind his own; they too had a car full of children. Two of the boys, seeing David in front of the chemjohn, burst out and dashed into the line behind him. The father was grinning; Tom caught his eye and looked away. He remembered seeing them pass a large bottle of expensive reclaimed-water around the car, the whole family guzzling it as though water grew on trees. Extros, that whole family. Almost criminal, the way people like that were allowed to run loose and increase the discomfort of everyone else. Now the father had left the car too. He had curly black hair; he was very plump. When he saw

Tom watching him he grinned broadly, waved towards the Tunnel and lifted his shoulders with a kind of humorous resignation.

Tom drummed on the wheel. The extros were lucky. You'd never catch them worrying unduly about the Tunnel. They had to get the kids out of the city, once in a while, like everybody else; the Tunnel was the only way in and out, so they shrugged and took it. Besides, there were so many rules and regulations now that it was hard to question them any more. You can't fight City Hall. The extros would neither dread the trip, the way Jeannie did, nor . . . Tom's fingers were rigid on the wheel. He clamped down, hard, on the thought in his mind. He had been about to say, *needed* it, the way he did.

David emerged from the chemjohn and slid back into his seat. The cars had just begun to move; in a moment they had resumed their crawl.

On the left of the Skyway they were coming to the development that was already called, facetiously, "Beer Can Mountain." So far there was nothing there except the mountainous stacks of shiny bricks, the metal bricks that had once been tin cans, and would soon be constructed into another badly needed housing development. Probably with even lower ceilings and thinner walls. Tom winced, involuntarily. Even at home, in a much older residential section, the ceilings were so low that he could never stand up without bending his head. Individual area-space was being cut down and cut down, all the time.

On the flatlands, to the right of the Skyway, stretched mile after garish mile of apartment buildings, interspersed with gasoline stations and parking lots. And beyond these flatlands were the suburbs of Long Island, cement-floored and stacked with gay-colored skyscrapers.

Here, as they approached the city, the air was raucous with the noise of transistor radios and TV sets. Privacy and quiet had disappeared everywhere, of course, but this was a lower-class unit and so noisy that the blare penetrated even the closed windows of the car. The immense apartment buildings, cement block and neon-lit, came almost to the edge of the Skyway, with ramps between them at all levels. The ramps, originally built for cars, were swarming now with people returning from their routine job-shifts or from marketing, or just carrying on the interminable business of leisuretime. They looked pretty apathetic, Tom thought. You couldn't blame them. There was so much security that none of the work anybody did was really necessary, and they knew it. Their jobs were probably even more monotonous and futile than his own. All he did, on his own job-shift, was verify figures in a ledger, then copy them into another ledger. Time-killing, like everything else. These people looked as though they didn't care, one way or the other.

But as he watched there was a quick scuffle in the crowd, a sudden, brief outbreak of violence. One man's shoe had scraped the heel of the woman ahead of him; she turned and swung her shopping bag, scraping a bloody gash down his cheek. He slammed his fist at her stomach. She kicked. A man behind them rammed his way past, his face contorted. The pair separated, both muttering. Around them other knots of people were beginning to mutter. The irritation was spreading, as it seemed to do from time to time, as though nobody wanted anything so much as the chance to strike out.

Jeannie had seen the explosion too. She gasped and turned away from the window, looking quickly back at the children, who were all asleep now. Tom pulled one of her pigtails, gently.

The skyline loomed ahead of them, one vast unified glass-walled cube of Manhattan. Light rays shot from it into the sunset; the spots of foliage that were the carefully planned block gardens, one at each level of the ninety-eight floors of the Unit, glowed dark green. Tom, as he always did, blessed the foresight that had put them there. Each one of his children had been allotted his or her weekly hour on the grass and a chance to play near the tree. There was even a zoo on each level, not the kind of elaborate one they had in Washington and London and Moscow, of course, but at least it had a cat and a dog and a really large tank of goldfish. When you came down to it, luxuries like that almost made up for the crowds and the noise and tiny rooms and feeling that there was never quite enough air to breathe.

They were just outside the Tunnel. Jeannie had put her knitting down; she was looking intently ahead, but as though she were listening rather than looking. In spite of his own arguments, Tom felt his fingers thudding on the dashboard. On the TV screen, Malenkovsky triumphantly moved a king.

They had reached the Tunnel entrance. Jeannie was silent. She glanced at her watch, irrationally. Tom pressed the tranquillizer button and the drawer shot out, but Jeannie shook her head.

"I hate this, Tom. I think it's an absolutely *lousy* idea."

Her voice sounded almost savage, for Jeannie, and Tom felt a little shocked.

"It's the fairest thing," he argued. "You know it perfectly well."

Jeannie's mouth had set in a stubborn line. "I don't care. There must be another way."

"This is the only fair way," Tom said again. "We take our chances along with everybody else."

His own heart was pounding, now, and his hands felt cold. It was the feeling he always had on entering the Tunnel, and he had never decided whether it was dread or elation, or both. He was no longer bored. He glanced at the children on the back seat. David was watching television again and gnawing on a fingernail; the three little ones were still asleep, sitting up as they had been taught to do, hands folded properly in their laps. Three blind mice.

The Tunnel was echoing and cold. White light slipped off the white tile walls that were clean and polished and air-tight. Wind rushed past, sounding as though the car were moving faster than it actually was. The Italian family was still behind them, following at a constant speed. Huge fans were set into the Tunnel ceiling; their roar reverberated over the roar of the giant invisible air-conditioning units, over the slow wind of the moving cars.

Jeannie had put her head down on the seat back as though she were asleep. The cars stopped for an instant, started again. Tom wondered if Jeannie felt the same vivid thrill that he felt. Then he looked at the line of her mouth and saw the fear.

The Tunnel was 8500 feet long. Each car took up seven feet, bumper to bumper. Allow five feet between cars. About seven hundred cars in the tunnel, then: more than three thousand people. It would take each car about fifteen minutes to go through. Their car was halfway through now.

They were three-quarters of the way through. Automatic signal lights were flashing at them from the catwalk under the Tunnel roof. Tom's foot moved to the gas pedal before he remembered the car was set on Automatic. It was an atavistic gesture: his hands and feet wanted a job to do. His body, for a minute, wanted to control the direction of its plunge. It was the way he always felt, in the Tunnel.

They were almost through. His scalp felt as though tiny ants were running along the hairs. He moved his toes, feeling the scratch of sand on the nerves between them. He could see the far end of the Tunnel. Maybe two minutes more. A minute.

They stopped again. A car, somewhere ahead, had swerved out of line to search for the right exit. Once out of the Tunnel it was legal to switch back to Manual drive, since it was necessary to pick the right exit out of ten, and all too easy to find yourself carried to the top level of Manhattan Unit before finding a place to turn off.

Tom's hand drummed at the wheel. The maverick ahead had edged back into line. They started movement again. They picked up speed. They were out of the Tunnel.

Jeannie picked up her knitting and shook it, sharply. Then she dropped it as though it had bitten her fingers. A bell was clanging over their heads, not too loud, but clear. Just behind their rear bumper a gate swung smoothly into place.

Jeannie turned to look back at the space behind them where the Italian family in the bright blue car, and others, had been. There were no cars there now. She turned back, to stare whitely through the windshield.

Tom was figuring. Two minutes for the ceiling sprays to work. Then the seven hundred cars in the Tunnel would be hauled out and emptied. Ten minutes for that, say. He wondered how long it was supposed to take for the giant fans to blow the cyanide gas away.

"Depopulation without Discrimination," they called it at election time. Nobody would ever admit voting for it, but almost everybody did. Aloud, you had to rationalize: it was the fairest way to do a necessary thing. But in the unadmitted places of your mind you knew it was more than that. A gamble, the one unpredictable element in the long, dreary process of survival. A game. Russian Roulette. A game you played to win? Or, maybe, to lose? The answer didn't matter, because the Tunnel was excitement. The only excitement left.

Tom felt, suddenly, remarkably wide awake. He switched to Manual Drive and angled the round nose of the Topolino over to the Fourth Level exit.

He began to whistle between his teeth. "Beach again next week-end, sweetie, huh?"

Jeannie's eyes were on his face. Defensively, he added, "Good for all of us, get out of the city, get a little fresh air once in a while."

He nudged her and pulled a pigtail gently, with affection.

1961

KIT REED

The New You

"NOW—the New You," the ad said. It was a two-page spread in one of the glossier fashion magazines, and it was accompanied by a shadowed, grainy art photograph that hinted at the possibility of a miraculous transformation which hovered—so the ad said—at every woman's fingertips.

Raptly, Martha Merriam hunched forward, pulling at her violet-sprigged housedress so that it almost covered plump knees, and bent once more over the magazine. Raptly she contemplated the photograph, the list of promises framed in elegant italics, absently chewing a string of wiry, dun-colored hair.

In her more wistful, rebellious moments, Martha Merriam forgot her dumpy body and imagined herself the svelte, impeccable Marnie, taller by six inches and lighter by forty pounds. When a suaver, better-dressed woman cut her at a luncheon or her husband left her alone at parties she would retreat into dialogues with Marnie. Marnie knew just the right, devastating thing to say to chic, overconfident women, and Marnie was expert in all the wiles that keep a man at home. In the person of Marnie, Martha could pretend.

"Watch the Old You Melt Away," Martha read aloud, and as she mouthed the words for the second time Marnie strained inside her, waiting for release. Martha straightened imperceptibly, patting her doughy throat with a stubby hand, and as her eyes found the hooker—the price tag for the New You in small print in the lower right hand corner, longing consumed her, and Marnie took cover.

"We could use a New You," Marnie said.

"But three thousand dollars." Martha nibbled at the strand of hair.

"You have those stocks," Marnie prompted.

"But those were Howard's wedding present to me—part of his *business*."

"He won't mind . . ." Marnie twisted and became one with the photograph.

"But a hundred shares . . ." The hank of hair was sodden now, and Martha was chewing faster.

"He won't mind when he sees us," Marnie said.

And Martha, eyes aglow, got up and went to the telephone almost without realizing what she was doing, and got her broker on the line.

The New You arrived as advertised two weeks later, and when it came, Martha was too excited to touch it, alone in the house as she was, with this impossibly beautiful future.

In mid-afternoon, when she had looked at the coffin-shaped crate from every possible angle and smoothed the ruffled, splintered edges of wood, she nerved herself to pull the ripcord the company had provided—and let her future begin. She jumped back with a little squeak as the hard crate sides fell away to reveal a black and richly molded box. Trembling, she twiddled the gold-plated clasp with the rosebud emblem and opened the lid.

For a moment, all she saw was an instruction booklet, centered on top of fold upon fold of purple tissue paper, but as she looked closer, she saw that the paper was massed to protect a mysterious, promising form which lay beneath. IMPORTANT: READ THIS BEFORE PROCEEDING, the booklet warned. Distracted, she threw it aside, reflecting as she did so that the last time she had seen paper folded in this way was around long-stemmed American Beauties—a dozen of them, which Howard had sent her a dozen years before.

The last piece of paper came away in her fingers, revealing the figure beneath, and Martha gasped. It was a long-stemmed American Beauty—everything she had hoped for. She recognized her own expression in its face, but it was a superb, glamorous version of her face, and at the same time it was Marnie, Helen, Cleopatra—more than she had dared anticipate. It was the new her. Quivering with impatience to get into it, she bent over it without another thought for the instruction book, and plunged her arms to the elbows in the rustling, rising swirl of purple tissue paper. The sudden aura of perfume, the movement of the paper, a sense of mounting excitement overcame her, and the last thing she remembered was clasping the figure's silken hands in her own stubby fingers and holding them to her bosom as the two figures, new and old, tossed on a rushing purple sea. Then the moiling sheets of purple kaleidoscoped and engulfed her and she lost consciousness.

She was awakened by a squashy thud. She lay in the midst of the purple tissue, stretching luxuriously, thinking that she ought to get up to see what the thud had been. She raised one knee, in the beginning of a movement to get to her feet, and then stopped, delighted by its golden sleekness. She stretched the leg she knew must be just beyond that perfect knee, and then hugged shoulders lithe and smooth as a jungle cat's in a gradual awareness of what had happened. Then, remembering that the new her was quite naked and that Howard would be home any minute, she pulled herself together in one fluid glide of muscles and got to her feet. With the air of a queen, she lifted one foot delicately and stepped out of the box.

She remembered the line from the advertisement "Watch the Old You Melt Away," and she smiled languidly as she flowed away from the box. Yawning, she reached in the closet, picked up her old quilted wrapper and discarded it for the silk kimono Howard had brought her from Japan. It had fitted her ten years before, and then it had gotten too small. She looped the sash twice about her middle and then—still not too good to be an orderly housewife—she began folding the tissue paper that seemed to have exploded all over the room, and putting it in the box. As she came to the side where the old her had first touched the gold-plated rosebud, she swooped up a whole armful of tissue in a gesture of exuberance—and dropped it with a little scream. Her toe had hit something. Not wanting to look, she poked at the remaining pieces of paper with a gilded toe-nail. Her foot connected with something soft. She made herself look down, and stifled a moan.

The old her had not melted away. It was still there, dowdy as ever in its violet-sprigged housedress. Its drab hair trailed like seaweed, and its hips seemed to spread where it lay, settling on the rug.

"But you promised!" the new, sleek Martha yelped. With a sudden sinking feeling, she rooted around in the rest of the purple tissue until she found the cast-off instruction book.

"Care must be exercised in effecting the transfer," the book warned in urgent italics. Then it went on with a number of complicated, technical directions about transfer and grounding, which Martha didn't understand. When she had grasped the new her's hands she had plunged right into the transfer, without a thought for the body she was leaving behind. And it had to be dematerialized at the time of transfer, no later. It was pointless to send botched jobs back to the company, the booklet warned. The company would send them back. Apparently, the new Martha was stuck with the old her.

"Ohh . . ." There was a little moan from the figure on the floor. And the old Martha sat up and looked dully around the room.

"You—" the new Martha looked at it with growing hatred. "You leave me alone," she said. She was about to lunge at it in a fit of irritation when there was a sound in the driveway. "Oh-oh. Howard." Without another thought, she pushed the lumpy, unresisting old her into the hall closet, locked it and pocketed the key.

Then, pulling the robe around her, she went to the door. "Howard, darling," she began.

He recognized her and he didn't recognize her. He stood just inside the doorway with the look of a child who has just been given a soda fountain, listening as she explained (leaving out certain details—the sale of his stock, the matter of the old her) in vibrant, intimate tones.

"Martha, darling," he said at last, pulling her toward him.

"Call me Marnie, dear. Hm?" she purred, and nestled against his chest.

Of course the change involved a new wardrobe, and new things for Howard too, as Marnie had read in a dozen glamour magazines how important an accessory a well-dressed man could be. The Merriams were swept up in a round of parties and were admitted, for the first time, to the city's most glittering homes. Howard's business flourished and Marnie, surrounded by admirers, far more attractive than the most fashionable of her rivals, thrived. There were parties, meetings, theatre dates, luncheon engagements with a number of attractive men. And what with one thing and another, Marnie didn't have much time for piddling around the house. The black box from the New You Company lay where she had left it, and the old her was still stacked—like an old vacuum cleaner, so far as she was concerned—unused, in the closet in the hall.

In the second week of her new life, Marnie began to notice things. The tissue paper around the New You box was disarrayed, and the instruction book was gone. Once, when she had stepped out of the bedroom for a moment, she thought she saw a shadow moving in the hall. "Oh, it's you," Howard said with an ambiguous look, when she returned to their room. "For a minute I thought . . ." He sounded almost wistful.

And there were crumbs—little trails of them—and empty food containers left in odd corners of the house.

Disturbed by the dirt which had begun to collect, Marnie refused two luncheon dates and a cocktail invitation and spent one of her rare afternoons at home. In slippers and the quilted house coat she had discarded the first day of her transformation, she began to clean the house. She was outraged to find a damp trail leading from the kitchen to the hall closet. With a rug-cleaning preparation she began scrubbing at the hall carpet, and she straightened her back, indignant, when she reached a particularly sordid little mixture of liquid and crumbs, right at the closet door. Fumbling in her pocket, she brought out the key and applied herself to the lock.

"You," she said disgustedly. She had almost forgotten.

"Yes—yes ma'am," the old her said humbly, almost completely cowed. The dumpy, violet-sprigged Martha was sitting in one corner of the closet, a milk carton in one hand and a box of marshmallow cookies open in her lap.

"Why can't you just . . . Why can't you . . ." Marnie snorted in disgust. There was chocolate at the corners of the creature's mouth, and it had gained another five pounds.

"A body has to live," the old her said humbly, trying to wipe away the chocolate. "You forgot—I had a key to the closet too."

"If you're going to be wandering around," Marnie said, tapping one vermilion fingernail on a flawless tooth, "you might as well be of some use. Come on," she said, pulling at the old her. "We're going to clear out the old maid's room. Move!"

The old Martha came to its feet and shambled behind Marnie, making little sounds of obedience.

The experiment was a flop. The creature ate constantly and had a number of (to Marnie) disgusting habits, and when Marnie invited some of Howard's more attractive business contacts in for dinner, it refused to wear a maid's cap and apron, and made a terrible mess of serving the soup. When she called it down at table, Howard protested mildly but Marnie was too engrossed in conversation with a Latin type who dealt in platinum to notice. Nor did she notice, in the days that followed, that Howard was putting on weight. She was slimmer even than she had been the first day of her new life, and she stalked the house impatiently, nervous and well-groomed as a high-bred horse. Howard seemed unusually quiet and withdrawn, and Marnie laid it to the effect of having the Old Her around, flat-footed and quiet in its violet-sprigged dress. When she caught it feeding Howard fudge cake at the kitchen table the very day she found he could no longer button his tuxedo, she knew the Old Her had to go.

She had a Dispose-All installed in her kitchen sink and began a quiet investigation into the properties of various poisons, in hopes of finding a permanent way of getting rid of it. But when she brought a supply of sharp-edged equipment into the house the violet-sprigged Martha seemed to sense what she was planning. It stood in front of her, wringing its hands humbly, until she noticed it.

"Well?" Marnie said, perhaps more sharply than she had intended.

"I—just wanted to say you can't get rid of me that way," it offered, almost apologetically.

"What way?" Marnie asked, trying to cover, and then, with a little gesture of indifference, she raised one eyebrow. "Okay, smarty, why not?"

"Killing's against the law," the creature said patiently.

"This would hardly be killing," Marnie said in her most biting tones. "It's like giving your old clothes to the rag man or the Good Will, or burning them. Getting rid of old clothes has never been murder."

"Not murder," the old her said, and it produced the instruction book. Patiently, it guided Marnie's eyes over the well-thumbed pages to a paragraph marked in chocolate. "Suicide."

Desperate, she gave it a thousand dollars and a ticket to California.

And for a few days, the gay life went on as it had before. The Merriams were entertained or entertaining day and night now, and Howard hardly had time to notice that the quiet old Martha was missing. Marnie's new autochef made her dinner parties the talk of the city's smarter social set, and she found herself the center of an inexhaustible crowd of attentive, handsome young men in tuxedoes. While Howard had abandoned the old her at parties, she saw little more of him now, because the good-looking young men adored her too much to leave her alone. She was welcome in the very best places and there wasn't a woman in town who dared exclude her from her invitation list. Marnie went everywhere.

If she was dissatisfied, it was only because Howard seemed lumpier and less attractive than usual, and the bumps and wrinkles in his evening clothes made him seem something less than the perfect accessory. She slipped away from him early in the evening each time they went out together, and she looked for him again only in the small hours, when it was time to collect him and go home.

But for all that, she still loved him, and it came as something of a blow when she discovered that it was no longer she who avoided him at parties—he was avoiding her. She first noticed it after an evening of dinner and dancing. She had been having a fascinating conversation with someone in consolidated metals, and it seemed to her the right touch—the final fillip—for the evening would be for the gentleman in question to see her standing next to Howard in the soft light, serene, beautiful, the doting wife.

"You must meet my husband," she murmured, stroking the metal magnate's lapel.

"Have you seen Howard?" she asked a friend nearby, and something in the way the friend shook his head and turned away from her made her a little uneasy.

Several minutes later, the metal magnate had taken his leave and Marnie was still looking for Howard. She found him at last, on a balcony, and she could have sworn that she saw him wave to a dark figure, which touched its hands to its lips and disappeared into the bushes just as she closed the balcony door.

"It's not very flattering, you know," she said, coiling around his arm.

"Mmmmm?" He hardly looked at her.

"Having to track you down like this," she said, fitting against him.

"Mmmm?"

She started to go on, but led him through the apartment and down to the front door. Even in the cab, she couldn't shake his reverie. She tucked his coattails into the cab with a solicitous little frown. And she brooded. There had been something disturbingly familiar about that figure on the balcony.

The next morning Marnie was up at an unaccustomed hour,

dressing with exquisite care. She had been summoned to morning coffee with Edna Hotchkiss-Baines. For the first time, she had been invited to help with the Widows' and Orphans' Fund Bazaar. ("I've found somebody wonderful to help with the planning," the chichi Edna had confided. "You'll never guess who.")

Superb in an outfit that could stand even Edna's scrutiny, Marnie presented herself at the Hotchkiss-Baines door and followed the butler into the Hotchkiss-Baines breakfast room.

Edna Hotchkiss-Baines barely greeted her. She was engrossed in conversation with a squat, unassuming figure that slumped across the table from her, shoes slit to accommodate feet that were spreading now, violet-sprigged dress growing a little tight.

Face afire, Marnie fell back. She took a chair without speaking and leveled a look of hatred at the woman who held the town's most fashionable social leader enthralled—the dowdy, frumpy, lumpy old her.

It was only the beginning. Apparently the creature had cashed in the California ticket and used the fare and the thousand dollars to rent a small flat and buy a modest wardrobe. Now, to Marnie's helpless fury, it seemed to be going everywhere. It appeared at cocktail parties in a series of matronly crepe dresses ranging in color from taupe to dove grey. It sat on the most important committees and appeared at the most elegant dinners. No matter how exclusive the guest list or how gay the company, no matter how high Marnie's hopes that it had not been included, somebody had always invited it. It appeared behind her in clothing store mirrors when she was trying on new frocks and looked over her shoulder in restaurants when she dined with one of her devastating young men. It haunted her steps, looking just enough like her to make everyone uncomfortable, enough like everything Marnie hated, to embarrass her.

Then one night she found Howard kissing it at a party.

At home a few hours later, he confronted her.

"Marnie, I want a divorce."

"Howard." She made clutching motions. "Is there . . ."

He sounded grave. "My dear, there's someone else. Well, it isn't exactly someone else."

"You don't mean—Howard, you can't be serious."

"I'm in love with the girl I married," he said. "A quiet girl, a grey-and-brown girl."

"That—" Her fashionable body was trembling. Her gemlike eyes were aflame. "That frumpy . . ."

"A home girl . . ." He was getting rhapsodic now. "Like the girl I married so many years ago."

"After all that money—the transformation—the new body—" Marnie's voice rose with every word. "The CHANGE?"

"I never asked you to change, Marnie." He smiled mistily. "You were so . . ."

"You'd drop me for that piece of suet?" She was getting shrill. "How could I face my *friends*?"

"You deserve somebody better looking," he said with a little sigh. "Somebody tall and slim. I'll just pack and go . . ."

"All right, Howard." She managed a noble tone. "But not just yet." She was thinking fast. "There has to be a Decent Waiting Period . . ."

A period would give her time to handle this.

"If you wish, my dear." He had changed into his favorite flannel bathrobe. In times past, the old Martha had sat next to him on the couch in front of the television, she in her quilted house coat, he in his faithful robe. He stroked its lapels. "I just want you to realize that my mind is made up—we'll all be happier . . ."

"Of course," she said, and a hundred plans went through her mind. "Of course."

She sat alone for the rest of the night, drumming opalescent nails on her dressing table, tapping one slender foot.

And by morning, she had it. Something Howard had said had set her mind churning. "You deserve somebody better looking."

"He's right," she said aloud. "I do." And by the time it had begun to get light she had conceived of a way to get rid of the persistent embarrassment of the old her and the homier elements of Howard at one stroke. As soon as Howard left for the office she began a series of long distance inquiries, and once she had satisfied her curiosity she called a number of friends and floated several discreet loans in the course of drinks before lunch.

There was a crate in the living room just two weeks later. "Howard," Marnie said, beckoning, "I have a surprise for you . . ."

He was just coming in, with the old Martha, from a date. They liked to sit in the kitchen over cocoa and talk. At a look from Marnie, the creature settled in a chair. It couldn't take its eyes off the coffin-shaped box. Howard stepped forward, brows wrinkling furrily. "What's this?" he asked, and then without waiting for her to answer, he murmured, "Didn't we have one of these around a few months ago?" and pulled the cord attached to the corner of the crate. It fell open—perhaps a little too easily—and the lid of the smooth ebony box sprang up under his fingers almost before he had touched the rosebud catch. The tissue paper was green this time, and if there had been an instruction book nestled on top, it was gone now.

Both the new Marnie and the old her watched raptly as Howard, oblivious of both of them, broke through the layers of tissue paper and with a spontaneous sound of pleasure grasped the figure in the box.

Both the new and the old woman watched as the papers began to swirl and rise, and they sat transfixed until there was a thud and the papers settled again.

When it was over, Marnie turned to the old her with a malicious grin. "Satisfied?" she asked. And then, eyes gleaming, she waited for the new Howard to rise from the box.

He came forth like a new Adam, ignoring both of them, and went to his own room for clothes.

While he was gone, the old Howard, a little frayed at the corners, almost buried under a fall of tissue, stirred and tried to rise.

"That's yours," Marnie said, giving the old her a dig in the ribs. "Better go help it up." And then she presented her face to the doorway, waiting with arms spread for the new Howard to reappear. After a few moments he came, godlike in one of Howard's pin-striped business suits.

"Darling," Marnie murmured, mentally cancelling dinner at the Hotchkiss-Bainses' and a Westport party with a new man.

"Darling," the new Howard said. And he swept past her to the old Martha, still scrabbling around in the tissue paper on the floor. Gently, with the air of a prince who has discovered the new Cinderella, he helped her to her feet. "Shall we go?" he asked.

Marnie watched, openmouthed.

They did.

On the floor, the old Howard had gotten turned on its stomach somehow, and was floundering like a displaced fish. Marnie watched, taut with rage, too stricken to speak. The old Howard flapped a few more times, made it to its knees and then slipped on the tissue paper again. Hardly looking at it, Marnie smoothed the coif she had prepared for the Hotchkiss-Baines dinner that night. There was always the dinner—and the party in Westport.

Dispassionately, she moved forward and kicked a piece of tissue out of the way. She drew herself up, supple, beautiful, and she seemed to find new strength. The old Howard flapped again.

"Oh get *up*," she said, and poked it with her toe. She was completely composed now. "Get up—*darling*," she spat.

1962

JOHN JAY WELLS & MARION ZIMMER BRADLEY

Another Rib

"REMEMBER, you requested it," Fanu murmured. The little alien's pronunciation was as toneless, as flat as ever, and yet, somehow, it carried sympathy and distress. "I am sorry, John."

John Everett slumped before the film viewer. At last, reluctantly, he leaned forward and underlined his shock with a second view. "When—when did you take this?" he asked.

"A—I do not know your words for it—a revolution ago. Do you wish for a current view, my friend?"

"No. God, no! This is bad enough. You're—sure of your identification?"

Fanu's three-fingered hand riffled expertly for a sheet of coordinates. Shaking, forcing his eyes and mind to activity, Everett checked the data, glancing back now and then at the viewer to verify. There was no doubt. That was Sol—that had been the Sun—that vast incandescent swirl covering . . . oh God, covering a range well beyond Pluto!

He became aware that he had been sitting quite still for many long minutes, stiff muscles and sluggish circulation forcing themselves, at last, even through the numbness of his brain. Fanu was waiting.

Fanu was always waiting. The alien had waited aeons. Not Fanu himself, of course, but his kind. Waiting; always waiting for other life forms, other intelligences, new civilizations—new enthusiasms. They had waited too long. There weren't many left.

"Looks like we've joined you," Everett muttered, bitterly, at last.

"I do not quite understand—?"

"You said—" he paused, groping for a kind word, "that your people were becoming extinct. Looks like mine are—already."

"Survivors—"

He got to his feet so quickly he knocked over the chair, and spent fumbling minutes setting it right. "But there are no survivors. We were the first probe. Out to the stars. All the way to Proxima Centauri. For what? An Earth-type planet. Fine, we found one—but for what? For whom? Oh, God, for whom!"

"John," softly, a three-fingered hand falling on his shoulder. "You are not alone, not as I am. You have your friends, your—your crew."

Everett walked over to the window, and stared out at the valley, dotted with the tiny huts of the expedition. "For now, yes. Sixteen men—a good crew. But we're mortal, Fanu. Human life is pitifully short, compared with yours. We're mortal—and we're all male. By your standards, we're—here today and gone tomorrow."

"Are you quite sure that need be, John?"

Everett turned to look into the alien's large green eyes, cursing the inevitable semantic differences, the inability to get a point across in a hurry. Suddenly the shock, the numbness broke into stark horror. He couldn't stand here painstakingly explaining the differences in the word *men* and the word *male* to a friendly alien, when he'd just found out . . . found out . . . his voice strangled. "Just take my word for it, Fanu," he said thickly, "in fifty years, homo sapiens will be a lot more extinct than your people. Now I've got to go and—and tell them—"

He stumbled blindly away and fumbled for the door, conscious of the big green eyes still fixed compassionately on his back.

*

He had managed to calm himself and speak quietly, but the men were as shocked as he had been, first numb in silent horror, then moving close together as if to draw comfort from their group, their solidity.

"There's—no mistake, Cap'n?" Chord asked timidly. He always spoke timidly; incongruous for such a giant.

"I've seen the plates myself, and the co-ordinates, Chord. And I have no reason to doubt Fanu's—the alien's—data. From what I've been able to gather, it must have happened about six months after we left. His equipment's superior to ours, but pretty soon we'll be able to see it for ourselves."

Somewhere in the back row of the group of men, there was a muffled sob. He could see the anguish on the other faces, men struggling with the idea of a future that was no future at all. Young Latimer from the drive room—the one they all called Tip—had bent over and buried his face in his hands. It was Tsen, the young navigator, who finally managed the question on all their minds.

"Then it's—just us, sir?"

"Just us." Everett waited a moment, then turned away, dismissing them with his back. It wasn't a thing you could make speeches about. One way or another, they'd have to come to terms with it, every man for himself.

He heard the rustle of Fanu's garments, and turned to smile a greeting. The two stood side by side on the hilltop, looking down at the men working in the little valley. "What is it to be?" Fanu finally inquired.

"It's—" Everett could not suppress an amused smile, "a hospital for you—and Garrett, the pharmacist's mate."

"Oh?" Fanu's features could not duplicate a smile, but his eyes blinked rapidly with pleasure. "That is most kind. Most kind."

"Hardly. It just takes care of one problem. The two of you can keep us in good health, I'm sure."

"Your race is so strong!" Fanu's toneless voice gave, nevertheless, an impression of amazement and awe. "My own people, under such a sentence as yours, gave themselves over to despair."

"You think we didn't?" Everett's jaw tightened, remembering the first few weeks; the dazed men, Garrett stopped in the very act of slashing his wrists. Then he straightened his back. "We've found that hard work is a remedy for despair, or at least—a good defense against it."

"I see," remarked the alien. "Or at least—I understand that it might be so. But how long can you work? Will you fill the valley with your superbly constructed buildings? For sixteen of your race?"

Everett shook his head, bitterly. "We'll all be dead before we can fill the valley. But at least we'll make ourselves comfortable, before we—go."

"There is no need to die."

He swung around to face the alien. "You've been hinting that and hinting that for the last two months! If there's one thing worse than despair it's false hope! Even if your people were immortal, and they're not—"

"I did not mean to anger you, John." The strange little paw uplifted in apology.

"Then quit hinting and say something."

"Mammals—" Fanu began, then halted, obviously groping for the proper terminology.

"Yes, we're mammals, technically," Everett snorted, "the mammalian characteristic perished with our solar system, though."

"That is not true—or it need not be true."

Everett stared at the alien, wishing for the thousandth time that he could read that dark expression. Fanu went on, “I have observed your race in undress, compared the information from your study reels—from your ship—the material you brought to me so graciously—I cannot thank you—”

“Yes, yes!” he broke in. Fanu was so damned polite. He liked the alien, but the only one of the Earthmen who really got along with him perfectly was Tsen, who was used to all this overdone courtesy.

“Forgive me, what I mean is, your . . . two sexual groups are so close together . . .”

Everett’s eyes widened. Then he laughed, embarrassed. “You just lost me. I mean, I don’t understand your statement, Fanu.”

“Your two sexual types are so exceptionally similar—”

“Oh, lord, vive la difference!” Everett laughed aloud, and some of the men in the valley glanced up, curious, pleased to see their captain laughing with the omnipotent, knowing alien. “If you mean our—females had two arms, two legs, and a head, yes, we were very similar, but—”

Fanu regarded John with compassion. “No, not that. I mean that, compared to our race, your own sexual differences seem minute. It would be a relatively simple matter to convert one to the other. I recall in the tapes several instances in which this sort of change occurred naturally, and others in which the changes were brought about medically.”

Everett knew his eyes were bulging, and he felt the anger rising in his throat. He beat it down. Fanu wouldn’t know. He could read about the taboos of another race without fully appreciating . . . in spite of his revulsion, Everett gave a spluttering laugh. “Yes, yes, I see your point, Fanu. It’s an interesting theory, but even if it would work, it, well, it wouldn’t work that way.”

"Why?"

"Well, it's a matter of—my men wouldn't stand for it. We're not guinea pigs," he finished, testily.

"No." The voice was compassionate again. "You are a race doomed to extinction, with a possible way out. My race had no such second chance."

Fanu glided away toward the laboratory and Everett stared after him, one thought drumming through his mind. "My God! He wasn't theorizing! He—he *meant* it!"

The slight noise finally made him look up. He hadn't heard anyone come in, and started involuntarily at seeing Chord's great hulk before him.

"Sorry to disturb you, Cap'n."

"That isn't necessary, Chord. What can I do for you?"

The big man smiled sheepishly. "Hard to break habits, sir. Guess I never will." Despite his size and demeanor, Chord was not stupid, though hampered by poor education and embarrassment for his giant clumsy body. Now he shifted uneasily from foot to foot as he mumbled. "I—guess I've been picked out as a representative, sir. For—for the men."

"Gripe committee? Look, I'm not really your superior any more, Chord. We're all together now."

"Yes, sir, but—you're still Captain."

Everett sighed, waited for the big man to continue. "Some—some of us would like to build private quarters, sir. I mean—not fights, or anything like that, we just—we'd like some privacy—you know—homes, sir, like—"

"Like back on Earth?" Chord nodded dumbly and Everett said, "Well, I see no objection to that. You didn't need to consult me."

"It's just—well, sir, some of the guys thought you might get the wrong idea, sir."

"Wrong idea?" Everett asked stupidly, startled by Chord's red face.

"Well, you know, a couple of men living alone. It's nothing like that, sir. Honest."

He waited until Chord left before he permitted the embarrassed amusement to boil over into his face; and knew that the amusement covered some strange unease that was almost fear.

"He actually worried about it," he laughed, telling Fanu later.

"Shouldn't he?" Fanu inquired gently. "John, don't stare. I'm not sure of the word in your tongue, but I think your people sense that the—the last person to approve of such a matter would be yourself."

Everett got to his feet, angrily. "Are you implying that my men would actually—"

"You said they were free agents. You said they were not your men."

Everett turned away, rubbing a tired hand across his eyes. "Yes, so I did. Habit."

"Habit in morals too, John?"

"Fanu! Look, I appreciate that you don't know our taboos, probably they're idiotic, but—they're *ours*. As for the men—"

"Do *you* know them, John?"

"Of course."

"How long did you expect to be here?"

He opened his mouth, then paused to consider, mentally counting. "Six months on planet, eight months coming, eight months back."

"How long have you been here now?"

"Eighteen—months." His face worked, remembering some of the material on those cursed tape reels. "Fanu, you're my friend, but what you're suggesting is ridiculous. You haven't known Earthmen long enough to make an adequate appraisal."

Fanu shook his head solemnly. "There is a folk saying on your tapes—we have a similar one—that one may be too close to the forest to see the trees." He gestured John to the window and pointed. "Count them, John. Seven small huts, and three are smaller than the others. Why?"

Trying to swallow the horror in his throat, the suspicion that both frightened and sickened him, he shook his head in denial. "They're friends. You wouldn't understand."

"No?" The voice sounded very sad. "Don't you think we had friends among our own? But you are blessed with bodies that will permit friends to become mates."

"Stop it!" Everett felt like screaming the words; he held a picture of a large whitewashed wall disintegrating before his eyes, of himself trying to hold it together with his bare hands, of his men standing by, staring at him. Fanu was gesturing again. Unwillingly, his eyes followed the pointing paw. The men had organized an impromptu ball game of some sort, rough house, much laughing, shouting, pushing and tussling. Two of them stumbled and fell together. They were slow in getting up and they moved apart with both reluctance and a touch of conscious guilt.

He jerked away from the window, trying to blot out the sight. The wall had large holes in it, the ravages of inevitability. His mind worked feverishly with brush and plaster; children, horseplaying, a reversion to adolescence—

"Put the question to your men!" For the first time, Fanu's tones were tense with the beginnings of anger. "You have a second chance, John! They have the right to choose for themselves if they want to die! You can't decide for them all! Put it to your men, or—" he swung around, to see that the little alien was actually trembling, "or I shall do so on my own initiative."

Everett felt a sour taste in his mouth. "All right," he shouted, "I'll put it to them—but don't blame me if they tear you to pieces afterward!"

The looks on their faces had been enough. The men knew Fanu, certainly. He was one of them now. They knew the tragic history of his people, respected his knowledge, even loved him. But he was an outsider, and he'd proved it. He didn't understand mankind.

The knock on the doorframe went through him like a shock.

It was Chord, and another man. Everett blinked in the half light, trying to pick him out. Young Latimer—the apprentice, the one they called Tip—just a kid—my God! Under his nose, right under his nose!

"Cap'n—" Chord began, then trailed off. The big man looked sick, stricken, and Everett became aware that his own expression must be one of outright condemnation. He—the mighty tolerant, benevolent skipper. We're all together now, eh? *In a pig's eye!* Did he think he was God? Everett suddenly hated his own guts, and struggled to bring his face to order. With a new humility, he said, "Come in, Chord. You too, Lat—Tip. What can I do for you?"

"About—about what you said, a couple of days ago. You know, about . . . the . . . about what Dr. Fanu said. Did he mean it?"

"Really mean it?" Tip added. Everett shifted his glance. Young, yes; but there was nothing simpering about him. Clear-eyes, unashamed, he met the Captain's eyes; a good-looking kid, the athletic, All-Academy type, but not *too* good-looking. Calloused hands. A faint residue of old acne scars along his jawline.

"Well," Everett said slowly, trying to keep his voice impersonal, "he says he means it."

"Dr. Fanu doesn't strike me as a joker," the boy continued. The alien had become "Doctor" to them after repairing several broken ribs and a fractured knee or ankle in the last few months.

"No, I don't think he was joking."

"How does he—I mean—"

"I didn't get the details," Everett cut in quickly. "But if he says he can—his race is advanced enough, biologically—he may be able to do what he says. Let us reproduce."

"Have babies," Tip amended. The bluntness shocked Everett. He'd never put it quite that way even to himself. "Will you—let us talk to him, Captain?"

Chord broke in, shamble-speeched as always. "Tip and me, we talked this over a long while. Funny part, we always—well—thought about something like this, then Dr. Fanu came along and said—thing is—well, will you take us to talk with him?"

He got up slowly, nodding. "If that's what you want." They nodded silently and he started toward the door, then turned, still torn by doubt and incredulity.

"Would you answer—one rather blunt question? Have you two—is this something that developed between you here on Prox, or were you—were you like this before touchdown?"

Both men suddenly looked dismayed, disgusted, their faith in an intelligent commander suddenly cracking across the top. Chord's lips curled in rage, but it was the boy who blurted out "For God's sake, sir, what do you think we are?"

"Sorry," he said quickly, "I—sorry. It's good of you to volunteer." He turned and led them toward the hilltop laboratory, but in his thoughts the unspoken answer drummed, over and over. "God in

Heaven, I don't know! I honestly don't know! And what's worse, I don't know what you're going to be, and neither will God!"

"It's really an elementary process from a surgical point of view," Fanu began academically.

Everett squirmed, his eyes straying toward the closed door of the hospital room, as Fanu went on. "Chemically, of course, we're on less sure ground. The hormones must be reproduced synthetically, pituitary stimulation, a great deal of chanciness. It's fortunate that your sexes produce enough of the hormones of each so that I could test them for synthesis. But there's no reason it shouldn't work."

He glared at the alien, taking out his emotion in fury at the scientific coldness of that voice. "In other words, they're just laboratory animals! Guinea pigs!"

"Not at all. It will work. It may take time for adjustment of the glandular system, and much will depend on physical adjustment. Now if I had been able to get him younger, before puberty—"

"Why Tip?" he demanded, interrupting, wanting to shift the attention from disgusting medical matters, hang on to his sanity. "I'd think Chord was so much bigger, he'd be better able to—"

"To carry a fetus? Not at all. Unfortunately it's a matter of pelvic development. Chord is much too masculine, his pelvis much too narrow to accommodate—"

Everett exploded in hysterical laughter. "Too masculine! That's a jolt, isn't it! Too masculine!"

"I can give you a sedative," the alien said tonelessly. "You sound as if you needed one." But the hand on his shoulder was faintly comforting. Everett pulled himself together a little, and Fanu said "John, it must be. If your race is to survive—"

"Maybe we shouldn't survive!" he snarled. "Wouldn't it be more decent to die, die clean and human and what we were intended to be, than as some—some obscene imitation of—*it's not natural*!"

"Neither is the presence of your race on this planet."

"That's different," he countered weakly. "That's mechanics. This—"

"You bred domestic animals into alternate phenotypes for your own use. You bred humans to some extent, with your limitations on marriage, compulsory sterilization for defective types—"

"I opposed that!" Everett defended. "That was different—"

"And so is your situation—different from anything that ever happened to your race," the alien said. The Earthman stared bleakly, his prejudices and his intelligence warring. "I asked you to put it to your men, John. You did. You considered it only fair that they should make their own decision. They did. Now you oppose it."

"I brought them here, didn't I?"

"Yes, and I thank you for that. Some day you shall thank yourself."

"I doubt that. Oh, I know by your reasoning, I'm an anachronism, but I still can't—" he trailed off, glancing back at the hospital door. "Why both of them, if you can only—convert one?"

Fanu blinked in surprise. "For their physical pleasure, John. I understand that is quite important to your species, whether or not as a means of reproduction. Certain anatomical rearrangements—"

"Spare me!" He saw the alien did not understand the phrase and made some elaboration.

"Oh," the alien murmured an apology. "I thought you would wish to know."

"I—" Everett swallowed. "I'd rather know about the scientific part of it. I still don't understand. I mean, there are males and there are females, and that's that."

"Not at all, not in your species. There are members, like your crew, with predominantly male organs and vestigial female organs, and—presumably, I've only seen films—predominantly female organs and only rudimentary male organs." He paused. "Shall I go on?"

The Captain found that he wanted a stiff drink, but nodded for Fanu to continue.

"There are vestigal organs, as I say, and certain common elements. The DNA factor can be cross-stimulated by hormones, certain chemicals—it was done long ago, to a limited extent, by your own scientists." Everett watched the alien doctor pick up a phial and hold the contents to the light. "It's most fortunate that your race comes equipped with pairs of everything, including the reproductive organs."

"It gives you a guinea pig expendable."

If Fanu had been capable of human expression, he would probably have looked hurt; Everett, increasingly sensitive to the alien gestures and intonations, knew he was wounded. He blinked solemnly. "It makes it possible for him, guinea pig if you prefer, to be both sexes. What must be done is to transfer one set of lobes, and the nature of these makes it possible to separate, and increase the chances of success. We can subject the interstitial tissue to massive doses of hormones, and DNA mutating materials." Everett evidently looked skeptical, for Fanu hurried to the laboratory animal cages and extracted a furry little native mammal, about the size of a squirrel. "It works, John. It works. This is proof. Not changed at infancy or at puberty, but as a full-grown male!"

Everett stroked the animal absently, glumly. "Yes, but it's not human. And—will they be?"

Fanu didn't answer. Everett hadn't expected him to answer.

*

A few of the comments were lewd, as he'd expected, but most of the men were kind. He had gone down to the recreation hall, gotten a glass of their home-brewed ale and listened, fading into the background. No more than three or four of the men had made cracks, and they were the ones who'd make cracks about anything, simply for lack of anything better to do. Good workers, but dense in the empathy department.

"May I sit down, sir?"

It was Tsen. Everett gestured and watched the little navigator seat himself. Tsen made an expression of distaste toward the gossipers. "You do not approve, either, of what Chord and the youngster have done?"

"It's not a question of approval, Tsen. It's a question of survival. They feel, and Fanu feels, it's the only way." He gave a short, bitter laugh. "They're right, of course."

"But you do not approve."

He took a long pull at his glass and muttered "I was taught it was a sin. *The* sin."

"It? Homosexuality?" Everett winced, saw Tsen's expression and tried to depersonalize himself. "But, Captain, wasn't the very base of that sinfulness, the fact that they could not reproduce?"

He stared. He knew his jaw was dropping, but he stared, anyway.

"Do you think Doctor Fanu would accept me as a second—volunteer?"

"You!" He looked around quickly and lowered his voice. "Tsen, I never suspected that—"

"That I am human, sir? We've been here nearly two years, and we are not monks, not ascetics. If anyone here has been reared in such a tradition of asceticism, it is myself. Yet affection, physical need—they overwhelm some people. We are not all blessed with your control, sir. Some seek satisfaction from themselves. For some, it requires an attraction to others, and if the others happen to be of the same sex, that is unfortunate, but—under these circumstances—unavoidable, sir."

Everett flinched. That was getting it straight between the eyes. "Who, if I might ask?"

"Would it make you feel better, sir, or only more bitter?" Everett, trapped in his own prejudice, could not look into the dark eyes. "Will Doctor Fanu accept me for consideration? Are things—well with Chord and Tip?"

"Fanu seems satisfied, and if he isn't, no one will be." Everett tilted up his glass, drained the dregs and set it down hard. "Yes, I'm sure Fanu will consider you. You think alike, modern. You should get along very well."

He hadn't thought about the situation for weeks. Tsen was out of the hospital, and there were other things to consider. Supplies from the ship were running out. Everett applied all his skill and energy to working out substitute methods, converting some machinery, utilizing native products. The men continued to surprise him with jury riggings and inspired minor inventions. The planet offered a mild climate and two growing seasons a year. Still, as their equipment disintegrated, they were forced to resort to native beasts of burden, and to do more manual labor.

How long had Chord been doing the work of two men on the community farm? He confronted the giant late one afternoon as they straggled back to the mess hall.

"I can handle it, Cap'n. I grew up on a farm."

"That's not the point, Chord. Where's Tip?"

"At home." There was no apology and no anger, mere honest confusion.

"Chord, it's not fair for you to do his work. I don't care if you're the strongest man here. He's imposing on you."

"No sir. No, he's not. He's sick. Doctor Fanu—"

But Everett was already striding purposefully toward the small hut shared by Chord and young Latimer. The big man loped behind him, protesting, but the Captain could think of nothing but the rotten laziness of the younger man, who would let his lover do his work, and idle here—

The hut was darkened, and for a moment he could not make out the shapes of things, Chord's words a muttered undercurrent in the background. He stepped over the high threshold, and looked around, finally making out the form on the bed in the corner.

"Latimer!"

The boy raised himself part way, pulling a blanket close around him. A blanket? Lord, it must be eighty-five or ninety in here! "What the hell is this—letting Chord do your assigned work?"

"Sir, I didn't—I can't get up!" The voice was pathetic, and Everett had to force himself to remember that the kid was malingering. "Has Garrett seen you yet?"

"N—no, sir. I—I—"

Everett pulled at the blanket, but the boy pulled it around himself with savage strength, shouting "Leave me alone!" then suddenly burst into tears and fell back on the bed. Chord grabbed Everett's arm. "Damn it, leave him alone!" Fury trembled the big man's voice. "Leave him alone—sir."

Tip's sobs from beneath the blanket were high, muffled, hysterical. Everett pulled his bruised arm loose from Chord's great fingers, looking down at the form beneath the blanket; a form strangely, unbelievably distorted—

"Oh, my God," he said, and left the hut almost running, heading for Fanu's hillside laboratory.

"But of course it worked, John. Didn't you believe me?"

Everett paced the floor, running his hands through his hair again and again. "My God, no, no, I—I didn't. I thought it was some sort of cruel, monstrous joke, a—a ghastly nightmare I couldn't wake up from."

"Do you want to?"

"Want to? Oh, Lord, Fanu, haven't you been listening? This is monstrous, it's—unholy!"

"The word is without meaning to me, John. It is without meaning to the men who wished this done."

He stopped pacing and sat down. "If you can do this, why can't you—test tubes—anything but this!"

"It might be possible."

"It might—then why in God's name this—blasphemy?"

"John, the word does not exist for me. I could create a fertilized ovum in that matter, but gestation would be tremendously difficult outside its natural element. It would require every moment of two or three men's time for the entire gestation period. And even if we had so many men at our disposal—"

"But—"

"Hear me out, John. Tip was a poor choice for the—first. I would not have consented. I warned them of the dangers, but Tip insisted. Chord had many reservations, but the younger man won out. He will have difficulty. But even so, incubating a fetus in his body is much safer and surer than any amount of laboratory work."

"Safer for the fetus."

"That's true."

He lunged to his feet, confronting the alien, furious. "You're gambling with that boy's life!"

"Yes, and he knows it. He said—he said that he wanted Chord's inheritance combined with his."

Everett turned away, hands to his face. "Oh, God, what am I trapped in? Why didn't the ship crash coming in?"

"Ask your God, John."

He jerked around, stunned.

"If you accept your deity's omnipotence, mustn't you accept the fact that he has permitted this development?"

"If that boy dies—Fanu, if you'd *seen* him—"

The alien blinked, solemnly. "Hysteria is perhaps natural," he confirmed. "Even though he has been prepared for this there is some amount of emotional shock remaining. You must remember, there is a certain chemical imbalance. Tsen will have an easier time."

John sat down again. The nightmare was rising above his ears, drowning him in its terrifying black waters. He didn't hear the alien go out.

The jokes had ceased. They concerned too many men now. The men who were concerned and still able did not look too kindly on lewd comments about their partners. Emotional patterns were developing, friendships becoming deeper, the new way of life more and more ingrained. Everett sometimes thought that he sounded like a reactionary preacher, mumbling to himself. They were all against him now. They knew how he felt, and they had stopped discussing it in his hearing. They made their reports when they must, and that was all, a habit not yet broken.

He kept his log. Some day he would either run out of paper or learn to make a substitute. That was something to consider. The one grain they'd been able to grow—he'd have to consult the record tapes; how did you make rice paper? Maybe among his study materials, Tsen had something that would tell him—the hell with Tsen! Why bother? He'd be dead, they'd all be dead before they ran out of paper. Then what use would the log be to any of them?

The rainy season between the two growing seasons was well under way when someone beat on his door, one night. He mumbled admission, not turning.

"Sir!"

"What? Chord, what is it?" The giant looked wild, his hair tousled, his eyes wide. "What is it, man?"

"It's Tip, sir. He's awful sick!"

"Hasn't he been, all along?"

"This is—no, sir, this is different. He . . . he hurts. He's in awful pain."

Everett gasped and had to suppress a hysterical laugh. "Oh. Well, isn't that just what you've been waiting for? He ought to have thought of that before he took Fanu's offer." He wondered insanely if he ought to offer congratulations.

The big man dug his thumbs into Everett's shoulders with painful force, his face livid with anger and fear. "Look, sir, I've had about enough of your—" he stopped and gulped and said, quite meekly for him, "Look, sir, I'm scared. It—it's not *time* yet. Not for about six weeks. And I'm—I'm scared, sir," he finished pitifully.

The two men hurried to Chord's hut through the blowing rain, and Everett suppressed another burst of crazy hysteria. Those corny old videocasts on a vanished world! Rainstorms, the black of night, a hurried summons—he found himself dismissing irrelevant, ribald thoughts of a midnight delivery of a . . . child . . . by two men.

But when he stepped into the hut the thoughts fled, beaten away by the pain of the youth on the bed. He was incredibly pale, sweating badly, trying desperately to muffle his outcries and not succeeding very well. His lips were white and blood-specked where he'd chewed on them. Everett found himself concerned, involved; whatever the cause, he could not ignore the agony in the young face. Tip gave the Captain one look, turned his face away and shut his eyes. "Couldn't you get—Garrett," he said weakly, and gasped.

"When did this start?" Everett asked, running over his memory quickly for things that would help, and for the first time wishing he'd listened more closely to Fanu's explanations.

"While ago." Tip made a smothered sound.

"*How* long ago?" he snapped, trying to be sympathetic in spite of his worry.

"Couple . . . couple hours." The boy suddenly threw his head back, muffling a groan, trembling violently. Everett glanced at his chronometer. The spasm lasted nearly two minutes. He kept his eyes averted from the swollen body, its distortion no longer concealable by the blanket. Tip, breathing hoarsely, murmured "How did our women ever—" then his eyes widened in surprise and he slumped back on the bed, unconscious.

"Tip! Tip! Wake up, kid—please," Chord pleaded, bending over the boy, shaking him gently, stroking the sweat-bathed forehead.

"That's no help." Everett felt frantic. Fanu would have to straighten this out. He *had* to. He couldn't let the boy die, not after a—sacrifice—like this!

"Can you carry him?" He helped Chord wrap the blanket around the unconscious figure, that still twisted silently, spasmodically beneath their hands. Chord picked him up, and they hurried through the rain, up toward the beacon lights of the alien laboratory.

"And he'd been conscious until then?" Fanu questioned gently, moving around the moaning figure.

"Yes, all the time," Chord answered. "It isn't time, is it? It isn't time? That's what he was scared of. He was afraid to say anything. He said it'd go away . . . all those books and tapes he read . . . he . . . by God, if he dies, I'll kill you!"

"I am not your God," Fanu said quietly, sadly. "Life and death are not in my hands, but I will do all that I can."

"Fanu—" Everett began, dragging his eyes away from the obscenely swollen body. He hadn't seen any of the . . . experiments . . . in clear light until now, and the sight stunned him, brought all this brutally home. Maybe he had been a fool. Why had he, alone, been kept in the dark? He realized only now; there had been a conspiracy of sorts, to keep Tip, and Tsen, and young Reading, the ComCon man, out of his way.

"You've got to do something. Chord says it isn't time."

"Seven and a half or better of your gestation counts. Better than I hoped."

"Fanu . . . the human male was never designed for . . . this . . ." he found himself wanting to giggle, more with fright than amusement. Tip was regaining consciousness, moaning slightly, grunting like an animal. Garrett was there, white-coated, his hand reassuring over Tip's, calm and matter of fact as he explored the boy's body briefly with a stethoscope. "Heartbeat fine so far, Dr. Fanu. But we can't monkey around too long."

"Chord, carry him in there. I must operate this time, I am afraid." As Tip's eyes focused on him, the alien's voice—and it no longer sounded toneless to Everett—said kindly "I'm sorry, Tip. You are too masculinely constructed. Remember, I warned you."

The boy nodded wordlessly, biting his lip. Then, as Chord picked him up, he gasped between his teeth "If it comes to a choice—remember what you promised me, Doc—"

Everett sank down in a chair and buried his face in his hands, and consciousness was swamped in black nightmare. The next thing he knew, Chord stumbled out of the operating room door, and Everett, feeling nightmarishly idiotic, watched him give a startling performance of expectant fatherhood.

"Female," Fanu announced, his tiny mouth curving in the nearest approach to a smile he could manage. Chord caught at the alien's clothing.

"Tip? *Tip?*"

"He's all right. Very weak, but fine. You can go in and see him. Be very gentle, though."

Chord's face went limp all over. "Oh, thank God," he muttered, "thank God! Cap'n, that idiot kid made the Doc promise—to save the kid if it came a choice—"

He pushed past them into the other room.

"Female?"

"Female," Fanu confirmed. "I arranged things that way—with all of them."

"But—"

"Did you think this was permanent?"

"Well—well, yes, I did."

Fanu made a sound of alien amusement. "That's what's been troubling you. No, John. In fifteen years your planet will have four or five nubile females, at least. The climate will aid precocity. In two generations you will be on firm footing. Your race is intelligent, hardy, ingenious, young—all the things mine wasn't. Tip's case was the most difficult. He'll have to wait two years before attempting this again."

"Again?" Everett gaped.

"His own request. I had difficulty making him agree even to that, or I should have taken measures to end it now. I shall, next time. When the females are grown, his chore will be done."

"When the females are grown—what happens to the—to the converted men then? The—attachments, the—the lovers, Fanu?"

Fanu blinked sadly. "I don't know, John. I shall not be here. I am old, John—old. But I'm sure you'll solve it."

Everett turned and walked over to the window, staring down at the twinkling lights from the huts, the rebirth of homo sapiens. Somewhere behind him he could hear an infant wailing. The rain had stopped, and stars were coming out, the strange stars of a strange world.

"All right," he said softly, "I was wrong. Now, for Your sake, tell us what's next?"

1963

SONYA DORMAN

When I Was Miss Dow

THESE hungry, mother-haunted people come and find us living in what they like to call crystal palaces, though really we live in glass places, some of them highly ornamented and others plain as paper. They come first as explorers, and perhaps realize we are a race of one sex only, rather amorphous beings of proteide; and we, even baby I, are Protean, also, being able to take various shapes at will. One sex, one brain lobe, we live in more or less glass bridges over the humanoid chasm, eating, recreating, attending races and playing other games like most living creatures.

Eventually, we're all dumped into the cell banks and reproduced once more.

After the explorers comes the colony of miners and scientists. The warden and some of the other elders put on faces to greet them, agreeing to help with the mining of some ores, even giving them a koota or two as they become interested in our racing dogs. They set up their places of life, pop up their machines, bang-bang, chug-chug; we put on our faces, forms, smiles and costumes; I am old enough to learn to change my shape, too.

The Warden says to me, "It's about time you made a change, yourself. Some of your friends are already working for these people, bringing home credits and sulfas."

My Uncle (by the Warden's fourth conjunction) made himself over at the start, being one of the first to realize how it could profit us.

I protest to the Warden, "I'm educated and trained as a scholar. You always say I must remain deep in my mathematics and other studies."

My Uncle says, "You have to do it. There's only one way for us to get along with them," and he runs his fingers through his long blond hair. My Uncle's not an educated person, but highly placed, politically, and while Captain Dow is around my Uncle retains this particular shape. The Captain is shipping out soon, then Uncle will find some other features, because he's already warned that it's unseemly for him to be chasing around in the face of a girl after the half-bearded boys from the space ships. I don't want to do this myself, wasting so much time, when the fourteen decimals even now are clicking on my mirrors.

The Warden says, "We have a pattern from a female botanist, she ought to do for you. But before we put you into the pattern tank, you'll have to approximate another brain lobe. They have two."

"I know," I say, sulkily. A botanist. A she!

"Into the tank," the Warden says to me without mercy, and I am his to use as he believes proper.

I spend four days in the tank absorbing the female Terran pattern. When I'm released, the Warden tells me, "Your job is waiting for you. We went to a lot of trouble to arrange it." He sounds brusque, but perhaps this is because he hasn't conjoined for a long time. The responsibilities of being Warden of Mines and Seeds come first, long before any social engagement.

I run my fingers through my brunette curls, and notice my Uncle is looking critically at me. "Haven't you made yourself rather old?" he asks.

"Oh, he's all right," the Warden says. "Thirty-three isn't badly matched to the Doctor, as I understand it."

Dr. Arnold Proctor, the colony's head biologist, is busy making radiograph pictures (with his primitive X-rays) of skeletal structures: murger birds, rodents, and our pets and racers, the kootas—dogs to the Terrans, who are fascinated by them. We breed them primarily for speed and stamina, but some of them carry a gene for an inherited structural defect which cripples them and they have to be destroyed before they are full grown. The Doctor is making a special study of kootas.

He gets up from his chair when I enter his office. "I'm Miss Dow, your new assistant," I say, hoping my long fingernails will stand up to the pressure of punch keys on the computer, since I haven't had much practise in retaining foreign shapes. I'm still in uncertain balance between myself and Martha Dow, who is also myself. But one does not have two lobes for nothing, I discover.

"Good morning. I'm glad you're here," the Doctor says.

He is a nice, pink man, with silver hair, soft-spoken, intelligent. I'm pleased, as we work along, to find he doesn't joke and wisecrack like so many of the Terrans, though I am sometimes whimsical. I like music and banquets as well as my studies.

Though absorbed in his work, Dr. Proctor isn't rude to interrupters. A man of unusual balance, coming as he does from a culture which sends out scientific parties that are ninety per cent of one sex, when their species provides them with two. At first meetings he is dedicated but agreeable, and I'm charmed.

"Dr. Proctor," I ask him one morning. "Is it possible for you to radiograph my koota? She's very fine, from the fastest stock available, and I'd like to breed her."

"Yes, yes, of course," he promises with his quick, often absent, smile. "By all means. You wish to breed only the best." It's typical of him to assume we're all as dedicated as he.

My Uncle's not pleased. "There's nothing wrong with your koota," he says. "What do you want to X-ray her for? Suppose he finds something is wrong? You'll be afraid to race or breed her, and she won't be replaced. Besides, your interest in her may make him suspicious."

"Suspicious of what?" I ask, but my Uncle won't say, so I ask him, "Suppose she's bred and her pups are cripples?"

The Warden says, "You're supposed to have your mind on your work, not on racing. The koota was just to amuse you when you were younger."

I lean down and stroke her head, which is beautiful, and she breathes a deep and gentle breath in response.

"Oh, let him go," my Uncle says wearily. He's getting disgusted because they didn't intend for me to bury myself in a laboratory or a computer room, without making more important contacts. But a scholar is born with a certain temperament, and has an introspective nature, and as I'm destined to eventually replace the Warden, naturally I prefer the life of the mind.

"I must say," my Uncle remarks, "you look the image of a Terran female. Is the work interesting?"

"Oh, yes, fascinating," I reply, and he snorts at my lie, since we both know it's dull and routine, and most of the time is spent working out the connections between my two brain lobes, which still present me with some difficulty.

My koota bitch is subjected to a pelvic radiograph. Afterwards, I stand on my heels in the small, darkened cubicle, looking at the film on the viewing screen. There he stands, too, with his cheekbones emerald in the peculiar light, and his hair, which is silver in daylight, looks phosphorescent. I resist this. I am resisting this

Doctor with the X-ray eyes who can examine my marrow with ease. He sees Martha's marrow, every perfect corpuscle of it.

You can't imagine how comforting it is to be so transparent. There's no need to pretend, adjust, advance, retreat or discuss the oddities of my planet. We are looking at the X-ray film of my prized racer and companion to determine the soundness of her hip joints, yet I suspect the Doctor, platinum-green and tall as a tower, is piercing my reality with his educated gaze. He can see the blood flushing my surfaces. I don't need to do a thing but stand up straight so the crease of fat at my waist won't distort my belly button, the center of it all.

"You see?" he says.

I do see, looking at the film in the darkness where perfection or disaster may be viewed, and I'm twined in the paradox which confronts me here. The darker the room, the brighter the screen and the clearer the picture. Less light! and the truth becomes more evident. Either the koota is properly jointed and may be bred without danger of passing the gene on to her young, or she is not properly jointed, and cannot be used. Less light, more truth! And the Doctor is green sculpture—a little darker and he would be a bronze—but his natural color is pink alabaster.

"You see," the Doctor says, and I do try to see. He points his wax pencil at one hip joint on the film, and says, "A certain amount of osteo-arthritic buildup is already evident. The cranial rim is wearing down, she may go lame. She'll certainly pass the defect on to some of her pups, if she's bred."

This koota has been my playmate and friend for a long time. She retains a single form, that of koota, full of love and beautiful speed; she has been a source of pleasure and pride.

Dr. Proctor, of the pewter hair, will discuss the anatomical defects of the koota in a gentle and cultivated voice. I am disturbed. There shouldn't be any need to explain the truth, which is evident. Yet it seems that to comprehend the exposures, I require a special education. It's said that the more you have seen, the quicker you are to sort the eternal verities into one pile and the dismal illusions into another. How is it that sometimes the Doctor wears a head which resembles that of a koota, with a splendid muzzle and noble brow?

Suddenly he gives a little laugh and points the end of the wax pencil at my navel, announcing: "There. There, it is essential that the belly button be attached onto the pelvis, or you'll bear no children." Thoughts of offspring had occurred to me. But weren't we discussing my racer? The radiograph film is still clipped to the view screen, and upon it, spread-eagled, appears the bony Rorschach of my koota bitch, her hip joints expressing doom.

I wish the Doctor would put on the daylight. I come to the conclusion that there's a limit to how much truth I can examine, and the more I submit to the conditions necessary for examining it, the more unhappy I become.

Dr. Proctor is a man of such perfect integrity that he continues to talk about bones and muscles until I'm ready to scream for mercy. He has done something that is unusual and probably prohibited, but he's not aware of it. I mean it must be prohibited in his culture, where it seems they play on each other, but not with each other. I am uneasy, fluctuating.

He snaps two switches. Out goes the film and on goes the sun, making my eyes stream with sensitive and grateful tears, although he's so adjusted to these contrasts he doesn't so much as blink. Floating in the sunshine I've become opaque. He can't see anything but my surface tensions, and I wonder what he does in his spare time. A part of me seems to tilt, or slide.

"There, there, oh dear, Miss Dow," he says, patting my back, rubbing my shoulder blades. His forearms and fingers extend gingerly. "You do want to breed only the best, don't you?" he asks. I begin within me a compulsive ritual of counting the elements; it's all I can do to keep communications open between my brain lobes. I'm suffering from eclipses: one goes dark, the other lights up, that one goes dark, the other goes nova.

"There, there," the Doctor says, distressed because I'm quivering and trying to keep the connections open; I have never felt clogged before. They may have to put me back into the pattern tank.

Profoundly disturbed, I lift my face, and he gives me a kiss. Then I'm all right, balanced again, one lobe composing a concerto for virtix flute, the other one projecting, "Oh Arnie, oh Arnie." Yes, I'm okay for the shape I'm in. He's marking my joints with his wax pencil (the marks of which can be easily erased from the film surface) and he's mumbling, "It's essential, oh yes, it's essential."

Finally he says, "I guess all of us colonists are lonely here," and I say, "Oh yes, aren't we," before I realize the enormity of the Warden's manipulations, and what a lot I have to learn. Evidently the Warden triple-carded me through the Colony Punch Center as a Terran. I lie and say, "Oh, yes. Yes, yes. Oh, Arnie, put out the light," for we may find some more truth.

"Not here," Arnie says, and of course he's right. This is a room for study, for cataloguing obvious facts, not a place for carnival. There are not many places for it, I discover with surprise. Having lived in glass all my life I expect everyone else to be as comfortable there as I am but this isn't so.

Just the same we find his quarters, after dark, to be comfortable and free of embarrassment. You wouldn't think a dedicated man of his age would be so vigorous, but I find out he spends his weekends at the recreation center hitting a ball with his hand. The ball bounces back off a wall and he hits it and hits it. Though he's given that up now because we're together on weekends.

"You're more than an old bachelor like me deserves," he tells me.

"Why are you an old bachelor?" I ask him. I do wonder why, if it's something not to be.

He tries to explain it to me. "I'm not a young man. I wouldn't make a good husband, I'm afraid. I like to work late, to be undisturbed. In my leisure time, I like to make wood carvings. Sometimes I go to bed with the sun and sometimes I'm up working all night. And then children. No. I'm lucky to be an old bachelor," he says.

Arnie carves kaku wood, which has a brilliant grain and is soft enough to permit easy carving. He's working on a figure of a murger bird, whittling lengthwise down the wood so the grain, wavy, full of flowing, wedge-shaped lines, will represent the feathers. The lamp light shines on his hair and the crinkle of his eyelids as he looks down and carves, whittles, turns. He's absorbed in what he doesn't see there but he's projecting what he wants to see. It's the reverse of what he must do in the viewing room. I begin to suffer a peculiar pain, located in the nerve cluster between my lungs. He's not talking to me. He's not caressing me. He's forgotten I'm here, and like a false projection, I'm beginning to fade. In another hour perhaps the film will become blank. If he doesn't see me, then am I here?

He's doing just what I do when absorbed in one of my own projects, and I admire the intensity with which he works: it's magnificent. Yes, I'm jealous of it. I burn with rage and jealousy. He has abandoned me to be Martha and I wish I were myself again, free in shape and single in mind. Not this sack of mud clinging to another. Yet he's teaching me that it's good to cling to another. I'm exhausted from strange disciplines. Perhaps he's tired, too; I see that sometimes he kneads the muscles of his stomach with his hands, and closes his eyes.

The Warden sits me down on one of my rare evenings home, and talks angrily. "You're making a mistake," he says. "If the Doctor finds out what you are, you'll lose your job with the colony. Besides, we never supposed you'd have a liaison with only one man. You were supposed to start with the Doctor, and go on from there. We need every credit you can bring in. And by the way, you haven't done well on that score lately. Is he stingy?"

"Of course he isn't."

"But all you bring home in credits is your pay."

I can think of no reply. It's true the Warden has a right to use me in whatever capacity would serve us all best, as I will use others when I'm a Warden, but he and my Uncle spend half the credits from my job on sulfadiazole, to which they've become addicted.

"You've no sense of responsibility," the Warden says. Perhaps he's coming close to time for conjunction again, and this makes him more concerned about my stability.

My Uncle says, "Oh, he's young, leave him alone. As long as he turns over most of those pay credits to us. Though what he uses the remainder for, I'll never know."

I use it for clothes at the Colony Exchange. Sometimes Arnie takes me out for an evening, usually to the Laugh Tree Bar, where the space crews, too, like to relax. The bar is the place to find joy babies; young, pretty, planet-born girls who work at the Colony

Punch Center during the day, and spend their evenings here competing for the attention of the officers. Sitting here with Arnie, I can't distinguish a colonist's daughter from one of my friends or relatives. They wouldn't know me, either.

Once, at home, I try to talk with a few of these friends about my feelings. But I discover that whatever female patterns they've borrowed are superficial ones; none of them bother to grow an extra lobe, but merely tuck the Terran pattern into a corner of their own for handy reference. They are most of them on sulfas. Hard and shiny toys, they skip like pebbles over the surface of the colonists' lives.

Then they go home, revert to their own free forms, and enjoy their mathematics, colors, compositions, and seedings.

"Why me?" I demand of the Warden. "Why two lobes? Why me?"

"We felt you'd be more efficient," he answers. "And while you're here, which you seldom are these days, you'd better revert to other shapes. Your particles may be damaged if you hold that woman form too long."

Oh, but you don't know, I want to tell him. You don't know I'll hold it forever. If I'm damaged or dead, you'll put me into the cell banks, and you'll be amazed, astonished, terrified, to discover that I come out complete, all Martha. I can't be changed.

"You little lump of protagon," my Uncle mumbles bitterly. "You'll never amount to anything, you'll never be a Warden. Have you done any of your own work recently?"

I say, "Yes, I've done some crystal divisions, and re-grown them in non-established patterns." My Uncle is in a bad mood, as he's kicking sulfa and his nerve tissue is addled. I'm wise to speak quietly to him, but he still grumbles.

"I can't understand why you like being a two-lobed pack of giggles. I couldn't wait to get out of it. And you were so dead against it to begin with."

"Well, I have learned," I start to say, but can't explain what it is I'm still learning, and close my eyes. Part of it is that on the line between the darkness and the brightness it's easiest to float. I've never wanted to practise only easy things. My balance is damaged. I never had to balance. It's not a term or concept that I understand even now, at home, in free form. Some impress of Martha's pattern lies on my own brain cells. I suspect it's permanent damage, which gives me joy. That's what I mean about not understanding it. I am taught to strive for perfection. How can I be pleased with this, which may be a catastrophe?

Arnie carves on a breadth of kaku wood, bringing out to the surface a seascape. Knots become clots of spray, a flaw becomes windblown spume. I want to be Martha. I'd like to go to the Laugh Tree with Arnie, for a good time, I'd like to learn to play cards with him.

You see what happens: Arnie is, in his way, like my original self, and I hate that part of him, since I've given it up to be Martha. Martha makes him happy, she is chocolate to his appetite, pillow for his weariness.

I turn for company to my koota. She's the color of morning, her chest juts out like an axe blade, her ribs spring up and back like wings, her eyes are large and clear as she returns my gaze. Yet she's beyond hope; in a little time, she'll be lame; she cannot race any more, she must not mother a litter. I turn to her and she gazes back into my eyes, dreaming of speed and wind on the sandy beaches where she has run.

"Why don't you read some tapes?" Arnie suggests to me, because I'm restless and I disturb him. The koota lies at my feet. I read tapes. Every evening in his quarters Arnie carves, I read tapes, the broken racer lies at my feet. I pass through Terran history this way. When the clown tumbles into the tub, I laugh. Terran history is full of clowns and tubs; at first it seems that's all there is, but you learn to see beneath the comic costumes.

While I float on the taut line, the horizon between light and dark, where it's so easy, I begin to sense what is under the costumes: staggering down the street dead drunk on a sunny afternoon with everyone laughing at you; hiding under the veranda because you made blood come out of Pa's face; kicking a man when he's in the gutter because you've been kicked and have to pass it on. Tragedy is what one of the Terrans called being a poet in the body of a cockroach.

"Have you heard the rumor?" Arnie asks, putting down the whittling tool. "Have you heard that some of the personnel in Punch Center aren't really humans?"

"Not really?" I ask, putting away the tape. We have no tragedy. In my species, family relationships are based only on related gene patterns; they are finally dumped into the family bank and a new relative is created from the old. It's one form of ancient history multiplying itself, but it isn't tragic. The koota, her utility destroyed by a recessive gene, lies sleeping at my feet. Is this tragedy? But she is a single form, she can't regenerate a lost limb, or exfoliate brain tissue. She can only return my gaze with her steadfast and affectionate one.

"What are they, then?" I ask Arnie. "If they're not human?"

"The story is that the local life forms aren't as we really see them. They've put on faces, like ours, to deal with us. And some of them have filtered into personnel."

Filtered! As if I were a virus.

"But they must be harmless," I say. "No harm has come to anyone."

"We don't know that for a fact," Arnie replies.

"You look tired," I say, and he comes to me, to be soothed, to be loved in his flesh, his single form, his search for the truth in the darkness of the viewing cubicle. At present he's doing studies of murger birds. Their spinal cavities are large, air-filled ovals, and their bone is extremely porous, which permits them to soar to great heights.

The koota no longer races on the wind-blown beaches; she lies at our feet, looking into the distance. The wall must be transparent to her eyes, I feel that beyond it she sees clearly how the racers go, down the long, bright curve of sand in the morning sun. She sighs, and lays her head down on her narrow, delicate paws. I look into the distance too: bright beaches and Arnie, carrying me from his ship. But he will not carry me again.

Arnie says, "I seem to be tired all the time." He puts his head on my breast. "I don't think the food's agreeing with me, lately."

"Do you suffer pains?" I ask him, curiously.

"Suffer," he mutters. "What kind of nonsense is that, with analgesics. No I don't suffer. I just don't feel well."

He's absorbed in murger birds, kaku wood, he descends into the bottom of the darks and rises up like a rocket across the horizon into the thin clarity above, while I float. I no longer dare to breathe, I'm afraid of disturbing everything. I do not want anything. His head lies gently on my breast and I will not disturb him.

"Oh. My God," Arnie says, and I know what it's come to, even before he begins to choke, and his muscles leap although I hold him in my arms. I know his heart is choking on massive doses of blood; the brilliance fades from his eyes and they begin to go dark while I tightly hold him. If he doesn't see me as he dies, will I be here?

I can feel, under my fingers, how rapidly his skin cools. I must put him down, here with his carvings and his papers, and I must go home. But I lift Arnie in my arms, and call the koota, who gets up rather stiffly. It's long after dark, and I carry him slowly, carefully, home to what he called a crystal palace, where the Warden and my Uncle are teaching each other to play chess with a set some space captain gave them in exchange for seed crystals. They sit in a bloom of light, sparkling, their old brains bent over the chessmen, as I breathe open the door and carry Arnie in.

First, my Uncle gives me just a glance, but then another glance, and a hard stare. "Is that the Doctor?" he asks.

I put Arnie down and hold one of his cold hands. "Warden," I say, on my knees, on eye level with the chessboard and its carved men. "Warden, can you put him in one of the banks?"

The Warden turns to look at me, as hard as my Uncle. "You've become deranged, trying to maintain two lobes," he says. "You cannot reconstitute or recreate a Terran by our methods, and you must know it."

"Over the edge, over the edge," my Uncle says, now a blond, six-foot, hearty male Terran, often at the Laugh Tree with one of the joy babies. He enjoys life, his own or someone else's. I have, too, I suppose. Am I fading? I am, really, just one of Arnie's projections, a form on a screen in his mind. I am not, really, Martha. Though I tried.

"We can't have him here," the Warden says. "You better get him out of here. You couldn't explain a corpse like that to the colonists, if they come looking for him. They'll think we did something to him. It's nearly time for my next conjunction, do you want your nephew to arrive in disgrace? The Uncles will drain his bank."

The Warden gets up and comes over to me. He takes hold of my dark curls and pulls me to my feet. It hurts my physical me, which is Martha. God knows Arnie, I'm Martha, it seems to me. "Take him back to his quarters," the Warden says to me. "And come back here immediately. I'll try to see you back to your own pattern, but it may be too late. In part, I blame myself. If you must know. So I will try."

Yes, yes, I want to say to him; as I was, dedicated, free; turn me back into myself, I never wanted to be anyone else, and now I don't know if I am anyone at all. The light's gone from his eyes and he doesn't see me, or see anything, does he?

I pick him up and breathe the door out, and go back through the night to his quarters, where the lamp still burns. I'm going to leave him here, where he belongs. Before I go, I pick up the small carving of the murger bird, and take it with me, home to my glass bridge where at the edge of the mirrors the decimals are still clicking perfectly, clicking out known facts; an octagon can be reduced, the planet turns at such a degree on its axis, to see the truth you must have light of some sort, but to see the light you must have darkness of some sort. I can no longer float on the horizon between the two because that horizon has disappeared. I've learned to descend, and to rise, and descend again.

I'm able to revert without help to my own free form, to re-absorb the extra brain tissue. The sun comes up and it's bright. The night comes down and it's dark. I'm becoming somber, and a brilliant student. Even my Uncle says I'll be a good Warden when the time comes.

The Warden goes to conjunction; from the cell banks a nephew is lifted out. The koota lies dreaming of races she has run in the wind. It is our life, and it goes on, like the life of other creatures.

1966

KATE WILHELM

Baby, You Were Great

JOHN Lewisohn thought that if one more door slammed, or one more bell rang, or one more voice asked if he was all right, his head would explode. Leaving his laboratories, he walked through the carpeted hall to the elevator that slid wide to admit him noiselessly, was lowered, gently, two floors, where there were more carpeted halls. The door he shoved open bore a neat sign, AUDITIONING STUDIO. Inside, he was waved on through the reception room by three girls who knew better than to speak to him unless he spoke first. They were surprised to see him; it was his first visit there in seven or eight months. The inner room where he stopped was darkened, at first glance appearing empty, revealing another occupant only after his eyes had time to adjust to the dim lighting.

John sat in the chair next to Herb Javits, still without speaking. Herb was wearing the helmet and gazing at a wide screen that was actually a one-way glass panel permitting him to view the audition going on in the next room. John lowered a second helmet to his head. It fit snugly and immediately made contact with the eight prepared spots on his skull. As soon as he turned it on, the helmet itself was forgotten.

A girl had entered the other room. She was breathtakingly lovely, a long-legged honey blonde with slanting green eyes and apricot skin. The room was furnished as a sitting room with two couches, some chairs, end tables and a coffee table, all tasteful and lifeless, like an ad in a furniture trade publication. The girl stopped at the doorway and John felt her indecision, heavily tempered with nervousness and fear. Outwardly she appeared poised and expectant, her smooth face betraying none of her emotions. She took a hesitant step toward the couch, and a wire showed trailing behind her. It was attached to her head. At the same time a second door opened. A young man ran inside, slamming the door behind him; he looked wild and frantic. The girl registered surprise, mounting nervousness; she felt behind her for the door handle, found it and tried to open the door again. It was locked. John could hear nothing that was being said in the room; he only felt the girl's reaction to the unexpected interruption. The wild-eyed man was approaching her, his hands slashing through the air, his eyes darting glances all about them constantly. Suddenly he pounced on her and pulled her to him, kissing her face and neck roughly. She seemed paralyzed with fear for several seconds, then there was something else, a bland nothing kind of feeling that accompanied boredom sometimes, or too-complete self-assurance. As the man's hands fastened on her blouse in the back and ripped it, she threw her arms about him, her face showing passion that was not felt anywhere in her mind or in her blood.

"Cut!" Herb Javits said quietly.

The man stepped back from the girl and left her without a word. She looked about blankly, her torn blouse hanging about her hips, one shoulder strap gone. She was very beautiful. The audition manager entered, followed by a dresser with a gown that he threw about her shoulders. She looked startled; waves of anger mounted to fury as she was drawn from the room, leaving it empty. The two watching men removed their helmets.

"Fourth one so far," Herb grunted. "Sixteen yesterday; twenty the day before . . . All nothing." He gave John a curious look. "What's got you stirred out of your lab?"

"Anne's had it this time," John said. "She's been on the phone all night and all morning."

"What now?"

"Those damn sharks! I told you that was too much on top of the airplane crash last week. She can't take much more of it."

"Hold it a minute, Johnny," Herb said. "Let's finish off the next three girls and then talk." He pressed a button on the arm of his chair and the room beyond the screen took their attention again.

This time the girl was slightly less beautiful, shorter, a dimply sort of brunette with laughing blue eyes and an upturned nose. John liked her. He adjusted his helmet and felt with her.

She was excited; the audition always excited them. There was some fear and nervousness, not too much. Curious about how the audition would go, probably. The wild young man ran into the room, and her face paled. Nothing else changed. Her nervousness increased, not uncomfortably. When he grabbed her, the only emotion she registered was the nervousness.

"Cut," Herb said.

The next girl was also brunette, with gorgeously elongated legs. She was very cool, a real professional. Her mobile face reflected the range of emotions to be expected as the scene played through again, but nothing inside her was touched. She was a million miles away from it all.

The next one caught John with a slam. She entered the room slowly, looking about with curiosity, nervous, as they all were. She was younger than the other girls, less poised. She had pale gold hair piled in an elaborate mound of waves on top of her head. Her eyes were brown, her skin nicely tanned. When the man entered, her emotion changed quickly to fear, then to terror. John didn't know when he closed his eyes. He was the girl, filled with unspeakable terror; his heart pounded, adrenalin pumped into his system; he wanted to scream but could not. From the dim unreachable depths of his psyche there came something else, in waves, so mixed with terror that the two merged and became one emotion that pulsed and throbbed and demanded. With a jerk he opened his eyes and stared at the window. The girl had been thrown down to one of the couches, and the man was kneeling on the floor beside her, his hands playing over her bare body, his face pressed against her skin.

"Cut!" Herb said. His voice was shaken. "Hire her," he said. The man rose, glanced at the girl, sobbing now, and then quickly bent over and kissed her cheek. Her sobs increased. Her golden hair was down, framing her face; she looked like a child. John tore off the helmet. He was perspiring.

Herb got up, turned on the lights in the room, and the window blanked out, blending with the wall. He didn't look at John. When he wiped his face, his hand was shaking. He rammed it in his pocket.

"When did you start auditions like that?" John asked, after a few moments of silence.

"Couple of months ago. I told you about it. Hell, we had to, Johnny. That's the six hundred nineteenth girl we've tried out! Six hundred nineteen! All phonies but one! Dead from the neck up. Do you have any idea how long it was taking us to find that out? Hours for each one. Now it's a matter of minutes."

John Lewisohn sighed. He knew. He had suggested it, actually, when he had said, "Find a basic anxiety situation for the test." He hadn't wanted to know what Herb had come up with.

He said, "Okay, but she's only a kid. What about her parents, legal rights, all that?"

"We'll fix it. Don't worry. What about Anne?"

"She's called me five times since yesterday. The sharks were too much. She wants to see us, both of us, this afternoon."

"You're kidding! I can't leave here now!"

"Nope. Kidding I'm not. She says no plug-up if we don't show. She'll take pills and sleep until we get there."

"Good Lord! She wouldn't dare!"

"I've booked seats. We take off at twelve-thirty-five. They stared at one another silently for another moment, then Herb shrugged. He was a short man, not heavy but solid. John was over six feet, muscular, with a temper that he knew he had to control. Others suspected that when he did let it go, there would be bodies lying around afterward, but he controlled it.

Once it had been a physical act, an effort of body and will to master that temper; now it was done so automatically that he couldn't recall occasions when it even threatened to flare anymore.

"Look, Johnny, when we see Anne, let me handle it. Right? I'll make it short."

"What are you going to do?"

"Give her an earful. If she's going to start pulling temperament on me, I'll slap her down so hard she'll bounce a week." He grinned. "She's had it all her way up to now. She knew there wasn't a replacement if she got bitchy. Let her try it now. Just let her try." Herb was pacing back and forth with quick, jerky steps.

John realized with a shock that he hated the stocky, red-faced man. The feeling was new; it was almost as if he could taste the hatred he felt, and the taste was unfamiliar and pleasant.

Herb stopped pacing and stared at him for a moment. "Why'd she call you? Why does she want you down, too? She knows you're not mixed up with this end of it."

"She knows I'm a full partner, anyway," John said.

"Yeah, but that's not it." Herb's face twisted in a grin. "She thinks you're still hot for her, doesn't she? She knows you tumbled once, in the beginning, when you were working on her, getting the gimmick working right." The grin reflected no humor then. "Is she right, Johnny, baby? Is that it?"

"We made a deal," John said. "You run your end, I run mine. She wants me along because she doesn't trust you, or believe anything you tell her anymore. She wants a witness."

"Yeah, Johnny. But you be sure you remember our agreement." Suddenly Herb laughed. "You know what it was like, Johnny, seeing you and her? Like a flame trying to snuggle up to an icicle."

At three-thirty they were in Anne's suite in the Skyline Hotel in Grand Bahama. Herb had a reservation to fly back to New York on the 6 P.M. flight. Anne would not be off until four, so they made themselves comfortable in her rooms and waited. Herb turned her screen on, offered a helmet to John, who shook his head, and they both seated themselves. John watched the screen for several minutes; then he, too, put on a helmet.

Anne was looking at the waves far out at sea where they were long, green, undulating; then she brought her gaze in closer, to the blue-green and quick seas, and finally in to where they stumbled on the sandbars, breaking into foam that looked solid enough to walk on. She was peaceful, swaying with the motion of the boat, the sun hot on her back, the fishing rod heavy in her hands. It was like being an indolent animal at peace with its world, at home in the world, being one with it. After a few seconds she put down the rod and turned, looking at a tall smiling man in swimming trunks. He held out his hand and she took it. They entered the cabin of the boat where drinks were waiting. Her mood of serenity and happiness ended abruptly, to be replaced by shocked disbelief, and a start of fear.

"What the hell . . . ?" John muttered, adjusting the audio. You seldom needed audio when Anne was on.

". . . Captain Brothers had to let them go. After all, they've done nothing yet—" the man was saying soberly.

"But why do you think they'll try to rob me?"

"Who else is here with a million dollars' worth of jewels?"

John turned it off and said, "You're a fool! You can't get away with something like that!"

Herb stood up and crossed to the window wall that was open to the stretch of glistening blue ocean beyond the brilliant white beaches. "You know what every woman wants? To own something worth stealing." He chuckled, a sound without mirth. "Among other things, that is. They want to be roughed up once or twice, and forced to kneel. . . . Our new psychologist is pretty good, you know? Hasn't steered us wrong yet. Anne might kick some, but it'll go over great."

"She won't stand for an actual robbery." Louder, emphatically, he added, "I won't stand for that."

"We can dub it," Herb said. "That's all we need, Johnny, plant the idea, and then dub the rest."

John stared at his back. He wanted to believe that. He needed to believe it. His voice was calm when he said, "It didn't start like this, Herb. What happened?"

Herb turned then. His face was dark against the glare of light behind him. "Okay, Johnny, it didn't start like this. Things accelerate, that's all. You thought of a gimmick, and the way we planned it, it sounded great, but it didn't last. We gave them the feeling of gambling, or learning to ski, of automobile racing, everything we could dream up, and it wasn't enough. How many times can you take the first ski jump of your life? After a while you want new thrills, you know? For you it's been great, hasn't it? You bought yourself a shiny new lab and closed the door. You bought yourself time and equipment and when things didn't go right, you could toss it out and start over, and nobody gave a damn. Think of what it's been like for me, kid! I gotta keep coming up with something new, something that'll give Anne a jolt and through her all those nice little people who aren't even alive unless they're plugged in. You think it's been easy? Anne was a green kid. For her everything was new and exciting, but it isn't like that now, boy. You better believe it is *not* like that now. You know what she told me last month? She's sick and tired of men. Our little hot-box Annie! Tired of men!"

John crossed to him and pulled him around toward the light. "Why didn't you tell me?"

"Why, Johnny? What would you have done that I didn't do? *I* looked harder for the right guy. What would you do for a new thrill for her? I worked for them, kid. Right from the start you said for me to leave you alone. Okay. I left you alone. You ever read any of the memos I sent? You initialed them, kiddo. Everything that's been done, we both signed. Don't give me any of that why didn't I tell you stuff. It won't work!" His face was ugly red and a vein bulged in his neck. John wondered if he had high blood pressure, if he would die of a stroke during one of his flash rages.

John left him at the window. He had read the memos. Herb was right; all he had wanted was to be left alone. It had been his idea; after twelve years of work in a laboratory on prototypes he had shown his—gimmick—to Herb Javits. Herb had been one of the biggest producers on television then; now he was the biggest producer in the world.

The gimmick was simple enough. A person fitted with electrodes in his brain could transmit his emotions, which in turn could be broadcast and picked up by the helmets to be felt by the audience. No words or thoughts went out, only basic emotions—fear, love, anger, hatred . . . That, tied in with a camera showing what the person saw, with a voice dubbed in, and you were the person having the experience, with one important difference—you could turn it off if it got to be too much. The "actor" couldn't. A simple gimmick. You didn't really need the camera and the sound track; many users never turned them on at all, but let their own imaginations fill in the emotional broadcast.

The helmets were not sold, only leased or rented after a short, easy fitting session. A year's lease cost fifty dollars, and there were over thirty-seven million subscribers. Herb had created his own network when the demand for more hours squeezed him out of regular television. From a one-hour weekly show, it had gone to one hour nightly, and now it was on the air eight hours a day live, with another eight hours of taped programming.

What had started out as A DAY IN THE LIFE OF ANNE BEAUMONT was now a life in the life of Anne Beaumont, and the audience was insatiable.

Anne came in then, surrounded by the throng of hangers-on that mobbed her daily—hairdressers, masseurs, fitters, script men . . . She looked tired. She waved the crowd out when she saw John and Herb were there. "Hello, John," she said, "Herb."

"Anne, baby, you're looking great!" Herb said. He took her in his arms and kissed her solidly. She stood still, her hands at her sides.

She was tall, very slender, with wheat-colored hair and gray eyes. Her cheekbones were wide and high, her mouth firm and almost too large. Against her deep red-gold suntan her teeth looked whiter than John remembered. Although too firm and strong ever to be thought of as pretty, she was a very beautiful woman. After Herb released her, she turned to John, hesitated only a moment, then extended a slim, sun-browned hand. It was cool and dry in his.

"How have you been, John? It's been a long time."

He was very glad she didn't kiss him, or call him darling. She smiled only slightly and gently removed her hand from his. He moved to the bar as she turned to Herb.

"I'm through, Herb." Her voice was too quiet. She accepted a whiskey sour from John, but kept her gaze on Herb.

"What's the matter, honey? I was just watching you, baby. You were great today, like always. You've still got it, kid. It's coming through like always."

"What about this robbery? You must be out of your mind . . ."

"Yeah, that. Listen, Anne baby, I swear to you I don't know a thing about it. Laughton must have been giving you the straight goods on that. You know we agreed that the rest of this week you just have a good time, remember? That comes over too, baby. When you have a good time and relax, thirty-seven million people are enjoying life and relaxing. That's good. They can't be stimulated all the time. They like the variety." Wordlessly John held out a glass, scotch and water. Herb took it without looking.

Anne was watching him coldly. Suddenly she laughed. It was a cynical, bitter sound. "You're not a damn fool, Herb. Don't try to act like one." She sipped her drink again, staring at him over the rim of the glass. "I'm warning you, if anyone shows up here to rob me, I'm going to treat him like a real burglar. I bought a gun after today's broadcast, and I learned how to shoot when I was ten. I still know how. I'll kill him, Herb, whoever it is."

"Baby," Herb started, but she cut him short.

"And this is my last week. As of Saturday, I'm through."

"You can't do that, Anne," Herb said. John watched him closely, searching for a sign of weakness; he saw nothing. Herb exuded confidence. "Look around, Anne, at this room, your clothes, everything. . . . You are the richest woman in the world, having the time of your life, able to go anywhere, do anything . . ."

"While the whole world watches—"

"So what? It doesn't stop you, does it?" Herb started to pace, his steps jerky and quick. "You knew that when you signed the contract. You're a rare girl, Anne, beautiful, emotional, intelligent. Think of all those women who've got nothing but you. If you quit them, what do they do? Die? They might, you know. For the first time in their lives they're able to feel like they're living. You're giving them what no one ever did before, what was only hinted at in books and films in the old days. Suddenly they know what it feels like to face excitement, to experience love, to feel contented and peaceful. Think of them, Anne, empty, with nothing in their lives but you, what you're able to give them. Thirty-seven million drabs, Anne, who never felt anything but boredom and frustration until you gave them life. What do they have? Work, kids, bills. You've given them the world, baby! Without you they wouldn't even want to live anymore."

She wasn't listening. Almost dreamily she said, "I talked to my lawyers, Herb, and the contract is meaningless. You've already broken it over and over. I agreed to learn a lot of new things. I did. My God! I've climbed mountains, hunted lions, learned to ski and water-ski, but now you want me to die a little bit each week . . . That airplane crash, not bad, just enough to terrify me. Then the sharks. I really do think it was having sharks brought in when I was skiing that did it, Herb. You see, you will kill me. It will happen, and you won't be able to top it, Herb. Not ever."

There was a hard, waiting silence following her words. *No!* John shouted soundlessly. He was looking at Herb. He had stopped pacing when she started to talk. Something flicked across his face—surprise, fear, something not readily identifiable. Then his face went blank and he raised his glass and finished the scotch and water, replacing the glass on the bar. When he turned again, he was smiling with disbelief.

"What's really bugging you, Anne? There have been plants before. You knew about them. Those lions didn't just happen by, you know. And the avalanche needed a nudge from someone. You know that. What else is bugging you?"

"I'm in love, Herb."

Herb waved that aside impatiently. "Have you ever watched your own show, Anne?" She shook her head. "I thought not. So you wouldn't know about the expansion that took place last month, after we planted that new transmitter in your head. Johnny boy's been busy, Anne. You know these scientist types, never satisfied, always improving, changing. Where's the camera, Anne? Do you ever know where it is anymore? Have you even seen a camera in the past couple of weeks, or a recorder of any sort? You have not, and you won't again. You're on now, honey." His voice was quite low, amused almost. "In fact the only time you aren't on is when you're sleeping. I know you're in love. I know who he is. I know how he makes you feel. I even know how much money he makes a week. I should know, Anne baby. I pay him." He had come closer to her with each word, finishing with his face only inches from hers. He didn't have a chance to duck the flashing slap that jerked his head around, and before either of them realized it, he had hit her back, knocking her into a chair.

The silence grew, became something ugly and heavy, as if words were being born and dying without utterance because they were too brutal for the human spirit to bear. There was a spot of blood on Herb's mouth where Anne's diamond ring had cut him. He touched it and looked at his finger. "It's all being taped now, honey, even this," he said. He turned his back on her and went to the bar.

There was a large red print on her cheek. Her gray eyes had turned black with rage.

"Honey, relax," Herb said after a moment. "It won't make any difference to you, in what you do, or anything like that. You know we can't use most of the stuff, but it gives the editors a bigger variety to pick from. It was getting to the point where most of the interesting stuff was going on after you were off. Like buying the gun. That's great stuff there, baby. You weren't blanketing a single thing, and it'll all come through like pure gold." He finished mixing his drink, tasted it, and then swallowed half of it. "How many women have to go out and buy a gun to protect themselves? Think of them all, feeling that gun, feeling the things you felt when you picked it up, looked at it . . ."

"How long have you been tuning in all the time?" she asked. John felt a stirring along his spine, a tingle of excitement. He knew what was going out over the miniature transmitter, the rising crests of emotion she was feeling. Only a trace of them showed on her smooth face, but the raging interior torment was being recorded faithfully. Her quiet voice and quiet body were lies; the tapes never lied.

Herb felt it too. He put his glass down and went to her, kneeling by the chair, taking her hand in both of his. "Anne, please, don't be that angry with me. I was desperate for new material. When Johnny got this last wrinkle out, and we knew we could record around the clock, we had to try it, and it wouldn't have been any good if you'd known. That's no way to test anything. You knew we were planting the transmitter . . ."

"How long?"

"Not quite a month."

"And Stuart? He's one of your men? He is transmitting also? You hired him to . . . to make love to me? Is that right?"

Herb nodded. She pulled her hand free and averted her face. He got up then and went to the window. "But what difference does it make?" he shouted. "If I introduced the two of you at a party, you wouldn't think anything of it. What difference if I did it this way? I knew you'd like each other. He's bright, like you, likes the same sort of things you do. Comes from a poor family, like yours . . . Everything said you'd get along."

"Oh, yes," she said almost absently. "We get along." She was feeling in her hair, her fingers searching for the scars.

"It's all healed by now," John said. She looked at him as if she had forgotten he was there.

"I'll find a surgeon," she said, standing up, her fingers white on her glass. "A brain surgeon—"

"It's a new process," John said slowly. "It would be dangerous to go in after them."

She looked at him for a long time. "Dangerous?"

He nodded.

"You could take it back out."

He remembered the beginning, how he had quieted her fear of the electrodes and the wires. Her fear was that of a child for the unknown and the unknowable. Time and again he had proved to her that she could trust him, that he wouldn't lie to her. He hadn't lied to her, then. There was the same trust in her eyes, the same unshakable faith. She would believe him. She would accept without question whatever he said. Herb had called him an icicle, but that was wrong. An icicle would have melted in her fires. More like a stalactite, shaped by centuries of civilization, layer by layer he had been formed until he had forgotten how to bend, forgotten how to find release for the stirrings he felt somewhere in the hollow, rigid core of himself. She had tried and, frustrated, she had turned from him, hurt, but unable not to trust one she had loved. Now she waited. He could free her, and lose her again, this time irrevocably. Or he could hold her as long as she lived.

Her lovely gray eyes were shadowed with fear, and the trust that he had given to her. Slowly he shook his head.

"I can't," he said. "No one can."

"I see," she murmured, the black filling her eyes. "I'd die, wouldn't I? Then you'd have a lovely sequence, wouldn't you, Herb?" She swung around, away from John. "You'd have to fake the story line, of course, but you are so good at that. An accident, emergency brain surgery needed, everything I feel going out to the poor little drabs who never will have brain surgery done. It's very good," she said admiringly. Her eyes were black. "In fact, anything I do from now on, you'll use, won't you? If I kill you, that will simply be material for your editors to pick over. Trial, prison, very dramatic . . . On the other hand, if I kill myself . . ."

John felt chilled; a cold, hard weight seemed to be filling him. Herb laughed. "The story line will be something like this," he said. "Anne has fallen in love with a stranger, deeply, sincerely in love with him. Everyone knows how deep that love is, they've all felt it, too, you know. She finds him raping a child, a lovely little girl in her early teens. Stuart tells her they're through. He loves the little nymphet. In a passion she kills herself. You are broadcasting a real storm of passion, right now, aren't you, honey? Never mind, when I run through this scene, I'll find out." She hurled her glass at him, ice cubes and orange slices flying across the room. Herb ducked, grinning.

"That's awfully good, baby. Corny, but after all, they can't get too much corn, can they? They'll love it, after they get over the shock of losing you. And they will get over it, you know. They always do. Wonder if it's true about what happens to someone experiencing a violent death?" Anne's teeth bit down on her lip, and slowly she sat down again, her eyes closed tight. Herb watched her for a moment, then said, even more cheerfully, "We've got the kid already. If you give them a death, you've got to give them a new life. Finish one with a bang. Start one with a bang. We'll name the kid Cindy, a real Cinderella story after that. They'll love her, too."

Anne opened her eyes, black, dulled now; she was so full of tension that John felt his own muscles contract. He wondered if he would be able to stand the tape she was transmitting. A wave of excitement swept him and he knew he would play it all, feel it all, the incredibly contained rage, fear, the horror of giving a death to them to gloat over, and finally, anguish. He would know it all. Watching Anne, he wished she would break now. She didn't. She stood up stiffly, her back rigid, a muscle hard and ridged in her jaw. Her voice was flat when she said, "Stuart is due in half an hour. I have to dress." She left them without looking back.

Herb winked at John and motioned toward the door. "Want to take me to the plane, kid?" In the cab he said, "Stick close to her for a couple of days, Johnny. There might be an even bigger reaction later when she really understands just how hooked she is." He chuckled again. "By God! It's a good thing she trusts you, Johnny boy!"

As they waited in the chrome and marble terminal for the liner to unload its passengers, John said, "Do you think she'll be any good after this?"

"She can't help herself. She's too life-oriented to deliberately choose to die. She's like a jungle inside, raw, wild, untouched by that smooth layer of civilization she shows on the outside. It's a thin layer, kid, real thin. She'll fight to stay alive. She'll become more wary, more alert to danger, more excited and exciting . . . She'll really go to pieces when he touches her tonight. She's primed real good. Might even have to do some editing, tone it down a little." His voice was very happy. "He touches her where she lives, and she reacts. A real wild one. She's one; the new kid's one; Stuart . . . They're few and far between, Johnny. It's up to us to find them. God knows we're going to need all of them we can get." His expression became thoughtful and withdrawn. "You know, that really wasn't such a bad idea of mine about rape and the kid. Who ever dreamed we'd get that kind of a reaction from her? With the right sort of buildup . . ." He had to run to catch his plane.

John hurried back to the hotel, to be near Anne if she needed him. But he hoped she would leave him alone. His fingers shook as he turned on his screen; suddenly he had a clear memory of the child who had wept, and he hoped Stuart would hurt Anne just a little. The tremor in his fingers increased; Stuart was on from six until twelve, and he already had missed almost an hour of the show. He adjusted the helmet and sank back into a deep chair. He left the audio off, letting his own words form, letting his own thoughts fill in the spaces.

Anne was leaning toward him, sparkling champagne raised to her lips, her eyes large and soft. She was speaking, talking to him, John, calling him by name. He felt a tingle start somewhere deep inside him, and his glance was lowered to rest on her tanned hand in his, sending electricity through him. Her hand trembled when he ran his fingers up her palm, to her wrist where a blue vein throbbed. The slight throb became a pounding that grew, and when he looked again into her eyes, they were dark and very deep. They danced and he felt her body against his, yielding, pleading. The room darkened and she was an outline against the window, her gown floating down about her. The darkness grew denser, or he closed his eyes, and this time when her body pressed against his, there was nothing between them, and the pounding was everywhere.

In the deep chair, with the helmet on his head, John's hands clenched, opened, clenched, again and again.

1967

JOANNA RUSS

The Barbarian

ALYX, the gray-eyed, the silent woman. Wit, arm, kill-quick for hire, she watched the strange man thread his way through the tables and the smoke toward her. This was in Ourdh, where all things are possible. He stopped at the table where she sat alone and with a certain indefinable gallantry, not pleasant but perhaps its exact opposite, he said:

"A woman—here?"

"You're looking at one," said Alyx dryly, for she did not like his tone. It occurred to her that she had seen him before—though he was not so fat then, no, not quite so fat—and then it occurred to her that the time of their last meeting had almost certainly been in the hills when she was four or five years old. That was thirty years ago. So she watched him very narrowly as he eased himself into the seat opposite, watched him as he drummed his fingers in a lively tune on the tabletop, and paid him close attention when he tapped one of the marine decorations that hung from the ceiling (a stuffed blowfish, all spikes and parchment, that moved lazily to and fro in a wandering current of air) and made it bob. He smiled, the flesh around his eyes straining into folds.

"I know you," he said. "A raw country girl fresh from the hills who betrayed an entire religious delegation to the police some ten years ago. You settled down as a picklock. You made a good thing of it. You expanded your profession to include a few more difficult items and you did a few things that turned heads hereabouts.

You were not unknown, even then. Then you vanished for a season and reappeared as a fairly rich woman. But that didn't last, unfortunately."

"Didn't have to," said Alyx.

"Didn't last," repeated the fat man imperturbably, with a lazy shake of the head. "No, no, it didn't last. And now" (he pronounced the "now" with peculiar relish) "you are getting old."

"Old enough," said Alyx, amused.

"Old," said he, "old. Still neat, still tough, still small. But old. You're thinking of settling down."

"Not exactly."

"Children?"

She shrugged, retiring a little into the shadow. The fat man did not appear to notice.

"It's been done," she said.

"You may die in childbirth," said he, "at your age."

"That, too, has been done."

She stirred a little, and in a moment a short-handled Southern dagger, the kind carried unobtrusively in sleeves or shoes, appeared with its point buried in the tabletop, vibrating ever so gently.

"It is true," said she, "that I am growing old. My hair is threaded with white. I am developing a chunky look around the waist that does not exactly please me, though I was never a ballet-girl." She grinned at him in the semi-darkness. "Another thing," she said softly, "that I develop with age is a certain lack of patience. If you do not stop making personal remarks and taking up my time—which is valuable—I shall throw you across the room."

"I would not, if I were you," he said.

"You could not."

The fat man began to heave with laughter. He heaved until he choked. Then he said, gasping, "I beg your pardon." Tears ran down his face.

"Go on," said Alyx. He leaned across the table, smiling, his fingers mated tip to tip, his eyes little pits of shadow in his face.

"I come to make you rich," he said.

"You can do more than that," said she steadily. A quarrel broke out across the room between a soldier and a girl he had picked up for the night; the fat man talked through it, or rather under it, never taking his eyes off her face.

"Ah!" he said, "you remember when you saw me last and you assume that a man who can live thirty years without growing older must have more to give—if he wishes—than a handful of gold coins. You are right. I can make you live long. I can insure your happiness. I can determine the sex of your children. I can cure all diseases. I can even" (and here he lowered his voice) "turn this table, or this building, or this whole city to pure gold, if I wish it."

"Can anyone do that?" said Alyx, with the faintest whisper of mockery.

"I can," he said. "Come outside and let us talk. Let me show you a few of the things I can do. I have some business here in the city that I must attend to myself and I need a guide and an assistant. That will be you."

"If you can turn the city into gold," said Alyx just as softly, "can you turn gold into a city?"

"Anyone can do that," he said, laughing; "come along," so they rose and made their way into the cold outside air—it was a clear night in early spring—and at a corner of the street where the moon shone down on the walls and the pits in the road, they stopped.

"Watch," said he.

On his outstretched palm was a small black box. He shook it, turning it this way and that, but it remained wholly featureless. Then he held it out to her and, as she took it in her hand, it began to glow until it became like a piece of glass lit up from the inside. There in the middle of it was her man, with his tough, friendly, young-old face and his hair a little gray, like hers. He smiled at her, his lips moving soundlessly. She threw the cube into the air a few times, held it to the side of her face, shook it, and then dropped it on the ground, grinding it under her heel. It remained unhurt.

She picked it up and held it out to him, thinking:

Not metal, very light. And warm. A toy? Wouldn't break, though. Must be some sort of small machine, though God knows who made it and of what. It follows thoughts! Marvelous. But magic? Bah! Never believed in it before; why now? Besides, this thing is too sensible; magic is elaborate, undependable, useless. I'll tell him—but then it occurred to her that someone had gone to a good deal of trouble to impress her when a little bit of credit might have done just as well. And this man walked with an almighty confidence through the streets for someone who was unarmed. And those thirty years—so she said very politely:

"It's magic!"

He chuckled and pocketed the cube.

"You're a little savage," he said, "but your examination of it was most logical. I like you. Look! I am an old magician. There is a spirit in that box and there are more spirits under my control than you can possibly imagine. I am like a man living among monkeys. There are things spirits cannot do—or things I choose to do myself, take it any way you will. So I pick one of the monkeys who seems brighter than the rest and train it. I pick you. What do you say?"

"All right," said Alyx.

"Calm enough!" he chuckled. "Calm enough! Good. What's your motive?"

"Curiosity," said Alyx. "It's a monkeylike trait." He chuckled again; his flesh choked it and the noise came out in a high, muffled scream.

"And what if I bite you," said Alyx, "like a monkey?"

"No, little one," he answered gaily, "you won't. You may be sure of that." He held out his hand, still shaking with mirth. In the palm lay a kind of blunt knife which he pointed at one of the whitewashed walls that lined the street. The edges of the wall burst into silent smoke, the whole section trembled and slid, and in an instant it had vanished, vanished as completely as if it had never existed, except for a sullen glow at the raw edges of brick and a pervasive smell of burning. Alyx swallowed.

"It's quiet, for magic," she said softly. "Have you ever used it on men?"

"On armies, little one."

So the monkey went to work for him. There seemed as yet to be no harm in it. The little streets admired his generosity and the big ones his good humor; while those too high for money or flattery he won by a catholic ability that was—so the little picklock thought—remarkable in one so stupid. For about his stupidity there could be no doubt. She smelled it. It offended her. It made her twitch in her sleep, like a ferret. There was in this woman—well hidden away—an anomalous streak of quiet humanity that abhorred him, that set her teeth on edge at the thought of him, though she could not have put into words just what was the matter. *For stupidity,* she thought, *is hardly—is not exactly—*

Four months later they broke into the governor's villa. She

thought she might at last find out what this man was after besides pleasure jaunts around the town. Moreover, breaking and entering always gave her the keenest pleasure; and doing so "for nothing" (as he said) tickled her fancy immensely. The power in gold and silver that attracts thieves was banal, in this thief's opinion, but to stand in the shadows of a sleeping house, absolutely silent, with no object at all in view and with the knowledge that if you are found you will probably have your throat cut—! She began to think better of him. This dilettante passion for the craft, this reckless silliness seemed to her as worthy as the love of a piece of magnetite for the North and South poles—the "faithful stone" they call it in Ourdh.

"Who'll come with us?" she asked, wondering for the fiftieth time where the devil he went when he was not with her, whom he knew, where he lived, and what that persistently bland expression on his face could possibly mean.

"No one," he said calmly.

"What are we looking for?"

"Nothing."

"Do you ever do anything for a reason?"

"Never." And he chuckled.

And then, "Why are you so fat?" demanded Alyx, halfway out of her own door, half into the shadows. She had recently settled in a poor quarter of the town, partly out of laziness, partly out of necessity. The shadows playing in the hollows of her face, the expression of her eyes veiled, she said it again, "Why are you so goddamned fat!" He laughed until he wheezed.

"The barbarian mind!" he cried, lumbering after her in high good humor. "Oh—oh, my dear!—oh, what freshness!" She thought:

That's it! and then

The fool doesn't even know I hate him.

But neither had she known, until that very moment.

They scaled the northeast garden wall of the villa and crept along the top of it without descending, for the governor kept dogs. Alyx, who could walk a taut rope like a circus performer, went quietly. The fat man giggled. She swung herself up to the nearest window and hung there by one arm and a toehold for fifteen mortal minutes while she sawed through the metal hinge of the shutter with a file. Once inside the building (he had to be pulled through the window) she took him by the collar with uncanny accuracy, considering that the inside of the villa was stone dark. "Shut up!" she said, with considerable emphasis.

"Oh?" he whispered.

"I'm in charge here," she said, releasing him with a jerk, and melted into the blackness not two feet away, moving swiftly along the corridor wall. Her fingers brushed lightly alongside her, like a creeping animal: stone, stone, a gap, warm air rising . . . In the dark she felt wolfish, her lips skinned back over her teeth; like another species she made her way with hands and ears. Through them the villa sighed and rustled in its sleep. She put the tips of the fingers of her free hand on the back of the fat man's neck, guiding him with the faintest of touches through the turns of the corridor. They crossed an empty space where two halls met; they retreated noiselessly into a room where a sleeper lay breathing against a dimly lit window, while someone passed in the corridor outside. When the steps faltered for a moment, the fat man gasped and Alyx wrung his wrist, hard. There was a cough from the corridor, the sleeper in the room stirred and murmured, and the steps passed on. They crept back to the hall. Then he told her where he wanted to go.

"What!" She had pulled away, astonished, with a reckless hiss of indrawn breath. Methodically he began poking her in the side and giving her little pushes with his other hand—she moving away, outraged—but all in silence. In the distant reaches of the building something fell—or someone spoke—and without thinking, they waited silently until the sounds had faded away. He resumed his continual prodding. Alyx, her teeth on edge, began to creep forward, passing a cat that sat outlined in the vague light from a window, perfectly unconcerned with them and rubbing its paws against its face, past a door whose cracks shone yellow, past ghostly staircases that opened up in vast wells of darkness, breathing a faint, far updraft, their steps rustling and creaking. They were approaching the governor's nursery. The fat man watched without any visible horror—or any interest, for that matter—while Alyx disarmed the first guard, stalking him as if he were a sparrow, then the one strong pressure on the blood vessel at the back of the neck (all with no noise except the man's own breathing; she was quiet as a shadow). Now he was trussed up, conscious and glaring, quite unable to move. The second guard was asleep in his chair. The third Alyx decoyed out into the anteroom by a thrown pebble (she had picked up several in the street). She was three motionless feet away from him as he stooped to examine it; he never straightened up. The fourth guard (he was in the anteroom, in a feeble glow that stole through the hangings of the nursery beyond) turned to greet his friend—or so he thought—and then Alyx judged she could risk a little speech. She said thoughtfully, in a low voice, "That's dangerous, on the back of the head."

"Don't let it bother you," said the fat man. Through the parting of the hangings they could see the nurse, asleep on her couch with her arms bare and their golden circlets gleaming in the lamplight, the black slave in a profound huddle of darkness at the farther door, and a shining, tented basket—the royal baby's royal house. The baby was asleep. Alyx stepped inside—motioning the fat man away from the lamp—and picked the governor's daughter out of her gilt cradle. She went round the apartment with the baby in one arm, bolting both doors and closing the hangings, draping the fat man in a guard's cloak and turning down the lamp so that a bare glimmer of light reached the farthest walls.

"Now you've seen it," she said, "shall we go?"

He shook his head. He was watching her curiously, his head tilted to one side. He smiled at her. The baby woke up and began to chuckle at finding herself carried about; she grabbed at Alyx's mouth and jumped up and down, bending in the middle like a sort of pocket-compass or enthusiastic spring. The woman lifted her head to avoid the baby's fingers and began to soothe her, rocking her in her arms. "Good Lord, she's cross-eyed," said Alyx. The nurse and her slave slept on, wrapped in the profoundest unconsciousness. Humming a little, soft tune to the governor's daughter, Alyx walked her about the room, humming and rocking, rocking and humming, until the baby yawned.

"Better go," said Alyx.

"No," said the fat man.

"Better," said Alyx again. "One cry and the nurse—"

"Kill the nurse," said the fat man.

"The slave—"

"He's dead." Alyx started, rousing the baby. The slave still slept by the door, blacker than the blackness, but under him oozed something darker still in the twilight flame of the lamp. "You did that?" whispered Alyx, hushed. She had not seen him move. He took something dark and hollow, like the shell of a nut, from the palm of his hand and laid it next to the baby's cradle; with a shiver half of awe and half of distaste Alyx put that richest and most fortunate daughter of Ourdh back into her gilt cradle. Then she said:

"Now we'll go."

"But I have not what I came for," said the fat man.

"And what is that?"

"The baby."

"Do you mean to steal her?" said Alyx curiously.

"No," said he, "I mean for you to kill her."

The woman stared. In sleep the governor's daughter's nurse stirred; then she sat bolt upright, said something incomprehensible in a loud voice, and fell back to her couch, still deep in sleep. So astonished was the picklock that she did not move. She only looked at the fat man. Then she sat by the cradle and rocked it mechanically with one hand while she looked at him.

"What on earth for?" she said at length. He smiled. He seemed as easy as if he were discussing her wages or the price of pigs; he sat down opposite her and he too rocked the cradle, looking on the burden it contained with a benevolent, amused interest. If the nurse had woken up at that moment, she might have thought she saw the governor and his wife, two loving parents who had come to visit their child by lamplight. The fat man said:

"Must you know?"

"I must," said Alyx.

"Then I will tell you," said the fat man, "not because you must, but because I choose. This little six-months morsel is going to grow up."

"Most of us do," said Alyx, still astonished.

"She will become a queen," the fat man went on, "and a surprisingly wicked woman for one who now looks so innocent. She will be the death of more than one child and more than one slave. In plain fact, she will be a horror to the world. This I know."

"I believe you," said Alyx, shaken.

"Then kill her," said the fat man. But still the picklock did not stir. The baby in her cradle snored, as infants sometimes do, as if to prove the fat man's opinion of her by showing a surprising precocity; still the picklock did not move, but stared at the man across the cradle as if he were a novel work of nature.

"I ask you to kill her," said he again.

"In twenty years," said she, "when she has become so very wicked."

"Woman, are you deaf? I told you—"

"In twenty years!" In the feeble light from the lamp she appeared pale, as if with rage or terror. He leaned deliberately across the cradle, closing his hand around the shell or round-shot or unidentifiable object he had dropped there a moment before; he said very deliberately:

"In twenty years you will be dead."

"Then do it yourself," said Alyx softly, pointing at the object in his hand, "unless you had only one?"

"I had only one."

"Ah, well then," she said, "here!" and she held out to him across the sleeping baby the handle of her dagger, for she had divined something about this man in the months they had known each other; and when he made no move to take the blade, she nudged his hand with the handle.

"You don't like things like this, do you?" she said.

"Do as I say, woman!" he whispered. She pushed the handle into his palm. She stood up and poked him deliberately with it, watching him tremble and sweat; she had never seen him so much at a loss. She moved round the cradle, smiling and stretching out her arm seductively. "Do as I say!" he cried.

"Softly, softly."

"You're a sentimental fool!"

"Am I?" she said. "Whatever I do, I must feel; I can't just twiddle my fingers like you, can I?"

"Ape!"

"You chose me for it."

"Do as I say!"

"Sh! You will wake the nurse." For a moment both stood silent, listening to the baby's all-but-soundless breathing and the rustling of the nurse's sheets. Then he said, "Woman, your life is in my hands."

"Is it?" said she.

"I want your obedience!"

"Oh no," she said softly, "I know what you want. You want importance because you have none; you want to swallow up another soul. You want to make me fear you and I think you can succeed, but I think also that I can teach you the difference between fear and respect. Shall I?"

"Take care!" he gasped.

"Why?" she said. "Lest you kill me?"

"There are other ways," he said, and he drew himself up, but here the picklock spat in his face. He let out a strangled wheeze and lurched backwards, stumbling against the curtains. Behind her Alyx heard a faint cry; she whirled about to see the governor's nurse sitting up in bed, her eyes wide open.

"Madam, quietly, quietly," said Alyx, "for God's sake!"

The governor's nurse opened her mouth.

"I have done no harm," said Alyx passionately, "I swear it!" but the governor's nurse took a breath with the clear intention to scream, a hearty, healthy, full-bodied scream like the sort picklocks hear in nightmares. In the second of the governor's nurse's shuddering inhalation—in that split second that would mean unmentionably unpleasant things for Alyx, as Ourdh was not a kind city—Alyx considered launching herself at the woman, but the cradle was between. It would be too late. The house would be roused in twenty seconds. She could never make it to a door—or a window—not even to the garden, where the governor's hounds could drag down a stranger in two steps. All these thoughts flashed through the picklock's mind as she saw the governor's nurse inhale with that familiar, hideous violence; her knife was still in her hand; with the smooth simplicity of habit it slid through her fingers and sped across the room to bury itself in the governor's nurse's neck, just above the collarbone in that tender hollow Ourdhian poets love to sing of. The woman's open-mouthed expression froze on her face; with an "uh!" of surprise she fell forward, her arms hanging limp over the edge of the couch. A noise came from her throat. The knife had opened a major pulse, and in the blood's slow, powerful, rhythmic tides across sheet and slippers and floor Alyx could discern a horrid similarity to the posture and appearance of the black slave. One was hers, one was the fat man's. She turned and hurried through the curtains into the anteroom, only noting that the soldier blindfolded and bound in the corner had managed patiently to work loose the thongs around two of his fingers with his teeth. He must have been at it all this time. Outside in the hall the darkness of the house was as undisturbed as if the nursery were that very Well of Peace whence the gods first drew (as the saying is) the dawn and the color—but nothing else—for the eyes of women. On the wall someone had written in faintly shining stuff, like snail-slime, the single word *Fever*.

But the fat man was gone.

Her man was raving and laughing on the floor when she got home. She could not control him—she could only sit with her hands over her face and shudder—so at length she locked him in and gave the key to the old woman who owned the house, saying, "My husband drinks too much. He was perfectly sober when I left earlier this evening and now look at him. Don't let him out."

Then she stood stock-still for a moment, trembling and thinking: of the fat man's distaste for walking, of his wheezing, his breathlessness, of his vanity that surely would have led him to show her any magic vehicle he had that took him to whatever he called home. He must have walked. She had seen him go out the north gate a hundred times.

She began to run.

To the south Ourdh is built above marshes that will engulf anyone or anything unwary enough to try to cross them, but to the north the city peters out into sand dunes fringing the seacoast and a fine monotony of rocky hills that rise to a countryside of sandy scrub, stunted trees and what must surely be the poorest farms in the world. Ourdh believes that these farmers dream incessantly of robbing travelers, so nobody goes there, all the fashionable world frequenting the great north road that loops a good fifty miles to avoid this region. Even without its stories the world would have no reason to go here; there is nothing to see but dunes and weeds and now and then a shack (or more properly speaking, a hut) resting on an outcropping of rock or nesting right on the sand like a toy boat in a basin. There is only one landmark in the whole place—an old tower hardly even fit for a wizard—and that was abandoned nobody knows how long ago, though it is only twenty minutes' walk from the city gates. Thus it was natural that Alyx (as she ran, her heart pounding in her side) did not notice the stars, or the warm night-wind that stirred the leaves of the trees, or indeed the very path under her feet; though she knew all the paths for twenty-five miles around. Her whole mind was on that tower. She felt its stones stick in her throat. On her right and left the country flew by, but she seemed not to move; at last, panting and trembling, she crept through a nest of tree-trunks no thicker than her wrist (they were very old and very tough) and sure enough, there it was. There was a light shining halfway between bottom and top. Then someone looked out, like a cautious householder out of an attic, and the light went out.

Ah! thought she, and moved into the cover of the trees. The light—which had vanished—now reappeared a story higher and so on, higher and higher, until it reached the top. It wobbled a little, as if held in the hand. So this was his country seat! Silently and with great care, she made her way from one pool of shadow to another. One hundred feet from the tower she circled it and approached it from the northern side. A finger of the sea cut in very close to the base of the building (it had been slowly falling into the water for many years) and in this she first waded and then swam, disturbing the faint, cold radiance of the starlight in the placid ripples. There was no moon. Under the very walls of the tower she stopped and listened; in the darkness under the sea she felt along the rocks; then, expelling her breath and kicking upwards, she rushed head-down; the water closed round, the stone rushed past and she struggled up into the air. She was inside the walls.

And so is he, she thought. For somebody had cleaned the place up. What she remembered as choked with stone rubbish (she had used the place for purposes of her own a few years back) was bare and neat and clean; all was square, all was orderly, and someone had cut stone steps from the level of the water to the most beautifully precise archway in the world. But of course she should not have been able to see any of this at all. The place should have been in absolute darkness. Instead, on either side of the arch was a dim glow, with a narrow beam of light going between them; she could see dancing in it the dust-motes that are never absent from this earth, not even from air that has lain quiet within the rock of a wizard's mansion for uncountable years. Up to her neck in the ocean, this barbarian woman then stood very quietly and thoughtfully for several minutes. Then she dove down into the sea again, and when she came up her knotted cloak was full of the tiny crabs that cling to the rocks along the seacoast of Ourdh. One she killed and the others she suspended captive in the sea; bits of the blood and flesh of the first she smeared carefully below the two sources of that narrow beam of light; then she crept back into the sea and loosed the others at the very bottom step, diving underwater as the first of the hurrying little creatures reached the arch. There was a brilliant flash of light, then another, and then darkness. Alyx waited. Hoisting herself out of the water, she walked through the arch—not quickly, but not without nervousness. The crabs were pushing and quarreling over their dead cousin. Several climbed over the sources of the beam, *pulling*, she thought, *the crabs over his eyes*. However he saw, he had seen nothing. The first alarm had been sprung.

Wizards' castles—and their country residences—have every right to be infested with all manner of horrors, but Alyx saw nothing. The passage wound on, going fairly constantly upward, and as it rose it grew lighter until every now and then she could see a kind of lighter shape against the blackness and a few stars. These were windows. There was no sound but her own breathing and once in a while the complaining rustle of one or two little creatures she had inadvertently carried with her in a corner of her cloak. When she stopped she heard nothing. The fat man was either every quiet or very far away. She hoped it was quietness. She slung the cloak over her shoulder and began the climb again.

Then she ran into a wall.

This shocked her, but she gathered herself together and tried the experiment again. She stepped back, then walked forward and again she ran into a wall, not rock but something at once elastic and unyielding, and at the very same moment someone said (as it seemed to her, inside her head) *You cannot get through.*

Alyx swore, religiously. She fell back and nearly lost her balance. She put out one hand and again she touched something impalpable, tingling and elastic; again the voice sounded close behind her ear, with an uncomfortable, frightening intimacy as if she were speaking to herself: *You cannot get through.* "Can't I!" she shouted, quite losing her nerve, and drew her sword; it plunged forward without the slightest resistance, but something again stopped her bare hand and the voice repeated with idiot softness, over and over *You cannot get through. You cannot get through—*

"Who are you!" said she, but there was no answer. She backed down the stairs, sword drawn, and waited. Nothing happened. Round her the stone walls glimmered, barely visible, for the moon was rising outside; patiently she waited, pressing the corner of her cloak with her foot, for as it lay on the floor one of the crabs had chewed his way to freedom and had given her ankle a tremendous nip on the way out. The light increased.

There was nothing there. The crab, who had scuttled busily ahead on the landing of the stair, seemed to come to the place himself and stood there, fiddling. There was absolutely nothing there. Then Alyx, who had been watching the little animal with something close to hopeless calm, gave an exclamation and threw herself flat on the stairs—for the crab had begun to climb upward between floor and ceiling and what it was climbing on was nothing. Tears forced themselves to her eyes. Swimming behind her lids she could see her husband's face, appearing first in one place, then in another, as if frozen on the black box the fat man had showed her the first day they met. She laid herself on the stone and cried. Then she got up, for the face seemed to settle on the other side of the landing and it occurred to her that she must go through. She was still crying. She took off one of her sandals and pushed it through the something-nothing (the crab still climbed in the air with perfect comfort). It went through easily. She grew nauseated at the thought of touching the crab and the thing it climbed on, but she put one hand involuntarily over her face and made a grab with the other (*You cannot* said the voice). When she had got the struggling animal thoroughly in her grasp, she dashed it against the rocky side wall of the tunnel and flung it forward with all her strength. It fell clattering twenty feet further on.

The distinction then, she thought, *is between life and death*, and she sat down hopelessly on the steps to figure this out, for the problem of dying so as to get through and yet getting through without dying, struck her as insoluble. Twenty feet down the tunnel (the spot was in darkness and she could not see what it was) something rustled. It sounded remarkably like a crab that had been stunned and was now recovering, for these animals think of nothing but food and disappointments only seem to give them fresh strength for the search. Alyx gaped into the dark. She felt the hairs rise on the back of her neck. She would have given a great deal to see into that spot, for it seemed to her that she now guessed at the principle of the fat man's demon, which kept out any conscious mind—as it had spoken in hers—but perhaps would let through . . . She pondered. This cynical woman had been a religious enthusiast before circumstances forced her into a drier way of thinking; thus it was that she now slung her cloak ahead of her on the ground to break her fall and leaned deliberately, from head to feet, into the horrid, springy net she could not see. Closing her eyes and pressing the fingers of both hands over an artery in the back of her neck, she began to repeat to herself a formula that she had learned in those prehistoric years, one that has to be altered slightly each time it is repeated—almost as effective a self-hypnotic device as counting backward. And the voice, too, whispering over and over *You cannot get through, you cannot get through—cannot—cannot—*

Something gave her a terrific shock through teeth, bones and flesh, and she woke to find the floor of the landing tilted two inches from her eyes. One knee was twisted under her and the left side of her face ached dizzily, warm and wet under a cushion of numbness. She guessed that her face had been laid open in the fall and her knee sprained, if not broken.

But she was through.

She found the fat man in a room at the very top of the tower, sitting in a pair of shorts in a square of light at the end of a corridor; and, as she made her way limping towards him, he grew (unconscious and busy) to the size of a human being, until at last she stood inside the room, vaguely aware of blood along her arm and a stinging on her face where she had tried to wipe her wound with her cloak. The room was full of machinery. The fat man (he had been jiggling some little arrangement of wires and blocks on his lap) looked up, saw her, registered surprise and then broke into a great grin.

"So it's you," he said.

She said nothing. She put one arm along the wall to steady herself.

"You are amazing," he said, "perfectly amazing. Come here," and he rose and sent his stool spinning away with a touch. He came up to where she stood, wet and shivering, staining the floor and wall, and for a long minute he studied her. Then he said softly:

"Poor animal. Poor little wretch."

Her breathing was ragged. She glanced rapidly about her, taking in the size of the room (it broadened to encompass the whole width of the tower) and the four great windows that opened to the four winds, and the strange things in the shadows: multitudes of little tables, boards hung on the walls, knobs and switches and winking lights innumerable. But she did not move or speak.

"Poor animal," he said again. He walked back and surveyed her contemptuously, both arms akimbo, and then he said, "Do you believe the world was once a lump of rock?"

"Yes," she said.

"Many years ago," he said, "many more years than your mind can comprehend, before there were trees—or cities—or women—I came to this lump of rock. Do you believe that?"

She nodded.

"I came here," said he gently, "in the satisfaction of a certain hobby, and I made all that you see in this room—all the little things you were looking at a moment ago—and I made the tower, too. Sometimes I make it new inside and sometimes I make it look old. Do you understand that, little one?"

She said nothing.

"And when the whim hits me," he said, "I make it new and comfortable and I settle into it, and once I have settled into it I begin to practice my hobby. Do you know what my hobby is?" He chuckled.

"My hobby, little one," he said, "came from this tower and this machinery, for this machinery can reach all over the world and then things happen exactly as I choose. Now do you know what my hobby is? My hobby is world-making. I make worlds, little one."

She took a quick breath, like a sigh, but she did not speak. He smiled at her.

"Poor beast," he said, "you are dreadfully cut about the face and I believe you have sprained one of your limbs. Hunting animals are always doing that. But it won't last. Look," he said, "look again," and he moved one fat hand in a slow circle around him. "It is I, little one," he said, "who made everything that your eyes have ever rested on. Apes and peacocks, tides and times" (he laughed) "and the fire and the rain. I made you. I made your husband. Come," and he ambled off into the shadows. The circle of light that had rested on him when Alyx first entered the room now followed him, continually keeping him at its center, and although her hair rose to see it, she forced herself to follow, limping in pain past the tables, through stacks of tubing and wire and between square shapes the size of stoves. The light fled always before her. Then he stopped, and as she came up to the light, he said:

"You know, I am not angry at you."

Alyx winced as her foot struck something, and grabbed her knee.

"No, I am not," he said. "It has been delightful—except for tonight, which demonstrates, between ourselves, that the whole thing was something of a mistake and shouldn't be indulged in again—but you must understand that I cannot allow a creation of mine, a paring of my fingernail, if you take my meaning, to rebel in this silly fashion." He grinned. "No, no," he said, "that I cannot do. And so" (here he picked up a glass cube from the table in back of him) "I have decided" (here he joggled the cube a little) "that tonight—why, my dear, what is the matter with you? You are standing there with the veins in your fists knotted as if you would like to strike me, even though your knee is giving you a great deal of trouble just at present and you would be better employed in supporting some of your weight with your hands or I am very much mistaken." And he held out to her—though not far enough for her to reach it—the glass cube, which contained an image of her husband in little, unnaturally sharp, like a picture let into crystal. "See?" he said. "When I turn the lever to the right, the little beasties rioting in his bones grow ever more calm and that does him good. A great deal of good. But when I turn the lever to the left—"

"Devil!" said she.

"Ah, I've gotten something out of you at last!" he said, coming closer. "At last you know! Ah, little one, many and many a time I have seen you wondering whether the world might not be better off if you stabbed me in the back, eh? But you can't, you know. Why don't you try it?" He patted her on the shoulder. "Here I am, you see, quite close enough to you, peering, in fact, into those tragic, blazing eyes—wouldn't it be natural to try and put an end to me? But you can't, you know. You'd be puzzled if you tried. I wear an armor plate, little beast, that any beast might envy, and you could throw me from a ten-thousand-foot mountain, or fry me in a furnace, or do a hundred and one other deadly things to me without the least effect. My armor plate has *in-er-tial dis-crim-in-a-tion*, little savage, which means that it lets nothing too fast and nothing too heavy get through. So you cannot hurt me at all. To murder me, you would have to strike me, but that is too fast and too heavy and so is the ground that hits me when I fall and so is fire. Come here."

She did not move.

"Come here, monkey," he said. "I'm going to kill your man and then I will send you away; though since you operate so well in the dark, I think I'll bless you and make that your permanent condition. What do you think you're doing?" for she had put her fingers to her sleeve; and while he stood, smiling a little with the cube in his hand, she drew her dagger and fell upon him, stabbing him again and again.

"There," he said complacently, "do you see?"

"I see," she said hoarsely, finding her tongue.

"Do you understand?"

"I understand," she said.

"Then move off," he said, "I have got to finish," and he brought the cube up to the level of his eyes. She saw her man, behind the glass as in a refracting prism, break into a multiplicity of images; she saw him reach out grotesquely to the surface; she saw his fingertips strike at the surface as if to erupt into the air; and while the fat man took the lever between thumb and forefinger and—prissily and precisely, his lips pursed into wrinkles, prepared to move it all the way to the left—

She put her fingers in his eyes and then, taking advantage of his pain and blindness, took the cube from him and bent him over the edge of a table in such a way as to break his back. This all took place inside the body. His face worked spasmodically, one eye closed and unclosed in a hideous parody of a wink, his fingers paddled feebly on the tabletop and he fell to the floor.

"My dear!" he gasped.

She looked at him expressionlessly.

"Help me," he whispered, "eh?" His fingers fluttered. "Over there," he said eagerly, "medicines. Make me well, eh? Good and fast. I'll give you half."

"All," she said.

"Yes, yes, all," he said breathlessly, "all—explain all—fascinating hobby—spend most of my time in this room—get the medicine—"

"First show me," she said, "how to turn it off."

"Off?" he said. He watched her, bright-eyed.

"First," she said patiently, "I will turn it all off. And then I will cure you."

"No," he said, "no, no! Never!" She knelt down beside him.

"Come," she said softly, "do you think I want to destroy it? I am as fascinated by it as you are. I only want to make sure you can't do anything to me, that's all. You must explain it all first until I am master of it, too, and then we will turn it on."

"No, no," he repeated suspiciously.

"You must," she said, "or you'll die. What do you think I plan to do? I have to cure you, because otherwise how can I learn to work all this? But I must be safe, too. Show me how to turn it off."

He pointed, doubtfully.

"Is that it?" she said.

"Yes," he said, "but—"

"Is that it?"

"Yes, but—no—wait!" for Alyx sprang to her feet and fetched from his stool the pillow on which he had been sitting, the purpose of which he did not at first seem to comprehend, but then his eyes went wide with horror, for she had got the pillow in order to smother him, and that is just what she did.

When she got to her feet, her legs were trembling. Stumbling and pressing both hands together as if in prayer to subdue their shaking, she took the cube that held her husband's picture and carefully—oh, how carefully!—turned the lever to the right. Then she began to sob. It was not the weeping of grief, but a kind of reaction and triumph, all mixed; in the middle of that eerie room she stood, and threw her head back and yelled. The light burned steadily on. In the shadows she found the fat man's master switch, and leaning against the wall, put one finger—only one—on it and caught her breath. Would the world end? She did not know. After a few minutes' search she found a candle and flint hidden away in a cupboard and with this she made herself a light; then, with eyes closed, with a long shudder, she leaned—no, sagged—against the switch, and stood for a long moment, expecting and believing nothing.

But the world did not end. From outside came the wind and the sound of the sea-wash (though louder now, as if some indistinct and not quite audible humming had just ended) and inside fantastic shadows leapt about the candle—the lights had gone out. Alyx began to laugh, catching her breath. She set the candle down and searched until she found a length of metal tubing that stood against the wall, and then she went from machine to machine, smashing, prying, tearing, toppling tables and breaking controls. Then she took the candle in her unsteady hand and stood over the body of the fat man, a phantasmagoric lump on the floor, badly lit at last. Her shadow loomed on the wall. She leaned over him and studied his face, that face that had made out of agony and death the most appalling trivialities. She thought:

Make the world? You hadn't the imagination. You didn't even make these machines; that shiny finish is for customers, not craftsmen, and controls that work by little pictures are for children. You are a child yourself, a child and a horror, and I would ten times rather be subject to your machinery than master of it.

Aloud she said:

"Never confuse the weapon and the arm," and taking the candle, she went away and left him in the dark.

She got home at dawn and, as her man lay asleep in bed, it seemed to her that he was made out of the light of the dawn that streamed through his fingers and his hair, irradiating him with gold. She kissed him and he opened his eyes.

"You've come home," he said.

"So I have," said she.

"I fought all night," she added, "with the Old Man of the Mountain," for you must know that this demon is a legend in Ourdh; he is the god of this world who dwells in a cave containing the whole world in little, and from his cave he rules the fates of men.

"Who won?" said her husband, laughing, for in the sunrise when everything is suffused with light it is difficult to see the seriousness of injuries.

"I did!" said she. "The man is dead." She smiled, splitting open the wound on her cheek, which began to bleed afresh. "He died," she said, "for two reasons only: because he was a fool. And because we are not."

And all the birds in the courtyard broke out shouting at once.

1968

JAMES TIPTREE, JR.

The Last Flight of Dr. Ain

DR. Ain was recognized on the Omaha-Chicago flight. A biologist colleague saw him in an aisle seat while coming back from the toilet. Five years before, this man had been jealous of Ain's huge grants. Now he nodded coldly and was surprised at the intensity of Ain's response. If he had not had the flu like everyone else that autumn, he would have turned back to speak with Ain, but he shuffled on to his seat.

The stewardess handing out coats after they landed remembered Ain too: a tall, thin, nondescript man with rusty hair. He held up the line, staring at her; and since he already had his raincoat with him, she decided it was some kooky kind of pass and waved him on.

They both saw Ain shamble off into the airport smog, apparently alone. Despite the big Civil Defense signs, O'Hare was late getting underground. Neither of them saw the woman.

The wounded, dying woman.

Nobody recalled him on the flight to New York, but the 2:40 jet carried an Ames on the checklist, which was thought to be a misspelling of Ain. It was. The plane had circled for an hour while Ain watched the smoky seaboard monotonously tilt, straighten, and tilt again.

The woman was weaker now. She coughed, picking weakly at the scabs on her face that were half-hidden behind her hair. Her hair, Ain saw, that great hair which had been so splendid, was drabbed and thinning. He looked to seaward, willing himself to think of cold, clean breakers. On the horizon he saw a vast spreading black rug. Somewhere a tanker had opened its vents. The woman coughed again. Ain closed his eyes. It was the dead time of afternoon.

He was picked up next while checking in for the BOAC flight to Glasgow. Kennedy-Underground was a boiling stew of people breathing each other's reek, the air-conditioning unequal to the hot September evening. The check-in line swayed and sweated, staring dully at the newscast. *Save the last Green Mansions*—a conservation group was protesting the defoliation and drainage of the Amazon basin. Several people recalled the beautifully colored shots of the new clean bomb. The line squeezed together to let a band of uniformed men go by. They were wearing buttons inscribed: *Who's Afraid?*

That was when a woman noticed Ain. He was holding a newssheet and she heard it rattling in his hand. Her family hadn't caught the flu, so she looked at him sharply. Sure enough, his forehead was sweaty. She herded her kids to the side away from Ain. He was using *Instac* throat spray, she remembered. She did not think much of *Instac*; her family used *Kleer*. While she was looking at him, Ain suddenly thrust his head down and stared in her face, with the spray still floating above him. That made her mad. Such inconsiderateness! She turned her back. She did not recall him talking to any woman, but she perked up her ears when the clerk read off Ain's destination. Moscow!

The clerk recalled that too, with disapproval. Ain checked in alone, he reported. No woman had been ticketed for Moscow, but it would have been easy enough to split up the tickets. By that time they were sure she was with him.

Ain's flight went via Iceland with an hour's delay at Kevlavik. Ain walked over to the airport park, breathing gratefully the sea-filled air. Every so often he shuddered. Under the whine of bulldozers, the sea could be heard running its huge paws up and down the keyboard of the land. In the little park were yellowed birches, and a flock of wheateaters foraged by the path. Next month they would be in North Africa. Two thousand miles of tiny wing-beats, Ain thought. He threw them some crumbs from a packet in his pocket.

The woman seemed stronger here. She was panting in the sea air, her large eyes fixed on Ain. He saw that the birches were as gold as those where he had first seen her, the day his life began. Squatting down to watch a shrewmouse, he had been, when he caught the falling ripple of green and recognized the shocking naked girl-flesh, creamy, pink-tipped among the golden bracken, coming towards him. Young Ain held his breath under stress, his nose on the sweet moss and his heart going *crash—crash*—and then he was staring at the outrageous fall of that hair down her narrow back, watching it dance around her heart-shaped buttocks while the shrewmouse ran over his paralyzed hand. The lake was utterly still, dusty silver under the misty sky, and she made no more than a muskrat's ripple to rock the floating golden leaves. The silence closed back, the trees burning silent like torches where the naked girl had walked the wild wood, and Ain's eye's were shining. For a time he believed he had seen an Oread.

Ain was last on board for the Glasgow leg. The stewardess recalled dimly that he had stayed awake. She could not identify the woman; there were a lot of women on board. And babies. Her passenger list had had several errors.

At Glasgow airport a waiter remembered that a man like Ain had called for Scottish oatmeal, and eaten two bowls, although of course it wasn't really oatmeal. A young mother with a pram saw him tossing crumbs to the birds. When he checked in at the BOAC desk, he was hailed by a Glasgow professor who was going to the same conference at Moscow. This man had been one of Ain's teachers. It was now known that Ain had done his postgraduate work in Europe. They chatted all the way across the North Sea.

"I wondered about that," the professor said later. "'Why have you come round about?'" I asked him. He told me the direct flights were booked up. (This was found to be untrue; Ain deliberately avoided going to Moscow apparently as an amateurish attempt to avoid attention.)

The professor spoke with relish of Ain's work.

"Brilliant? Oh, aye—and stubborn, too, very stubborn. It was as though a concept—often the simplest relation, mind you—would stop him in his tracks, fascinate him, so he would hunt all 'round it instead of going on to the next thing, as a more docile mind would. Truthfully, I wondered at first if he could be just a bit thick. But you recall who it was said that the capacity for wonder at matters of common acceptance occurs in the superior mind? And of course, so it proved when he shook us all up over that enzyme coding business. A pity your government took him away from his line, there . . . No, *he* said nothing of this, *I* say it to you, young man. We spoke in fact largely of my work. I was surprised to find he'd kept up. He asked me what my *sentiments* about it were, which surprised me again . . . Now, understand, I'd not seen the man for five years, but he seemed—well, perhaps just tired, as who is not? I'm sure he was glad to have a change; he jumped out for a leg-stretch wherever we came down. Oslo, even at Bonn. Oh yes, he did feed the birds, but that was nothing new for Ain . . . His social life when I knew him? Radical causes? Young man, I've said what I've said because of who it was that introduced you, but I'll have you know it is an impertinence in you to think ill of Charles Ain, or that he could do a harmful deed . . . Good evening."

The professor said nothing of the woman in Ain's life. Nor could he have, although Ain had been much with her in the university time. No one had seen how he was obsessed with the miracle, the wealth of that body . . . her inexhaustibility. They met privately at his every spare moment, sometimes even in public, pretending to be casual strangers under his friends' noses, pointing out a pleasing view to each other, gravely formal. And later—what doubled intensity of love! He revelled in her, possessed her and searched over every atom of her—the sweetest springs and shadowed places and the white rounded glory in the moonlight—finding always more, always new ways to never-failing delights. The danger of her frailty was far off then in the rush of birdsongs and the springing leverets of the meadow. On dark days she might cough a bit, but so did he. In those years he had had no thought to the urgent study of disease . . .

At the Moscow conference nearly everyone noticed Ain at some point or another, which was to be expected in view of his professional stature. Ain was late in; a day's reports were over, and his was to be on the third and last. It was a small high-calibre meeting. Many people spoke with Ain, and several sat with him at meals. No one was surprised that he spoke little, since he was a retiring man except on a few memorable occasions of hot argument. He did strike some of his friends as a bit tired and jerky. An Indian molecular engineer who saw him with the throat spray kidded him about bringing over Asian flu. A Swedish colleague recalled that Ain had been called away to the transAtlantic phone at lunch; and when he returned Ain had volunteered the information that something had turned up missing in his home lab. There was another joke, and Ain said cheerfully, "Oh yes, quite active." At that point one of the Chicom biologists swung into his daily propaganda chore about bacteriological warfare and accused Ain of manufacturing biotic weapons. Ain took the wind out of his sails by saying: "You're perfectly right." By tacit consent, there was very little talk about military applications, industrial dusting, or subjects of that type. And nobody recalled seeing Ain with any woman other than old Madame Vialche, who could scarcely have played Mata Hari.

Ain's own speech was bad, even for him. He always had a poor public voice, but his ideas were usually expressed with the lucidity so typical of the first-rate original mind. This time he seemed muddled, with little new to say. His audience excused this as the muffling effects of security. He then got somehow into a tangled point about the course of evolution in which he seemed to be trying to show that something was very wrong indeed. When he wound up with a reference to Hudson's bell bird "singing for a later race," several listeners wondered if he were drunk.

The big security break came right at the end, when he suddenly began to describe the methods he had used to mutate and redesign a leukemia virus. He explained the procedure with admirable clarity in four sentences and paused. Then he said other sentences about the effects of the mutated strain. It was maximal only on the higher primates, he said; recovery rate among the lower mammals and other orders was close to 100%. As to vectors, he went on, any warm-blooded animal served. In addition, the virus retained viability in most environmental media and performed very well airborne. Contagion rate was of course extremely high. Almost offhand, he added that no test primate or accidentally exposed human had survived beyond the twenty-second day.

These words fell into a silence broken only by the running feet of a Chicom delegate making for the door. Then a gilt chair went over as an American bolted after him. Ain seemed unaware that his audience was in a state of unbelieving paralysis. It had all come so fast. A man who had been blowing his nose was staring popeyed around his handkerchief. Another who had been lighting a pipe grunted as his fingers singed. Two men chatting by the door had missed his words entirely, and their laughter chimed into a dead silence in which echoed Ain's words: "—really no point in attempting."

Later they found he had been explaining that the virus utilized the body's own immunomechanisms, and so defense was by definition hopeless.

That was all. Ain looked around vaguely for questions and then started down the aisle. By the time he got to the door, people were swarming after him. He wheeled about and said rather crossly, "Yes, of course it is very wrong. I told you that. We are all wrong. Now it's over."

An hour later they found he had gone, having apparently reserved a Sinair flight to Karachi. Our security men caught up with him at Hong Kong. By then he seemed really very ill, and went with them peacefully. They started back to the States via Hawaii. His captors were civilized types; they saw he was gentle and treated him accordingly. They took him out handcuffed for a stroll at Osaka. He had no weapons or drugs on him, and they let him feed his crumbs to the birds, and listened with interest to his account of the migration routes of the common brown sandpiper. He was very hoarse. At that point, he was wanted only for the security thing. There was no question of a woman at all.

*

He dozed most of the way to the islands; but when they came in sight, he pressed to the window and began to mutter. The security man behind him got the first inkling that there was a woman in it, and turned on his recorder.

". . . blue, blue and green until you see the scabs. Oh my girl! Oh beautiful, you won't die. I won't let you die. I tell you, my girl, it's all over now, hold on, it's over . . . Lustrous eyes, look at me, let me see you now alive my girl. Oh great queen, my sweet body, my girl, have I saved you? Oh terrible to know, and noble—Chaos' girl green-robed and blue, in golden light . . . the thrown and spinning ball of life against black space. Have I saved you?"

On the last leg, he was obviously feverish.

"She may have tricked me, you know," he said confidentially to the government man. "You have to be prepared for that, of course. I know her!" He chuckled confidentially. "She's no small thing. But wring your heart out—"

Coming over San Francisco, he was merry. "Don't you know the otters will go back in there? I'm certain of it. That fill won't last, there'll be a bay there again."

They got him on a stretcher at Hamilton Air Base, and he went unconscious shortly after takeoff. Before he collapsed, he'd insisted on throwing the last of his birdseed on the field.

"Birds are of course, warm-blooded," he confided to the agent who was handcuffing him to the stretcher. Then Ain smiled gently and lapsed into inertness. He stayed that way almost the whole remaining ten days of his life. By then, of course, no one really cared. Both the government men had died quite early, just after they finished analyzing the birdseed and throat-spray. The woman who had seen him at Kennedy was only just then feeling sickish.

The tape-recorder they had put by his bed functioned right on through, but if anybody cared to replay it, they would have found little babbling. "Gaea Gloriatrix!" he crooned. At times he was grandiose and tormented. "Our life, your death!" he yelled. "Our death would have been your death too, no need for that, no need—" At other times he was accusing. "What did you do about the dinosaurs?" he demanded. "How did you fix *them*? Did they annoy you? Cold. Queen, you're too cold! You came close to it this time, my girl," he raved. And then he wept and caressed the bedclothes and was maudlin.

Only at the end, lying in his filth and thirst, still chained where they had forgotten him, he was suddenly coherent. In a light, clear voice, as one might ask one's lover what to take on a summer picnic, he asked the recorder happily:

"Have you ever thought about *bears*? They have so much—funny they never came along further. By any chance were you saving them, girl?" And he chuckled in his ruined throat until he died.

1969

URSULA K. LE GUIN

Nine Lives

SHE was alive inside but dead outside, her face a black and dun net of wrinkles, tumors, cracks. She was bald and blind. The tremors that crossed Libra's face were mere quiverings of corruption. Underneath, in the black corridors, the halls beneath the skin, there were crepitations in darkness, ferments, chemical nightmares that went on for centuries. "O the damned flatulent planet," Pugh murmured as the dome shook and a boil burst a kilometer to the southwest, spraying silver pus across the sunset. The sun had been setting for the last two days. "I'll be glad to see a human face."

"Thanks," said Martin.

"Yours is human to be sure," said Pugh, "but I've seen it so long I can't see it."

Radvid signals cluttered the communicator which Martin was operating, faded, returned as face and voice. The face filled the screen, the nose of an Assyrian king, the eyes of a samurai, skin bronze, eyes the color of iron: young, magnificent. "Is that what human beings look like?" said Pugh with awe. "I'd forgotten."

"Shut up, Owen, we're on."

"Libra Exploratory Mission Base, come in please, this is *Passerine* launch."

"Libra here. Beam fixed. Come on down, launch."

"Expulsion in seven E-seconds. Hold on." The screen blanked and sparkled.

"Do they all look like that? Martin, you and I are uglier men than I thought."

"Shut up, Owen. . . ."

For twenty-two minutes Martin followed the landing craft down by signal and then through the cleared dome they saw it, small star in the blood-colored east, sinking. It came down neat and quiet, Libra's thin atmosphere carrying little sound. Pugh and Martin closed the headpieces of their imsuits, zipped out of the dome air-locks, and ran with soaring strides, Nijinsky and Nureyev, toward the boat. Three equipment modules came floating down at four-minute intervals from each other and hundred-meter intervals east of the boat. "Come on out," Martin said on his suit radio, "we're waiting at the door."

"Come on in, the methane's fine," said Pugh.

The hatch opened. The young man they had seen on the screen came out with one athletic twist and leaped down onto the shaky dust and clinkers of Libra. Martin shook his hand, but Pugh was staring at the hatch, from which another young man emerged with the same neat twist and jump, followed by a young woman who emerged with the same neat twist, ornamented by a wriggle, and the jump. They were all tall, with bronze skin, black hair, high-bridged noses, epicanthic fold, the same face. They all had the same face. The fourth was emerging from the hatch with a neat twist and jump. "Martin bach," said Pugh, "we've got a clone."

"Right," said one of them, "we're a tenclone. John Chow's the name. You're Lieutenant Martin?"

"I'm Owen Pugh."

"Alvaro Guillen Martin," said Martin, formal, bowing slightly. Another girl was out, the same beautiful face; Martin stared at her and his eye rolled like a nervous pony's. Evidently he had never given any thought to cloning and was suffering technological shock. "Steady," Pugh said in the Argentine dialect, "it's only excess twins." He stood close by Martin's elbow. He was glad himself of the contact.

It is hard to meet a stranger. Even the greatest extravert meeting even the meekest stranger knows a certain dread, though he may not know he knows it. Will he make a fool of me wreck my image of myself invade me destroy me change me? Will he be different from me? Yes, that he will. There's the terrible thing: the strangeness of the stranger.

After two years on a dead planet, and the last half year isolated as a team of two, oneself and one other, after that it's even harder to meet a stranger, however welcome he may be. You're out of the habit of difference, you've lost the touch; and so the fear revives, the primitive anxiety, the old dread.

The clone, five males and five females, had got done in a couple of minutes what a man might have got done in twenty: greeted Pugh and Martin, had a glance at Libra, unloaded the boat, made ready to go. They went, and the dome filled with them, a hive of golden bees. They hummed and buzzed quietly, filled up all silences, all spaces with a honey-brown swarm of human presence. Martin looked bewildered at the long-limbed girls, and they smiled at him, three at once. Their smile was gentler than that of the boys, but no less radiantly self-possessed.

"Self-possessed," Owen Pugh murmured to his friend, "that's it. Think of it, to be oneself ten times over. Nine seconds for every motion, nine ayes on every vote. It would be glorious." But Martin was asleep. And the John Chows had all gone to sleep at once. The dome was filled with their quiet breathing. They were young, they didn't snore. Martin sighed and snored, his Hershey-bar-colored face relaxed in the dim afterglow of Libra's primary, set at last. Pugh had cleared the dome and stars looked in, Sol among them, a great company of lights, a clone of splendors. Pugh slept and dreamed of a one-eyed giant who chased him through the shaking halls of Hell.

From his sleeping bag Pugh watched the clone's awakening. They all got up within one minute except for one pair, a boy and a girl, who lay snugly tangled and still sleeping in one bag. As Pugh saw this there was a shock like one of Libra's earthquakes inside him, a very deep tremor. He was not aware of this and in fact thought he was pleased at the sight; there was no other such comfort on this dead hollow world. More power to them, who made love. One of the others stepped on the pair. They woke and the girl sat up flushed and sleepy, with bare golden breasts. One of her sisters murmured something to her; she shot a glance at Pugh and disappeared in the sleeping bag; from another direction came a fierce stare, from still another direction a voice: "Christ, we're used to having a room to ourselves. Hope you don't mind, Captain Pugh."

"It's a pleasure," Pugh said half truthfully. He had to stand up then wearing only the shorts he slept in, and he felt like a plucked rooster, all white scrawn and pimples. He had seldom envied Martin's compact brownness so much. The United Kingdom had come through the Great Famines well, losing less than half its population: a record achieved by rigorous food control. Black marketeers and hoarders had been executed. Crumbs had been shared. Where in richer lands most had died and a few had thriven, in Britain fewer died and none throve. They all got lean. Their sons were lean, their grandsons lean, small, brittle-boned, easily infected. When civilization became a matter of standing in lines, the British had kept queue, and so had replaced the survival of the fittest with the survival of the fair-minded. Owen Pugh was a scrawny little man. All the same, he was there.

At the moment he wished he wasn't.

At breakfast a John said, "Now if you'll brief us, Captain Pugh—"

"Owen, then."

"Owen, we can work out our schedule. Anything new on the mine since your last report to your Mission? We saw your reports when *Passerine* was orbiting Planet V, where they are now."

Martin did not answer, though the mine was his discovery and project, and Pugh had to do his best. It was hard to talk to them. The same faces, each with the same expression of intelligent interest, all leaned toward him across the table at almost the same angle. They all nodded together.

Over the Exploitation Corps insigne on their tunics each had a nameband, first name John and last name Chow of course, but the middle names different. The men were Aleph, Kaph, Yod, Gimel, and Samedh; the women Sadhe, Daleth, Zayin, Beth, and Resh. Pugh tried to use the names but gave it up at once; he could not even tell sometimes which one had spoken, for all the voices were alike.

Martin buttered and chewed his toast, and finally interrupted: "You're a team. Is that it?"

"Right," said two Johns.

"God, what a team! I hadn't seen the point. How much do you each know what the others are thinking?"

"Not at all, properly speaking," replied one of the girls, Zayin. The others watched her with the proprietary, approving look they had. "No ESP, nothing fancy. But we think alike. We have exactly the same equipment. Given the same stimulus, the same problem, we're likely to be coming up with the same reactions and solutions at the same time. Explanations are easy—don't even have to make them, usually. We seldom misunderstand each other. It does facilitate our working as a team."

"Christ yes," said Martin. "Pugh and I have spent seven hours out of ten for six months misunderstanding each other. Like most people. What about emergencies, are you as good at meeting the unexpected problem as a nor . . . an unrelated team?"

"Statistics so far indicate that we are," Zayin answered readily. Clones must be trained, Pugh thought, to meet questions, to reassure and reason. All they said had the slightly bland and stilted quality of answers furnished to the Public. "We can't brainstorm as singletons can, we as a team don't profit from the interplay of varied minds; but we have a compensatory advantage. Clones are drawn from the best human material, individuals of IIQ ninety-ninth percentile, Genetic Constitution alpha double A, and so on. We have more to draw on than most individuals do."

"And it's multiplied by a factor of ten. Who is—who was John Chow?"

"A genius surely," Pugh said politely. His interest in cloning was not so new and avid as Martin's.

"Leonardo Complex type," said Yod. "Biomath, also a cellist and an undersea hunter, and interested in structural engineering problems and so on. Died before he'd worked out his major theories."

"Then you each represent a different facet of his mind, his talents?"

"No," said Zayin, shaking her head in time with several others. "We share the basic equipment and tendencies, of course, but we're all engineers in Planetary Exploitation. A later clone can be trained to develop other aspects of the basic equipment. It's all training;

the genetic substance is identical. We *are* John Chow. But we are differently trained."

Martin looked shell-shocked. "How old are you?"

"Twenty-three."

"You say he died young—had they taken germ cells from him beforehand or something?"

Gimel took over: "He died at twenty-four in an air car crash. They couldn't save the brain, so they took some intestinal cells and cultured them for cloning. Reproductive cells aren't used for cloning, since they have only half the chromosomes. Intestinal cells happen to be easy to despecialize and reprogram for total growth."

"All chips off the old block," Martin said valiantly. "But how can . . . some of you be women . . . ?"

Beth took over: "It's easy to program half the clonal mass back to the female. Just delete the male gene from half the cells and they revert to the basic, that is, the female. It's trickier to go the other way, have to hook in artificial Y chromosomes. So they mostly clone from males, since clones function best bisexually."

Gimel again: "They've worked these matters of technique and function out carefully. The taxpayer wants the best for his money, and of course clones are expensive. With the cell manipulations, and the incubation in Ngama Placentae, and the maintenance and training of the foster-parent groups, we end up costing about three million apiece."

"For your next generation," Martin said, still struggling, "I suppose you . . . you breed?"

"We females are sterile," said Beth with perfect equanimity. "You remember that the Y chromosome was deleted from our original cell. The males can interbreed with approved singletons, if they want to. But to get John Chow again as often as they want, they just reclone a cell from this clone."

Martin gave up the struggle. He nodded and chewed cold toast. "Well," said one of the Johns, and all changed mood, like a flock of starlings that change course in one wingflick, following a leader so fast that no eye can see which leads. They were ready to go. "How about a look at the mine? Then we'll unload the equipment. Some nice new models in the roboats; you'll want to see them. Right?" Had Pugh or Martin not agreed they might have found it hard to say so. The Johns were polite but unanimous; their decisions carried. Pugh, Commander of Libra Base 2, felt a qualm. Could he boss around this superman/woman-entity-of-ten? and a genius at that? He stuck close to Martin as they suited for outside. Neither said anything.

Four apiece in the three large airjets, they slipped off north from the dome, over Libra's dun rugose skin, in starlight.

"Desolate," one said.

It was a boy and girl with Pugh and Martin. Pugh wondered if these were the two that had shared a sleeping bag last night. No doubt they wouldn't mind if he asked them. Sex must be as handy as breathing to them. Did you two breathe last night?

"Yes," he said, "it is desolate."

"This is our first time off, except training on Luna." The girl's voice was definitely a bit higher and softer.

"How did you take the big hop?"

"They doped us. I wanted to experience it." That was the boy; he sounded wistful. They seemed to have more personality, only two at a time. Did repetition of the individual negate individuality?

"Don't worry," said Martin, steering the sled, "you can't experience no-time because it isn't there."

"I'd just like to once," one of them said. "So we'd know."

The Mountains of Merioneth showed leprotic in starlight to the east, a plume of freezing gas trailed silvery from a vent-hole to the west, and the sled tilted groundward. The twins braced for the stop at one moment, each with a slight protective gesture to the other. Your skin is my skin, Pugh thought, but literally, no metaphor. What would it be like, then, to have someone as close to you as that? Always to be answered when you spoke; never to be in pain alone. Love your neighbor as you love yourself. . . . That hard old problem was solved. The neighbor was the self: the love was perfect.

And here was Hellmouth, the mine.

Pugh was the Exploratory Mission's E.T. geologist, and Martin his technician and cartographer; but when in the course of a local survey Martin had discovered the U-mine, Pugh had given him full credit, as well as the onus of prospecting the lode and planning the Exploitation Team's job. These kids had been sent out from Earth years before Martin's reports got there and had not known what their job would be until they got here. The Exploitation Corps simply sent out teams regularly and blindly as a dandelion sends out its seed, knowing there would be a job for them on Libra or the next planet out or one they hadn't even heard about yet. The government wanted uranium too urgently to wait while reports drifted home across the lightyears. The stuff was like gold, old-fashioned but essential, worth mining extraterrestrially and shipping interstellar. Worth its weight in people, Pugh thought sourly, watching the tall young men and women go one by one, glimmering in starlight, into the black hole Martin had named Hellmouth.

As they went in their homeostatic forehead-lamps brightened. Twelve nodding gleams ran along the moist, wrinkled walls. Pugh heard Martin's radiation counter peeping twenty to the dozen up ahead. "Here's the drop-off," said Martin's voice in the suit intercom, drowning out the peeping and the dead silence that was around them. "We're in a side-fissure, this is the main vertical vent in front of us." The black void gaped, its far side not visible in the headlamp beams. "Last vulcanism seems to have been a couple of thousand years ago. Nearest fault is twenty-eight kilos east, in the Trench. This area seems to be as safe seismically as anything in the area. The big basalt-flow overhead stabilizes all these substructures, so long as it remains stable itself. Your central lode is thirty-six meters down and runs in a series of five bubble caverns northeast. It is a lode, a pipe of very high-grade ore. You saw the percentage figures, right? Extraction's going to be no problem. All you've got to do is get the bubbles topside."

"Take off the lid and let 'em float up." A chuckle. Voices began to talk, but they were all the same voice and the suit radio gave them no location in space. "Open the thing right up. —Safer that way. —But it's a solid basalt roof, how thick, ten meters here? —Three to twenty, the report said. —Blow good ore all over the lot. —Use this access we're in, straighten it a bit and run slider rails for the robos. —Import burros. —Have we got enough propping material? —What's your estimate of total payload mass, Martin?"

"Say over five million kilos and under eight."

"Transport will be here in ten E-months. —It'll have to go pure. —No, they'll have the mass problem in NAFAL shipping licked by now, remember it's been sixteen years since we left Earth last Tuesday. —Right, they'll send the whole lot back and purify it in Earth orbit. —Shall we go down, Martin?"

"Go on. I've been down."

The first one—Aleph? (Heb., the ox, the leader)—swung onto the ladder and down; the rest followed. Pugh and Martin stood at the chasm's edge. Pugh set his intercom to exchange only with Martin's suit, and noticed Martin doing the same. It was a bit wearing, this listening to one person think aloud in ten voices, or was it one voice speaking the thoughts of ten minds?

"A great gut," Pugh said, looking down into the black pit, its veined and warted walls catching stray gleams of headlamps far below. "A cow's bowel. A bloody great constipated intestine."

Martin's counter peeped like a lost chicken. They stood inside the dead but epileptic planet, breathing oxygen from tanks, wearing suits impermeable to corrosives and harmful radiations, resistant to a 200-degree range of temperatures, tear-proof, and as shock-resistant as possible given the soft vulnerable stuff inside.

"Next hop," Martin said, "I'd like to find a planet that has nothing whatever to exploit."

"You found this."

"Keep me home next time."

Pugh was pleased. He had hoped Martin would want to go on working with him, but neither of them was used to talking much about their feelings, and he had hesitated to ask. "I'll try that," he said.

"I hate this place. I like caves, you know. It's why I came in here. Just spelunking. But this one's a bitch. Mean. You can't ever let down in here. I guess this lot can handle it, though. They know their stuff."

"Wave of the future, whatever," said Pugh.

The wave of the future came swarming up the ladder, swept Martin to the entrance, gabbled at and around him: "Have we got enough material for supports? —If we convert one of the extractor servos to anneal, yes. —Sufficient if we miniblast? —Kaph can calculate stress." Pugh had switched his intercom back to receive them; he looked at them, so many thoughts jabbering in an eager mind, and at Martin standing silent among them, and at Hellmouth and the wrinkled plain. "Settled! How does that strike you as a preliminary schedule, Martin?"

"It's your baby," Martin said.

Within five E-days the Johns had all their material and equipment unloaded and operating and were starting to open up the mine. They worked with total efficiency. Pugh was fascinated and frightened by their effectiveness, their confidence, their independence. He was no use to them at all. A clone, he thought, might indeed be the first truly stable, self-reliant human being. Once adult it would need nobody's help. It would be sufficient to itself physically, sexually, emotionally, intellectually. Whatever he did, any member of it would always receive the support and approval of his peers, his other selves. Nobody else was needed.

Two of the clone stayed in the dome doing calculations and paperwork, with frequent sled trips to the mine for measurements and tests. They were the mathematicians of the clone, Zayin and Kaph. That is, as Zayin explained, all ten had had thorough mathematical training from age three to twenty-one, but from twenty-one to twenty-three she and Kaph had gone on with math while the others intensified study in other specialties, geology, mining, engineering, electronic engineering, equipment robotics, applied atomics, and so on. "Kaph and I feel," she said, "that we're the element of the clone closest to what John Chow was in his singleton lifetime. But of course he was principally in biomath, and they didn't take us far in that."

"They needed us most in this field," Kaph said, with the patriotic priggishness they sometimes evinced.

Pugh and Martin soon could distinguish this pair from the others, Zayin by gestalt, Kaph only by a discolored left fourth fingernail, got from an ill-aimed hammer at the age of six. No doubt there were many such differences, physical and psychological, among them; nature might be identical, nurture could not be. But the differences were hard to find. And part of the difficulty was that they never really talked to Pugh and Martin. They joked with them, were polite, got along fine. They gave nothing. It was nothing one could complain about; they were very pleasant, they had the standardized American friendliness. "Do you come from Ireland, Owen?"

"Nobody comes from Ireland, Zayin."

"There are lots of Irish-Americans."

"To be sure, but no more Irish. A couple of thousand in all the island, the last I knew. They didn't go in for birth control, you know, so the food ran out. By the Third Famine there were no Irish left at all but the priesthood, and they all celibate, or nearly all."

Zayin and Kaph smiled stiffly. They had no experience of either bigotry or irony. "What are you then, ethnically?" Kaph asked, and Pugh replied, "A Welshman."

"Is it Welsh that you and Martin speak together?"

None of your business, Pugh thought, but said, "No, it's his dialect, not mine: Argentinean. A descendant of Spanish."

"You learned it for private communication?"

"Whom had we here to be private from? It's just that sometimes a man likes to speak his native language."

"Ours is English," Kaph said unsympathetically. Why should they have sympathy? That's one of the things you give because you need it back.

"Is Wells quaint?" asked Zayin.

"Wells? Oh, Wales, it's called. Yes, Wales is quaint." Pugh switched on his rock-cutter, which prevented further conversation by a synapse-destroying whine, and while it whined he turned his back and said a profane word in Welsh.

That night he used the Argentine dialect for private communication. "Do they pair off in the same couples or change every night?"

Martin looked surprised. A prudish expression, unsuited to his features, appeared for a moment. It faded. He too was curious. "I think it's random."

"Don't whisper, man, it sounds dirty. I think they rotate."

"On a schedule?"

"So nobody gets omitted."

Martin gave a vulgar laugh and smothered it. "What about us? Aren't we omitted?"

"That doesn't occur to them."

"What if I proposition one of the girls?"

"She'd tell the others and they'd decide as a group."

"I am not a bull," Martin said, his dark, heavy face heating up. "I will not be judged—"

"Down, down, *machismo*," said Pugh. "Do you mean to proposition one?"

Martin shrugged, sullen. "Let 'em have their incest."

"Incest is it, or masturbation?"

"I don't care, if they'd do it out of earshot!"

The clone's early attempts at modesty had soon worn off, unmotivated by any deep defensiveness of self or awareness of others. Pugh and Martin were daily deeper swamped under the intimacies of its constant emotional-sexual-mental interchange: swamped yet excluded.

"Two months to go," Martin said one evening.

"To what?" snapped Pugh. He was edgy lately, and Martin's sullenness got on his nerves.

"To relief."

In sixty days the full crew of their Exploratory Mission were due back from their survey of the other planets of the system. Pugh was aware of this.

"Crossing off the days on your calendar?" he jeered.

"Pull yourself together, Owen."

"What do you mean?"

"What I say."

They parted in contempt and resentment.

Pugh came in after a day alone on the Pampas, a vast lava plain the nearest edge of which was two hours south by jet. He was tired but refreshed by solitude. They were not supposed to take long trips alone but lately had often done so. Martin stooped under bright lights, drawing one of his elegant masterly charts. This one was of the whole face of Libra, the cancerous face. The dome was otherwise empty, seeming dim and large as it had before the clone came. "Where's the golden horde?"

Martin grunted ignorance, cross-hatching. He straightened his back to glance round at the sun, which squatted feebly like a great red toad on the eastern plain, and at the clock, which said 18:45. "Some big quakes today," he said, returning to his map. "Feel them down there? Lots of crates were falling around. Take a look at the seismo."

The needle jigged and wavered on the roll. It never stopped dancing here. The roll had recorded five quakes of major intensity back in midafternoon; twice the needle had hopped off the roll.

The attached computer had been activated to emit a slip reading, "Epicenter 61′ N by 42′ 4″ E."

"Not in the Trench this time."

"I thought it felt a bit different from usual. Sharper."

"In Base One I used to lie awake all night feeling the ground jump. Queer how you get used to things."

"Go spla if you didn't. What's for dinner?"

"I thought you'd have cooked it."

"Waiting for the clone."

Feeling put upon, Pugh got out a dozen dinnerboxes, stuck two in the Instobake, pulled them out. "All right, here's dinner."

"Been thinking," Martin said, coming to table. "What if some clone cloned itself? Illegally. Made a thousand duplicates—ten thousand. Whole army. They could make a tidy power grab, couldn't they?"

"But how many millions did this lot cost to rear? Artificial placentae and all that. It would be hard to keep secret, unless they had a planet to themselves. . . . Back before the Famines when Earth had national governments, they talked about that: clone your best soldiers, have whole regiments of them. But the food ran out before they could play that game."

They talked amicably, as they used to do.

"Funny," Martin said, chewing. "They left early this morning, didn't they?"

"All but Kaph and Zayin. They thought they'd get the first payload above ground today. What's up?"

"They weren't back for lunch."

"They won't starve, to be sure."

"They left at seven."

"So they did." Then Pugh saw it. The air tanks held eight hours' supply.

"Kaph and Zayin carried out spare cans when they left. Or they've got a heap out there."

"They did, but they brought the whole lot in to recharge." Martin stood up, pointing to one of the stacks of stuff that cut the dome into rooms and alleys.

"There's an alarm signal on every imsuit."

"It's not automatic."

Pugh was tired and still hungry. "Sit down and eat, man. That lot can look after themselves."

Martin sat down but did not eat. "There was a big quake, Owen. The first one. Big enough it scared me."

After a pause Pugh sighed and said, "All right."

Unenthusiastically, they got out the two-man sled that was always left for them and headed it north. The long sunrise covered everything in poisonous red jello. The horizontal light and shadow made it hard to see, raised walls of fake iron ahead of them which they slid through, turned the convex plain beyond Hellmouth into a great dimple full of bloody water. Around the tunnel entrance a wilderness of machinery stood, cranes and cables and servos and wheels and diggers and robocarts and sliders and control huts, all slanting and bulking incoherently in the red light. Martin jumped from the sled, ran into the mine. He came out again, to Pugh. "Oh God, Owen, it's down," he said. Pugh went in and saw, five meters from the entrance, the shiny moist, black wall that ended the tunnel. Newly exposed to air, it looked organic, like visceral tissue. The tunnel entrance, enlarged by blasting and double-tracked for robocarts, seemed unchanged until he noticed thousands of tiny spiderweb cracks in the walls. The floor was wet with some sluggish fluid.

"They were inside," Martin said.

"They may be still. They surely had extra air cans—"

"Look, Owen, look at the basalt flow, at the roof, don't you see what the quake did, look at it."

The low hump of land that roofed the caves still had the unreal look of an optical illusion. It had reversed itself, sunk down, leaving a vast dimple or pit. When Pugh walked on it he saw that it too was cracked with many tiny fissures. From some a whitish gas was seeping, so that the sunlight on the surface of the gas pool was shafted as if by the waters of a dim red lake.

"The mine's not on the fault. There's no fault here!"

Pugh came back to him quickly. "No, there's no fault, Martin— Look, they surely weren't all inside together."

Martin followed him and searched among the wrecked machines dully, then actively. He spotted the airsled. It had come down heading south, and stuck at an angle in a pothole of colloidal dust. It had carried two riders. One was half sunk in the dust, but his suit meters registered normal functioning; the other hung strapped onto the tilted sled. Her imsuit had burst open on the broken legs, and the body was frozen hard as any rock. That was all they found. As both regulation and custom demanded, they cremated the dead at once with the laser guns they carried by regulation and had never used before. Pugh, knowing he was going to be sick, wrestled the survivor onto the two-man sled and sent Martin off to the dome with him. Then he vomited and flushed the waste out of his suit, and finding one four-man sled undamaged, followed after Martin, shaking as if the cold of Libra had got through to him.

The survivor was Kaph. He was in deep shock. They found a

swelling on the occiput that might mean concussion, but no fracture was visible.

Pugh brought two glasses of food concentrate and two chasers of aquavit. "Come on," he said. Martin obeyed, drinking off the tonic. They sat down on crates near the cot and sipped the aquavit.

Kaph lay immobile, face like beeswax, hair bright black to the shoulders, lips stiffly parted for faintly gasping breaths.

"It must have been the first shock, the big one," Martin said. "It must have slid the whole structure sideways. Till it fell in on itself. There must be gas layers in the lateral rocks, like those formations in the Thirty-first Quadrant. But there wasn't any sign—" As he spoke the world slid out from under them. Things leaped and clattered, hopped and jigged, shouted Ha! Ha! Ha! "It was like this at fourteen hours," said Reason shakily in Martin's voice, amidst the unfastening and ruin of the world. But Unreason sat up, as the tumult lessened and things ceased dancing, and screamed aloud.

Pugh leaped across his spilt aquavit and held Kaph down. The muscular body flailed him off. Martin pinned the shoulders down. Kaph screamed, struggled, choked; his face blackened. "Oxy," Pugh said, and his hand found the right needle in the medical kit as if by homing instinct; while Martin held the mask he struck the needle home to the vagus nerve, restoring Kaph to life.

"Didn't know you knew that stunt," Martin said, breathing hard.

"The Lazarus Jab, my father was a doctor. It doesn't often work," Pugh said. "I want that drink I spilled. Is the quake over? I can't tell."

"Aftershocks. It's not just you shivering."

"Why did he suffocate?"

"I don't know, Owen. Look in the book."

Kaph was breathing normally and his color was restored; only the lips were still darkened. They poured a new shot of courage and sat down by him again with their medical guide. "Nothing about cyanosis or asphyxiation under 'Shock' or 'Concussion.' He can't have breathed in anything with his suit on. I don't know. We'd get as much good out of *Mother Mog's Home Herbalist*. . . . 'Anal Hemorrhoids,' fy!" Pugh pitched the book to a crate table. It fell short, because either Pugh or the table was still unsteady.

"Why didn't he signal?"

"Sorry?"

"The eight inside the mine never had time. But he and the girl must have been outside. Maybe she was in the entrance and got hit by the first slide. He must have been outside, in the control hut maybe. He ran in, pulled her out, strapped her onto the sled, started for the dome. And all that time never pushed the panic button in his imsuit. Why not?"

"Well, he'd had that whack on his head. I doubt he ever realized the girl was dead. He wasn't in his senses. But if he had been I don't know if he'd have thought to signal us. They looked to one another for help."

Martin's face was like an Indian mask, grooves at the mouth corners, eyes of dull coal. "That's so. What must he have felt, then, when the quake came and he was outside, alone—"

In answer Kaph screamed.

He came off the cot in the heaving convulsions of one suffocating, knocked Pugh right down with his flailing arm, staggered into a stack of crates and fell to the floor, lips blue, eyes white. Martin dragged him back onto the cot and gave him a whiff of oxygen, then knelt by Pugh, who was sitting up, and wiped at his cut cheekbone. "Owen, are you all right, are you going to be all right, Owen?"

"I think I am," Pugh said. "Why are you rubbing that on my face?"

It was a short length of computer tape, now spotted with Pugh's blood. Martin dropped it. "Thought it was a towel. You clipped your cheek on that box there."

"Is he out of it?"

"Seems to be."

They stared down at Kaph lying stiff, his teeth a white line inside dark parted lips.

"Like epilepsy. Brain damage maybe?"

"What about shooting him full of meprobamate?"

Pugh shook his head. "I don't know what's in that shot I already gave him for shock. Don't want to overdose him."

"Maybe he'll sleep it off now."

"I'd like to myself. Between him and the earthquake I can't seem to keep on my feet."

"You got a nasty crack there. Go on, I'll sit up a while."

Pugh cleaned his cut cheek and pulled off his shirt, then paused.

"Is there anything we ought to have done—have tried to do—"

"They're all dead," Martin said heavily, gently.

Pugh lay down on top of his sleeping bag and one instant later was wakened by a hideous, sucking, struggling noise. He staggered up, found the needle, tried three times to jab it in correctly and failed, began to massage over Kaph's heart. "Mouth-to-mouth," he said, and Martin obeyed. Presently Kaph drew a harsh breath, his heartbeat steadied, his rigid muscles began to relax.

"How long did I sleep?"

"Half an hour."

They stood up sweating. The ground shuddered, the fabric of the dome sagged and swayed. Libra was dancing her awful polka again, her *Totentanz.* The sun, though rising, seemed to have grown larger and redder; gas and dust must have been stirred up in the feeble atmosphere.

"What's wrong with him, Owen?"

"I think he's dying with them."

"Them— But they're all dead, I tell you."

"Nine of them. They're all dead, they were crushed or suffocated. They were all him, he is all of them. They died, and now he's dying their deaths one by one."

"Oh, pity of God," said Martin.

The next time was much the same. The fifth time was worse, for Kaph fought and raved, trying to speak but getting no words out, as if his mouth were stopped with rocks or clay. After that the attacks grew weaker, but so did he. The eighth seizure came at about four-thirty; Pugh and Martin worked till five-thirty doing all they could to keep life in the body that slid without protest into death. They kept him, but Martin said, "The next will finish him." And it did; but Pugh breathed his own breath into the inert lungs, until he himself passed out.

He woke. The dome was opaqued and no light on. He listened and heard the breathing of two sleeping men. He slept, and nothing woke him till hunger did.

The sun was well up over the dark plains, and the planet had stopped dancing. Kaph lay asleep. Pugh and Martin drank tea and looked at him with proprietary triumph.

When he woke Martin went to him: "How do you feel, old man?" There was no answer. Pugh took Martin's place and looked into the brown, dull eyes that gazed toward but not into his own. Like Martin he quickly turned away. He heated food concentrate and brought it to Kaph. "Come on, drink."

He could see the muscles in Kaph's throat tighten. "Let me die," the young man said.

"You're not dying."

Kaph spoke with clarity and precision: "I am nine-tenths dead. There is not enough of me left alive."

That precision convinced Pugh, and he fought the conviction. "No," he said, peremptory. "They are dead. The others. Your brothers and sisters. You're not them, you're alive. You are John Chow. Your life is in your own hands."

The young man lay still, looking into a darkness that was not there.

Martin and Pugh took turns taking the Exploitation hauler and a spare set of robos over to Hellmouth to salvage equipment and protect it from Libra's sinister atmosphere, for the value of the stuff was, literally, astronomical. It was slow work for one man at a time, but they were unwilling to leave Kaph by himself. The one left in the dome did paperwork, while Kaph sat or lay and stared into his darkness and never spoke. The days went by, silent.

The radio spat and spoke: the Mission calling from the ship. "We'll be down on Libra in five weeks, Owen. Thirty-four E-days nine hours I make it as of now. How's tricks in the old dome?"

"Not good, chief. The Exploit team were killed, all but one of them, in the mine. Earthquake. Six days ago."

The radio crackled and sang starsong. Sixteen seconds' lag each way; the ship was out around Planet II now. "Killed, all but one? You and Martin were unhurt?"

"We're all right, chief."

Thirty-two seconds.

"*Passerine* left an Exploit team out here with us. I may put them on the Hellmouth project then, instead of the Quadrant Seven project. We'll settle that when we come down. In any case you and Martin will be relieved at Dome Two. Hold tight. Anything else?"

"Nothing else."

Thirty-two seconds.

"Right then. So long, Owen."

Kaph had heard all this, and later on Pugh said to him, "The chief may ask you to stay here with the other Exploit team. You know the ropes here." Knowing the exigencies of Far Out life, he wanted to warn the young man. Kaph made no answer. Since he had said, "There is not enough of me left alive," he had not spoken a word.

"Owen," Martin said on suit intercom, "he's spla. Insane. Psycho."

"He's doing very well for a man who's died nine times."

"Well? Like a turned-off android is well? The only emotion he has left is hate. Look at his eyes."

"That's not hate, Martin. Listen, it's true that he has, in a sense, been dead. I cannot imagine what he feels. But it's not hatred. He can't even see us. It's too dark."

"Throats have been cut in the dark. He hates us because we're not Aleph and Yod and Zayin."

"Maybe. But I think he's alone. He doesn't see us or hear us, that's the truth. He never had to see anyone else before. He never was alone before. He had himself to see, talk with, live with, nine other selves all his life. He doesn't know how you go it alone. He must learn. Give him time."

Martin shook his heavy head. "Spla," he said. "Just remember when you're alone with him that he could break your neck one-handed."

"He could do that," said Pugh, a short, soft-voiced man with a scarred cheekbone; he smiled. They were just outside the dome airlock, programming one of the servos to repair a damaged hauler. They could see Kaph sitting inside the great half-egg of the dome like a fly in amber.

"Hand me the insert pack there. What makes you think he'll get any better?"

"He has a strong personality, to be sure."

"Strong? Crippled. Nine-tenths dead, as he put it."

"But he's not dead. He's a live man: John Kaph Chow. He had a jolly queer upbringing, but after all every boy has got to break free of his family. He will do it."

"I can't see it."

"Think a bit, Martin bach. What's this cloning for? To repair the human race. We're in a bad way. Look at me. My IIQ and GC are half this John Chow's. Yet they wanted me so badly for the Far Out Service that when I volunteered they took me and fitted me out with an artificial lung and corrected my myopia. Now if there were enough good sound lads about would they be taking one-lunged short-sighted Welshmen?"

"Didn't know you had an artificial lung."

"I do then. Not tin, you know. Human, grown in a tank from a bit of somebody; cloned, if you like. That's how they make replacement organs, the same general idea as cloning, but bits and pieces instead of whole people. It's my own lung now, whatever. But what I am saying is this, there are too many like me these days and not enough like John Chow. They're trying to raise the level of the human genetic pool, which is a mucky little puddle since the population crash. So then if a man is cloned, he's a strong and clever man. It's only logic, to be sure."

Martin grunted; the servo began to hum.

Kaph had been eating little; he had trouble swallowing his food, choking on it, so that he would give up trying after a few bites. He had lost eight or ten kilos. After three weeks or so, however, his appetite began to pick up, and one day he began to look through the clone's possessions, the sleeping bags, kits, papers which Pugh had stacked neatly in a far angle of a packing-crate alley. He sorted, destroyed a heap of papers and oddments, made a small packet of what remained, then relapsed into his walking coma.

Two days later he spoke. Pugh was trying to correct a flutter in the tape-player and failing; Martin had the jet out, checking their maps of the Pampas. "Hell and damnation!" Pugh said, and Kaph said in a toneless voice, "Do you want me to do that?"

Pugh jumped, controlled himself, and gave the machine to Kaph. The young man took it apart, put it back together, and left it on the table.

"Put on a tape," Pugh said with careful casualness, busy at another table.

Kaph put on the topmost tape, a chorale. He lay down on his cot. The sound of a hundred human voices singing together filled the dome. He lay still, his face blank.

In the next days he took over several routine jobs, unasked. He undertook nothing that wanted initiative, and if asked to do anything he made no response at all.

"He's doing well," Pugh said in the dialect of Argentina.

"He's not. He's turning himself into a machine. Does what he's programmed to do, no reaction to anything else. He's worse off than when he didn't function at all. He's not human any more."

Pugh sighed. "Well, good night," he said in English. "Good night, Kaph."

"Good night," Martin said; Kaph did not.

Next morning at breakfast Kaph reached across Martin's plate for the toast. "Why don't you ask for it?" Martin said with the geniality of repressed exasperation. "I can pass it."

"I can reach it," Kaph said in his flat voice.

"Yes, but look. Asking to pass things, saying good night or hello, they're not important, but all the same when somebody says something a person ought to answer. . . ."

The young man looked indifferently in Martin's direction; his eyes still did not seem to see clear through to the person he looked toward. "Why should I answer?"

"Because somebody has said something to you."

"Why?"

Martin shrugged and laughed. Pugh jumped up and turned on the rock-cutter.

Later on he said, "Lay off that, please, Martin."

"Manners are essential in small isolated crews, some kind of manners, whatever you work out together. He's been taught that, everybody in Far Out knows it. Why does he deliberately flout it?"

"Do you tell yourself good night?"

"So?"

"Don't you see Kaph's never known anyone but himself?"

Martin brooded and then broke out. "Then by God this cloning business is all wrong. It won't do. What are a lot of duplicate geniuses going to do for us when they don't even know we exist?"

Pugh nodded. "It might be wiser to separate the clones and bring them up with others. But they make such a grand team this way."

"Do they? I don't know. If this lot had been ten average inefficient E.T. engineers, would they all have got killed? What if, when the quake came and things started caving in, what if all those kids ran the same way, farther into the mine, maybe, to save the one who was farthest in? Even Kaph was outside and went in. . . .

It's hypothetical. But I keep thinking, out of ten ordinary confused guys, more might have got out."

"I don't know. It's true that identical twins tend to die at about the same time, even when they have never seen each other. Identity and death, it is very strange. . . ."

The days went on, the red sun crawled across the dark sky, Kaph did not speak when spoken to, Pugh and Martin snapped at each other more frequently each day. Pugh complained of Martin's snoring. Offended, Martin moved his cot clear across the dome and also ceased speaking to Pugh for some while. Pugh whistled Welsh dirges until Martin complained, and then Pugh stopped speaking for a while.

The day before the Mission ship was due, Martin announced he was going over to Merioneth.

"I thought at least you'd be giving me a hand with the computer to finish the rock analyses," Pugh said, aggrieved.

"Kaph can do that. I want one more look at the Trench. Have fun," Martin added in dialect, and laughed, and left.

"What is that language?"

"Argentinean. I told you that once, didn't I?"

"I don't know." After a while the young man added, "I have forgotten a lot of things, I think."

"It wasn't important, to be sure," Pugh said gently, realizing all at once how important this conversation was. "Will you give me a hand running the computer, Kaph?"

He nodded.

Pugh had left a lot of loose ends, and the job took them all day. Kaph was a good co-worker, quick and systematic, much more so than Pugh himself. His flat voice, now that he was talking again, got on the nerves; but it didn't matter, there was only this one day left to get through and then the ship would come, the old crew, comrades and friends.

During tea break Kaph said, "What will happen if the Explore ship crashes?"

"They'd be killed."

"To you, I mean."

"To us? We'd radio SOS signals and live on half rations till the rescue cruiser from Area Three Base came. Four and a half E-years away it is. We have life support here for three men for, let's see, maybe between four and five years. A bit tight, it would be."

"Would they send a cruiser for three men?"

"They would."

Kaph said no more.

"Enough cheerful speculations," Pugh said cheerfully, rising to get back to work. He slipped sideways and the chair avoided his hand; he did a sort of half-pirouette and fetched up hard against the dome hide. "My goodness," he said, reverting to his native idiom, "what is it?"

"Quake," said Kaph.

The teacups bounced on the table with a plastic cackle, a litter of papers slid off a box, the skin of the dome swelled and sagged. Underfoot there was a huge noise, half sound, half shaking, a subsonic boom.

Kaph sat unmoved. An earthquake does not frighten a man who died in an earthquake.

Pugh, white-faced, wiry black hair sticking out, a frightened man, said, "Martin is in the Trench."

"What trench?"

"The big fault line. The epicenter for the local quakes. Look at the seismograph." Pugh struggled with the stuck door of a still-jittering locker.

"Where are you going?"

"After him."

"Martin took the jet. Sleds aren't safe to use during quakes. They go out of control."

"For God's sake man, shut up."

Kaph stood up, speaking in a flat voice as usual. "It's unnecessary to go out after him now. It's taking an unnecessary risk."

"If his alarm goes off, radio me," Pugh said, shut the head-piece of his suit, and ran to the lock. As he went out Libra picked up her ragged skirts and danced a belly dance from under his feet clear to the red horizon.

Inside the dome, Kaph saw the sled go up, tremble like a meteor in the dull red daylight, and vanish to the northeast. The hide of the dome quivered, the earth coughed. A vent south of the dome belched up a slow-flowing bile of black gas.

A bell shrilled and a red light flashed on the central control board. The sign under the light read Suit 2 and scribbled under that, A. G. M. Kaph did not turn the signal off. He tried to radio Martin, then Pugh, but got no reply from either.

When the aftershocks decreased he went back to work and finished up Pugh's job. It took him about two hours. Every half hour he tried to contact Suit 1 and got no reply, then Suit 2 and got no reply. The red light had stopped flashing after an hour.

It was dinnertime. Kaph cooked dinner for one and ate it. He lay down on his cot.

The aftershocks had ceased except for faint rolling tremors at long intervals. The sun hung in the west, oblate, pale red, immense. It did not sink visibly. There was no sound at all.

Kaph got up and began to walk about the messy, half-packed-up, overcrowded, empty dome. The silence continued. He went to the player and put on the first tape that came to hand. It was pure music, electronic, without harmonies, without voices. It ended. The silence continued.

Pugh's uniform tunic, one button missing, hung over a stack of rock samples. Kaph stared at it a while.

The silence continued.

The child's dream: There is no one else alive in the world but me. In all the world.

Low, north of the dome, a meteor flickered.

Kaph's mouth opened as if he were trying to say something, but no sound came. He went hastily to the north wall and peered out into the gelatinous red light.

The little star came in and sank. Two figures blurred the airlock. Kaph stood close beside the lock as they came in. Martin's imsuit was covered with some kind of dust so that he looked raddled and warty like the surface of Libra. Pugh had him by the arm.

"Is he hurt?"

Pugh shucked his suit, helped Martin peel off his. "Shaken up," he said, curt.

"A piece of cliff fell onto the jet," Martin said, sitting down at the table and waving his arms. "Not while I was in it though. I was parked, see, and poking about that carbon-dust area when I felt things humping. So I went out onto a nice bit of early igneous I'd noticed from above, good footing and out from under the cliffs. Then I saw this bit of the planet fall off onto the flyer, quite a sight it was, and after a while it occurred to me the spare aircans were in the flyer, so I leaned on the panic button. But I didn't get any radio reception, that's always happening here during quakes, so I didn't know if the signal was getting through either. And things went on jumping around and pieces of the cliff coming off. Little rocks flying around, and so dusty you couldn't see a meter ahead. I was really beginning to wonder what I'd do for breathing in the small hours, you know, when I saw old Owen buzzing up the Trench in all that dust and junk like a big ugly bat—"

"Want to eat?" said Pugh.

"Of course I want to eat. How'd you come through the quake here, Kaph? No damage? It wasn't a big one actually, was it, what's the seismo say? My trouble was I was in the middle of it. Old Epicenter Alvaro. Felt like Richter fifteen there—total destruction of planet—"

"Sit down," Pugh said. "Eat."

After Martin had eaten a little his spate of talk ran dry. He very soon went off to his cot, still in the remote angle where he had removed it when Pugh complained of his snoring. "Good night, you one-lunged Welshman," he said across the dome.

"Good night."

There was no more out of Martin. Pugh opaqued the dome, turned the lamp down to a yellow glow less than a candle's light, and sat doing nothing, saying nothing, withdrawn.

The silence continued.

"I finished the computations."

Pugh nodded thanks.

"The signal from Martin came through, but I couldn't contact you or him."

Pugh said with effort, "I should not have gone. He had two hours of air left even with only one can. He might have been heading home when I left. This way we were all out of touch with one another. I was scared."

The silence came back, punctuated now by Martin's long, soft snores.

"Do you love Martin?"

Pugh looked up with angry eyes: "Martin is my friend. We've worked together, he's a good man." He stopped. After a while he said, "Yes, I love him. Why did you ask that?"

Kaph said nothing, but he looked at the other man. His face was changed, as if he were glimpsing something he had not seen before; his voice too was changed. "How can you . . . How do you . . ."

But Pugh could not tell him. "I don't know," he said, "it's practice, partly. I don't know. We're each of us alone, to be sure. What can you do but hold your hand out in the dark?"

Kaph's strange gaze dropped, burned out by its own intensity.

"I'm tired," Pugh said. "That was ugly, looking for him in all that black dust and muck, and mouths opening and shutting in the ground. . . . I'm going to bed. The ship will be transmitting to us by six or so." He stood up and stretched.

"It's a clone," Kaph said. "The other Exploit Team they're bringing with them."

"Is it then?"

"A twelveclone. They came out with us on the *Passerine*."

Kaph sat in the small yellow aura of the lamp seeming to look past it at what he feared: the new clone, the multiple self of which he was not part. A lost piece of a broken set, a fragment, inexpert at solitude, not knowing even how you go about giving love to another individual, now he must face the absolute, closed self-sufficiency of the clone of twelve; that was a lot to ask of the poor fellow, to be sure. Pugh put a hand on his shoulder in passing. "The chief won't ask you to stay here with a clone. You can go home. Or since you're

Far Out maybe you'll come on farther out with us. We could use you. No hurry deciding. You'll make out all right."

Pugh's quiet voice trailed off. He stood unbuttoning his coat, stooped a little with fatigue. Kaph looked at him and saw the thing he had never seen before, saw him: Owen Pugh, the other, the stranger who held his hand out in the dark.

"Good night," Pugh mumbled, crawling into his sleeping bag and half asleep already, so that he did not hear Kaph reply after a pause, repeating, across darkness, benediction.

1969

BIOGRAPHICAL NOTES

Elizabeth Mann Borgese (April 24, 1918–February 8, 2002) was born Elisabeth Mann in Munich, the fifth of Nobel laureate Thomas Mann and Katia (Pringsheim) Mann's six children. Fleeing Nazi Germany with her famous family, she finished her education at the Conservatory of Music in Zurich, where she studied piano and cello, and arrived in the United States in 1938. In 1939, she married literature professor Giuseppe Antonio Borgese, with whom she moved to Chicago and had two children. She became an American citizen in 1941 and made frequent public appearances throughout the 1940s, lecturing on subjects including European politics and "Women and the Future"; toward the end of the decade she became a proponent of world government, joining the Committee to Frame a World Constitution and editing its journal *Common Cause*. Her husband died in 1952.

While raising her daughters as a single parent, Borgese experimented with SF writing, placing three stories in SF magazines over the course of 1959. Although Borgese was known for her optimism and energy, most of her speculative tales are dark and pessimistic, revolving around near-future worlds whose dangerous scientific and technological arrangements are reflected in damaged human psyches and distorted human bodies. The most significant of these are collected in her 1960 anthology, *To Whom It May Concern*.

In 1963 Borgese published *Ascent of Woman*, which argued that sociological trends would eventually "produce superior women, men's true equals." Becoming a senior fellow at the Center for Study of Democratic Institutions in Santa Barbara in 1964, she began to focus on environmental issues facing the world's oceans and the law of the sea. She organized the 1970 Pacem in Maribus Conference, which led to the United Nations Convention on the Law of the Sea; helped to establish the International Ocean Institute at the Royal University of Malta; and published *The Drama of the Oceans* (1975). She moved to Halifax, Nova Scotia, in 1978, taking Canadian citizenship, teaching political science at Dalhousie University, and writing subsequent books on maritime subjects. A global "Ambassador of the Seas," she received numerous honorary degrees; was ordained a Member of the Order of Canada in 1988; and won Germany's most prestigious award, the Commander's Cross of the Order of Merit, in 2001. Borgese died in St. Moritz, Switzerland, at eighty-three.

Leigh Brackett (December 7, 1915–March 18, 1978), known among SF fans as the "Queen of Space Opera," was born Leigh C. Brackett in Los Angeles, California, the only child of Margaret (Douglass) Brackett and William Franklin Brackett, an accountant and aspiring writer. Her father died in 1918 during the flu pandemic and Brackett was raised by her mother and maternal grandparents in Santa Monica, where she attended a private girls' school. Family financial difficulties forced her to decline a college scholarship.

Joining the Los Angeles Science Fiction Society in 1939, Brackett published her first story, "Martian Quest," in the February 1940 *Astounding Science Fiction*; by the end of World War II she had become a prolific contributor to SF magazines, including *Astonishing Stories*, *Comet*, *Planet Stories*, *Super Science Stories*, and *Thrilling Wonder Stories*. Her first novel, *No Good from a Corpse* (1944)—a work of detective fiction—attracted the attention of director Howard Hawks, who hired her to work with William Faulkner and Jules Furthman on the screenplay for *The Big Sleep* (1946), based on Raymond Chandler's novel. Busy in Hollywood, she asked her friend Ray Bradbury to complete her novella "Lorelei of the Red Mist," published jointly in 1946. The same year, she married author Edmond Hamilton, moving with him to rural Kinsman, Ohio.

Brackett began publishing novel-length SF with "Shadow over Mars" in the Fall 1944 issue of *Startling Stories*; it appeared in book form in 1951. She followed this with *The Starmen* (1952), *The Sword of Rhiannon* (1953), *The Big Jump* (1955), *The Long Tomorrow* (1955), *The Galactic Breed* (1955), *Alpha Centauri or Die!* (1963), *The Ginger Star* (1974), *The Hounds of Skaith* (1974), and *The Reavers of Skaith* (1976). At the same time, she published crime novels, Westerns, and other fiction, and earned screenwriting credit for *Rio Bravo* (1959), *Hatari!* (1962), *El Dorado* (1966), *Rio Lobo* (1970), and *The Long Goodbye* (1973). Several of her own works—including the crime novels *An Eye for an Eye* (1957) and *The Tiger Among Us* (1957)—were adapted for television. Brackett also famously collaborated on the screenplay for *The Empire Strikes Back* (1980, with Lawrence Kasdan), completing an early draft shortly before her death. *The Best of Leigh Brackett*, edited by Edmond Hamilton, was published in 1977, just one year before Brackett died of lung cancer in Lancaster, California. Since her death, Brackett's contributions to the development of SF as a modern genre have been recognized in the form of a Hugo Award for Best Dramatic Presentation (*The Empire Strikes Back*, 1981), a Cordwainer Smith Rediscovery Award, and induction into the Science Fiction Hall of Fame (2014).

Marion Zimmer Bradley (June 3, 1930–September 25, 1999) was born Marion Eleanor Zimmer on a farm near Albany, New York. Her parents Evelyn P. (Conklin) Zimmer and Leslie R. Zimmer, a truck driver and carpenter, later had two sons.

As a child, Bradley enjoyed reading SF and fantasy authors Henry Kuttner, Edmond Hamilton, C. L. Moore, and Leigh Brackett (the latter two of whom are also featured in this anthology). At seventeen, she began writing for, illustrating, and publishing the fanzine *Astra's Tower*; contributors included her younger brother Leslie and her future husband Robert Alden Bradley, more than thirty years her senior, whom she married in 1949 after an epistolary courtship. Leaving upstate New York for Abilene, Texas, she had a son, David, in 1950; she also started publishing professionally, winning an *Amazing Stories* contest for "Outpost" in December 1949 and selling "Women Only" to *Vortex Science Fiction* in 1953. The first novels in her multivolume Darkover series appeared in magazine form in the late 1950s, to be published separately early in the next decade: *Falcons of Narabedla* (1964) and *The Planet Savers* (1962). Her first separately published novel, *Lesbian Love* (1960), was one of eight lesbian pulps she is known to have written from 1960 to 1966 under pseudonyms including Marlene Longman, Lee Chapman, Miriam Gardner, Morgan Ives, and John Dexter. She collected her early stories in *The Dark Intruder & Other Stories* (1964).

Bradley graduated from Hardin-Simmons University in Abilene in 1964 and headed to Berkeley, California, to continue her education in psychology. She divorced her first husband and married numismatist Walter H. Breen in Marin, California, the same year; they had two children, Patrick in 1964 and Moira in 1966. Along with future literary collaborator Diana L. Paxson, she is credited with helping to found the Society for Creative Anachronism on May Day, 1966. In 1981, along with Paxson and others, she incorporated the Center for Non-Traditional Religion in Berkeley. Bradley was well-known for her active interest in SF and fantasy fandom, coediting a number of fanzines, publishing her own *Lord of the Rings* fan fiction, and encouraging fans to write stories in her own Darkover universe (a practice she ended when she found herself in a skirmish with a fan over intellectual property issues).

Moving to Staten Island, New York, in 1968, Bradley edited the influential anthology series *Sword and Sorceress* (1984–99) and began the magazine *Marion Zimmer Bradley's Fantasy* (1988–99), serving as editor and publisher. In 1984, she received the Locus Award for Best Novel for her bestselling Arthurian fantasy, *The Mists of Avalon* (1983), and in 2000 she posthumously won a World Fantasy Award for Lifetime Achievement. Dying of a heart attack in Berkeley at sixty-nine, she was credited as the author of over six dozen novels.

For many years Bradley was best remembered for *The Mists of Avalon*. However, posthumous allegations of child abuse have muddied her reputation. Bradley divorced Walter H. Breen in 1990 following his arrest on child sex abuse charges for which he was later imprisoned; they had separated earlier, in 1979, but remained business partners and friends. Having helped to edit Breen's pseudonymously published treatise *Greek Love* in 1964, Bradley was certainly aware of her husband's theoretical advocacy of pedophilia. In 1963–64, the SF community debated the exclusion of Breen on related grounds from Pacificon II, in what became known as "Breendoggle." In 2014, Bradley's daughter Moira Greyland accused Bradley of abusing her and her younger brother; in 2017 she published *The Last Closet*, a memoir of her childhood.

Rosel George Brown (March 15, 1926–November 26, 1967), born Rosel George in New Orleans, Louisiana, was the second of Sam and Elizabeth Rightor George's three children; she grew up in Bay St. Louis, Mississippi, and New Orleans, where her father worked as a nurseryman. Graduating from Sophie Newcomb College in 1946 with a degree in ancient Greek, she married Tulane student and returning veteran W. Burlie Brown the following year. Continuing her education in the classics at the University of Minnesota, she specialized in fifth-century Greece, a lifelong interest, and began writing a life of Alcibiades. Returning to New Orleans, where her husband joined the history department at Tulane, she had two daughters (in 1954 and 1959) and worked as a teacher and welfare visitor.

Brown's first published story, "From an Unseen Censor," appeared in *Galaxy* in September 1958; that same year, she received a Hugo nomination for the best new SF or fantasy author. Brown went on to publish nearly two dozen more speculative stories in the next five years, many of which were featured in her 1963 collection, *A Handful of Time*. She was a charter member of the Science Fiction Writers of America, and in 1966 she published two novels, *Earthblood* (in collaboration with Keith Laumer) and *Sibyl Blue*

Sue (retitled *Galactic Sibyl Blue Sue* for the paperback edition), the latter featuring a future-detective main character Judith Merril described as "the swingingest mama since—well, *since*."

Brown's promising career was tragically cut short when she died at forty-one of lymphoma. As Daniel F. Galouye recalls in his memorial piece from *Nebula Award Stories* (1969), Brown was a "crisp stylist" whose signal accomplishment was the production of short stories "rich in emotion and satirical content" while the character of Sibyl Blue Sue was "a landmark in science fiction" that underscored Brown's "skill at cloaking unconventional protagonists with vividly drawn credibility." *The Waters of Centaurus*, a sequel to *Sibyl Blue Sue*, was published posthumously in 1970.

Doris Pitkin Buck (January 3, 1898–December 4, 1980) started her career as a writer of speculative fiction relatively late in life, publishing her first story—"Aunt Agatha," in the October 1952 *Magazine of Fantasy and Science Fiction*—at fifty-four. She was born in New York City, where her father Lucius Pitkin owned a chemical and metallurgical consulting laboratory. Though he hoped someday to rename his firm "Pitkin and Daughter" and hand it down, she studied literature instead, graduating from Bryn Mawr in 1920 and teaching at the Brearley School in Manhattan while completing her master's degree in English at Columbia in 1925. Marrying architect Richard S. Buck Jr. in 1926, she moved with her husband to Columbus, Ohio, where both taught at Ohio State; in 1932 she had a son. The family relocated to the suburbs of Washington, D.C., in the 1940s, where she joined the Little Theatre of Alexandria and wrote a radio play, "Wish Upon a Star" (1944).

Buck contributed dozens of stories and poems to genre magazines before her death in 1980. While she was most closely associated with the literary experiments of *The Magazine of Fantasy and Science Fiction*, she was proud of her status as a scientist's daughter who did careful research for her art. As she told *The Washington Post* in 1963, "real science fiction is based on science." Her short story, "The Little Blue Weeds of Spring," made the first ballot for the 1967 Nebula Awards and her short story "Cacophony in Pink and Ochre" is one of the stories slated to appear in Harlan Ellison's still-unpublished *Last Dangerous Visions* anthology.

Buck actively contributed to the development of the modern SF community in other ways as well. She helped found the Science Fiction Writers of America (now the Science Fiction and Fantasy Writers of America) and was a regular participant at the Milford Writers' Conference, an annual SF event organized by Damon Knight and Kate Wilhelm. She also wrote articles on traveling and gardening and, with her husband, on landscaping and remodeling. She died at eighty-two in a Hyattsville, Maryland, nursing home. A final poem, "Travel Tip," appeared posthumously in the June 1981 issue of *The Magazine of Fantasy and Science Fiction*.

Mildred Clingerman (March 14, 1918–February 26, 1997) was born Mildred McElroy in Allen, Oklahoma, the first of two daughters of Arthur McElroy, a railroad construction superintendent, and Meda (Bush) McElroy, who worked for a mining company boardinghouse; her parents divorced in 1925. Raised in Iowa, Missouri, California, Texas, and New Mexico, she moved to Arizona with her mother and sister in 1929, attending Tucson High School. She married Stuart Clingerman, a wholesale milkman and later construction project manager, in 1937, and had a son and daughter in 1940 and 1942, attending the University of Arizona in 1941.

During World War II, while her husband served as an army paratrooper, she worked at a Tucson flight training school. In subsequent decades she was active in the Tucson Writer's Club and the Tucson Press Club.

Clingerman noted late in her career that she had "firmly kept [her] writing life secondary to other joys," calling it "an avocation," but she was relatively productive, publishing almost two dozen works of speculative short fiction from 1952 to 1975, most in *The Magazine of Fantasy and Science Fiction*. In 1958, Anthony Boucher dedicated the seventh volume of *The Best from Fantasy and Science Fiction* to her, calling Clingerman "the most serendipitous of discoveries." She also published speculative fiction in mainstream magazines, including *Collier's* and *Woman's Home Companion*, and at least one story in a local paper, the *Arizona Daily Star*; additionally she contributed nongenre fiction to the *Philadelphia Inquirer* and *Good Housekeeping*. A collection of her stories, *A Cupful of Space*, appeared in 1961. Clingerman died of heart failure at seventy-eight, in McKinney, Texas, and received a posthumous Cordwainer Smith Rediscovery Award in 2014. *The Clingerman Files: Collected Works*, containing previously uncollected and unpublished stories, appeared in 2017.

Sonya Dorman (June 4, 1924–February 14, 2005), born Sonya Gloria Hess in New York City, was raised by foster parents on a farm in West Newbury, Massachusetts; her mother, a dancer and model, died while she was an infant. Unable to afford more than a year of agricultural college, she worked as a stablehand, maid, fish canner, riding instructor, and tuna boat cook while giving herself an education, reading widely in world literature. After a brief first marriage in 1945–46, she married Jack Dorman, an engineer, in 1950, and had a daughter, Sherri, in 1959. Moving from Stony Point, New York, to West Mystic and then New London, Connecticut, during the 1970s, the family bred Akitas and other dogs and exhibited at dog shows.

Dorman published approximately two dozen SF stories from 1961 to 1980, gathering three of these as a young adult novel, *Planet Patrol*, in 1978; she also published fiction in *The Saturday Evening Post*, *Redbook*, and other nonspecialist magazines. Dorman was particularly associated with SF's New Wave of edgy, experimental writing, and indeed, her short story "Go, Go, Go, Said the Bird" was featured in Harlan Ellison's groundbreaking *Dangerous Visions* anthology (1967). Her experimental novel "Onyx" was rejected by publishers in 1971, but her collected *Poems* appeared in 1970, followed by *Palace of Earth* (1984), *Constellations of the Inner Eye* (1991), *Carrying What You Love* (1996), and other volumes of poetry. She moved to Taos, New Mexico, after her divorce in 1986, publishing once again under her maiden name, and died there at eighty. Dorman's recognition from the SF community includes a 1978 Science Fiction Poetry Association Rhysling Award for "The Corruption of Metals" and a 1995 James Tiptree, Jr. retroactive award for "When I Was Miss Dow" (1966, reprinted in this anthology).

Carol Emshwiller (b. April 12, 1921) was born Agnes Carolyn Fries in Ann Arbor, Michigan, the eldest of Charles and Agnes (Carswell) Fries's four children. Growing up, she spent several years in France and Germany while her father, a professor of English and linguistics, was on sabbatical. Graduating from the University of Michigan with a BA in music in 1945, she joined the Red

Cross, aiding U.S. troops in postwar Italy, then returned to Ann Arbor for art school. She married fellow art student Ed Emshwiller in 1949. Together, they attended the École Nationale Supérieure des Beaux-Arts (1949–50), toured Europe on a motorcycle, and eventually settled in Levittown, New York, where they had three children, in 1955, 1957, and 1959.

Emshwiller began publishing SF in the mid-1950s, after being introduced to key people within the genre by her husband, who became one of the principal genre artists of the era. During the 1960s, Emshwiller and her husband expanded their circle to include avant-garde musicians, painters, poets, and filmmakers—as she put it, "we were enmeshed. Embedded. *Passionate* about that sixties world and nothing else." Not surprisingly, her experimental stories were often associated with SF's New Wave, and at the 1962 Hugo Awards she received an honorable mention for her short story "Adapted"—the first of many such honors she would accumulate in subsequent decades.

In 1974 Emshwiller became an adjunct assistant professor at New York University and published her first story collection, *Joy in Our Cause*. She has continued to publish almost nonstop since then. Her novels include *Carmen Dog* (1998), *The Mount* (2002), *Mister Boots* (2005), and *The Secret City* (2007). Her contemporary, Ursula K. Le Guin, praised her as a "major fabulist, a marvelous magical realist, one of the strongest, most complex, most consistently feminist voices in fiction"; to date, Emshwiller has won one World Fantasy Award, one Philip K. Dick Award, two Nebula Awards, and a World Fantasy Award for Lifetime Achievement (in 2005). Since her husband's death in 1990, she has divided her time between New York City and Owens Valley, California.

Alice Glaser (December 3, 1928–August 22, 1970) was born in New York City and raised on Long Island by her father, a Russian-born lawyer, and her mother, a homemaker from Pittsburgh. At Woodmere High School, from which she graduated in 1946, she worked on the student *Bulletin* and won praise for her poetry; at Radcliffe, she wrote a senior thesis on Joseph Conrad. Afterwards she moved to Paris, working at various U.S. government agencies, marrying and divorcing Jean-Paul Surmain, and finding friends in the expatriate SF community. Returning to New York in 1958, she began a career at *Esquire* magazine, rising to assistant and then associate editor during the 1960s.

At *Esquire*, Glaser solicited articles and stories (some from SF writers, including Fritz Leiber) and contributed articles of her own; her best known, an account of a week spent in India with Allen Ginsberg, appeared in 1963 as "Back on the Open Road for Boys." "The Tunnel Ahead," published in *The Magazine of Fantasy and Science Fiction* in 1961, is her only known work of speculative fiction. "The Tunnel Ahead" is one of the most frequently anthologized of modern SF stories, and in 2016 Norwegian filmmaker André Øvredal (director of the critically acclaimed *Trollhunter*, 2010) released a short film adaptation of it that went on to win the prize for Best Overall Short Film at the Calgary International Film Festival. Glaser also reviewed books for the *Chicago Tribune* and is said to have written a roman à clef about life at *Esquire*. She died after a fall, reportedly by suicide, at forty-one.

Clare Winger Harris (January 18, 1891–October 26, 1968) is credited as the first woman to publish fiction under her own name in the SF specialist magazines of the 1920s. She was born Clare M.

Winger in Freeport, Illinois. Her mother, Mary Stover Winger, was the daughter of the town's richest man (inventor and industrialist D. C. Stover), and her father, Frank S. Winger, was an electrical contractor and SF writer who published *The Wizard of the Island; or, The Vindication of Prof. Waldinger* in 1917. As a child, Harris "preferred . . . the stories of Jules Verne and H. G. Wells" to more conventional girls' fare. Graduating from Lake View High School in Chicago in 1910, she entered Smith College, but married in 1912 before completing her degree. She travelled in Europe and the Middle East, then went with her husband Frank Clyde Harris to California and Kansas, where he finished his education in architecture and engineering and where, in 1915, 1916, and 1918, she had three sons.

After moving with her family to Fairfield, Iowa, Harris published a historical novel, *Persephone of Eleusis: A Romance of Ancient Greece* (1923), and her first SF story, "A Runaway World," in the July 1926 issue of *Weird Tales*. "The Fate of the *Poseidonia*," published in June 1927, earned Harris third place (and $100) in a contest organized by *Amazing Stories* publisher Hugo Gernsback and secured her place as a leading voice in the genre. "The Ape Cycle," which appeared in the Spring 1930 issue of *Science Wonder Quarterly*, was her last-known story but she continued to actively participate in the SF community; her August 1931 letter to the editors at *Wonder Stories*, entitled "Possible Science Fiction Plots," constitutes one of the earliest pieces of SF criticism.

By the time of the 1940 census, Harris was divorced and living in Pasadena, California. Gathering eleven of her works in the self-published volume *Away from the Here and Now: Stories in Pseudo-Science* in 1947, she noted that her sons had "inherited their mother's love of science" and produced a "third generation of scientists" in the form of three grandchildren. *Away from the Here and Now* earned Harris one of the very first genre awards, granted to her by the Los Angeles Science Fiction Society. About a year before her death at seventy-seven, Harris inherited one-quarter of her grandfather's estate, valued in excess of two million dollars. It was contested in the courts for almost sixty years.

Zenna Henderson (November 1, 1917–May 11, 1983) was born Zena Chlarson in Tucson, Arizona (she began spelling her name "Zenna" in the early 1950s), the second of five children; her mother Emily Vernell (Rowley) Chlarson, a housekeeper for a private family, had emigrated from Mexico in 1912 after the destruction of Colonia Díaz, a Mormon settlement, and her father, Louis Rudolph Chlarson, worked as a chauffeur, railroad carpenter, and dairyman. A graduate of Phoenix Union High School and Arizona State Teachers' College, Henderson had a lifelong career as a teacher, mostly of elementary school children in the Tucson area. However, she also taught at the Gila River Relocation Center, an internment camp for Japanese Americans (1942–43); on a U.S. military base in France (1956–58); and at Seaside Children's Hospital in Waterford, Connecticut (1958–59). She married Richard H. Henderson, a miner, in 1944, divorcing him in 1951 and subsequently completing her master's degree at Arizona State.

Henderson published her first SF story, "Come On, Wagon!," in *The Magazine of Fantasy and Science Fiction* in December 1951 and was quickly singled out for praise by Sam Merwyn in an essay celebrating what was then seen as a new boom of women SF writers. In 1959, her long story "Captivity" received a Hugo nomination.

She is most widely remembered for "The People," a series of stories first published from 1952 to 1980 about a group of humanoid aliens stranded on Earth who represent our better selves. Along with *Pilgrimage: The Book of the People* (1961) and *The People: No Different Flesh* (1966), Henderson's short fiction is collected in *The Anything Box* (1965) and *Holding Wonder* (1971). *The People*, a made-for-TV movie based on her series of the same name and starring Kim Darby and William Shatner, was released in 1972. *Ingathering: The Complete People Stories* (1995), including previously uncollected material, was published after Henderson's death in Tucson, at the age of sixty-five.

Alice Eleanor Jones (March 30, 1916–November 6, 1981) was born in Philadelphia, where her father, Henry Stayton Jones worked, as a photoengraver for a publishing firm and her mother, Lucy A. (Schuler) Jones, stayed home to raise Jones and her sister. Jones graduated from the University of Pennsylvania in 1936, continuing her education in the English department, from which she earned her PhD in 1944, writing a dissertation on the seventeenth-century dramatist Shakerly Marmion. She married fellow graduate student Homer Nearing Jr. and moved with him to Swarthmore, Pennsylvania. They had two sons, Geoffrey and Gregory, in 1944 and 1948.

Jones had an intense but brief career as a writer of speculative fiction, publishing five stories in genre magazines from April to December 1955. In April of 1955, she published her first short story, "Life, Incorporated," in *The Magazine of Fantasy and Science Fiction* under her maiden name. In June of the same year, Jones published "Created He Them," her most successful speculative fiction work. Somewhat ironically—given that "Created He Them" details the deprivations suffered by an average housewife in the wake of World War III—Jones used the first check from that story to go on a shopping spree, buying herself "an extra special dress, the sort that wives of professors normally only look at in shops."

Jones focused her subsequent literary energies on better-paying mainstream publications, including *Redbook*, *Ladies' Home Journal*, *The Saturday Evening Post*, *Woman's Day*, *American Girl*, and *Seventeen*, to which she contributed both fiction and nonfiction well into the 1960s. She died in 1981 and is buried in Bala Cynwyd, Pennsylvania. Her stories are now available in podcast form at *Strange Horizons*.

Ursula K. Le Guin (October 21, 1929–January 22, 2018), born Ursula Kroeber in Berkeley, California, was the daughter of Theodora (Kracaw) Kroeber, an anthropology student and later a writer, and Alfred Kroeber, head of the University of California anthropology department; she had three older brothers and stepbrothers, with whom she spent summers on the family's small ranch in the Napa Valley. At ten or eleven she submitted one of her early literary productions to *Astounding Science Fiction*, of which she was a devoted reader.

Graduating from Berkeley High School in 1947, Le Guin attended Radcliffe College and then Columbia University, from which she earned a master's degree in Renaissance French and Italian Language and Literature in 1952. The following year, on the way to France as a Fulbright scholar to pursue her doctorate, she met fellow Fulbright recipient Charles Alfred Le Guin, and they married in Paris. Returning to the U.S., both began teaching, first at Mercer University in Macon, Georgia (he in the history department, she in

French), then at the University of Idaho. Settling permanently in Portland, Oregon, they raised three children, born in 1957, 1959, and 1964, respectively.

Le Guin's first published works—"Folksong from the Montayna Province" (*Prairie Poet*, Fall 1959) and "An die Musik" (*Western Humanities Review*, Summer 1961)—began her series set in the fictional European nation of Orsinia, later expanded with the story collection *Orsinian Tales* (1976) and the novel *Malafrena* (1979). She began to appear in genre magazines with the time-travel story "April in Paris," in the September 1962 *Fantastic Stories of the Imagination*, and published her first SF novel, *Rocannon's World*, in 1966.

Le Guin's subsequent works include the multiple-award-winning novel *The Left Hand of Darkness* (1969), *The Lathe of Heaven* (1971), *The Dispossessed: An Ambiguous Utopia* (1974), and *Tehanu: The Last Book of Earthsea* (1990); story collections *The Wind's Twelve Quarters* (1975), *The Compass Rose* (1982), *Changing Planes* (2003), and others; and collections of essays and poetry. In 1993, with Brian Attebery, she edited *The Norton Book of Science Fiction: North American Science Fiction, 1960–1990*. Le Guin's accomplishments have long been recognized by her peers: in 1975 she was named the sixth Gandalf Grand Master of Fantasy; in 1989 the Science Fiction Research Association granted her a Pilgrim Award for Lifetime Achievement; in 2001 she was inducted into the Science Fiction Hall of Fame, and in 2003 she became the Science Fiction and Fantasy Writers of America's twentieth Grand Master. Elected to the American Academy of Arts and Letters in 2017, before her death in Portland Le Guin was revising and adding new material to her 1985 novel *Always Coming Home*, for a new edition in the Library of America series.

Katherine MacLean (b. January 22, 1925) was born in Glen Ridge, New Jersey, and raised in Flushing, New York. She was the daughter of chemical engineer Gordon MacLean and homemaker Ruth (Crawford) MacLean, who raised her along with two older brothers. Beginning in high school, MacLean worked at a wide variety of jobs, including "nurse's aide, store detective, pollster, econ graph-analyst, antibiotic lab researcher, food factory quality controller, office manager, payroll bookkeeper, college teacher, reporter." After a brief first marriage to Charles Dye, she married David Mason, with whom she had a son in 1957.

MacLean published her first short story, "Defense Mechanism," in the October 1949 issue of *Astounding Science Fiction* while she was still an economics undergraduate at Barnard and working part-time as a lab technician. By the time her first collection, *The Diploids*, appeared in 1962 she had over two dozen stories in print, many of which were celebrated for their innovative adaptation of ideas from the hard sciences and for their celebration of the social sciences. Along with a second story collection, *The Trouble with You Earth People* (1980), she is the author of four novels: *Cosmic Checkmate* (1962, with Charles V. De Vet), *The Man in the Bird Cage* (1971), *Missing Man* (1975), and *Dark Wing* (1979, with Carl West).

In the late 1960s, MacLean moved to Maine to care for her invalid mother, and in 1979 she married fellow SF author Carl P. West. She currently lives near Portland, Maine. The quality of MacLean's work has long been recognized by the SF community: in 1962 fellow author and editor Damon Knight noted that "as a science fiction writer, [MacLean] has few peers"; and in 1971 she won a Nebula Award for her novella "Missing Man." She was the professional Guest of Honor at the first WisCon, held in 1977 (WisCon is the largest and oldest feminist SF convention in the world), and in 2003 she was honored by the Science Fiction Writers of America as Author Emeritus. In 2011, she received the Cordwainer Smith Rediscovery Award.

Judith Merril (January 21, 1923–September 12, 1997) was the principal pseudonym under which Judith Josephine Grossman published stories, novels, and criticism beginning in 1947. Born in Boston, she moved to the Bronx after her freshman year in high school; her father Samuel Solomon ("Shlomo") Grossman, a columnist and drama critic for a Yiddish newspaper, had committed suicide when she was six, and her mother Ethel (Hurwitch) Grossman had accepted a job running a settlement house for juvenile offenders. Graduating in 1939, she met Dan Zissman at a Trotskyist Youth picnic the following year. They married and in 1942 had a daughter, Merril, who was raised during her infancy on military bases across the country.

Moving to Greenwich Village after the war, Merril became one of the few female members of the Futurians (the men included Isaac Asimov, James Blish, C. M. Kornbluth, and Frederik Pohl; other women included Leslie Perri and Virginia Kidd). She published a SF fanzine, *TEMPER!*, and contributed two stories under her married name to *Crack Detective*. Separated in 1946, she turned to writing and editing to support herself and her daughter, working briefly for Bantam Books and selling more than a dozen sports stories, under the pseudonyms Eric Thorstein and Ernest Hamilton, to pulp magazines. Her first SF story, "That Only a Mother" (*Astounding Science Fiction*, June 1948), was her first publication as Judith Merril and was written to win a bet with *Astounding* editor John W. Campbell, who claimed that women couldn't write SF good enough to appear in his magazine. Not only did Merril win that bet, but "That Only a Mother" has gone on to be one of the most widely anthologized SF stories since its initial appearance.

Merril collected her subsequent short fiction in *Out of Bounds* (1960), *Daughters of Earth* (1968), *Survival Ship and Other Stories* (1974), and *The Best of Judith Merril* (1976). Her first novel, *Shadow on the Hearth* (1950)—adapted for television in 1954 as *Atomic Attack*—was followed by *The Tomorrow People* in 1960. She also wrote two novels in collaboration with C. M. Kornbluth, *Gunner Cade* and *Outpost Mars*; both appeared in 1952 under the joint pseudonym Cyril Judd. Along with these works, Merril was a prolific reviewer and edited SF anthologies, including *Shot in the Dark* (1950), *England Swings SF* (1968), and the annual series *S–F: The Year's Greatest Science Fiction and Fantasy* (1956–68).

Married to Frederik Pohl from 1948 to 1953, Merril had a second daughter, Ann, in 1950. She later cofounded and served on the board of the Milford Science Fiction Writers' Conference (1956–60) and in 1960 married union organizer Dan Sugrue, separating three years later. In 1968, after a year in England, she immigrated to Canada, joining the staff of Rochdale College in Toronto and helping to organize the Committee to Aid Refugees from Militarism (CARM). Her private book collection, donated to the Toronto Public Library in 1970 to form the "Spaced Out Library," became the nucleus of the Merril Collection of Science Fiction, Speculation, and Fantasy, now numbering over 70,000 volumes. She died in Toronto of heart failure the same year she became a Science Fiction and Fantasy Writers of America Author Emeritus. Her posthumously published autobiography, *Better to Have Loved* (2003), earned a Hugo Award for Best Related Book, and in 2013 she was inducted into the Science Fiction Hall of Fame.

C. L. Moore (January 24, 1911–April 4, 1987), the eldest child of Indiana natives Otto Moore and Maude Jones Moore, was born Catherine Lucille Moore in Indianapolis, where her father was an inventor and mechanical engineer. An often sickly child "reared on a diet of Greek mythology, Oz books, and Edgar Rice Burroughs," she entered Indiana University in 1929, publishing stories in *The Vagabond*, a student magazine, but left in the middle of her sophomore year. Working as a stenographer in an Indianapolis bank through the Great Depression, she began to sell her stories; the first, "Shambleau," appeared in *Weird Tales* in November 1933. (*Weird Tales* editor Farnsworth Wright was reportedly so impressed upon receiving it that he closed his offices for the day in celebration.) Moore continued to write stories featuring "Shambleau" protagonist Northwest Smith (a swashbuckling rogue adventurer who went on to inspire characters including Han Solo) while publishing a series of sword-and-sorcery tales featuring the first female protagonist in that subgenre, Jirel of Joiry.

Moore's work attracted an admiring letter in 1936 from aspiring author Henry Kuttner, who addressed her as "Mr. Moore." The confusion was soon cleared up and the two married in 1940, thereby initiating a prolific, collaborative literary relationship. Using pennames including Lewis Padgett, C. H. Liddell, and Lawrence O'Donnell, Moore and Kuttner published dozens of stories (including mystery, detective, and suspense as well as speculative fiction) and several novels. They also completed their undergraduate degrees in English, at the University of Southern California, in 1954.

Separately, Moore published the novels *Judgment Night* (1952) and *Doomsday Morning* (1957) and was nominated for a Hugo Award for her 1955 novella "Home There's No Returning." After Kuttner's death in 1958, she turned to television writing, completing scripts for *Tales of Frankenstein* (1958), *The Alaskans* (1959),

77 Sunset Strip (1960), and *Maverick* (1961). In 1963 she married businessman Thomas Reggie. In 1981, the onset of Alzheimer's disease prevented her from personally accepting the World Fantasy Lifetime Achievement Award. She died at seventy-six in Hollywood, California, and was posthumously inducted into the Science Fiction Hall of Fame. In 2004 she posthumously received the Cordwainer Smith Rediscovery Award.

Andrew North (February 17, 1912–March 17, 2005) was a pseudonym SF author Andre Norton used occasionally in the 1940s and 1950s. Born Alice Mary Norton and taking the name "Andre" with the publication of her first novel in 1934, she was the younger of two daughters of Adalbert Freely Norton, a carpet salesman, and Daisy Bertha (Stemm) Norton. A native of Cleveland, Ohio, she graduated from Collingwood High School, where she edited the literary page of *The Collingwood Spotlight*, and spent a year at Western Reserve University. Leaving school in 1931 in the wake of the Great Depression, she took a job as a children's librarian at the Cleveland Public Library, where she remained, with a brief hiatus in 1940–41 as an archivist at the Library of Congress and as the owner of an independent bookstore, until 1950. Forced by disability to retire (she suffered from what she described as "continuing attacks of vertigo"), she supported herself, working from bed, as an editorial reader for the SF specialist Gnome Press (c. 1952–58), and eventually with her own fiction.

Norton began her notably prolific literary career as a writer of boys' adventure stories, publishing *The Prince Commands* (1934), *Ralestone Luck* (1938), and several other novels. She first turned to SF with "The People of the Crater," featured on the cover of *Fantasy Book* in July 1947, and with the novel *Star Man's Son: 2250*

A.D. (1952). Her novel *Witch World* (1963) is perhaps her best known; the fictional universe that it began ultimately included dozens of novels and stories, many coauthored and some completed posthumously.

In 1966, Norton moved to Winter Park, Florida, with her mother, with whom she lived for most of her life. In 1997, after her mother's death, she relocated to Murfreesboro, Tennessee, where she founded High Hallack, a retreat and research library for genre writers. Norton was the first woman to win the Gandalf Grand Master of Fantasy Award and the Nebula Grand Master Award for Lifetime Achievement from the Science Fiction Writers of America. She was nominated for the World Fantasy Award for Lifetime Achievement three times and won it in 1998. She was also nominated twice for the Hugo Award. She died of congestive heart failure; in lieu of a funeral, she was cremated with copies of her first and last novels. In 2005 the Science Fiction and Fantasy Writers of America established the annual Andre Norton Award for Young Adult Science Fiction and Fantasy in her honor.

Leslie Perri (April 27, 1920–January 31, 1970) was born Doris Marie Claire ("Doë") Baumgardt in Brooklyn, New York, to German-immigrant bank manager Fritz Perri and housewife Marie Baumgardt. She joined the Science Fiction League and then the Futurian Society (whose members included Judith Merril, Virginia Kidd, Frederik Pohl, and Isaac Asimov) in New York while still a teenager. She attended the first Worldcon in 1939 and helped to circulate fanzines as a founding member of the Fantasy Amateur Press Association. During her brief first marriage (1940–42) to fellow Futurian Frederik Pohl, Perri edited (and reportedly largely wrote) the romance pulp *Movie Love Stories*. Later, she had a daughter (1944–?) by her second husband, the painter Thomas Owens, and a son by her third (1951–65), the former Futurian Richard Wilson.

Baumgardt took on the penname Leslie Perri when she began writing, illustrating, editing, and otherwise contributing to SF fandom in the late 1930s. She is credited as the author of numerous sketches and short items in fanzines, including *Future Art*, *Futurian News*, *Le Vombiteur Literaire*, *Mind of Man*, *Mutant*, and *Fantasy Fictioneer*. During this time, Perri also published three professional SF stories, the first of which was "Space Episode" for the December 1941 issue of *Future Combined with Science Fiction*. "Space Episode" provoked a great deal of controversy with its depiction of a heroic female astronaut who sacrifices her life to save her male companions: predictably, women found the story compelling and realistic while male readers dismissed it as sour grapes (and editor Donald Wollheim happily fanned the flames of controversy). Moving from Brooklyn to New City, New York, Perri worked intermittently as a journalist while raising her children. She died of cancer at forty-nine.

Kit Reed (June 7, 1932–September 24, 2017) was born Lillian Hyde Craig in San Diego, California; her infant nickname "Kitten" was later shortened to "Kit." The only surviving child of naval officer John R. Craig and teacher Lillian (Hyde) Craig, she grew up on and around military bases in Connecticut, Florida, Hawaii, and elsewhere. After her father's death in 1943 (he was lost at sea in the Pacific as lieutenant commander of the submarine USS *Grampus*), she attended high schools in Florida, North Carolina, and Washington, D.C., and in 1954 graduated from the College of Notre Dame of Maryland. She married Joseph Reed Jr. in 1955 while working as a reporter for the *St. Petersburg Times*. Her salary at the *New Haven Register*, where she won awards for her reporting on the juvenile justice system, helped to put her husband through graduate school. Moving to Middletown, Connecticut, in the early 1960s, the couple had three children; both taught at Wesleyan University for most of the rest of their lives.

Reed's earliest-known SF story, "Space Traveler," appeared in the Sunday magazine of the *St. Petersburg Times* in July 1955. "The Wait," published in the April 1958 *Magazine of Fantasy and Science Fiction*, set her on a professional writing career that ultimately included almost a dozen story collections, more than a dozen novels, and occasional nonfiction as well. Principally known as a writer of speculative fiction, she published works in a variety of genres, including the comic novel *Mother Isn't Dead, She's Only Sleeping* (1961), psychological thrillers under the pseudonym (a variation of her maiden name) Kit Craig, and the horror novel *Blood Fever* (1986, as Shelley Hyde). She died in Los Angeles at eighty-five of an inoperable brain tumor. Reed's honors include a Guggenheim Fellowship, a five-year grant from the Abraham Woursell Foundation, three nominations for the James Tiptree, Jr., Award, and the Young Adult Library Services Alex Award (for her 2005 novel *Thinner Than Thou*).

Joanna Russ (February 22, 1937–April 29, 2011), often cited as the author of the landmark feminist SF novel *The Female Man* (1975), was also a prolific reviewer and essayist and published several collections of short fiction, including *Alyx* (1976), *The Zanzibar Cat* (1983), *Extra(ordinary) People* (1984), and *The Hidden*

Side of the Moon (1988). Born Joanna Ruth Russ in the Bronx to public school teachers Evarett and Bertha (Zinner) Russ, she demonstrated early aptitude in the sciences (becoming a finalist in the 1953 Westinghouse Science Talent Search for her project "Growth of Certain Fungi Under Colored Light and in Darkness") but turned to literature at Cornell, where she studied with Vladimir Nabokov and published in undergraduate magazines. After college, she attended the Yale School of Drama, earning an MFA in playwriting in 1960, and began a career as an English professor at Queensborough Community College in New York.

Russ read SF as a teenager because it promised a world "where things could be different," and sold her first SF story, "Nor Custom Stale," while still in graduate school. In 1963 she married journalist Albert Amateau and then in 1967 divorced him. During this period Russ established herself as a leading voice in SF's New Wave, one who embraced the radical politics of her time—especially its feminist variants—and who wove it into her stories accordingly. As she noted in a letter to Susan Koppelman, Russ saw anger as an important part of both politics and art, noting that "from now on, I will not trust anyone who isn't angry." While some members of the SF community were uneasy with Russ's political views, others recognized the innovative nature of her fiction, and in 1968 she received a Hugo nomination for her first novel, *Picnic on Paradise*, which follows the adventures of a female mercenary named Alyx. Alyx (who stars in Russ's "The Barbarian," featured in this anthology) is both an homage to C. L. Moore's groundbreaking 1940s adventuress Jirel of Joiry (also featured in this anthology, in the story "The Black God's Kiss") and the template for nearly every strong female protagonist in contemporary SF.

Teaching subsequently at Cornell, SUNY Binghamton, the University of Colorado at Boulder, and the University of Washington (from which she retired in ill health in the 1990s), Russ published influential feminist literary criticism (including *How to Suppress Women's Writing* (1983) and *To Write Like a Woman: Essays in Feminism and Science Fiction* (1995) alongside her fiction. Her story "When It Changed" won a 1973 Nebula Award; "Souls" received both Hugo and Locus Awards in 1983. In 1995, Russ received retrospective Tiptree Awards (for the best explorations of sex and gender in speculative fiction) for "When It Changed" and *The Female Man.* She died in Tucson after a series of strokes, and was posthumously inducted into the Science Fiction and Fantasy Hall of Fame and named a Science Fiction and Fantasy Writers of America Grand Master. Her papers are archived at the University of Oregon.

Margaret St. Clair (February 17, 1911–November 22, 1995) was born Eva Margaret Neeley in Hutchinson, Kansas. The only child of Eva Margaret (Hostetler) Neeley and George Neeley, a recently elected congressman, she spent some of her early years in Washington, D.C. When her father died of influenza in 1919, St. Clair moved with her mother to Lawrence, Kansas, and then, in 1928, to Los Angeles, where she finished high school. She married Raymond Earl ("Eric") St. Clair shortly after completing her Berkeley undergraduate degree in 1932; two years later Berkeley awarded her a master's degree in Greek Classics. After a trip to China, the couple settled in El Sobrante, California, where they owned St. Clair Rare Bulb Gardens (1937–41) and where she raised and sold Dachshunds. During World War II, she took a "brief and unsatisfactory" job as a welder.

St. Clair started her career as a professional writer in the mid-1940s, publishing both detective fiction (beginning with "Letter from the Deceased" in the May 1945 *Street & Smith's Detective Story Magazine*) and SF (beginning with "Rocket to Limbo" in *Fantastic Adventures*, November 1946). By the 1950s she had focused on the latter genre: more than seventy of her SF stories appeared in print over the course of that decade (some under the pseudonym Idris Seabright or Wilton Hazzard) along with her first novels, *Agent of the Unknown* (1956) and *The Green Queen* (1956). St. Clair's stories were popular with readers and television viewers alike; her short story "Mrs. Hawk" (1950) was filmed for the 1961 season of *Thriller*, while "The Boy Who Predicted Earthquakes" (1950) and "Brenda" (1954) were filmed as segments for the 1971 season of Rod Serling's *Night Gallery*.

St. Clair's later writings, particularly *Sign of the Labrys* (1963) and *The Shadow People* (1969), reflect an increasing interest in neopaganism; in 1966, she and her husband were inducted into the Wiccan religion under the names Froniga and Weyland. In a 1981 interview, she reported she was at work on two novels, "The Euthanasiasts" and "The Once and Future Queen," which were never published. After her husband's death in 1986 she moved to a retirement community in Santa Rosa, California, where she died at eighty-four. Her papers are archived at the University of California–Riverside.

Wilmar H. Shiras (September 23, 1908–December 23, 1990) was born Wilmar Alberta House in Boston, her father a machinist and both of her parents Massachusetts natives. She married in 1927 at eighteen, after a year at Boston University, and moved with her husband, a newly graduated chemical engineer, to the suburbs of Los Angeles. There and in Oakland, California, beginning in the early 1940s, they raised three girls and two boys. In 1946 she published an autobiographical account of her conversion to Catholicism, *Slow Dawning*, under the pseudonym Jane Howes, as a reviewer for *New Catholic World* and other magazines and as a translator of Catholic theology and philosophy. Going back to school, she earned her bachelor's degree from the College of the Holy Names in Oakland in 1955, and a master's degree in History at Berkeley in 1956.

Shiras is principally remembered for her first published story—the widely anthologized "In Hiding" (*Astounding Science Fiction*, November 1948)—and for the Children of the Atom series, collected as the novel *Children of the Atom* in 1953. "Whatever else I wrote," she later remarked, "came back with a note asking for another 'In Hiding.'" These stories, which follow the adventures of mutant geniuses who are created by exposure to nuclear radiation, are often identified by SF fans and critics as important precursors to Marvel's X-Men series.

Leslie F. Stone (June 8, 1905–March 21, 1991) was born Leslie Francis Rubenstein in Philadelphia to homemaker Lillian A. (Spellman) Rubenstein and clothing merchant George S. Rubenstein. Stone published her first fantasy stories in local newspapers as a teenager while finishing high school in Norfolk, Virginia. Marrying labor reporter William Silberberg in 1927, she raised two sons in and around Washington, D.C., and won prizes as a gardener and ceramist. After her husband's death in 1957, she worked at the National Institutes of Health in Bethesda, Maryland.

Stone was one of the first women to publish in the new SF specialist magazines, contributing over twenty stories from 1929 to 1940. Though "Stone" was a pseudonym and "Leslie F." ambiguously gendered, she was an openly female author. Not only did Stone's portrait appear alongside her works, but editors were quick to correct readers who mistook her gender. While Stone could write space operas and thought-experiments as well as her male counterparts, she made her mark (and occasionally upset readers) by writing some of the first stories that featured female and black protagonists who are the heroes of their own stories (including 1931's "The Conquest of Gola," featured in this anthology). Stone stopped publishing SF at midcentury, attributing her early retirement from the field to changes in both science and SF—namely, the "horrifying use" of atomic weapons (which made it difficult to imagine positive high-tech futures) and an increase in "sexist experiences" with some of the male editors who entered the field around World War II, including John W. Campbell Jr. and Horace Gold.

During the 1960s and 1970s Stone revisited her literary career, revising "Out of the Void" as a stand-alone novel and appearing as an invited guest at SF conventions in Baltimore, offering reminiscences in 1974 later published as "Day of the Pulps." Her work is featured in anthologies, including Groff Conklin's *The Best of Science Fiction* (1946), Isaac Asimov's *Before the Golden Age* (1974), and *Wesleyan Anthology of Science Fiction* (2010).

James Tiptree, Jr. (August 24, 1915–May 19, 1987) was the primary pseudonym of Alice Bradley Sheldon. Born Alice Hastings Bradley in Chicago, Illinois, to author Mary Hastings Bradley and lawyer and naturalist Herbert Bradley, Tiptree was educated at the University of Chicago Laboratory Schools and then at finishing schools in Lausanne, Switzerland, and Tarrytown, New York. As a child, she accompanied her parents on three safari expeditions to Africa, becoming the child-celebrity protagonist and illustrator of her mother's books *Alice in Jungleland* (1927) and *Alice in Elephantland* (1929). In 1934, after a year at Sarah Lawrence, she married Princeton undergraduate William Davey; both attended the University of California at Berkeley and then New York University without taking degrees. An aspiring painter, she exhibited her work at the Art Institute of Chicago and the Corcoran Gallery in Washington, D.C.

After her divorce in 1941, Tiptree worked as an art critic for the *Chicago Sun* before enlisting in the Women's Army Auxiliary Corps, where she trained as a photo-intelligence analyst and rose to the rank of major. Stationed in Europe in 1945–46, she married fellow intelligence officer Huntington Denton Sheldon. After their return to the United States, the Sheldons ran an ill-fated chicken hatchery before joining the newly minted CIA in 1953, where Tiptree helped expand the agency's photo-intelligence section and later specialized in the analysis of African politics. After completing her undergraduate education at American University in 1959, Tiptree studied psychology at George Washington University, earning her PhD in 1967 and publishing "Preference for Familiar Versus Novel Stimuli as a Function of the Familiarity of the Environment" in the *Journal of Comparative and Physiological Psychology* in 1969.

Tiptree invented her famous pseudonym in 1967 when she began submitting to SF magazines, inspired by a jar of Tiptree marmalade she saw at the supermarket. As her stories began to appear in print and to attract attention—she won the 1974 Hugo Award for

"The Girl Who Was Plugged In," the 1974 Nebula Award for "Love Is the Plan the Plan Is Death," and both Hugo and Nebula Awards in 1977 for "Houston, Houston, Do You Read?"—Sheldon withheld details about her identity, offering "Tip" as an increasingly elaborate persona both for publication and in her extensive private correspondence with writers, including Philip K. Dick, Harlan Ellison, Ursula K. Le Guin, and Joanna Russ. She also published a handful of items as Raccoona Sheldon, ostensibly one of Tiptree's female friends. Tiptree was publicly exposed as Sheldon early in 1977, prompting a rather good-natured embarrassment among critics who had discerned "something inherently masculine" in Tiptree's prose and wide discussion of the relationship between reading, writing, and gender.

Tiptree collected her stories in *Ten Thousand Light-Years from Home* (1973), *Warm Worlds and Otherwise* (1975), *Star Songs of an Old Primate* (1978), *Out of the Everywhere, and Other Extraordinary Visions* (1981), *The Starry Rift* (1986), and other volumes; she also published two novels, *Up the Walls of the World* (1978) and *Brightness Falls from the Air* (1985). At seventy-one, increasingly suffering from depression and ill health, she took her own life at home in McLean, Virginia, in a murder-suicide pact with her husband. The James Tiptree, Jr. Literary Award, conceived in 1991, honors work that explores and expands ideas about gender.

John Jay Wells (b. February 12, 1933), a pseudonym Juanita Coulson used only once, was born Juanita Ruth Wellons in Anderson, Indiana. Her parents Grant and Ruth (Omler) Wellons were both employed in a local auto parts factory. Coulson graduated from Anderson High School, where she worked on *The X-Ray*, a student newspaper. She was introduced to Robert Coulson at a meeting of the Eastern Indiana Science Fiction Association in 1953, and they married the following year; together, they published the fanzine *Yandro* (1953–86), winner of a 1965 Hugo Award for best amateur magazine. Graduating from Ball State University in 1954 and earning her master's degree in Education in 1961, Coulson briefly taught second grade; she had a son in 1957.

Coulson was coauthor with Marion Zimmer Bradley of "Another Rib," published in *The Magazine of Fantasy and Science Fiction* in June 1963. This was Coulson's first published story and the only time she employed the Wells pseudonym. The story "had a vaguely sexual theme, and the editor was a little nervous, it being 1963," Coulson later recalled; "he thought that [it] needed masculine names on it." After "Another Rib," Coulson went on to write more than a dozen SF novels under her own name, beginning with *Crisis on Cheiron* (1967). Her most recent is *Star Sister* (1990). She has also published historical romance and mystery novels and some short fiction. After the death of her husband in 1999, she moved to London, Ohio, where she works part-time in the mayor's office and attends "as many cons as money will allow." An active filker (or SF-folk music performer) since the 1940s, she received the Pegasus Award for Best Filk Writer/Composer in 2012.

Kate Wilhelm (June 8, 1928–March 8, 2018), born Kate Gertrude Meredith in Toledo, Ohio, was the fourth child of Jesse and Ann (McDowell) Meredith, both natives of Kentucky; at twelve, she moved with her family to Louisville, where her father worked in a flour mill. Soon after her graduation from Louisville Girls' High School she married Joseph Wilhelm and had two sons, in 1949 and 1953. Her first published story, "The Pint-Size Genie," appeared in *Fantastic* in October 1956, and she became a regular contributor to genre magazines thereafter, collecting her stories in *The Mile-Long Spaceship* (1963), *The Downstairs Room and Other Speculative Fiction* (1968), *Abyss* (1971), *The Infinity Box* (1975), *Somerset Dreams and Other Fictions* (1978), *Listen, Listen* (1981), *Children of the Wind* (1989), and *And the Angels Sing* (1992).

Divorcing her first husband, in 1963 Wilhelm married fellow writer Damon Knight; together, they raised five children from previous marriages and had a son of their own. As hosts of the Milford Science Fiction Writers' Conference from their home in Milford, Pennsylvania, and later as cofounders of the Clarion Science Fiction and Fantasy Workshop, they began a tradition of literary mentorship and mutual criticism that has influenced many careers and continues to the present. They also both lectured on speculative fiction at universities around the world.

Wilhelm won Nebula Awards in 1969 (for "The Planners"), 1987 (for "The Girl Who Fell into the Sky"), and 1988 (for "Forever Yours, Anna"); her 1976 novel *Where Late the Sweet Birds Sang* received both Hugo and Locus Awards, and in 2003 she was inducted into the Science Fiction Hall of Fame. Along with speculative fiction she has also published more than a dozen mystery novels, her first, *More Bitter Than Death*, in 1963 and her most recent, cowritten with Richard Wilhelm and featuring her noted detective protagonist Barbara Holloway, *Mirror, Mirror* in 2017. She died in Eugene, Oregon, where she had lived since the 1970s.

NOTES

In the notes below, the reference numbers denote page and line of this volume (the line count includes headings but not blank lines). For further information about the authors in this volume and women's SF during this period, along with references to other studies, see Brian Attebery, *Decoding Gender in Science Fiction* (2002); Eric Leif Davin, *Partners in Wonder: Women and the Birth of Science Fiction, 1926–1965* (2005); Jane Donawerth, *Frankenstein's Daughters: Women Writing Science Fiction* (1997); Justine Larbalestier, *The Battle of the Sexes in Science Fiction* (2002), and *Daughters of Earth: Feminist Science Fiction in the Twentieth Century* (2006); Helen Merrick, *The Secret Feminist Cabal: A Cultural History of Science Fiction Feminisms* (2010); Robin Roberts, *A New Species: Gender and Science in Science Fiction* (1993); Lisa Yaszek, *Galactic Suburbia: Recovering Women's Science Fiction* (2008); and Lisa Yaszek and Patrick B. Sharp, eds., *Sisters of Tomorrow: The First Women of Science Fiction* (2016).

9.6 television] The first television broadcast experiments were taking place in both Europe and the United States around the time "The Miracle of the Lily" was published in Hugo Gernsback's *Amazing Stories* in April 1928; Gernsback himself began regular "radio television" broadcasts from his New York radio station WRNY in August 1928.

19.27 *Ex Terreno*] Latin: from the earth.

25.1 the nine planets] Pluto became the ninth planet of the solar system on its discovery in February 1930, just over a year before Stone published "The Conquest of Gola." (It was reclassified as a dwarf planet in 2006, after scientists discovered other objects of similar size in the Kuiper belt.)

89.6 Oak Ridge] Tennessee city established in 1942 as headquarters for the Manhattan Project, responsible for atomic bomb development; it housed a pilot plutonium reactor and uranium enrichment plants.

94.13 WACs] Members of the Women's Army Corps, created as an auxiliary branch of the U.S. Army in 1942 and disbanded in 1978 when women soldiers were integrated into the regular military.

105.12 the ink-pool in the Kipling stories,"] See Kipling's "The Finest Story in the World," first published in the *Contemporary Review* in July 1891.

119.19 Macaulay] Thomas Babington Macaulay (1800–1859), British historian and politician often described as a child prodigy.

140.19 in 'Through the Looking Glass,'] Like Tim's story, Lewis Carroll's *Through the Looking-Glass and What Alice Found There* (1872) dramatizes a game of chess.

163.26–27 Deerslayer, John Clayton, Lord Greystoke] Deerslayer (also known as Natty Bumppo) is the hero of James Fenimore Cooper's five-volume Leatherstocking Tales series (*The Pioneers*, 1823; *The Last of the Mohicans*, 1826; *The Prairie*, 1827; *The Pathfinder*, 1840; *The Deerslayer*, 1841); John Clayton, Lord Greystoke (also known as Tarzan), first appeared in Edgar Rice Burroughs's novel *Tarzan of the Apes* (1914).

197.2 *Ararat*] In the Old Testament, Noah's ark comes to rest "on the mountains of Ararat" after the great flood (see Genesis 8:4).

206.5 Pan] In Greek mythology, a bestial nature god associated with fertility and usually depicted as part man, part goat.

321.29 Neo-Helots] The helots were a class of serfs or slaves in ancient Sparta.

327.28–29 the Cheshire Cat's grin . . . *Wonderland*."] See Chapter VI of Lewis Carroll's novel *Alice's Adventures in Wonderland* (1865).

340.3 Topolino] Nickname for the earliest-model Fiat 500, an Italian city car produced from 1936 to 1955; literally, "little mouse."

449.4 BOAC] British Overseas Airway Corporation, an English state-owned airline created in 1940. BOAC merged with British European Airways in 1974 to form today's British Airways.

449.8 *Save the last Green Mansions*] See William Henry Hudson's 1904 novel *Green Mansions: A Romance of the Tropical Forest.*

449.12 *Who's Afraid?*] See Edward Albee's 1962 play *Who's Afraid of Virginia Woolf?*, which examines the breakdown of a middle-aged couple's marriage.

450.22 Oread] In Greek mythology, a mountain nymph.

453.2 Chicom] Vietnam-era U.S. military slang for "Chinese communist."

453.8 Mata Hari] Stage name of Dutch exotic dancer and courtesan Margaretha Geertruida MacLeod (1876–1917), convicted and executed as a German spy during World War I.

453.16 Hudson's bell bird "singing for a later race,"] See Hudson's *Green Mansions*, Chapter X: "O mystic bell-bird of the heavenly race of the swallow and the dove, the quetzal and the nightingale! When the brutish savage and the brutish white man that slay thee, one for food, the other for the benefit of science, shall have passed away, live still, live to tell thy message to the blameless spiritualized race that shall come after us to possess the Earth, not for a thousand years, but for ever."

454.20 Sinair] Singapore Airlines.

455.20 Hamilton Air Base] U.S. airfield in Marin County, California, decommissioned in 1974.

456.2 Gaea] In Greek mythology, a primordial earth-mother goddess.

458.9 Nijinsky and Nureyev] Vaslav Nijinsky (1889–1950) and Rudolf Nureyev (1938–1993), prominent ballet dancers.

458.24 bach] A word apparently invented by Le Guin; perhaps an honorific, like the Japanese -*san*. (Also page 481, line 12, in the present volume.)

466.29 Heb.] Hebrew.

471.20 the golden horde] A phrase also used to describe a Mongol khanate established in the thirteenth century.

472.7 spla] A word apparently invented by Le Guin; another character later gives "insane" and "psycho" as synonyms (see page 480, lines 11–12, in the present volume).

478.1 *Totentanz*] The dance of death or *danse macabre*, an allegorical theme that emerged in late medieval European art and literature, typically featuring a personified Death leading the living to the grave. Composers including Franz Liszt, Camille Saint-Saëns, and Arnold Schoenberg subsequently set the theme to music.

SOURCES & ACKNOWLEDGMENTS

This volume contains twenty-five stories first published in the period 1928 to 1969. The texts of all stories have been taken from their original magazine printings, with the exception of Ursula K. Le Guin's "Nine Lives," the text of which is taken from the first book edition.

Great efforts have been made to locate all owners of copyrighted material. Any owner who has inadvertently been omitted will gladly be acknowledged in future printings.

Clare Winger Harris, "The Miracle of the Lily," *Amazing Stories* 3.1 (April 1928): 48–54.

Leslie F. Stone, "The Conquest of Gola," *Wonder Stories* 2.11 (April 1931): 1278–87.

C. L. Moore, "The Black God's Kiss," *Weird Tales* 24.4 (October 1934): 402–21. Copyright © 1934 by *Weird Tales*. Reprinted by permission of Don Congdon Associates, Inc.

Leslie Perri, "Space Episode," *Future Combined with Science Fiction* 2.2 (December 1941): 106–12.

Judith Merril, "That Only a Mother," *Astounding Science Fiction* 41.4 (June 1948): 88–95. Later collected in *Homecalling and Other Stories* (NESFA Press, 2005). Copyright © 1948, 1976 by Judith Merril. Reprinted by permission of the Estate of Judith Merril and the Virginia Kidd Agency, Inc.

Wilmar H. Shiras, "In Hiding," *Astounding Science Fiction* 42.3 (November 1948): 40–70. Reprinted by permission of the Estate of Wilmar H. Shiras.

Katherine MacLean, "Contagion," *Galaxy* 1.1 (October 1950): 114–40. Later collected in *The Trouble With You Earth People* (Donning, 1979). Copyright © 1950, 1978 by Katherine MacLean. Reprinted by permission of the author and the Virginia Kidd Agency, Inc.

Margaret St. Clair, "The Inhabited Men," *Planet Stories* 5.2 (September 1951): 44–49. Copyright © 1951, 1978 by Margaret St. Clair. Reprinted by permission of McIntosh and Otis, Inc.

Zenna Henderson, "Ararat," *The Magazine of Fantasy and Science Fiction* 3.6 (October 1952): 103–22. Later collected in *Ingathering: The Complete People Stories*

(NESFA Press, 1995). Copyright © 1952, 1980 by Zenna Henderson. Reprinted by permission of the Estate of Zenna Henderson and the Virginia Kidd Agency, Inc.

Andrew North, "All Cats Are Gray," *Fantastic Universe* 1.2 (August–September 1953): 129–34. Reprinted by permission of the Estate of Andre Norton.

Alice Eleanor Jones, "Created He Them," *The Magazine of Fantasy and Science Fiction* 8.6 (June 1955): 29–36. Reprinted by permission of the Estate of Alice Eleanor Jones.

Mildred Clingerman, "Mr. Sakrison's Halt," *The Magazine of Fantasy and Science Fiction* 10.1 (January 1956): 122–27. Later collected in *The Clingerman Files* (Size 5½ B Publishing, 2017). Reprinted by permission of A Cupful of Space LLC.

Leigh Brackett, "All the Colors of the Rainbow," *Venture Science Fiction* 1.6 (November 1957): 108–28. Reprinted by permission of Spectrum Literary Agency on behalf of the Huntington National Bank.

Carol Emshwiller, "Pelt," *The Magazine of Fantasy and Science Fiction* 15.5 (November 1958): 102–10. Reprinted by permission of the author.

Rosel George Brown, "Car Pool," *If* 8.6 (July 1959): 80–94.

Elizabeth Mann Borgese, "For Sale, Reasonable," *The Magazine of Fantasy and Science Fiction* 17.1 (July 1959): 70–72.

Doris Pitkin Buck, "Birth of a Gardener," *The Magazine of Fantasy and Science Fiction* 20.6 (June 1961): 50–59.

Alice Glaser, "The Tunnel Ahead," *The Magazine of Fantasy and Science Fiction* 21.5 (November 1961): 54–61.

Kit Reed, "The New You," *The Magazine of Fantasy and Science Fiction* 23.3 (September 1962): 100–109. Reprinted by permission of the author.

John Jay Wells & Marion Zimmer Bradley, "Another Rib," *The Magazine of Fantasy and Science Fiction* 24.6 (June 1963): 111–26. Reprinted by permission.

Sonya Dorman, "When I Was Miss Dow," *Galaxy* 24.5 (June 1966): 153–63. Copyright © 1966, 1994 by Sonya Dorman. Reprinted by permission of the Estate of Sonya Dorman and the Virginia Kidd Agency, Inc.

Kate Wilhelm, "Baby, You Were Great," *Orbit 2*, ed. Damon Knight (New York: G. P. Putnam's Sons, 1967), 19–36. Reprinted by permission of InfinityBox Press LLC.

Joanna Russ, "The Barbarian," *Orbit 3*, ed. Damon Knight (New York: G. P. Putnam's Sons, 1968), 84–108. Copyright © 1968 by Joanna Russ. Reprinted by permission of the Diana Finch Literary Agency on behalf of the Estate of Joanna Russ.

James Tiptree, Jr., "The Last Flight of Dr. Ain," *Galaxy* 28.2 (March 1969): 121–27. Later collected in *Her Smoke Rose Up Forever* (Arkham House, 1990). Copyright © 1969 by James Tiptree, Jr. (Alice B. Sheldon), renewed 1997 by Jeffrey D. Smith. Reprinted by permission of Jeffrey D. Smith and the Virginia Kidd Agency, Inc.

Ursula K. Le Guin, "Nine Lives," *The Wind's Twelve Quarters* (New York: Harper & Row, 1975), 129–60. First published in *Playboy* in November 1969 under the byline U. K. Le Guin (imposed to conceal her gender) and in a version edited without her involvement. Later collected in *The Unreal and the Real* (Small Beer Press, 2012). Copyright © 1969 by Ursula K. Le Guin. Reprinted by permission of Curtis Brown, Ltd.

This book is set in 10.5 Georgia Regular, a face designed for digital composition by Matthew Carter and rendered by Tom Rickner in 1993 for the Microsoft Corporation; it was initially created specifically for use and readability on computer screens. (The font's name is a reference to a tabloid headline, "Alien heads found in Georgia.") Adobe Garamond Pro Italic and Alternate Gothic No. 2 are used as display fonts. The paper is a cream-white opaque stock with an eggshell finish and exceeds the requirements for permanence of the American National Standards Institute.

The binding material is Arrestox B-Cloth, a poly cotton blend fabric with an aqueous acrylic coating to resist stains and mildew. Design and composition by Dedicated Book Services. Printing and binding by LSC Communications.